JASMINE IN PARIS

CLARE FLYNN

Storm

Ebook ISBN: 978-1-80508-437-2
Paperback ISBN: 978-1-80508-438-9

Previously published in 2021 by Cranbrook Press.

Cover design: Debbie Clement
Cover images: Shutterstock

Published by Storm Publishing.
For further information, visit:
www.stormpublishing.co

ALSO BY CLARE FLYNN

ONE

NAIROBI, KENYA

March 1949

The girl took a deep breath. The smell of animal dung in the *bomas* – the corrals where the natives lived and kept their livestock – mingled with that of parched earth, along with the aromas of cooking, of firewood burning under pots.

Since Jasmine had returned to Kenya after six months on the island of Penang in Malaya, there had been no rain. The vegetation was brown and brittle, with compacted earth everywhere. Over the past few days, however, she'd been aware of a change in the air: an intangible expectation but nonetheless real. The herds of zebra and impala seemed imbued with a manic energy, but Jasmine, once her attention fixed on this change, understood perfectly. Rain was coming.

It had finally arrived the previous evening, with thunder and lightning striking as the family sat down to dinner. They'd moved outside onto the veranda to witness the quenching miracle.

Today, she was accompanying Arthur, her stepfather, as she often did when he went to meet with tribesmen and their elders. Problems were always bubbling just beneath the surface: tribal disputes, petty resentments, cattle thefts and land grabs. But after what she had experienced in Penang, Jasmine had no desire to be drawn into a closer understanding of local politics. When one had been held at gunpoint and believed death was imminent, an argument over a missing goat seemed trivial.

In the aftermath of the rain, the hot dusty earth, burned by months of relentless sun, gave off a new, unmistakable scent – the indescribable tang of water meeting dry ground. Jasmine drew it deep into her lungs, feeling a new energy course through her, before turning back to her sketch-pad.

She was drawing children at play. There was a plentiful supply of them in this tribal village. Working rapidly and roughly, she tried to capture their postures, their constant move-ments and changing expressions. Later, at home, she would use these to work on more detailed paintings. It was vital to keep up her painting and sketching, and continue to develop her skills, if she were to gain a place at art school in Paris later in the year.

The settlement was surrounded by a wall made of acacia branches, packed with mud. The villagers' houses were constructed with mud walls, cracked in places like the veins of a leaf, where the mud and straw had dried under the powerful sun. The huts were like natural parts of the land, as though they grew like trees out of the bare earth. Even the roofs were plas-tered with mud – or possibly dung. So different from the stilted houses with their *attap*-thatched roofs in Penang.

Regardless of gender, the children, like their parents, had closely-shaved heads. Their beauty lay entirely in their facial features and the grace of their bodies. Again, the contrast with Penang was all too apparent. Glossy shining dark hair was the Malays' birthright. For them to shave it off – unless they became monks – was unimaginable.

A memory surfaced of Bintang's lustrous hair: Bintang was the Malay chauffeur Jasmine had fallen in love with in Penang.

As he drove, she would sit behind him in the back of the car, her eyes fixed on the back of his beautiful head, imagining what it would feel like to reach a hand out and stroke it. She pushed the image away before it morphed into the vision of Bintang lying dead on the ground in a pool of blood. Jasmine had to concentrate on the present and the future and forget the past. If she let herself think about Bintang and what had happened in Penang, she would enter a very dark place. She had to protect herself against that.

The children were laughing, chasing each other around the *boma*, small sticks in their hands mimicking the spears their fathers carried. The mothers sat apart, gossiping as they pounded millet in stone bowls. They had no need of hair in order to be beautiful – their white teeth and expansive smiles, the multiple decorative hoops dangling from pierced lobes, were enough. Their clothing was bright, in vibrant contrast to the dull earth tones of their surroundings, so that they seemed to burst out of the virtual canvas in Jasmine's mind. Vivid oranges, ripe ruby reds, sunshine yellows.

As she swung her gaze between her subjects and the paper, Jasmine wondered why she'd once disliked Kenya so much. Now, she was able to see it for itself and celebrate its unique qualities with every mark she made with her pencil. She needed to drink it all in, fix it, not only on the paper, but imprint it on her brain, to offer her sustenance and inspiration when she got to Paris.

The sun was fierce, even though far away on the horizon she could see gathering cumulonimbus clouds. More rain soon. Jasmine adjusted her straw hat, an affectionately-preserved relic from her time in Malaya. Glancing up, she saw Arthur walking towards her, so she stowed away her sketch-pad in her satchel.

'Ready to roll?' he asked with a smile.

'Aye aye, Captain. Did you achieve what you needed?'

He nodded. 'I didn't actually need anything. Just a routine

call. An excuse to get out of the office and talk to people. Far better than reading reports. I get more from half an hour chatting with those men than from reading volumes of reports.'

They climbed into Arthur's shooting-brake. 'I'm beginning to understand why you love Africa so much,' Jasmine said. 'I know I'll never love it as much as Penang, but I'm starting to like it.'

Arthur took a hand off the steering-wheel and gave her arm a squeeze. 'Didn't I tell you? You just have to open yourself up to it. Let it happen. Drink it all in.'

'You're right.' She twisted in her seat to look at him. 'When I was at school last year I was so caught up in missing Malaya that I resented Kenya – simply for being different. I didn't really give the place a chance.' She leaned back, extending her legs into the footwell. 'But after my time back in Penang I now see different can sometimes be good.'

'Food for the brain, Jazz.' He drummed his fingers on the dashboard. 'Important for an artist to create memories, build a store of treasures to draw on.'

'Why are you so wise?' She turned to look out at the endless plain stretching away towards the Ngong Hills. She loved Arthur. Not in the same way she loved her stepmother, Evie – she couldn't imagine loving Mummy more if she were her actual mother. Her fondness for Arthur was more about closeness of minds. They didn't talk a lot. They didn't need to. Jasmine knew he understood her without need for explanation. It was a deep-rooted shared understanding, a spiritual kinship. Perhaps because they both loved Evie so much. The realisation dawned that she'd actually known Arthur longer than Mummy had. He'd been Daddy's best friend, present in her life from when she was a baby, before Evie came to Penang to marry Daddy, when Jasmine was seven.

Thinking about her father made Jasmine's stomach lurch, knowing she couldn't delay any longer in telling Arthur the secret that had been gnawing away inside her since she'd returned to Nairobi.

Taking a gulp of air, she said, 'Hugh and I have a brother.'

It was out now and couldn't be unsaid. Oddly, she felt better already for unburdening herself.

She looked at Arthur, wondering at first if he'd heard her. She saw the frown crease his forehead and knew that he had.

They were approaching a collection of wooden kiosks on stilts along the side of the dirt road. She turned away from him, gazing at the gourds, melons and bags of white onions hanging from the roofs of these makeshift shelters, wondering what he was thinking. Arthur drove on in silence until they'd passed the kiosks and people gathering to buy fruit and vegetables. When they reached a stretch of open road, he steered off the track and came to a halt.

'You'd better tell me everything, Jazz. That's quite something to drop into the conversation.'

'His name's Amir. He's a few months younger than Hugh,' she blurted, referring to her nine-year-old half-brother, Hugh.

'Amir? But that's the name—'

'Yes. Of the boy Mary and Reggie are adopting.'

Mary and Reggie Hyde-Underwood, friends of Evie and Arthur, had been Jasmine's hosts during the six months she had stayed in Penang.

'I told you how Amir's mother was murdered in front of us by that horrible British army officer – but I didn't tell you who the father was.' She looked down, twisting her fingers together. 'I didn't want to upset Mummy. It was such a betrayal by Daddy.' Looking up at him she added, 'When I saw Amir's mother, I remembered her from that day when I was a child and Mummy and Mary and I stopped at Batu Lembah so I could use the bathroom, and Daddy was with a Malayan lady. Afterwards Mummy cried and cried for days and I thought it was my fault.' Jasmine fidgeted with the cotton skirt of her dress, pleating it nervously with her fingers. 'I didn't understand then what was going on as I was only a child but as soon as I saw the woman again, I knew.'

Arthur took off his glasses and polished them with a handkerchief extracted from his shirt pocket. 'What makes you think the boy is Doug's?'

'Nayla, Amir's mother, told me herself. But she didn't need to. He looks exactly like Hugh, but darker. Like Daddy too. As soon as I saw him, I knew.'

'I see.' Arthur replaced his spectacles. Jasmine saw him clench his jaw and felt a rush of anguish; perhaps she should have kept quiet. She scrabbled in her satchel, pulled out a photograph and handed it to him. 'Here he is. See what I mean?'

Arthur studied it without comment, then handed it back. 'Do Mary and Reggie know who he is?'

She nodded. 'I promised them I'd tell Mummy but, Arthur, I don't want to hurt her so I've kept putting it off.'

'Did your father know?'

'According to Nayla, she didn't know herself until she'd left Batu Lembah. She says when she found out she was pregnant her family made her marry an old man in Selangor. He used to beat her, and she had a horrible time. He died just before the Japanese invaded, so she went back to Batu Lembah to find Daddy, but he was dead by then. She stayed on as a housekeeper on the estate.' Her eyes welled with tears. 'What shall I do? I don't want to upset Mummy. Do you think she has to know?'

He took her hands in his. 'It would be wrong for you and the Hyde-Underwoods, and now me, to know the truth and for Evie to be in the dark. Imagine if one day she found out. How would she feel?' He reached into the glove compartment, took out a pack of cigarettes and lit one – a rare occurrence. Expelling a slow plume of smoke, he said, 'I'll tell her. I'll find the right moment. Don't worry. You did the right thing telling me.'

Jasmine closed her eyes, relief washing over her.

'So, what's he like, this secret half-brother?'

Her face broke into a smile. 'Oh, Arthur, he's adorable. Sweet and gentle and so intelligent. The poor lamb saw his mother shot, so you can imagine what kind of state he was in. He was holding her hand when it happened. But Mary and Reggie are so caring and understanding. And little Frances adores him.' As she thought of the boy, she felt tears pricking her eyes. 'I do too.'

That night Jasmine went to her room straight after supper. She lay on her bed staring up at the ceiling, wondering when Arthur would tell Evie about Amir.

She was drifting off to sleep when there was a knock at her door and Evie put her head around. 'You're still awake. Can I come in for a moment?'

Jasmine pulled herself up and propped the pillows behind her.

'Arthur's told me.' Evie sat down on the edge of the bed and took Jasmine's hand in hers. 'It can't have been easy telling him that. Thank you.'

'I was scared to tell you myself. I thought it would be better to come from him. I hope you don't mind?'

'Of course not.'

'I didn't want to hurt you. To cause you pain.'

Evie smiled. 'The pain I felt about your father's infidelity is in the past. It can't hurt me now. I have never been happier in my life than I am with Arthur. That Douglas fathered another child is a shock. I can't deny that. But it can't hurt me. Not anymore.' She stroked Jasmine's hair. 'Arthur said Douglas never knew. Is that so?'

Jasmine nodded. 'Amir's mother, Nayla, told me she didn't know herself when Daddy sent her away from Batu Lembah.'

'It must have been a shock to find this out about your father.'

Jasmine smiled at her mother. 'I suppose somewhere in my subconscious I already knew what had happened between you and Daddy, but I was too young and later I didn't want to think about that time when you were so unhappy.'

Evie pulled her into her arms. 'My dear sweet girl.'

'You're not angry?'

'No. Sad, perhaps. Thinking about how you lost your father. And how that little boy lost his mother and never knew his father. In a funny way I'm sad for Douglas as well. That he died without ever knowing he had another son.'

'Amir has the Hyde-Underwoods now. They'll be wonderful parents to him.'

'No one better.' Evie was about to get up when she said, 'Arthur says you have a snap of Amir. May I see it?'

Jasmine stretched over the side of the bed and grabbed her satchel. She handed the small photograph to her mother.

Evie's lips tightened. 'Yes. There's no mistaking it. A darker version of Hugh.' She handed it back. 'He looks a sweet boy.'

'He is. And clever. I'd love Hugh to meet him.'

'One day he will, I'm sure. But in the meantime, I'd rather you said nothing about this to him. He's still very young, and he never knew your father. I don't want him to grow up thinking badly of Douglas. And it would be a confusion that's unnecessary. No need to tell him about this boy thousands of miles away. It would only unsettle him.'

Jasmine nodded. Mummy was right.

Evie kissed her daughter goodnight and left the room.

On the days when Arthur worked from his office in Nairobi – which was most days – Jasmine stayed at home, painted, and worked on her French. There was still no news regarding her application for a place to study at the École des Beaux-Arts. She was anxious but refused to give up hope.

Setting up an easel on the veranda which skirted the substantial colonial bungalow, she spent the mornings painting. After lunch, she walked in the garden with her mother, went with her to the sports club to swim, or swotted up on her French.

'I never expected to see the day when you'd bury your head in a French grammar book,' said Evie, one afternoon, on finding Jasmine curled up in a chair reading. 'You hated it at school.'

'It's not grammar. It's a novel. Arthur picked it up for me last week at the Alliance Française in Nairobi.' Jasmine held up the book.

'Ah! *Madame Bovary*,' said Evie knowingly, as she slid into a chair beside her. 'A bit grim, don't you think? I read it several years ago – but in translation of course. Jolly good show to tackle the original.' She smiled. 'But I'm sure you can find a better model for living your life than Emma Bovary.'

'I don't need to find one. I've already got two. You and Mary. But yes, it's depressing. I hope all French people aren't like that. So much misery and despair.' She sighed. 'Assuming I ever get to find out, which I'm starting to doubt.'

Evie adopted a confident tone. 'The start of term is months away. It must take a great deal of time for them to assess all the applicants. You did say it's frightfully popular.'

'They've never even acknowledged receiving my portfolio. It went ages ago. I'm worried it might have gone astray.'

'Don't be silly, darling. The British Embassy will have delivered it.'

'It was good of Arthur to arrange that.' Jasmine hesitated, frowning. 'Gosh. They won't think I'm trying to pull favours, will they? That might count against me.'

'Of course, they won't. The people at the Beaux-Arts won't

even know we used the diplomatic bag. The portfolio will have been dropped off by a courier, not the British ambassador himself, for heaven's sake! Stop worrying.'

'I was crazy to think they might accept me. They turned down Rodin!'

'Maybe they don't like sculptors.'

'They have a sculpture course, too. But their standards are so high. How could I have ever thought that a school that taught Monet and Renoir would want me?'

Evie looked at her stepdaughter with a sad expression. 'You really want this, don't you?'

'More than anything, Mummy.'

'Then I'm sure you'll get in. I have a powerful feeling. It means, though, that I'll have to give you up again. And this time it could be for years. Maybe forever.' Evie looked stricken.

Jasmine stood up and moved across to her stepmother. Standing behind her chair, she bent over and wrapped her arms around Evie's neck. 'I'll miss you too. But I'll come home in the long summer break.'

Evie looked at her, doubtfully, but said nothing.

Gichinga, the houseboy, arrived with a pot of tea. When he'd gone, Evie said, 'You're bound to fall in love in Paris. Apparently everyone does. There must be something in the air there. You'll marry a handsome Frenchman and all I'll have of you is a letter once a year with a Christmas card.' She gave Jasmine a playful smile.

'I don't intend to marry anyone at all. I will dedicate my life to art.' Jasmine was conscious of sounding overdramatic and immature, but she wanted to make light of the trip to her anxious mother. 'I'll live in a garret in Montmartre with views over the rooftops and spend all day painting. At night I'll emerge and spend the evenings drinking absinthe and smoking smelly French cigarettes in seedy basement bars.'

Evie looked horrified, then laughed. 'You'd better not!'

'Look, Mummy, you've no need to worry that I'll stay in Paris forever. I'm not a city girl. And you know I'll hate the winters. Remember London.'

'You've never been to Paris. How do you know you'll hate it?'

'Because it's full of buildings and people and traffic and smoke.' She began counting on her fingers. 'Because it's bound to be grey. Because it's not wild and open like it is here. Because it's not green and alive and surrounded by sea like Penang.'

'Don't cast judgement before you've experienced the place. You used to loathe being here and now you seem quite fond of it.'

'I am. But mainly because you and Arthur and Hugh are here – and because I don't have to go to that hideous school anymore.'

Evie sipped her tea. 'I don't know Paris well, but when I was a girl, I visited it a few times *en route* to the South of France for summer holidays. I found it charming. Once you've settled, I may well pay you a visit.'

Jasmine broke into a smile. 'I'd love that. Bring Arthur too.' She looked wistful. 'I hope I won't be lonely there. I won't know anyone.'

'Darling, it doesn't sound to me as if you really want to go at all. You can always change your mind. Even if they make you an offer. There are other things you could do, like go to teacher training college––'

'No! I want to go to the Beaux-Arts. I *have* to go. I'm desperate to learn more. Everything I do now is just experimentation. I know nothing of technique. I'm hugely ignorant and if I don't get proper training, I'll stagnate. And it's my chance to be among genuine artists. I can learn so much.'

Evie gave a long sigh. 'You have natural talent. It's all that experimentation that keeps you fresh. I'd hate them to train that spontaneity out of you. I think it was George Bernard Shaw who said, "Those who can, do; those who can't, teach."'

'That's harsh. What about Mary? She's a teacher and one of the most capable people we know. And, besides, you just suggested I go to teacher training college. You can't have it both ways, Mummy!' She gave Evie a playful shove.

'I did, didn't I? You're quite right. I'm just clutching at straws.'

'Actually, you've given me an idea. I really loved helping Mary out at the village school on the estate. Do you think Arthur might arrange for me to work as a volunteer here at one of the local schools? I don't mean a place like my rotten old convent with only white girls, but a village school. I could do what I did at Bella Vista – hear them reading, help out with games and maybe set up an art class.' She felt a rush of excitement. 'Part-time. I'll need time to paint and be with you, but it would give me something else to focus on and keep my mind off worrying about my application. When I've visited settlements with Arthur, the children are so sweet and some of them have no schooling at all. I'd love to help.'

Evie looked thoughtful, then said, 'I don't see why not. We'll ask Arthur tonight and find out if it's possible. It's all good experience, isn't it? Yes, I think it's a jolly good idea, my love.'

Over dinner that night, Arthur had another idea. 'Jazz, I was talking to the French cultural attaché today. Did you know they're running conversation classes at the new Alliance Française? They also have a programme of French films and lectures on all kinds of topics.'

'Really?'

'They're putting a lot of energy behind it. I think some classes there would make more sense for you right now than helping in a village school.'

'Arthur's right. Conversation classes would be just the ticket. And talking to actual French people will help you enormously with pronunciation.'

Arthur got up from the table. 'I picked up a flyer with the times of the classes and another with the programme of events. Hang on, it's in my briefcase.' He went into the room he used as a study and returned with a couple of mimeographed sheets.

Jasmine studied them. 'There's a film there tomorrow afternoon. *Les Enfants du Paradis*. Gosh. Over three hours long. That's a bit of a marathon. Sounds an ordeal.'

Evie was looking at the other sheet. 'Beginners' conversation classes every morning. Oh dear, that interferes with your painting time.'

'She's not a beginner.' Arthur leaned back in his chair, studying Jasmine. 'You must be at least intermediate, if not advanced. You only need help with pronunciation and a broadening of your vocabulary from whatever useless nonsense they stuff into you for the school certificate.'

'Arthur!' Evie arched an eyebrow. 'Anyway, the classes don't begin until next term, so the question's academic.'

'Next term?' Jasmine frowned. 'That's a couple of weeks away. That's terrible!'

'Considering you weren't even aware of the existence of the classes until a few minutes ago, there's no need to turn it into a tragedy, darling,' said Evie. 'Until then, you can go along and watch the film shows.'

The following afternoon, Jasmine went into Nairobi to see *Les Enfants du Paradis*.

Entering the building, she was surprised how many people were there. The French diplomatic wives were out in force, as well as several groups of students, both African and European. As soon as the titles came up, Jasmine lost herself in the theatrical world of the beautiful Garance and her admirers, and was transported to the streets of nineteenth-century Paris, captivated by the magic of the experience and the powerful performances of the actors.

There was a break between Parts One and Two of the film, and she went to the ladies' room. Afterwards, in the lobby, people were gathered around in small groups, chatting and drinking tea. Jasmine knew no one and, feeling shy, headed back into the room where the film was being shown, keen not to break the spell the film had cast over her.

Waiting for the film to start again, she asked herself how, if she were fortunate enough to get a place at the Beaux-Arts, she would ever get over her shyness enough to make friends, let alone contribute to any discussions in classes. Somehow, that crowd of people in the foyer, who all seemed to know each other, made her want to shrink away and hide. It would have been bad enough had they all been speaking English, but among all those French people she felt an absolute outsider. Perhaps it was just as well she hadn't heard from the Beaux-Arts selection committee. Maybe it was time to find another occupation.

After the film was over, Jasmine had intended to walk to Arthur's office for a lift home, but to her surprise and delight, his car was waiting for her outside when she left the building. She realised it was already after six o'clock, so absorbed in *Les Enfants du Paradis* had she been.

'You're finished early,' she said.

Arthur shrugged. 'For once.'

On the short journey home, she enthused about the drama of the film and how it was like no other she had seen.

'There was a cultural attaché from the French embassy who gave a short talk afterwards about all the challenges of making the film during the German occupation. And I actually understood most of what he was saying. I concentrated so hard during the film I stopped noticing it was in French!' She gave a little laugh. 'Obviously there were parts of the dialogue I couldn't understand but mostly it was easier than I expected.'

'Total immersion,' said Arthur. 'I told you your French is better than you give yourself credit for.'

When they came through the door of the house, all thoughts of the film left Jasmine. Evie was waiting in the hallway, a large envelope in her hands. 'I thought you'd never get home!'

Jasmine glanced at Arthur. 'That's why you came to pick me up, isn't it?' She rushed over and took the envelope from Evie. 'My hands are shaking. I don't think I can bear to open it.'

'Don't be silly, darling. If it was a "No", there'd only be a single piece of paper. This is a big fat envelope. It can only mean one thing.'

Jasmine tore it open and read, frowning. 'It's all formal flowery language. I can't take in what it means.' Jasmine passed the package to Arthur. 'Please put me out of my misery.'

Arthur scanned the covering letter, glanced at the rest of the contents, put them back into the envelope and returned it to Jasmine. 'This calls for a celebration. You, clever girl, have won a place at the art school, provided you fulfil two conditions.'

Jasmine's face fell. 'What conditions?'

'Firstly, you have to be interviewed in French by someone at the French embassy here. If he judges your command of the language is insufficient, you must enrol in a recognised course prior to coming to Paris.' He winked at her. 'But you're planning to do that anyway, aren't you? Secondly, one of the entrance requirements is a series of drawings of classical sculptures. The committee observes that your portfolio does not contain this.'

Jasmine let out a groan.

'Hold your horses! Let me finish.' Arthur accepted the Scotch and soda Evie handed him. 'The admissions committee is prepared to make an exception in your case based on the talent your work demonstrates and the fact that living in Kenya and Malaya without access to museums and art galleries has limited your access to classical sculpture. They've accepted you, on condition you undertake to complete a series of classical drawings before the September term begins and reach a sufficient standard to justify your inclusion in the course.'

Jasmine was lost for words.

'Come on. Let's sit on the veranda. We've got half an hour before supper. Gichinga has had a bottle of champagne chilling on ice since the letter arrived this afternoon.' Evie wrapped her arms around her daughter. 'I couldn't be prouder of you, my darling girl. But, gosh, I'm going to miss you so much.'

Jasmine couldn't wait to set off for Paris, but the following three months flew by too quickly for Evie. Her offer to accompany Jasmine on the voyage to France was politely rebuffed. Jasmine wanted to undertake the journey alone.

'Once I'm in Paris, I'll have to fend for myself, Mummy, so I may as well begin now.'

'But travelling all that way alone on a ship...'

'I travelled back from Penang on my own. Besides, Arthur and Hugh need you here.'

Evie stroked her daughter's hair, overwhelmed with tenderness tinged with sadness. For the first time, she felt her own increasing age, the irresistible pull of time. Having a nine-year-old son helped her to feel youthful, but a daughter grown up enough to travel unescorted across the world and embark on a new life in a foreign city terrified Evie and made her feel prematurely old. Then she remembered she'd done the same thing herself. Ten years ago she had accepted an offer to marry Jasmine's father, after meeting him only once. She'd grabbed the offer with both hands and left England for a new life in Malaya. What an adventure those last ten years had proved to be. What a tangle of emotions. A melange of the deepest despair and grief with the unbridled joy of having a new family and eventually finding true love with Arthur. She shivered despite the heat of the afternoon, wondering what lay ahead for Jasmine. But her daughter had to make her own mistakes, enjoy her own triumphs, face inevitable setbacks and unexpected joys. Evie must let her go; set her free to find her path. But that didn't stop her sorrow at the prospect of a long separation.

In early July, the family of four drove together to Mombasa, the back of Arthur's shooting-brake heavy with Jasmine's luggage and art materials. Arthur had arranged for some old Colonial Office colleagues, now posted in Paris, to put Jasmine up for a couple of weeks until she found a place of her own to stay. She'd have plenty of time to look before the influx of students for the new term as Paris would be quiet during the summer vacation.

When they reached the port, the family saw Jasmine safely installed in her cabin before she dismissed them.

'There's no need for you to worry about me. I'm going to miss you all dreadfully but I promise to write every week.'

Arthur raised an eyebrow sceptically. 'We won't hold you to that, Jazz. Once the charms of Paris get to you the desire to write to us will be inversely related to the amount of fun you're having.'

'Don't have *too* much fun,' said Evie, smiling. 'That's guaranteed to get me worrying.'

Arthur put his arm round his wife. 'Jasmine's a sensible girl. She's not going to do anything we wouldn't approve of. Having fun is one thing I hope she won't stint on.'

'Well, I think going to live in a big ugly city will be very, very boring.' Hugh folded his arms. 'Beats me why anyone would want to do that when we have lions and monkeys and zebras here. Who wants to look at a load of old buildings?'

They all laughed, and Arthur tousled Hugh's hair. The realisation that Jasmine did not know when she'd see her parents and little brother again pierced her heart. Suddenly she wanted them gone. Prolonging the pain of separation was unbearable.

'Please don't wait till we sail. It makes it harder. Let's say goodbye now,' she said, lip trembling. Evie frowned but understood. She gathered Jasmine into her arms and kissed her. Evie waited while the others said goodbye before, fighting back tears, she led Hugh and Arthur down the gangway and off the ship.

TWO

FRANCE

July 1949

When the ship docked in Marseille three weeks later, Jasmine felt a surge of excitement mixed with fear. It was finally happening. As she went down the gangway and set foot for the first time on French soil, her skin tingled with anticipation.

It was odd hearing voices everywhere speaking French. She breathed deeply, savouring the sensations – salt-soaked air, strong coffee, the sharp powerful smell of fish, the sweet pungency of garlic – all undercut with the stink of rotting vegetables and rubbish. She looked about her at the people. Men wearing cloth caps or berets, many scruffily dressed, stevedores pushing carts weighed down with sacks unloaded from ships, sailors in uniform, street vendors. Above the city the Cathedral of Notre Dame de la Garde rose on a craggy outcrop, with a tall statue-topped tower and a dome presiding over the buildings below.

Jasmine took a taxi from the port to the Gare Saint Charles to join the train to Paris. Drinking in the sights, she saw

Marseille was nothing like London. Yes, there were smoke-blackened buildings and the buzz of commerce, but the atmosphere was very different. She remembered London as gloomy, battered, and smog-filled. Marseille offered an interesting dichotomy: near the port were narrow alleys with bare-foot children in evident poverty but in the city centre, wide boulevards with elegantly-dressed people. The narrow side-streets were dark, monochromatic with washing hanging between the buildings and litter strewn on the ground. Yet she sensed an energy, a *joie de vivre* in the atmosphere. On the affluent boulevards, there were colourful signs above the shops, tabacs and bars advertising the acclaimed *savon de Marseille*. She asked the driver to stop so she could buy a few bars of lavender-scented soap as a gift for her hosts in Paris. Stepping onto the street, she felt the sunshine warm her skin. That differed from London too. She was going to enjoy being in France.

After the overnight journey north, the train pulled into the Gare de Lyon in a cloud of steam. Jasmine alighted and looked around for a porter. A rush of nerves took her by surprise, and she was relieved that, at least for the initial period, she'd be staying with an English family.

Passengers crowded the platform, so Jasmine hung back, allowing those who knew where they were going to overtake her. She didn't know what the Hendersons looked like, so waited for the crowds to disperse. A posse of nuns hurried past her – giant black-plumaged birds, their oversized head-dresses like white crested crowns. She shrank back, giving way as they swept by. A young shabbily-dressed woman, a jaunty beret on her head, was bending over a wooden box at the side of the platform where a man waited, one foot on the box as she polished his shoe. In Penang or Nairobi, a woman would never perform such a task – let alone a European woman. Jasmine watched the rapid operation, as the loudspeakers announced the departure of other trains, and the sound echoed under the glass-panelled roof.

Reaching the main concourse of the station, Jasmine looked about. Maybe the Hendersons had forgotten? Most of the people from the train had already disappeared onto the streets of the city. Then she noticed an elegant woman appraising her. Could this be Mrs Henderson?

'Mademoiselle Barrington?' The accent was French. The Hendersons' housekeeper, perhaps.

The woman was wearing a tailored linen suit. Chic. Expensive. Not the housekeeper, then.

'I am Madame Courbet. You are my guest. Come. The car is outside.' She spoke slowly in English, evidently doubting that Jasmine would be capable of understanding French.

'Mais je m'attendais à Monsieur et Madame Henderson.' Jasmine tried out her French. Better to start immediately.

Madame Courbet replied in English. 'The 'endersons 'ave returned to England. A family matter, so they ask my husband and I to accommodate you. They write a letter to explain.' The woman handed Jasmine an envelope, turned and, saying something in rapid French to the waiting porter, gestured to Jasmine to follow them.

Another way in which things were different here in Paris – Madame Courbet was driving her own car. When they had settled into it, she looked sideways at Jasmine and said, 'The Gare de Lyon is to the east of Paris. We live in Passy on the west. Let us hope there is not too much traffic.' She gave Jasmine a frosty smile.

Jasmine's mood of excited anticipation was already dissipating. Madame Courbet was clearly less than delighted that the

Hendersons had asked her to step in. Jasmine told herself she was being silly. Maybe this was just the way French people behaved. She'd heard they were sometimes very formal and correct, so it was up to her to be patient and polite and hope once Madame Courbet had got to know her, she would relax a little.

Trying again to use her French, she worked out in her head what she wanted to say first, then asked whether Mr Henderson was a colleague of Monsieur Courbet.

Jasmine realised her accent was making her hostess wince.

Again, the reply was in English. 'We are neighbours. Mr 'enderson works at the British embassy. My 'usband is a senior administrator in the French government.' She pronounced it *goo-vern-a-mont*.

'I see.' Defeated, Jasmine gave up trying to speak French. It was annoying. There was an implication that her French could not possibly match up to Madame's English. Or perhaps French people assumed it was acceptable to speak English with a French accent whereas the other way round was not.

Silence ruled as they negotiated the streets of Paris. Jasmine opened the envelope to find a card welcoming her to Paris and apologising for the Hendersons' absence which was due to the imminent demise of Mr Henderson's mother. It was signed by Mrs Henderson and had clearly been written in haste. Looking on the bright side, Jasmine told herself that maybe the Hendersons' absence was a good thing as this way she would have an immediate experience of life in a French home.

She stared through the windows, her enthusiasm reviving. She had no sense of where they were, and Madame Courbet did not point out landmarks or offer any sense of orientation. Jasmine allowed the city to flow by as she soaked it all up: cafés with tables and chairs on the pavements with Parisians sipping cold drinks and coffee in the late morning sunshine. The car wove in and out of back streets as Madame was clearly an enthusiast of shortcuts and determined to manoeuvre the vehicle out of any potential traffic jams. Through the open window Jasmine absorbed the distinctive smells of Paris, gripping the edge of her seat as yet another sudden sharp turn threatened to throw her off balance.

Eventually they arrived *chez* Courbet, a large art nouveau apartment building in pale sandstone. The area was clearly affluent. Like many of the surrounding buildings, it was topped with ornate turrets, its windows bearing decorative black wrought-iron balconies. Madame Courbet parked the car and called to the waiting concierge, who took Jasmine's bags. Speaking so fast that Jasmine struggled to understand, Madame Courbet instructed the woman to bring the luggage up to her apartment.

It was on the third floor and accessed by a terrifying, creaking lift that rose through the centre of the stairwell. This was the first time Jasmine had ever been in such a lift. The prospect of the mechanism failing and her being stuck in that cage behind the creaking metal doors was scary, so she decided to use the stairs in future.

When they emerged from the lift, Madame Courbet marched towards a pair of enormous double doors. Inside, the imposing square hallway was hung with gloomy portraits and adorned with a large floral display. The wooden floor was parquet, in an intricate design with a border of darker wood in front of the skirtings. The place gave off an air of faded grandeur.

'Have you lived here long, Madame Courbet?'

'Since my marriage.' The woman didn't elaborate when that might have been. Jasmine found it difficult to guess her age but settled on somewhere in her fifties.

'Do you and Monsieur Courbet have children?'

'You ask a lot of questions. We have a son. Married.' Turning away from Jasmine, she called out, 'Marielle!'

A uniformed maid appeared.

'Show Mademoiselle Barrington to her room,' Madame Courbet said in French. Turning to Jasmine, she said, 'Marielle will show you what you need. I have an engagement now. I am already late. My husband and I will dine out this evening. Marielle will prepare a cold supper for you.' She gave her a smile that didn't reach as far as her eyes. With that, she swept from the hallway through one of the doors, leaving Jasmine alone and starting to think that her presence here was *de trop*.

The room the maid showed her to was small and sparsely but adequately furnished. Her luggage was already waiting for her. Surprised, she turned to Marielle to ask in her shaky French how it had got there when the concierge had whisked it away into the interior of the building.

The maid looked puzzled, then smiled. '*L'escalier de service*,' she said at last and Jasmine gathered there was another behind-the-scenes route to conceal unsightly items such as luggage and servants.

When the maid left, Jasmine moved to the window. It looked over a small internal courtyard. No views of the Paris rooftops then, just pigeons and the walls of the apartment block.

She flung herself onto the narrow bed and asked herself whether coming to Paris had been a dreadful mistake. The gloom didn't last long. It was a beautiful, sunny day. Madame Courbet had gone out and Jasmine was free to explore. Besides, she wouldn't be staying here long. She must find somewhere to live, somewhere more in line with her ideal of being an art student in Paris. Maybe in the Latin Quarter, Montparnasse or Montmartre. Not here in stuffy, posh Passy.

Quickly, she unpacked and hung her clothes in the wardrobe, stowing the cases on the top. Marielle had indicated the door to a nearby bathroom, which she told her was for her exclusive use. Relieved not to be sharing with the Courbets, Jasmine freshened up after the long train journey, using one of the lavender soaps she had bought for the Hendersons. No point in offering them to Madame Courbet. It was all too easy to picture her curling her lip in disdain.

Feeling brighter, she put on a pretty dress. It was time to get out of this place and explore. The change in arrangements would not dampen her spirits.

She was leaving the room when she remembered something. Dragging one of the cases down from the wardrobe, she reached inside the side pocket and drew out an unopened envelope with a Malayan postmark. By mistake she'd put it in the case that had gone in the ship's hold rather than the one she'd used on the voyage. At last, she would read what Howard Baxter had to say.

Jasmine didn't know how far she'd walked nor exactly where she was. Hoping to rely on her inner compass, she'd headed in a more or less straight line in one direction, assuming she'd eventually come upon a landmark she might recognise. But the streets of Passy were lined with belle époque buildings, all very stern, grand and imposing – and all blocking the view of anything beyond. The people on the street were elegant – like Madame Courbet – and Jasmine felt small, insignificant and out of place. This was not the Paris she had dreamt of. She must find somewhere else to live as soon as possible: somewhere that was a closer fit with her artistic aspirations.

Hot and thirsty, she sat down at a table at the most modest pavement café she could see. Everywhere else she'd passed seemed likely to be very expensive, albeit chic, and she felt under-dressed in her simple cotton frock and sandals. She ordered a lemon soda and sipped it while watching the passers-by. She tried to relax and pretend she was French, but knew the briefest glance at her would indicate she was not.

She reached into her satchel for her pocket-sized sketch-pad and a pencil, wanting something discreet, so no one would notice her drawing. As she did so, her hand closed on the letter from Howard Baxter. She took that out instead, opened it, smiled on seeing how long the letter was, and began to read.

My dear Jasmine,
You haven't replied properly to my last letter so I'm writing again. I know you must be busy preparing for your grand adventure in France, but I had hoped you might manage more than a picture postcard. Take pity on me! Imagine the pain of knowing I can no longer jump in the car, take the ferry to Penang and find you at Bella Vista. I visit the Hyde-Underwoods about once a month – being up there makes me feel closer to you – but the pain of your absence is sharp. When I'm sitting on the veranda drinking a stengah with Reggie and Mary, talking about the Emergency, I keep expecting to hear your voice asking a question or making a comment. I suppose I ought to be thankful that it means I have no chance to put my foot in it with you by saying the wrong thing. I'd give anything to see you – even if you were to force me to eat humble pie for my numerous faux pas. See! I'm even trying my schoolboy French out on you!

Jasmine could almost hear Howard's voice. She couldn't help a grin spreading across her face.

In your absence I'm working on becoming more careful about what I say. Yes, actually trying to make use of the old grey matter before opening my mouth! When we meet again, whenever that may be, you will be astonished at how much I am a changed man.
I know you told me to forget you and not wait for your return to Penang. But since you now have a brother here, as well as the Hyde-Underwoods, I can't help nurturing the hope that you will come before too long. Last week I was on the island with a couple

of the chaps from Guthrie's and we went to that beach. I think of it as "our" beach. Remember – with the big rock you hid behind to change into your costume? The chaps loved it but I just felt sad. It wasn't the same without you.

Jasmine sipped her drink and stared, unseeing, into the middle distance. She could hardly bear to read any more. The longing for Penang swept over her. That day at the beach had been the first time she'd got past what she'd believed to be Howard's brash big-headed behaviour to the real person beneath. She remembered she'd been worried that he might try to take advantage of her. But Howard had been a complete gentleman. They had swum together, enjoyed a picnic and lain on towels on the edge of the beach, talking properly for the first time.

Sitting here now, alone and friendless in the Paris sunshine, Jasmine wished he was with her. But it was impossible to picture Howard here. She closed her eyes and saw him – in shorts, legs tanned, sipping a cold beer. He'd be a fish out of water. A rubber planter had no place on the streets of Paris.

Picking the letter up again, she focused on his reassurances about Amir's well-being. She smiled again, reading that the boy was settling in well with his new family, was flourishing at school and that the Hyde-Underwoods hoped he might win a coveted place at the Penang Free School in George Town to prepare for his school certificate in four or five years.

Reggie clearly dreams of Amir becoming a rubber planter and eventually taking over Bella Vista, but I get the impression Mary's not so keen. I think she harbours hopes of him going to university and making use of his evident talents by entering the government service and helping his country.

Jasmine mused on this. If Amir were to play a part in

creating a post-colonial Malaya that would be something to be proud of. Then she thought of the young Malayan man she had fallen for the previous year. Bintang had once been a pupil at the Free School – but the Japanese invasion and the destruction of his family had put a stop to his education. He'd had dreams about the future of Malaya – but had channelled them in the wrong direction by joining the communists, only to be killed by them. It was thanks to Howard Baxter's rapid reactions that Jasmine was alive today, sipping lemonade outside a Parisian café instead of lying beside Bintang's body with a hole in her head. But she didn't want to think about Bintang. It was too sad.

No doubt you're wondering about the Emergency and how things have been going since you left Malaya. Not a lot to report on that front – we're still on high alert here at Batu Lembah and never go anywhere on the estate without a gun.

Talking of guns, there's a bit of a stink about the execution of an Indian trade unionist – you might have read about it in the papers. He was apprehended back in March on a rubber estate in Selangor by the manager. According to the planter, he had a revolver and tried to put up a fight. The police took him and claimed he had six rounds of live ammo as well as the gun. Last month they hanged the poor devil for illegal possession. Lots of people are saying it was a stitch-up. A big fuss – questions in Parliament and protests by the Indian government. I've no idea what the truth is but, bearing in mind he was the head of the Pan Malayan Federation of Trade Unions and a volunteer with the Indian National Army, the British authorities probably had it in for him. It does seem rather fishy as they didn't even hear the poor chap's appeal before they put him to death – and to dole out the death sentence for possessing a gun does seem excessive. He probably was a communist – he'd been a jungle fighter against the Japs – but I can't help thinking the powers that be were too hasty. Mind you, I wouldn't be saying that if I'd been staring down the barrel of his gun.

Jasmine didn't want to read about that kind of thing. She'd put the conflict in Malaya behind her and it made her shiver, remembering how close she herself had come to death at the wrong end of a gun. It seemed unreal now. She didn't want to think about whether it was right or wrong to execute a man for having a gun. It was nothing to do with her anymore. All that was in her past. Now she wanted to concentrate on her future, and on her art.

The final part of the letter returned to Howard's favourite topic: Jasmine herself.

I know you told me to forget you, but you were asking the impossible. That's like asking me to forget that the moon goes round the earth and the earth goes round the sun.

Did they? Jasmine's grasp of interplanetary movements was not strong. It was so typical of Howard, she thought, unable to suppress her annoyance. Showing off again, making her feel small and rather stupid.

I don't think you meant it though. Why ask me to keep you in the picture about Amir's progress? Surely it was to give me an excuse to write to you. I'm going to tell myself that anyway. Please write back soon – and with more than a lousy postcard of the African plains. Much as I enjoyed seeing the herds of zebra, I'd far rather have a proper letter from you or, instead of a picture postcard, at least a sketch done by your own fair hand. Preferably a self-portrait.

She gave an audible groan. He was cringingly corny.

*I can't tell you how proud I am that you've been accepted by that
fancy French art school and I know you will impress all those
French professors. I have very high expectations!
Please write soon with your address in Paris. I hope this letter
catches you before you leave Africa. I've bought a photographic
book of Paris so I can look at the pictures and imagine you in
each image.
With all my love, Howard.*

He was infuriating. Part of her loved being in his company
– and the other part hated it. If only he could be content with
friendship. Why did he persist in this schoolboy fantasy of
being in love with her? They were too different. He was not the
kind of man she wanted to imagine spending her life with.
Being stuck on a rubber estate on the peninsula. Too awful to
contemplate. Jasmine stuffed the letter back in her satchel, paid
the bill and carried on with her walk.

After a while, the street flowed into an enormous circular
area with roads radiating outwards like spokes and a pair of
grand matching buildings on the opposite side. The helpful
blue Paris street sign told her she was at Place du Trocadéro.
The Eiffel Tower was visible on the other side between the
buildings. She wandered around the circumference to the space
between the wings of the Palais de Chaillot – and stepped out
onto a terraced area with a stone balustrade. Beyond the wall,
the ground fell away, revealing formal gardens, a view of the
Seine, and the perfect complete view of the Eiffel Tower. She
gave a gasp of pleasure.

'Did you know Adolf Hitler had his photograph taken on
the exact spot where you're standing?'

Jasmine jumped. The accent was American. She turned to
look at him.

A black man stood beside her, his hair short and wiry, his
eyes concealed by a large pair of dark glasses resting on a broad

nose, a cigarette dangling from his lips. Instead of a tie, a silk scarf was draped at his open neckline. He smiled at her, revealing bright white teeth against ebony skin.

'He only came to Paris once. He was driven to the Palais Garnier – the Paris Opera, and the Madeleine and then came here. Checking out the landmarks. At least those that interested him.'

The man had a lilting voice, sonorous, musical. Unlike those gangsters in the Hollywood films who spoke out of the side of their mouths, he had a way of emphasising the vowel sounds as though he was savouring them, rolling them around on his tongue. He offered his hand. 'I'm Stan,' he said, 'Stan Tyson.' He eased his sunglasses away from his eyes so she could see them. Large brown pools that fixed on hers intently. Although taken aback by his familiar manner, Jasmine instinctively liked him.

She shook his hand. 'Jasmine Barrington.'

He chuckled. 'English. Not another American then.'

'Technically, yes, I'm English, but I was born in Malaya and my family live in Africa. In Kenya. I've only spent about six months in England so I don't tend to think of myself as that at all.'

'How *do* you think of yourself?' He gazed at her intently then put his sunglasses on again so she couldn't see his eyes anymore. But a slight movement of the lips indicated he was amused.

Jasmine frowned. It was not a question she had given much thought to. 'Malayan I suppose... but obviously not a native Malay. I'm classed as British but don't feel that at all. Gosh, I really don't know how I think of myself. I can't claim to be Malayan when I no longer live there and both my parents were English. Although my half-brother *is* half-Malay. I suppose that makes me an outsider.'

His expression was sardonic. 'So, even being part of a colonial power has its drawbacks, you reckon? You should try being a negro.'

She felt the blood rush to her face. Had she offended him? Was she behaving like a spoilt colonial brat? She picked at the surface of the stone wall with her fingernail. 'I mean I know we had all the privileges. But I feel I don't actually belong anywhere.' Glancing at him, she added, 'But I'm not complaining – not belonging is actually exciting. I'm incredibly lucky that I've lived in so many different countries and now have the chance to be here.'

'So, you're an exile in Paris, like me. What brings you here? Vacation?'

It was an inquisition. Jasmine took a breath and said proudly. 'I'm about to begin my studies at L'École Supérieure des Beaux-Arts. It's an art school.'

'I know what it is. I'm staying around the corner from it.' He studied her with interest. 'So are you a painter or a sculptor or are you still finding out?'

'A painter.' She smiled at him shyly. 'Well, I'm hoping they'll help me to become a proper one.'

'The only way to do that is to paint. Throw yourself into it. Body and soul.'

She looked at him, surprised. 'Are you a painter then?'

'I wish! No. I'm a writer.' He leaned with one elbow against the stone balustrade and directed a broad smile at her. 'Or trying to become a proper one. I do have friends who are painters though. Paris is full of painters. And writers. Anyway, if you want to do something creative well, it amounts to the same thing whether it's art or writing. You have to keep on doing it. Give yourself up to it.'

'Where are you from?'

'The mighty USA. Born in Chicago. Couldn't wait to get away.'

'Do you like Paris?'

He chuckled. 'I like it well enough. It suits where I am in my life right now. Like you, I don't really belong anywhere.'

She wanted to ask him how he came to be in Paris. 'Did you serve over here in the war? Is that how you knew about Hitler being here?'

He jerked his head back and raised his eyebrows over the top of those dark sunglasses. Jasmine wished he'd take them off as being unable to see his eyes was disconcerting. She couldn't tell whether he was laughing at her or was annoyed by her.

'Yes, I was a GI. After the war I stayed in Europe. Did some French language classes. Back in the States, I heard lots of negroes were getting their GI Bill education entitlements refused. It was easier to claim from here. And I couldn't face going back to America.'

Something stopped her asking him why that might be. Instead she said, 'What kind of writing do you do? Are you writing about Paris? As a journalist?'

He smiled. 'I'm writing a novel. Not *about* Paris – but maybe *in* Paris.'

'What's it about?'

He considered for a moment, then said, 'Identity. Alienation. Love. Hate. Making choices.' He folded his arms. 'But I don't like talking about my work. Not until it's finished. How long you been in Paris? And why are you here when the Beaux-Arts is shut for the summer?'

'I have to submit some classical drawings before term begins. I didn't have access to any classical sculpture in Nairobi or Penang, so they made the offer of my place conditional. Apparently, I can have access to the school's classical galleries where there are lots of plaster casts of Greek and Roman pieces – and of course there's the Louvre too. If my portfolio is up to scratch I get my place on the course. If not...'

'How's it going?'

'I haven't started yet. I only arrived today.' She found

herself telling him about Madame Courbet and her misgivings about staying in the apartment.

'Then it's fortunate you met me, Jasmine. I have friends who might be able to help you find somewhere to stay. It won't be as grand as Passy, but you don't want to be stuck there. The cool cats live on the Left Bank. You need to be in the Quartier Latin, or Montparnasse. Closer to the art school and surrounded by interesting people. You'll suffocate in Passy. It's all bankers, politicians and businessmen.' He tapped the underside of his nose. 'Very haughty and probably very boring.'

'You know of somewhere?'

'No, but I know people who might. Be prepared for a small room. Probably a *chambre de bonne*. Possibly no running water. Lots of stairs and no lift. But cheap. You OK with that, Jasmine?'

A vision of a garret with roof top views filled her head. 'Oh yes! That sounds perfect.' Hesitating, she added, 'What's a *chambre de bonne*?'

'Maid's room. Too small to swing a mouse, let alone a cat.' Stan glanced at his wrist-watch. 'Time I was going, Miss Jasmine. I work a few nights a week in a café. Pays the bills. Tell you what – how about we meet on Wednesday evening at about six? I'm not working then. A place not far from the Beaux-Arts.' He took a scrap of paper and a pencil stub from his trouser pocket and scribbled down the address. 'Hey, you mind if I call you Jazz? I'm a big fan of jazz music so it would be a compliment.'

She beamed. 'I'd be delighted, Stan. My stepfather Arthur calls me that too, so it will remind me of him.'

'See you Wednesday, then, Jazz.' He gave her a thumbs up and walked away towards the Métro.

Jasmine watched him go. There was a swagger about him, yet with an underlying grace. And a very individual style – the silk scarf, knotted so casually in place of a tie, the very dark sunglasses. It was hard to imagine him in a GI uniform. A writer. Less than twenty-four hours in Paris and she had already met someone interesting. Someone who had promised to introduce her to other interesting people. She shivered despite the warmth of the late afternoon sun. A shiver of excitement. A shiver of anticipation.

THREE

When Jasmine returned to the apartment building in Passy, the concierge let her in before she could ring the doorbell. The elderly woman had a tiny room beside the front door, allowing her to keep one eye on the street and the other glued to her copy of *France-Soir*. Jasmine gave her a bright smile but was offered only a curt nod in response. Why was everyone in Paris so hostile? Entering the inner gloom of the lobby beyond the court-yard, her spirits, raised by her encounter with Stan, plummeted. Avoiding the metal cage, she trudged up the stairs to the third floor.

Madame Courbet hadn't offered a key, so Jasmine tapped gingerly on the large double doors. There was no response so, cursing her stupidity for failing to enquire of the maid about access, she knocked louder, only for the door to be flung open by the lady of the house herself, her expression one of irritation.

'No need to hammer the door down. Show some patience.' The woman stood aside to let Jasmine in.

Jasmine started to apologise but Madame Courbet brushed it away with a flick of her wrist.

'I have asked Marielle to get a key cut for you tomorrow. My husband and I are going out now. Marielle has left your meal in the kitchen.' Madame Courbet gestured towards the kitchen and moved off, presumably back to an area of the apartment she had no wish for Jasmine to enter. Deflated, Jasmine went to investigate what had been left for her solitary supper. She intended to eat quickly, then return to her room to read and sketch before having an early night.

On the kitchen table was a large tray, its contents covered with an embroidered cloth. Next to it was a glass tumbler, an open bottle of red wine with the cork pushed back in, an empty water pitcher, a napkin and cutlery. Realising she was hungry, Jasmine eased out a chair and sat down. She lifted the cloth, to find a bowl of mixed salad, a plate of cold meats, cheeses and a baguette. Next to these was a slice of what looked like apple tart and a small bowl of cream. Ignoring the wine, she moved to the sink, filled the water jug, poured some into a glass then sat down to eat.

As she was serving herself with a helping of salad, the door opened and a man came into the room. He looked her up and down as though she were a piece of porcelain he was appraising.

'Here you are, Mademoiselle Barrington. *Enchanté*.' He was short and stocky with an expansive but rather smug smile. He was wearing a pale grey suit and smelled of a lemony cologne. With an outstretched hand, he reached for hers then bent over and kissed it.

Jasmine stiffened.

'*Je suis* Bernard,' he said grandly as if he were the Emperor Napoleon. '*Comment t'appelles-tu?*'

Why was he asking her name when he'd just greeted her by it? And using the familiar *tu*, when they were meeting for the first time? The need for formality had been drummed into her during her French language classes. Had the teacher got it wrong?

He reached for the wine bottle. 'Or do you prefer to speak

in English? It will be *une bonne pratique* for me. My English is not as good as my wife's.'

'No, I prefer to speak French,' she told him in French. Then, remembering he had asked her name, added, *'Je m'appelle* Jasmine.'

He took a pair of glass tumblers from a cupboard and poured wine into each, handing one to Jasmine. He gestured with his glass towards her. *'Enchanté*, Jasmine. *A ta santé.'*

'No wine for me, thank you.' Jasmine reached for her water.

'Mon Dieu! You cannot dine without wine.' His expression was one of horror.

Jasmine didn't know how to counter this so she accepted the wine, gave him a weak smile, took a sip and muttered, *'A votre santé.'* She put down her cutlery. She wasn't going to eat with Monsieur Courbet standing there watching her.

He was about to speak, when the voice of Madame Courbet called out 'Bernard! *Le taxi est arrivé. Dépêche-toi!'*

Monsieur Courbet pouted at Jasmine, shrugged in resignation and moved to the door. He turned as he left the kitchen and said, *'À la prochaine.'*

Jasmine sat, frozen, until the sound of the heavy front door closing behind the Courbets echoed through the apartment. She took another sip of the wine, grateful for the warming sensation in her mouth and throat. What an odd couple they were: Madame, tall, waspish, skinny, and exuding *froideur*; Monsieur like a tubby Napoleon. While friendlier than his wife, his wasn't a natural warmth that made Jasmine feel comfortable. Rather it was a condescending, proprietorial manner, as though she ought to be grateful he was bestowing his patronage upon her. And that hand kiss. She shuddered. Creepy. If only she'd been staying with the Hendersons as planned. Things would be so much easier with an English family to explain French customs and help ease her into the Parisian way of life.

She lifted her fork and picked at the salad, remembering how Monique, her French teacher in Nairobi, had warned her not to judge the French by Parisians, who she claimed were a different species. At the time, Jasmine had been amused and thought Monique, who came from Provence, must be exaggerating. Now she wasn't so sure.

The following morning, to Jasmine's relief, when she ventured forth from her bedroom she met Marielle in the passageway and was told that Monsieur Courbet had left for the office and Madame never rose before ten. The maid led her into the kitchen where a basket of warm brioches was waiting, along with a dish of jam and pats of soft butter. Jasmine took a seat and Marielle passed her a large cup of milky coffee, with a smile.

They spoke in French and to Jasmine's delight Marielle was easy to understand. She asked Jasmine whether she minded eating her meals in the kitchen? Jasmine wanted to tell her that, on the contrary, it was a huge relief. The prospect of making polite conversation with the rather frosty wife and the over-familiar husband was a terrifying one. Instead, she settled on saying that it was perfectly fine.

Marielle, who Jasmine guessed was in her late forties, pulled out a chair and sat down opposite to drink her coffee too. 'Before I forget, Madame asked me to give you a key to the apartment so you won't disturb her. You don't need one for the street door as the concierge will let you in.'

Jasmine took it gratefully.

The French maid smiled at her with what Jasmine realised was sympathy. 'It is very rude of Madame Courbet to make you eat in here with me. She is not a kind woman.' The maid gave a disdainful sniff. '*Très snob.*' She lowered her voice. 'Have you met *him* yet?'

'Briefly. Last night. While I was eating my supper.'

The maid nodded. *'Attention!* He has *les mains baladeuses.'*

Jasmine wasn't clear what she meant, but hoped she'd be able to work it out as the maid continued.

'Since the end of the war they have had an au pair from England every year. To help me with the housework and for Madame to improve her English. But they never stayed long. Now, no more.' She clapped her hands together and leaned forward conspiratorially. 'Either they left because they didn't like his behaviour or, if they were prepared to put up with it, Madame dismissed them.'

Jasmine felt herself blushing. She realised Marielle's reference must have been to wandering hands. 'You aren't suggesting he will try that with me?'

'Mais oui. You are a pretty girl. As I said, *faites attention!'* The woman studied Jasmine, then added, 'You know Madame plans for you to be the new au pair. She will expect you to perform household duties in exchange for staying here.'

'But my stepfather made an arrangement to pay for my board.'

Marielle shrugged. 'That doesn't mean Madame won't try to treat you as another servant. She'll wait a few days then she will start giving you orders.'

'I can't work as an au pair. I'm here to study. I have a place at the École des Beaux-Arts. I'll be there every day, except the weekends.'

The maid smiled. 'Well, I have warned you. That's all I can do.' She moved over to the door, opened it and looked down the corridor. 'She'll still be sleeping. A good two hours yet.' Marielle sat down again and tore a croissant apart, dipping a piece into her coffee. 'She's often out at the ballet or the theatre. He doesn't go with her. Only when they dine with friends. When she's out you need to be careful. It's always the same thing. First, he'll come in here when you're alone and ask to read aloud in English for you to correct his pronunciation. That's how it starts with all of them. Agatha Christie. He will bring you pastries and chocolates. Invite you into the *salon* for an aperitif. Then he will pounce.' She jerked her hands forward like claws.

Jasmine stared at her, mute, unsure whether she'd understood correctly and too embarrassed to ask.

Removing all doubt, Marielle said, 'Make sure to lock your bedroom door. They sleep in separate rooms and she takes a pill to help her sleep. That's when he will try to seduce you.'

Jasmine couldn't believe what she was hearing.

'Susan, the girl who was here last summer only stayed three weeks.' Marielle shook her head, looking doleful. 'Emily was next and she was prepared to put up with it. He bought her jewellery and gave her extra cash. A nice little arrangement.' She dunked another piece of croissant. 'Until one evening Madame came home early with a headache and caught them.' She gave Jasmine a knowing look. 'On the best Aubusson carpet in the salon. Bags packed and in the hall before the evening was done. She doesn't want him herself. But she doesn't want anyone else to have him either.' Leaning forward, she added, 'Like most women, she's happy to look the other way if he's discreet. But doing it in the middle of the apartment on her best carpet is another matter.'

Jasmine bit her lip. Most women? What on earth had she walked into? 'Has he... has he tried ... with you?'

Marielle gave a gutsy laugh. 'No, *ma petite*. I'm far too old and ugly for his taste. He may be a fat old man himself, but he likes them young and pretty. Just like you. That's why she's unfriendly to you. She knows he's going to try it on. It's just a matter of time.'

Jasmine took a gulp of coffee, but it had gone cold. 'I won't be staying long. I was supposed to stay with an English family. The Hendersons.'

'The Hendersons live upstairs. Next floor. His mother's

dying. That's why they went back to England suddenly. Their maid says they won't be back for some time. Maybe never. A nice couple. You'd have been all right with them. *Tant pis.*' Marielle glanced up at the clock on the wall above the sink. '*Eh, bien!* I must get on. She'll be annoyed if the bathroom's not sparkling clean when she gets up for her bath. If I were you, I'd spend as little time here as possible.'

'*Merci*, Marielle. I'll start looking for somewhere to live right away.'

Jasmine was due to meet the principal that afternoon at the art school. When she came out of the apartment building, the air in the street was noticeably colder than on the previous day and she was glad she'd worn a cardigan. She took the Métro to Étoile, changing onto the red line towards Château Vincennes, intending to spend her free morning exploring the Louvre.

Inside the Métro, there was a stale unpleasant smell, a mix of cigarette smoke and what she couldn't help but recognise as urine. The French seemed to have a strangely practical attitude to urination. Yesterday as she had strolled around, she had noticed all the odd-looking *pissoirs,* where men slipped behind a flimsy green metal partition to relieve themselves, the effluent often flowing across the pavement. She'd also come across metal signs on walls, bearing the words '*Défense d'uriner*'. Why should it be necessary to tell people not to urinate against a wall in a busy thoroughfare?

The train rattled through the stations, most of her fellow passengers with their heads in books. Jasmine carried her trusty battered satchel across her shoulder, with sketch-pads, pencils and charcoal inside, ready to start her classical drawings. The meeting with Bernard Courbet last night had unsettled her – and Marielle's revelations had shocked her to the core. Feeling lonely, she scrabbled in her satchel and took out the letter from Howard. The words that had annoyed her yesterday were oddly comforting now. She would give anything for him to be here with her right now. He wouldn't let Bernard Courbet lay a finger on her or allow his wife to bully her. She imagined Howard punching him on the nose – and putting the hoity-toity Madame Courbet in her place. But Howard wasn't here.

Jasmine knew she mustn't let the maid's possibly unfounded warning derail her adventure. She'd be meeting Stan in a couple of days and he might be able to help her find somewhere to live. Surely she could cope with the Courbets for a few more days?

Jasmine gazed up at the façade of the Louvre, as she stood in the courtyard, the Cour Napoléon, taking in the grandeur of the building. Its vastness dwarfed her – making her insignificant – if it was possible to feel any smaller than she already had since arriving in Paris.

Snap out of it, Jasmine, she told herself. How long have you dreamt of standing here, on the threshold of the Louvre, moments from seeing some of the greatest works of art in the world? She took a deep breath and headed for the entrance.

Deciding to start on her drawing project before she met her tutor, she went straight to the classical sculpture galleries. After wandering amongst the white figures, she settled on a bench in front of a statue of Aphrodite. Jasmine stared at the cold marble, examining its shape and form. She'd never attempted to draw anything like that before. Solid, motionless, monochrome. Arthur had once told her that white Greek statues had originally been a riot of colours. What was the word he'd used? Polychromatic. Maybe she ought to draw it now with coloured pencils, giving it the vibrancy she imagined it might once have had.

She was about to start, when she reminded herself that the requirement for the classical portfolio was to test her drawing skills not her powers of imagination. There was already evidence of that in the rest of her portfolio.

A sigh escaped her as she studied the white goddess before her. Aphrodite had one breast bared but there was nothing brazen about her. The rest of her body was draped in a robe which, despite being carved from stone, seemed to be of a diaphanous fabric, clearly intended to seem wet, so that it clung to each curve, leaving little to the imagination. The thin drapery followed every bodily contour, drawing the eye to the triangle at the top of the legs. Jasmine remembered that Aphrodite was, like the Roman Venus, the goddess of love, beauty and sex. Her expression was serene, one hand holding out an apple, the other holding up her robe. One leg was bent, the other straight. Whilst she had an air of modesty, that triangle at the top of her legs was clearly intended by the sculptor to draw the eye. Jasmine marvelled at the way that ancient Athenian had managed to create such a soft effect from the hard stone. She gazed at the sculpture, imagining a flesh and blood model standing in front of the artist. Was that how the Greeks did it? Did a young woman remove her clothes and stand wrapped in a sheet of damp muslin for hours while the sculptor worked? Or did he first attempt to draw the woman, only later hammering away to bring her forth out of the cold hard stone?

Another sigh. Drawing a statue seemed a strange and gratuitous exercise – recreating something that itself was an attempt to recreate and capture the fluidity in movement of a physical woman – who herself was imitating a mythical goddess rising from the sea. Wheels within wheels.

Surely it was better to draw from life or from the imagination – not from another artist's work. This was more like draughtsmanship than art – slavishly copying something that had sprung from someone else's hands and head – even if many hundreds of years earlier. It was not only difficult, it seemed pointless.

Her eyes darted between the statue and her drawing-pad as she struggled to reproduce on the page what she saw in front of her. After half an hour, she held the drawing out at arm's length and compared it against the original.

The proportions were all wrong. The legs were too short and the hand which held the edge of the flimsy garment above one shoulder looked ugly and clumsy.

What had she been thinking? How could she have had the nerve to presume she merited a place in the school where artists such as Delacroix, Fragonard, Seurat and Sisley had studied? The school which turned down two applications from Cézanne? How could she, an untrained dabbler, deserve to be admitted? What arrogance! It was hopeless.

Tears of frustration and shame stung her eyes. She pictured herself back in Nairobi admitting to her family that she hadn't made the cut. Or returning to Penang and the Hyde-Underwoods, telling them – and worse, Howard Baxter – that she was a failure. After the humiliation she would never be able to recapture the spontaneity and joy that had driven her art until now. It would be the end.

The thought was intolerable. She wasn't going to be cowed by a piece of old marble. She wasn't going down without a fight.

Grabbing her drawing-pad and pencils she moved further down the gallery to where the famous *Venus de Milo* stood regally on a marble pedestal. At least there were no awkward hands to draw. And, rather than translucent damp voile, this goddess was partly clothed in a more substantial fabric which hung in heavy folds over her nether regions. No suggestive triangle at the top of these legs. Taking up her pencil she began to draw again.

Two hours later, Jasmine decided she'd made a creditable stab at drawing the armless statue. She glanced at her wristwatch. Time to go. She didn't intend to risk being late for her appointment. She wanted to walk there rather than plunging into the claustrophobic depths of the Métro again.

On her way out of the Louvre, Jasmine passed through a gallery hung with enormous oils and paused in front of a painting of a reclining nude. She'd seen this painting before in art books and encyclopaedias. *La Grande Odalisque* by Ingres. The concubine reclined on a bed, her back to the viewer, surrounded by lush drapery and holding a peacock feather fan. Ingres was another alumnus of the Beaux-Arts and had won the prestigious *Prix de Rome*, awarded annually to the most talented student. As she studied the painting, Jasmine realised the body of the naked woman was distorted. Her back, hips and bottom were impossibly elongated. Grotesquely stretched. Ingres must have made a mistake to have exaggerated the length and curvature of her spine. No woman was ever shaped that way. Jasmine felt vindicated. When she left the Louvre she was smiling.

Crossing the river to the left bank via the Pont des Arts, she walked westwards, with the Louvre across the water on the other side. She imagined others walking these same cobbled streets: artists, poets, writers, musicians. The very air of Paris was pregnant with the dreams fulfilled, or not, of others for generations before her. Remembering her meeting with Stan the previous day, she tried to picture how the city must have been just five years earlier, with Nazi soldiers everywhere.

The École des Beaux-Arts was in Rue Bonaparte. When all those famous men whose works adorned the walls of the Louvre had studied here, did they dream of a future where people would stand in awed silence in front of their paintings? It was odd to think that long after they were gone, their legacy would live on to be admired for generations. Jasmine shuddered again. She was an imposter.

Trying to push away her nerves, she gulped a breath of air then stepped through the gateway between two stone pillars, both surmounted by large stone busts of what she presumed to be long-dead artists. A tall column topped by a statue rose in front of her. The building itself was decorated with stone carvings depicting yet more great men. Replicas of ancient columns and plinths were dotted around the courtyard, a kind of outdoor museum to the classical origins of architecture. The whole place was intimidating in its grandeur and its celebration of artistic achievement.

Jasmine stepped beneath a stone triumphal arch into an inner courtyard and entered the Palais des Études. At the centre of the building was an enormous glass-roofed court, filled with plaster casts of more classical statuary, dominated by a gigantic replica of Doric columns from the Parthenon. Jasmine was awed. She was tempted to turn and run but a caretaker approached her. She gave her name. He nodded and told her to follow him.

Monsieur Rochambeau, the principal, slouched in his chair, looking Jasmine up and down as she waited nervously for him to invite her to sit. She guessed he was in his late fifties, with thick black hair white at the temples and a long straight nose. His nostrils flared and his heavy black brows narrowed as he studied her. Jasmine sensed he had taken an instant dislike to her. Imagining him thinking her a foolish young girl, wasting his time, she pulled back her shoulders and forced herself to speak, asking him whether she might be permitted to sit.

He didn't answer but nodded towards the empty chair on her side of his desk. 'At least you speak French,' he said at last, in English, while lighting a cigarette. 'The Americans rarely bother to try.'

'I'm British,' she said.

'I know that.' He waved a paper at her and she saw it was

her application form. 'I can read. Do you understand why you are here?'

'To complete a series of classical drawings in order for my admission to be confirmed.' She tried to assert herself, when all she really wanted to do was curl up in a ball and disappear.

'You understand correctly.'

'I'm grateful for the opportunity to prove myself.'

Rochambeau gave a dismissive wave of his hand.

Her portfolio lay on the desk and she swallowed, aware that she was shaking as he opened it.

'Where did you study painting?'

'I didn't. I just started to do it. Since I was a small child, I've loved to draw. My mother encouraged me but my school didn't have an art teacher, so I experimented and looked at books.'

He flipped the sheets over, pausing when he came to a watercolour she had done of Evie on the boat when they went back to Penang last year.

'Your work is naive. My colleagues on the admissions board believe you deserve a chance. I do not share their faith. I hope you prove me wrong, but I fear, Miss Barrington, that you won't.'

She gulped, her stomach hollow.

'You will have access to the plaster casts here at the Beaux-Arts for the next two weeks. I would encourage you also to use the Louvre. You are expected to produce a portfolio of no fewer than twenty detailed pencil drawings of a range of subjects. When these are complete I will meet with my colleagues and we will determine whether you merit a place. We will be looking for visual accuracy, an understanding of form, proportions and perspective, and a demonstration of the techniques of light and shade.' His black eyebrows moved together like a pair of fat hairy caterpillars. 'Is that clear?'

Jasmine nodded.

Raising his voice, he called through an open side door into

the adjacent office. 'Mademoiselle Daudin, take this prospective student to Monsieur Robertson please. He should be in his atelier.'

A small woman, her grey hair scraped into a bun, came into the room, and offered Jasmine a beaming smile. '*Allons-y!*' she said, shepherding her out of the office. Once they had moved down the corridor, the woman smiled again. 'Monsieur Rochambeau *fait plus de bruit que de mal*,' explaining that the tutor's bark was worse than his bite.

Shaking with nerves after her brief encounter with the principal, Jasmine followed the woman deeper into the building. As they were passing a heavy door the secretary paused and pushed it open so that Jasmine could look inside.

'This is the Salle de Prix, where the *Prix de Rome* and other prizes are presented. And that is our hemicycle,' she said proudly, indicating a spectacular mural. 'We are very proud of this beautiful room. Our students cannot fail but be inspired in such surroundings.'

Banked seating rose, amphitheatre-style, and behind, covering the semicircular wall, was the mural. Jasmine wanted to stand gazing at it, at the rich colours, at the scale and scope of the work. It depicted a classical temple structure which hosted an assembly of men deep in discussion.

'All the greatest artists since antiquity,' said the secretary.

Scores of men in costumes from togas to monastic robes, from regal gowns to doublet and hose, stood grouped in front of the classical façade, clearly locked in learned debate. In the centre, an almost naked woman was half kneeling as she cast forth laurel crowns as though bestowing them on the fortunate prizewinners in the room.

'Who are the men on the thrones in the middle?'

'Phidias, the ancient Greek sculptor, Ictinus the architect and Apelles the painter, each representing the disciplines studied here at the school. It was painted by Paul Delaroche.'

If Jasmine had been feeling presumptuous before, it was nothing to the sense of inadequacy she experienced now. Inspired and intimidated at the same time, she followed Mademoiselle Daudin along another corridor, across a courtyard until the secretary stopped at a door, knocked then ushered her in, whispering, 'You'll like Monsieur Robertson.'

The studio was large, bright and scattered with easels. In the corner, his back to the room, stood a man cleaning brushes at a sink. He turned to greet them. The secretary lifted her eyebrows to Jasmine as though affirming what she'd just said, then slipped away, leaving Jasmine alone with him.

Jasmine stared. The art teacher was slightly above average height, with a heavy beard and overlong dark brown hair. He was wearing a paint-spattered shirt and corduroy trousers. His brown eyes were warm, his smile broad and engaging. Undeniably handsome.

He moved across the room, weaving between the empty easels towards Jasmine. To her surprise and relief, he addressed her in English – with a Scottish accent. 'Lachlan Robertson,' he said, grasping her hand firmly. 'You're Jasmine Barrington? For your sins, you've been assigned to my atelier.' He smiled, his eyes crinkling, and she decided Mademoiselle Daudin was right. It would be hard not to like the Scotsman.

'You're Scottish,' she said stating the obvious.

'Aye, I canna deny it,' he said. 'My father is Scottish but my mother is French so I'm a bit of both.' He gave her a broad smile and to her chagrin she realised she was blushing. 'I teach in French, but they tend to wheel me out for those foreigners who struggle with the language. We usually have a lot of Americans. The GI Bill has encouraged many to study overseas. Although this year I think there's only one, so maybe studying art in Paris is falling out of fashion with the Yanks.'

'*Je parle français*,' she said, immediately wishing she hadn't.

'Let's get something to drink. I have nothing here so we'll go outside. I suggest you choose coffee as the French don't understand how to make tea.' He looked at her and smiled again.

She decided he was the smiliest person she'd ever met.

'I want to know all about you, Jasmine. Then I'll tell you what you'll need to do to satisfy old Beetle Brows.'

Jasmine giggled at his description of Monsieur Rochambeau. 'Does everyone call him that?'

'God, no! No one would dare, in case it got back to him. But we're safe speaking English. He can't manage more than a few phrases. By the way, call me Lachlan. I can't abide formality.'

Lachlan grabbed his jacket from where it was flung over the corner of an easel and shrugged it on. Jasmine, smiling with relief to have a tutor she was certain she'd get on with, followed him back through the corridors and courtyards. Her heart was lighter.

He took her to a small near-empty bar in a street close to the École. The owner greeted Lachlan like a friend, shaking hands vigorously before reaching for a bottle of whisky.

'*Pas encore*, Patrice, *nous prenons deux cafés.*' Lachlan waved away the offered whisky. 'I'm with a student. Allow me to present Jasmine.'

The bartender inclined his head and murmured, '*Enchanté, Mademoiselle.*'

They went to sit at a small round table at the rear of the bar and Patrice brought the coffees over to them. Jasmine was nervous. Not in the way she'd been with the intimidating Monsieur Rochambeau, but with an urge to impress and a desperate desire not to appear as young and foolish as she felt.

'I was impressed with your portfolio,' Lachlan said, slugging his coffee down in a single gulp. 'Your sense of colour, the bold use of form. There's a natural exuberance that seems to jump off the paper.'

She felt the blood rush to her face. 'Gosh!' Then, anxious

he'd think her stupid, added, 'I was worried because Monsieur Rochambeau accused my work of being naive.'

Lachlan smiled. 'Och, that for him is actually a compliment.' He gazed at her and she felt her face heat up again.

'Naive painting is not an insult. It is a term for artists like you, who have not received formal training – or for trained artists who deliberately adopt a more primitive style.'

She listened intently.

'Have ye heard of Henri Rousseau?'

Jasmine shook her head, embarrassed. Her art education was non-existent.

'He was untrained. Other artists mocked and ridiculed him until one day Picasso picked up a canvas of his in Les Puces.'

'Les Puces?'

'It's a flea market. It was being sold for someone to paint over, but Picasso recognised the brilliance of the work and set about making sure others knew of him. Some of Picasso's own work has a primitive style that could be described as naive, although he studied at art school and was taught by his father too. But it all came naturally to the untutored Rousseau.' He reached into his jacket pocket, extracted a pouch of tobacco and some papers and rolled a cigarette. 'You'll no longer be able to lay claim to the term naive, Jasmine, once you've been trained here.' He made a fist. 'But I will make it my mission to ensure that as you learn skills and techniques you don't lose the spontaneity and joy that characterises your work so far.'

Jasmine didn't know how to respond. She looked at him, awed by his words.

Lachlan drew on his cigarette and studied her face. She felt her cheeks reddening again, uncomfortable that someone like him was showing so much interest in her. His gaze was intense, and she felt exposed.

After a few moments she said, 'I won't get the chance to learn the techniques if I can't produce the drawings Monsieur

Rochambeau expects, and judging by the mess I made in the Louvre this morning...' Her voice trailed away.

'Show me.'

Jasmine wished she'd kept her mouth shut. Reaching into her satchel she handed him her sketch-pad and barely dared to breathe as he opened it.

He flipped through the pages then closed the book and put it down. 'You didn't find that much fun, did you?'

She shook her head. Was it so obvious? 'It seemed a point-less exercise. And very hard.'

'Why did you find it so difficult?'

'Because it was copying. What's the point of that? No one wants to look at a copy of an old statue.'

He drew on his roll-up. 'What do you think is the most important part of an artist's anatomy?'

Jasmine frowned. Had she misunderstood the question? But they were speaking English and she'd heard every word. 'Hands I suppose. Without them we wouldn't be able to draw or paint.'

'There are people who have no hands who learn to use their feet or their mouths.'

'Head?' She spoke tentatively, then with more confidence. 'Yes, the brain, the source of imagination.'

He pushed his chair back. It made a scraping sound on the tiled floor. He crossed one ankle over the other knee. 'The eyes,' he said. He tapped the cover of her drawing-pad. 'You didn't use them enough in this exercise. You drew what you thought you saw, not what was actually there.' He smiled. 'Don't look so glum, Jasmine. It's why you're here. There'd be nae point if you knew it all already. Your portfolio shows what an incredible raw talent you have. You've an innate understanding of composition, of colour, of light and shade, but now I will give you the tools to underpin it all.'

Jasmine twirled a finger through her hair. She still felt

miserable, deflated. Her work today must be truly dreadful if it didn't merit even a comment.

As though sensing what she felt, Lachlan opened the drawing-pad again. 'You did this first?' he asked indicating the drawing of the Aphrodite statue.

'Yes. And I know I got the proportions all wrong. Her legs are too short. And the hands are terrible. I'm poor at hands. I mostly stick to faces, or loose shapes of bodies without going in close on the details.' She hesitated, then added, 'But I noticed as I was leaving, that even Ingres got his proportions wrong. I was looking at that painting of the naked woman with the incredibly long back.'

Lachlan gave a little tilt of his head. 'Well spotted. Tell me more.'

'I could see there was something not right but I couldn't work out what at first. Then it hit me. I'd seen a picture of the painting before but it hadn't occurred to me until I was in front of the real thing that he'd painted a woman who couldn't possibly have looked like that, unless she was a freak.'

'And do ye think the great Ingres knew nothing of proportions? Or had an off-day?'

She felt foolish again. She had a premonition that he was going to tell her something she didn't want to hear.

'Ingres was a master at drawing the human form. Drawing her that way must have been deliberate. He wasn't making a photographic rendition of a reclining woman.' He rolled another cigarette, keeping his eyes fixed on her as he did it, before bending his head to lick the edge of the paper and seal it. 'She was symbolic. He was making a point. Do you know what an odalisque is?'

She didn't but she could guess.

Without waiting for an answer he said, 'A concubine. There to serve the pleasure of men. What else did you notice about her?'

Jasmine tried to recreate the painting in her memory. 'She had a peacock fan. The bed was covered with lots of fabrics. Her back was facing the viewer and her head was turned to look straight at me.'

'Aye! Well observed. No one can know for certain what Ingres intended, but it's probable he wanted to contrast the difference between her true self – a proud, almost disdainful, woman and the image and function men ascribed to her – a body to be used for their pleasure. Hence the long back and overlarge pelvic area.'

Jasmine wished now she'd never brought the subject up.

'Save your blushes, lassie. You'll need to get used to talking about bodies and looking at them in great detail.'

Jasmine felt as though she were about twelve. She pulled back her shoulders and sat upright, trying to project a more confident image.

'Did ye look at any more of Ingres' works? If you did, you'll be all too aware there's no lack of understanding of human anatomy and bodily proportions. Once you've mastered the rules you're free to break them.'

'I can't believe I ever will.'

'Calm doon, Jasmine. I'm going to teach you all about proportions. About anatomy, perspective, symmetry. Right now you're probably wishing you stayed in Kenya. But I promise you, you're going to love it.' He turned the page, flicked through the rest of her drawings. 'See how even in the time you spent today the work has got better. Still not as good as they will be, but already better than you managed with Aphrodite. Did you show these to Beetle Brows?'

She was horrified. 'No.'

'Good. He'd have said you were wasting your time coming here and will never achieve the standard needed.'

'He did that anyway.' She gave him a baleful smile.

'Well he's wrong.' Lachlan leaned across the table and put

his hand over hers, giving it a gentle squeeze. 'You're going to prove that to him. I'll help ye show him.' He exaggerated his Scottish burr. 'Och, he's talking oot his arse.'

She felt a rush of excitement. 'You think I can prove him wrong? In only two weeks?'

'With my help you can. We'll have a braw time. Tomorrow I am going to set you to work to draw a cast. I'm going to make you do it multiple times. You'll hate me for it but you'll learn so much.'

Jasmine couldn't even conceive of the possibility of hating this charismatic man.

He turned and called to Patrice. *'Un pichet de rouge, mon ami.'* He handed the sketch-pad back to Jasmine. 'You can put that away for today and tell me all about yourself over a drink. Then tomorrow we begin work.'

It was after seven when Jasmine and Lachlan left the bar. By then the place had filled up with people and the noise level was rising. Unused to drinking, and having helped her teacher get through two *pichets* of red wine, Jasmine felt slightly unsteady on her feet. Once outside in the cooling air of the early evening, she began to feel more herself.

They walked down narrow streets to the Seine and along the waterfront towards the towering presence of Notre Dame.

This was the Paris Jasmine had dreamt of. A city bathed in soft light, with ancient buildings, narrow streets, something to draw her eye wherever she walked. And now, to be walking along experiencing it all at the side of her handsome and inspiring teacher gave her a warm glow of happiness. Already, after just a few hours, she realised she was developing a crush. She looked sideways at him, at his purposeful stride, his glossy dark brown hair which at the back of his neck spilled over onto his collar, the dark beard which afforded him an added artistic cachet. Lachlan was the sort of person she expected her mother would describe as bohemian. She glanced down at her neat blouse and skirt, feeling stuffy and overdressed by comparison. She remembered Stan with his silk scarf loosely tied around his neck. Clearly, if Jasmine were to immerse herself in the artistic life of this magical city, she must start dressing the part.

They crossed the river via the Île de la Cité, taking the Pont Saint-Michel and passing over the island to the Pont au Change. Down below them, along the embankment, groups of people were clustered together, some sleeping under blankets, many talking quietly, one or two folding up items of clothing they'd washed and left to dry on the stone quays. An old man in tattered trousers was playing an accordion.

'Who are all those people?' she asked Lachlan.

He looked to where she was pointing. 'Homeless people. *Clochards*.'

'Tramps,' she said, understanding. 'Why don't the police tell them to go away? Surely they don't allow them to sleep down there? It looks so awful, so many people huddled together with all their belongings, spoiling the beautiful riverbanks.'

Lachlan frowned. 'They're not tramps by choice, Jasmine.' Did she detect censure in his tone? 'Many are refugees. God knows what some of them have been through. There's a dire housing shortage in Paris. Not to mention unemployment. And what housing there is, is often little better than sleeping under the stars.'

Realising she'd said something tactless, she lapsed into silence, wishing she hadn't asked him. Lachlan must think her a spoilt brat. She'd been used to seeing beggars before in the Far East and in Africa, but these looked like French people, or from other European countries. It shocked her.

'People were displaced in the war. Many lost their homes and families. Cities like Paris can be a magnet, but once here, they discover there's nothing much for them.' Lachlan gave his head a slow shake. 'The French aren't renowned for charitable giving beyond their families. The government does nothing. These people have no choice. All they've got is each other.'

Jasmine felt a rush of shame. Remembering the elegant apartment in Passy and her family's beautiful home in Nairobi, she felt even worse. Her life was privileged – pampered even. What must it be like to have nowhere at all to rest your head, other than the cold unyielding stone of an embankment?

Ahead of them the elegant Tour Saint-Jacques rose up like a sentinel against a darkening sky, now turning blue-black. To Jasmine's left, a rosy glow suffused the sky as the sun disappeared. Forgetting her *faux pas* over the *clochards*, she sighed with pleasure. Looking up at the skyline, lost in a romantic rapture, she was taken by surprise when Lachlan suddenly said goodbye.

'I head off here. I'm going that way.' He indicated the direction with a nod of his head. 'The Métro's just over there. You want the red line. See you tomorrow.' With a cheery wave he began to walk off, stopping to call back to her that he wouldn't be in until around eleven and she was to make a start on drawing the plaster casts in the Grand Court. 'Choose the simplest statue or fragment you can find. When I get in, we'll work in my atelier.'

Jasmine watched him walk away, hoping he would turn round, but he didn't. She remained rooted to the spot until he vanished around a distant corner. She had been nursing an expectation that the evening would go on. That perhaps they might eat together. But now he was gone she realised the silliness of her romantic fantasies. Lachlan was her tutor, not a prospective boyfriend. He was merely being kind and friendly towards her. And yet...

The world was empty now, as if a light had gone out. Just as the departing sun had left a darkened sky, Lachlan's absence made everything seem duller. Jasmine had only known her tutor for a few hours but she was already under his spell. The resolve to make a success of her studies burned like a flame inside her. She would absorb every word he said, soak it all up hungrily and work harder than she'd ever worked before. She couldn't let him down. All that mattered now was hearing words of praise from Lachlan. Whatever it took, she was determined to make him proud and prove Monsieur Rochambeau wrong.

Deciding against another descent into the smelly Métro, she began to walk along the Rue de Rivoli, the dark bulk of the Louvre on her left. She was determined not to be intimidated by the artistic greatness all around her here in Paris. Instead, it would inspire her. She was blessed – not just with natural talents but with the means to use them. It would be an insult to all those poor *clochards* if she were to fritter away her time in the capital when she had so many opportunities on a plate. And with Lachlan to guide her, how could she possibly fail? She intended to throw herself into her art, body and soul. That meant she must be diligent over the next two weeks and focus her mind and energy on those classical drawings, no matter how much her heart resisted.

Realising she was ravenously hungry, Jasmine went into a café and ordered an omelette. As she ate, she allowed herself to replay the conversation they'd had in the bar. It had been rather one-sided, she realised now. Lachlan had bombarded her with questions about her life, about Penang, her experiences during the war and her time in Australia, but he had told her little of himself. She had spoken a lot about the Malayan Emergency but had glossed over her own near encounter with death. Nor had she mentioned her short-lived passion for Bintang, the Hyde-Underwoods' driver. Every time she had asked the Scotsman anything, he'd batted the question away, saying there was plenty of time for that another day. She wondered if perhaps she'd overstepped the mark in asking in the first place.

As her tutor, he probably considered his private life to be none
of her business.

She'd talked about her love for the island of Penang, of how
her childhood memories had inspired her during the years
during and after the war when she was far away from there. 'I
think that's what drew me into painting in the first place –
trying to recreate the place I'd loved, on paper. I was scared that
if it was only a memory in my head it would eventually fade
away. Then, when I was unhappy at school in Nairobi, it helped
me reconnect with Malaya.'

'But you draw from life too – your portfolio is full of paintings of native children, of women at work, and of the country-
side. They can't have been from memory?'

'No, of course. I love painting from life. But living breathing
people, trees that move in the breeze, waves on the beach. Not
crumbly old statues of dead Greeks.'

Lachlan had laughed. When he did, his eyes shone and
Jasmine leaned in closer to him, mesmerised.

'Och, you'll have plenty of chance soon enough to draw real
people. Just get through this stage, Jasmine. It's not as bad as
you fear. You may even get to enjoy it.'

Leaving the café, Jasmine walked on, past the Tuileries
Gardens, across the Place de la Concorde and into the Champs-
Élysées. The wide boulevard was lined with cafés, with terraces
where people were enjoying the still warm evening as they
sipped their digestifs. All around her was the soft hum of
conversation. The huge bulk of the Arc de Triomphe rose up in
front of her; she remembered those wartime photographs of it
draped with an enormous swastika flag. The war had ended
only four years ago, and yet there was little evidence of it in
these prosperous people, unlike the less fortunate ones living on
the banks of the Seine. Just five years ago, before the Allies
liberated Paris, German uniformed officers would have been

lounging at these café tables, drinking champagne and seducing women.

To Jasmine's intense relief all was quiet in the Courbet home when she arrived back just before ten. It seemed the couple were dining out again or had already retired for the night. She slipped off her sandals and crept quietly along the corridor to her tiny bedroom. Following Marielle's advice, she locked the door.

Once tucked up in bed with her book – she had bought a copy of *La Peste* by Albert Camus from a bookstall that morning – Jasmine found she couldn't concentrate. Her head was buzzing. Taking her sketch-book from her bag she did a rapid drawing. This was what she loved: drawing from her mind's eye, from her memory, making patterns and bold shapes rather than attempting verisimilitude. The drawing was of the *clochards* gathered on the wide stone quays of the Seine. It was impressionistic: soft shading, shadowy forms, the overlapping bodies of the huddled people. Real living people, not cold stones.

Remembering what Lachlan had told her, she vowed that no matter how much she disliked drawing ancient statues, she would give it her all and view it as skill-building, not as art in itself. She flipped back through the pages to the sketches she had done in the Louvre. Her tutor was right. She hadn't used her eyes. If she was to earn the right to draw and paint in the way she wanted, she must knuckle under and do as she was told. And how much better to have the warm and sympathetic Scot telling her, than the stern and dismissive Monsieur Rochambeau. She would embrace classical drawing with gusto and determination.

Pushing the drawing-pad back into her satchel, Jasmine's

hand touched the letter from Howard Baxter. Dear old Howard. Much as she was fond of him – cared for him, even – he was the past. They could never have a future together. They were far too different. Now her life was going to be full of interesting creative people like Lachlan and Stan. There was no room for sentimental feelings for a man who was on the other side of the world and who shared none of her artistic passions. A rubber planter for heaven's sake! What could be duller? She crumpled his letter into a ball and dropped it back into the bag before switching off the light.

FOUR

PENANG, MALAYA

July 1949

It was raining. A heavy, tropical downpour, so intense that Howard could see only a few yards in front of him. He listened to the water hammering against the armour plating that enveloped his jeep, grateful that it was cooling the furnace that was the interior. Since the so-called Emergency had begun the previous year with the shooting of three British rubber planters by rebel communist fighters, it was a foolhardy planter who ventured beyond his estate without the protection of steel plating. Better to endure the suffocating heat than risk a bullet through the head as you drove into an ambush.

Over the past few months, there had been little sign of the insurgency at Batu Lembah, the rubber estate where Howard was Assistant Manager. The communist terrorists, or bandits as everyone called them, appeared to be focusing their efforts further south in the Kinta Valley. Once he was safely on the ferry across the straits to the island of Penang, he'd take the heavy metal plates off and stow them in the back. Cut off from their rapid escape routes into the impenetrable jungle that ran the length of the Malay peninsula, the terrorists weren't active on the island.

Driving onto the boat, Howard felt the lift in his spirits that he always experienced on Penang, underlaid with a deep ache of sadness, knowing Jasmine wouldn't be there. Not that she'd always been pleased to see him when he'd turned up at Bella Vista – often she'd be moody and touchy and chew his head off about something trivial. He had to admit he had a talent for saying the wrong thing at the wrong time. But when Jasmine had smiled at him, thrown back her head and laughed, eyes sparkling, or leaned in to listen intently to something he said, his heart had lifted with joy. No one else he had met before or since had the capacity to make him feel this way.

As the ferry docked at Weld Quay, Howard remembered the last time he'd seen Jasmine, when he'd come to the port to see her off on the voyage to rejoin her family in Nairobi. She'd stood on the quayside, telling him about her plans to study art in Paris, and he'd been overwhelmed with love for her – the pain of watching her leave remained with him even now. Even though he'd longed to persuade her to stay in Penang, he loved her too much to ask that. Jasmine was like a beautiful butterfly, needing to fly out into the world. It would have been wrong to hold her back, to cage her.

Although the pain of her absence still cut through him, leaving him raw, he wanted her to chase her dreams. Otherwise, she'd live the rest of her life steeped in regret and disappointment. And she had such talent. There was a brilliance and beauty in her art that even an ignorant brute like him could recognise. Folded in his wallet he carried a small pencil sketch she'd made when they'd swum together on a deserted beach. His most treasured possession. It was all he had to remember her, apart from a few scrawled lines on the back of a picture postcard of the African plains.

· · ·

The Hyde-Underwoods were sitting on the veranda of their large Victorian-built bungalow when Howard's jeep approached. On the grass in front of them, their adopted son, Jasmine's half-brother, Amir, was trying in vain to teach their small daughter Frances to hit a ball with a cricket bat. The two children dropped the bat and ball and rushed to greet Howard as he got out of the vehicle. He tousled Amir's hair, then picked Frances up and spun her around so she giggled in delight.

'All right! That's enough of that!' called Mary to her daughter who was now tugging at Howard's trouser leg, trying to persuade him to do it again. 'It's bedtime in half an hour, darling, and I don't want you too excited to sleep. Daddy and I want to have a chance to talk to our guest before we have dinner.'

Howard bounded up the steps to the veranda, kissed Mary's cheek and had his hand shaken vigorously by Reggie, who pressed a glass tumbler of whisky and soda into his other hand. 'More ice in your *stengah*?'

'No thanks. It looks perfect. It's so good to be up here. A haven of peace.' He indicated the lush lawn and the surrounding mature trees. 'Much cooler and fresher than at Batu Lembah.'

'Any trouble lately?' Reggie asked.

'Fortunately, nothing much at all. The local police station was attacked but it was a half-hearted affair and no one was hurt. Now that we've been issued with Sten guns that actually work, as well as plenty of ammo, the bandits seem to be backing off a bit.'

'Good show,' said Reggie. 'Can't be much fun having to be on your guard all the time. And after that nasty business last year when poor Jasmine nearly copped it, you don't want any more trouble at BL.'

Howard swallowed. Already they were talking of Jasmine. He turned his head to look out over the lawn at the children playing. 'Have you heard from her recently? I imagine she must have left for Paris by now.'

The Hyde-Underwoods exchanged glances. The complicity of the married couple. Mary answered, 'Actually, we had a letter yesterday. Airmail makes such a difference. It used to take weeks but nowadays it's so fast. She sent it as she was leaving Nairobi. Have you heard from her?'

'Just a postcard. Months ago. Nothing since.' He took a swig of his scotch. 'I suppose she doesn't have much time to write. And probably little inclination.' He drained the glass. 'At least to write to me.'

Saved from further discussion by the arrival of Jinjiang, the Hyde-Underwoods' housekeeper, to announce supper, Howard followed his hosts into the dining-room.

Conversation over the meal centred on the political situation. Reggie and Mary were always keen to stay up to date with what was happening on the peninsula, as Penang in general and Bella Vista in particular were removed from the action. Here, situated at the summit of the island, Bella Vista was a calm oasis where it was hard to imagine the precautions needed on most other rubber estates. Yet the conflict had reached them once on the lawns of Bella Vista when Amir's mother, Nayla, had been brutally and unjustifiably shot dead by a British army officer who had maintained she was a member of the *Min Yuen*, the banned civilian group which supported the insurgents, supplying them with food and cash.

'Amir seems to have settled in well,' said Howard.

'He misses his mother of course, but he does seem less anxious. And he now calls us Mummy and Daddy.' She reached for Reggie's hand. 'And Frances is his shadow. She follows him everywhere. Her big brother.'

'Have you formalised the adoption?'

'It's going through,' said Mary. 'But they move at a snail's pace. All being well it should be legal by the end of the year.'

'Have you seen anything more of Lieutenant Ellis?' Howard was referring to the man who had cold-bloodedly shot Nayla and had tried to force himself on Jasmine.

'Was about to ask you the same question.' Reggie steepled his fingers under his nose. 'After I made a formal complaint, they shipped him over to Perak somewhere, rather than court martial the bastard. He's something in Admin. That slimy devil needs to be wading through swamps and pulling leeches off his balls, not pushing a pen like the filthy coward he is.'

'Reggie. Enough.' Mary laid a hand on her husband's forearm. 'You don't want to send your blood pressure soaring.'

Reggie looked sheepish. 'Sorry.'

Mary got up from the table, went over to the sideboard and returned with a letter. 'Here's Jasmine's letter, Howard. Why don't you take it onto the veranda and read it and we'll join you once we've checked on the children.'

The strident noise of crickets pierced the darkness around the bungalow. Moths clustered around the lantern that illuminated the veranda. Howard opened the flimsy airmail paper and saw Jasmine's boldly-inked pen-strokes. Her handwriting was confident, flowing, artistic. Like her.

The letter was full of the minutiae of life in Nairobi. She wrote of the paintings she had been working on, her growing pleasure in the French language and the films she'd seen at the Institut Français to help improve her knowledge of it. The margins were filled with little drawings – a caricature of her brother Hugh, an elegant image of a gazelle – executed with just a few sweeping strokes of her pen. At the end of the letter was a more detailed watercolour study of a sunset. Even the airmail envelope was decorated with a border of fruits and flowers. Such care, such love, such an outpouring of her passion for painting and drawing. Howard bit his lip. It made the scribbled lines on the back of a picture postcard seem like a pointed insult. Jasmine simply didn't care enough for him to send him a part of herself.

He folded up the letter and released a long sigh. Yet, if it were a choice between a dashed-off postcard or nothing at all, he'd settle for the postcard. At least that card meant that for a few measly moments he had inhabited her head.

FIVE

PARIS

July 1949

Jasmine was deep in concentration. She was in La Cour Vitrée, the covered courtyard of the Palais des Études, drawing a cast of a man's foot and it was taking every ounce of willpower to stay focused on it.

Before beginning, she'd studied the naked foot thoroughly, trying to imagine it wasn't a foot but a random shape she'd never seen before and was seeing now for the first time. She had noted the proportion between toes and foot, the angle of the turn in the heel, the varying sizes of the individual toes and their placement relative to each other. Then, nervously, she'd begun to draw, building up layers on the paper, shading and cross-hatching until the foot was complete. As she held it up to compare it with the plaster model in front of her, she knew at once it was wrong. She must start again. Absorbed in the task, she didn't hear Lachlan approaching across the covered courtyard.

'Nice cross-hatching, good observation of light and shade. But you know where you're going wrong don't you?'

Jasmine jumped. He was standing right behind her. 'I was so careful. I worked out the actual proportions on the cast and then used them in the drawing but it's completely wrong.'

'No one's taught you about foreshortening?' he asked, leaning over her shoulder.

'No one's taught me about anything.'

He dangled a paper bag in front of her. 'I have croissants and remembered to bring a packet of tea. Let's go to my atelier and I'll explain while I brew up.'

Half an hour later, refreshed by a warm croissant and a cup of strong tea, Jasmine was buzzing with excitement as well as frustration at herself. 'Now you've explained foreshortening to me it's obvious. How could I have been so stupid?'

'Och, you're nae stupid at all. It took until the Renaissance before anyone figured it out. Thousands of years after men starting painting on cave walls. How could you expect to work it out for yersel'? Here, let me show you something.' He moved across to a large cabinet of narrow drawers, opened one and shuffled through some papers.

'Here's a grand example. It's by the Italian painter Andrea Mantegna. *The Lamentation over the Dead Christ.* We're looking at Christ's body from the perspective of the foot of the bed. Now compare the proportions of the legs, which are nearer to you, with the torso and arms which are further away.' He continued to explain, showing her another drawing of a man upright to highlight the difference. 'The eye plays tricks on us. If Mantegna had drawn the dead Christ according to the exact proportions of an upright man it would look odd – too elongated.' He did a quick pencil sketch to illustrate his point. 'But, strictly speaking, if he'd been entirely faithful to the principles, Mantegna would have made Christ's feet even bigger as they're closest to the viewer. But he chose not to. Probably to ensure the viewer's focus is on Christ's face. A great artist can choose when to go for the most realistic approach and when to allow his own artistry to take over. Like the Ingres painting you mentioned yesterday.' He placed a hand on her shoulder. 'It's only when all the tools are at your disposal that you can choose when and how to use or reject them. Your task right now, Jasmine, is to learn the techniques and understand them.'

For Jasmine it was a revelation, like discovering the keys to a box of treasures. Her gratitude and happiness made her light-headed.

He set her to work, drawing a series of plaster cast hands and feet, positioning them in relation to different angles. She became so absorbed in her task that the hours flew by.

'It's nearly six,' said Lachlan, emerging from behind the easel where he had been working all day on his own canvas.

Jasmine was dying to see what he'd produced but hesitated to ask, aware that some artists were sensitive about their works in progress. Once she knew him a little better, she'd pluck up the courage to ask him to show her.

'Ready for a drink?' he asked.

It was only then that she remembered the arrangement to meet Stan. Now bereft at having to forego her tutor's company, she told herself there was always tomorrow. Making her apologies, she left the studio and hurried up the Rue Bonaparte.

The address Stan had written on the scrap of paper was of a café called Les Deux Magots and, according to her trusty street map, it was where Rue Bonaparte joined the Boulevard Saint-Germain. Even the names of the streets were magical. If only she could find somewhere to live here in the Quartier Latin. She didn't care how basic it was. It was enough to be here in the midst of life on the Left Bank. Here – or in nearby Montparnasse which she understood was the hub of the artistic community.

It was a balmy evening and although Stan had told her the French deserted Paris during August, all the pavement tables were occupied. She went inside Les Deux Magots, looking around for her new friend. He was at the back of the room, the table in front of him covered with sheets of paper. He was bent over one, writing furiously.

'Hello, Stan,' she said. 'I'm interrupting your work?'

He gave her a welcoming smile. 'Take a seat, Jazz. I'm done. Some days it flows like a river and today was one of them. Tomorrow I'll read it again and probably tear it to shreds.'

'Then don't read it. Just keep writing.'

He chuckled. 'I wish it was that simple. I'm one of those writers cursed by the need to edit their work as they go. Constantly striving for perfection but finding it's always out of reach.'

She slid onto the banquette opposite him. 'It's the same for painters. Nothing's as good as the idea you have in your head.'

He summoned the waiter and ordered a pastis for himself and asked her what she would like. 'I got paid yesterday so I'm feeling flush.' He wasn't wearing his sunglasses so she could now see his eyes. They were large under heavy, hooded lids and were smiling now. Despite the smile there was an underlying sadness in them.

She asked for a glass of red wine. She was developing a taste for it. 'Do you always write here? Don't they mind?'

'Sometimes here, but mostly in Flore just opposite. I know the waiters better there. They like to cultivate artists and intellectuals. Seem to think the tourists like it. At Flore I work upstairs. Both these places have been a haven for writers for decades.' He jerked his head towards a table on the other side of the room. A short man with hair combed back from his brow and wearing rounded spectacles appeared to be holding court to a group of people. 'You know who he is?'

Jasmine shook her head.

'Heard of Jean-Paul Sartre?'

She had but wasn't sure why or for what reason. 'Isn't he a writer too?'

'A writer. A philosopher. A political theorist. And the woman opposite him is Simone de Beauvoir.'

Jasmine had never heard of her but was too embarrassed to admit it.

As if sensing her discomfort, Stan told her De Beauvoir had just published a book that was the talk of Paris. *Le Deuxième Sexe.*

'Have you read it?' she asked him.

'Not yet, but I'm sure I will. Although as a black man and a homosexual I happen to think being a woman is surely a much lighter burden to bear – at least that's the case back home.'

Jasmine was taken aback and felt herself flushing. A man openly admitting to being a homosexual. That would never happen with an English man. Maybe Americans were more relaxed about such things. Or perhaps it was because they were in Paris. She was already getting the feeling that the French viewed such matters in a different way. Suppressing her surprise, she asked, 'Is that what her book's about? Women being wrongly seen as inferior to men?' She was curious now and decided she would drop into a bookshop and pick up a copy.

Stan waved a hand airily. 'I believe so, but as I said, I haven't read it yet. Now, tell me Jazz, how's it going at the art school?'

She heaved a long sigh. 'Harder than I expected. I have to complete twenty detailed pencil drawings of classical objects and they must pass muster with the head of the admissions board or I will be denied my place when term begins.'

'Is that so hard?'

'Dreadful!' It was a relief to tell someone who was not part of the school about her struggles. 'I've never had any art lessons and I'm more used to painting from the heart, not copying old statues.' Then, feeling guilty after all the kindness Lachlan had shown her, added, 'But I'm learning so much. I have a wonderful tutor and he is teaching me so many new things. He's awfully encouraging. I'm going to work as hard as I can to produce the best set of drawings I've ever done in my life.'

Stan smiled, nodding sagely. 'Then you will. You seem a very determined young woman. How's posh Passy?'

Jasmine rolled her eyes. 'Frightful. Madame has made it clear that I am staying there on sufferance and, according to the maid, Monsieur is one of those dreadful men who creep up and pounce on women.' She gave him a shy smile. 'I lock the bedroom door, just in case.'

'Bad as that, eh?' His lip curled. 'Maybe you need to give him a copy of Simone's book.'

'I have to find somewhere else to live.' She looked at him, hoping he'd remember his offer to help her find a place to stay. 'Passy's so dull and suburban. Quiet and boring. I'd like to be closer to the École and the places around here.'

'For someone who's only been here a couple of days you seem to have already made your mind up about it.'

She blushed. 'Sorry. I don't mean to be dismissive. It's just—'

'No need to explain, Jazz. If I was told I had to live in the *seizième*, I'd be on the next ship back across the Atlantic.' Seeing her horrified expression he gave a dry laugh. 'I'm joking, Jasmine.' He pronounced her full name with a stress on the second syllable, Jasm*ee*ne.

She was tempted to correct him but decided she liked it and anyway he mostly shortened it to Jazz.

'Nothing would convince me to return to the US of A.' He started to gather up the papers on the table in front of him. 'No, ma'am, I'm staying in Europe. I'll probably end up living in the south when I'm done with Paris. On the Côte d'Azur in the sunshine. You must go. Painters love it.' He gathered the papers loosely and stuffed them into a canvas bag on the bench beside him. 'Drink up, Jazz. We're moving on. I'm going to introduce you to some of my friends.'

. . .

Stan took her to another bar, somewhere in the maze of nearby streets.

Following close behind him as he pushed open the door into the dimly-lit interior, Jasmine felt a frisson of nerves. She barely knew Stan. Was she right to trust him? What would Evie have said about her daughter befriending a man she'd met by chance in the street? But then what would Evie have said about the awful circumstances of her accommodation in Passy, with the predatory Monsieur Courbet and the cold bitchiness of Madame?

The bar had looked empty from the outside but, inside, Jasmine's ears were assaulted by the clink of glasses and the sound of animated voices. As her eyes adjusted to the gloom, she realised it was crowded. Stan squeezed past the clientele clustered near the zinc-topped bar and headed toward a group of people around a table at the rear. They all looked up and greeted him; he reached behind him, put a hand on Jasmine's shoulder and drew her in front of him to present her to the group.

'This is Jasmine. She's new in town,' he said, in slow awkward French. 'From darkest Africa. A British colonial. Here in Paris to become a great artist. She needs a place to stay. I'm hoping one of you might be able to help her.'

There was a scraping of chairs as the occupants of the table made room for them to sit down. Jasmine slipped onto a proffered chair, nervous, as Stan took a seat on the far side of the table. This would be a test for her language skills – after speaking in English with both Stan and Lachlan.

She was relieved, but slightly nonplussed when, instead of conversing with her, the people at the table immediately returned to their chatter. On her left-hand side was a young woman, around her own age, with dark brown hair drawn back into a ponytail. The woman spoke in rapid and hard-to-follow French with the person on Jasmine's right, a short, olive-skinned man with tousled over-long hair. They leaned forward to hear each other over the surrounding din, so that Jasmine was forced to lean back to accommodate them. She struggled to follow the nuances of what they were discussing so intensely and strained to make out the words which flew in a fast argot.

Someone had thrust a tumbler of wine in her direction and she accepted it gratefully. When she took a sip, it tasted robust, rough, but warming; it helped to calm her nerves.

Across the table she could see the top of Stan's head; he was bent over, deep in conversation with an older man who looked rather like a Spanish gypsy. As the two interlocutors beside her continued their increasingly heated debate, Jasmine's gaze took in the rest of the table. It was a motley crew. Men and women of a variety of ages, probably nationalities too. One person was in a man's linen suit, but with an over-large silk *foulard* knotted flamboyantly at the neck and an exaggeratedly made-up face and perfect, ruby red, Cupid's bow lips. Jasmine was unable to determine gender. His/her glossy black hair was cropped short at the sides with a tidal wave of a quiff rising up, then tumbling down to meet over-plucked eyebrows, above heavily mascaraed lashes. The combination of theatrical make-up and costume should have made the individual look ridiculous, but Jasmine found the effect mesmerising and was unable to take her eyes from the strange beauty of the exotic creature.

After several minutes, the man on her right banged his fist on the table, gave a snarl of contempt and jerked back his chair. He issued a barrage of what Jasmine took to be parting shots in his argument with the young woman, gave Jasmine a nod – his first acknowledgement of her since she'd sat down – then left. Jasmine turned to the girl, who raised her eyes towards the ceiling and said, *'Les hommes,'* in a tone that combined resignation with contempt.

The girl tapped a soft packet of cigarettes on the table so that one popped up. Withdrawing it with her lips, she offered the pack to Jasmine, who shook her head.

'He was rather angry,' Jasmine ventured. 'Is he a close friend?'

'No. I've never met him before.'

Surprised, Jasmine said, 'Gosh. That was a pretty intense argument then. May I ask what you were talking about?'

'De Beauvoir's book, of course. That's what everyone argues about these days. It's all becoming rather a bore.' She released a deep sigh. 'What's your name? I'm Corrine.'

Jasmine told her.

'So you're one of Stan's protegés? Everyone loves Stan.' She blew a smoke ring. 'Everyone except Stan himself.'

Jasmine leaned forward, expecting Corrine to elucidate, but the young woman said, 'So you need a place to stay? Stan says you're at the Beaux-Arts.'

Jasmine took a sip of the wine, surprised that Stan must have spoken about her in some detail to these friends. 'Yes. I start next term but I have to complete some drawings before they'll confirm my place. I'm working on them with my tutor.'

'Let me guess. They have put you in Robbo's atelier,' Corrine said.

'Robbo?' Then realising the woman must mean Lachlan Robertson, said, 'Is that what people call Lachlan? Are you at the school yourself?'

Corrine blew another smoke ring. 'I am not capable to hold a pencil. No, I sometimes work there as a life model. I get paid to take off my clothes and shiver to death – in front of a one-bar electric heater if I'm extremely lucky, which mostly I'm not – while you students draw or paint me.' Crushing out what was left of her cigarette, she added, 'I have to live. I'm starting my second year, studying philosophy at the Sorbonne and my family aren't wealthy. Life modelling pays the rent. Better than becoming *une putain* which is the only other way to get by. How about you? Rich *maman et papa?*'

Jasmine felt her face reddening. 'I'm lucky. My adoptive parents are very supportive but I have a small monthly allowance from my late father. Not a lot, but enough to get by.'

'So why do you need to find a place? Sounds as if you can afford to live somewhere decent. Not that decent means much in Paris. Everywhere is pretty run-down in this city.'

'I don't want to be different,' Jasmine said in a rush. 'I'll need money to pay for materials and to travel to see my family in the long vacation. Anyway, while I'm in Paris I want to live like everyone else.'

Corrine looked sceptical. 'Wait till you see what that involves. I bet you'll change your tune then. Want to come and look now?'

'You have a place?'

'That's why you're here, isn't it? That's what Stan told me. If you don't take it someone else will. There's more demand than supply in Paris. You don't want to end up sleeping on the *quais* with the *clochards*, do you? Most of the students will be back in Paris in the next couple of weeks and everywhere will be taken in an instant.'

Jasmine didn't want the chance to pass by. 'I definitely want a place. I don't care how small. Please, can you help me?'

'*Eh bien. Allons-y!*' Corrine pushed back her chair, called a brief farewell to the others around the table. Stan was now talking intently to the exotic character with the perfect *maquillage*. He glanced up briefly to give Jasmine a casual wave, and she found herself scurrying behind Corrine out of the bar.

Outside, it was still light. Jasmine glanced at her wristwatch. Not quite eight o'clock. Corrine was striding off up the cobbled street and Jasmine had to hurry to keep pace with her.

'It's in the Quartier and about equal distance between the Sorbonne for me and the Beaux-Arts for us both,' she said.

'Don't expect a lot. It's a typical student hotel. No bathrooms, but there's a shared toilet and wash-basin.'

Taking a sharp breath, Jasmine asked, 'What do you do for a bath?'

'Use the public ones. There's often a queue, so you need to pick the right times. And they're only open Thursdays through Sundays.' She shrugged. 'But they're free of charge.'

Jasmine swallowed, then told herself that Paris didn't compare with the sultry heat of the tropics where she'd been used to showering and changing her clothes several times a day. If everyone else managed, so would she.

The Hotel Lutèce was a shabby-looking building of several storeys. Inside, Corrine led Jasmine to a cubby-hole office where an elderly woman, Madame Trenet, got her to sign a book and pay a week's rent in advance.

'You're next door to me,' said Corrine. 'Fifth floor. No lift. Come on and I'll show you.' She bounded up the stairway and Jasmine followed.

The room was barely bigger than a broom cupboard. There was a narrow bed, a small armoire and a tiny table. No view, as the only window looked onto an air shaft. Grim. Depressing.

Intuiting her thoughts, Corrine said, 'We all live like this in Paris. Poor housing. Nothing repaired. Rents are controlled so there's no incentive for landlords to build new homes. Why do you think all those people sleep out on the quaysides?' She swept an arm around the tiny room. 'This is better than most places. Madame Trenet downstairs keeps it clean. There's a toilet on each floor and running water on the landings. Many buildings don't even have that. And the people here are fun and friendly. Most of them are students. Besides, you only need a room to sleep in. You'll be at the school all day, in the bars and cafés when you have some cash and being a *passante* when you don't.'

'A *passante*?'

'A *flâneur* but female.'

Jasmine still looked blank.

Corrine rolled her eyes. 'A *flâneur* spends his time strolling the streets as an observer, a leisurely wanderer. Haven't you read any Baudelaire?'

Jasmine shook her head.

'Proust?'

The blood rushed to Jasmine's cheeks.

'I'm going to have to educate you. So, when are you moving in?'

'At the weekend?'

Corrine gave a little shake of the head. '*Ça va.*'

It was almost nine that night when Jasmine got back to the apartment. She opened the door to find Bernard Courbet in the hallway.

He gave her a quizzical look. 'Already going out in the evenings, *chérie?* You have been in Paris less than a week. You must make friends very quickly, *non?*' He was blocking her way along the corridor that led to her bedroom, giving no indication he would stand aside to let her pass. He leaned forward, smiling, and held open the door to what she knew to be the drawing-room, which she had never entered. 'We will take a glass of wine together, *oui?*' It wasn't a question.

'*Merci, Monsieur*, but I am very tired.' Then, remembering she needed to tell her hosts she would be leaving at the weekend, she said, 'Is Madame at home? I need to speak to her.'

'My wife is visiting her sister.' He gave Jasmine a little wink, followed by a smile that made her shudder involuntarily. She could see his lips were wet, with a small white spot of spittle in one corner. She shuddered again.

'Claudine won't be back until tomorrow evening.'

He leaned against the door jamb, his eyes narrowing. 'You

must tell me while we enjoy our wine.' He ushered her into the room then moved towards an ornately-carved sideboard. 'Or would you prefer something stronger?'

'As I said, Monsieur, I am tired. I have been working very hard at the school today. I can speak to Madame when she returns. I think she'll be pleased to know I've found accommodation with another student so won't be imposing on your hospitality any longer. I will be leaving on Saturday.'

'It is no intrusion, *ma petite*. A pretty face such as yours is a pleasure to encounter. Tell me where you intend to live.'

She hesitated before deciding to lie. 'I can't remember the address. A student hostel. Somewhere between the Beaux-Arts and the Sorbonne.'

Courbet's lip curled. 'Why would you choose to live in a run-down room on the Left Bank when you can live here?' He indicated the elegant drawing-room, before pouring wine into two long-stemmed glasses. He lowered his head over one of them to breathe in the aroma and sighed. 'I opened this bottle especially for you. St Émilion Premier Grand Cru. 1934 was an excellent year for Bordeaux.' He handed her a glass. 'We will drink to your time here in Paris.' He took her by the arm and led her to the sofa, lowering himself to sit beside her, his body turned towards hers. Raising his glass, he said, '*À ta santé.*'

She lifted her own glass, avoiding his eye.

'*Non, non, ma petite!* You must keep the eye contact when you make the toast in France. Or you have very bad fortune – for seven years.' He gave her a patronising smile and wagged his finger at her. 'But you are new to our French customs, so we will repeat and this time you must look me in the eye. *C'est très important.*'

She did as he said, squirming in her seat and lowering her eyes as soon as he'd repeated the toast. Taking a sip of the wine, she said, 'Now, thank you very much, Monsieur, but I must pack.'

He shook his head rapidly, pointing his finger at her. 'You must call me Bernard. Never mind the packing. Plenty of time. And Marielle will help you.' He twirled his glass by the stem. 'But I repeat. Better to remain here where there are plenty of comforts.' He waved a hand around the large drawing-room, which was furnished with overstuffed belle époque furniture, and the walls hung with gloomy portraits, pastoral landscapes and fading tapestries. 'I am sure you will regret it if you accept an offer of a room on the Left Bank. Most of those buildings have no water supply. They are fit only to be demolished.' His nostrils flared in disdain. 'Do you want to live like *une clocharde? Mais, non!*'

'I will be perfectly comfortable. It's a nice room. And close to the school.'

'You are very young, Jasmine. Twenty?'

'Eighteen.'

Courbet's eyebrows rose. 'And your parents are happy for you to travel alone to a strange country? Most unusual.'

'They've always encouraged me to be independent. I may be young but I've lived through a lot. The war. Being in different countries.' She stopped, reluctant to tell him anything else about herself and her life.'

'And you are here to study art?' He looked puzzled. 'Why?'

'I love painting. It's what I want to do.'

'A pleasant hobby for a girl, but to take up a place in *une grande école* is not good.' He tutted. 'Being an artist is not a suitable role for a young woman. Women lack skill. Besides, you will marry soon and by accepting the place you have prevented a young man from studying there. It is irresponsible.'

'I have no intention of marrying. And if I did, I'd continue to paint. It's a calling, not a job.'

Courbet gave a dry laugh. 'But you understand you are expected to paint naked models? Men as well as women.'

Jasmine felt her face reddening, in anger as well as embarrassment. Eventually she said, 'An understanding of human anatomy is an essential part of any artist's studies.'

He looked at her in silence for a few moments. He was wearing a pale grey suit with a yellow patterned silk tie. Undoing the tie, he leaned back into the seat, legs spread wide as he sniffed his wine between sips, savouring it before placing it on the table beside him.

Jasmine felt increasingly uncomfortable. Should she get up and go to her room? Would he try to stop her? She put her own glass down on a matching side-table and prepared to stand.

Without warning, his hand was on her leg. He slipped it beneath the hem of her dress and began caressing her bare thigh, moving his hand dangerously higher between her legs. Shocked and disgusted, Jasmine pushed him away, and leapt to her feet, ready to make her escape.

He anticipated this and wrenched her arm, jerking her back onto the couch. Jasmine cried out at the sudden sharp pain. Courbet pushed her up against the corner of the sofa, both hands clamping her shoulders. His eyes narrowed as he studied her face. 'I can make you very happy *ma petite*. We will have a wonderful time. Let me make love to you. Let me take you, give you pleasure. I am a very skilled lover.' He lunged forward, his mouth seeking hers, but she twisted her head away in time. 'I know what girls like you want. The kind of girl who leaves her family to travel abroad alone. The kind of girl who is happy to make drawings of naked men.'

'Let me go. Now! Or I will tell your wife.'

He gave a little laugh. *'Ma femme est une femme sans passion.* We have an understanding. She overlooks my little indiscretions in return for a generous allowance. This is the French way. As long as I keep paying the bills for her very expensive taste in jewellery, she will say nothing.' He sighed. 'Claudine is past her best years. She takes no pleasure in making love. She has always been a cold woman. A man has important needs that must be satisfied.'

Courbet was pinning Jasmine down, the bulk of his body preventing her from moving, a mixture of wine and garlic on his breath. 'Perhaps you have scruples about our being under the same roof so I propose to put you in a beautiful little apartment I own in the *deuxième arrondissement*. Very discreet. Very convenient.' His voice was breathless, and a bead of sweat dripped from his face onto hers. 'I will visit you two or three evenings each week. We will make love, drink fine wine, dine in fine restaurants and the rest of the time you will be free to meet your friends and pursue your studies.'

Jasmine was paralysed with fear and rage. How was this happening? The man didn't even know her. She was a guest in his house. But she lacked the physical strength to stop him. She wanted to scream.

He turned his head to try to kiss her again. Summoning all her strength, she twisted her head away. But he was too strong. He jerked her head back, his elbow digging painfully into her shoulder, and pushed his mouth onto hers. His tongue forced her lips apart and pushed its way inside her mouth. Jasmine gagged. Disgusting.

'Now, you can do some private study of *my* anatomy.' His hand worked to undo his flies while his body weight pinned her down.

In the struggle to escape his hold, Jasmine kicked out a leg. Her foot struck his glass of red wine on the side table. It fell onto the polished parquet floor, sending an arc of ruby-red wine all over the ivory-coloured antique rug beyond.

Courbet jumped up as if stung. '*Putain!* You stupid fool. Do you know what that carpet is worth? It's an antique. Aubusson. Eighteenth century. My wife—'

Jasmine didn't wait to hear the rest. She sprinted across the drawing-room as though fired from a cannon, bursting through the double doors and dashing down the corridor to her bedroom, where she locked the door and, to be absolutely sure Courbet couldn't get in, placed the back of the chair under the door handle.

Her heart was beating a military tattoo inside her chest. A lucky escape. If it hadn't been for the wine spillage, Courbet would certainly have seen his plan through. Jasmine would have been powerless to prevent him having his way.

Tears stung her eyes. Fury and adrenaline had torn the breath out of her. Desperate to use the bathroom, she was afraid to risk leaving her bedroom. There was a large ceramic wash-bowl on the chest of drawers. She'd have to use that and empty it in the morning.

When she climbed into bed she lay staring through the window at a black starless sky. To lose her virginity to a man such as Courbet, to be forced, was too horrible to think about. If and when she were ever to give herself to a man it would only be because she loved him. As for accepting Courbet's offer to be set up as his mistress in a fancy apartment in a fashionable district – she'd rather be sleeping on the cold stones with the *clochards*.

SIX

The following morning it was raining. Jasmine stood at her bedroom window, looking over the roofs of the surrounding buildings at a gunmetal-grey sky. It was almost eight o'clock but she was terrified to leave her room in case Courbet hadn't yet gone to work. She sat cross-legged on the bed, her mind running over what had happened the night before.

Was it her fault? Had she been too friendly the first time they'd met? Did she look like a girl with loose morals? It was unthinkable that anyone would assume she would be willing to become the mistress of a married man. Surely it wasn't normal for young French women to become the mistresses of middle-aged men? What had she done to give Courbet the impression she would welcome his advances?

Perhaps it was because, as a young single woman, she had come to Paris alone. Had Monsieur Courbet assumed she was a good-time girl, out for herself? It made Jasmine nauseous. She was here to study, not have amorous adventures, and certainly not with a horrible man who was old enough to be her father – maybe even her grandfather.

She slid off the bed and crammed her belongings into her

suitcases. There was no possibility of her remaining here. She'd told Corinne not to expect her until the weekend, but she wasn't staying a minute longer than necessary under the same roof as Bernard Courbet.

Marielle was at the table reading a newspaper when Jasmine walked into the kitchen. The Frenchwoman raised one eyebrow. '*Bonjour*! I hear you spoiled one of their fancy carpets last night. I imagine it was thanks to *Monsieur 'Lubrique'*. Did he misbehave?'

Jasmine sat down, mortified. 'Will Madame find out about the carpet? Is it very badly damaged?'

Marielle shrugged. 'A carpet specialist is coming this morning to treat it. Madame will notice of course, no matter how good a job they do. But she will say nothing as she will guess the reason why. I suppose he pounced on you?'

Jasmine nodded, ashamed. Would the maid also think she was cheap?

But Marielle gave her a sad smile and shook her head. 'That man will never learn. He believes he can get away with what he does as Madame will never speak out against him. It's not in her interests.' The maid folded her newspaper, got up from the table and went to pour a coffee for Jasmine. 'I hope he didn't hurt you. I presume that's why you spilled the wine.'

Jasmine felt her cheeks reddening. 'It was horrible. He was on top of me. I couldn't move. I kicked over the wine glass and that's how I got him off me. If I hadn't...'

Marielle reached out and patted her hand. 'You don't need to tell me. I know. Something similar happened to me when I was a girl, in Alsace. Many years ago.' She sucked her lips inwards. 'I don't talk about it, but I understand. Men are pigs. Now, forget about it and eat a brioche while they are still warm.' She lifted the napkin covering the bread basket and passed it to Jasmine. 'Monsieur Courbet says you are leaving. Is it because of what he did?'

'No. I was going anyway. I intended to wait until the weekend but after what happened last night...'

'I'll be sorry to see you go, but I understand.'

'I've found a room between Saint-Germain-des-Près and Montparnasse. I'm moving my things today.'

'Since Madame is away from home I'd offer to help you, but I have to be here to admit the carpet cleaner. If you can wait until he has finished his work, I will help you carry your things. It is very bad weather today.'

'Don't worry, I'll take a taxi.'

She reached into her satchel, pulled out one of the bars of Marseille soap and handed it to the maid. 'You've been very kind, Marielle.'

To Jasmine's surprise, the woman flung her arms around her. *'Merci beaucoup, mademoiselle. Vous êtes très gentille.'*

It was still raining when Jasmine arrived at the École des Beaux-Arts and she had to make two trips to transport her bags inside the building after the driver dropped her at the gates. She piled her cases up in a corner of La Cour Vitrée and hoped she wouldn't be reprimanded by anyone.

She set to work on that day's assignment, a detailed pencil drawing of a cast of a man's head that Lachlan had selected the previous day. After she'd been working for about forty minutes, she sensed someone behind her and presuming it was her tutor, turned to greet him with a smile, only to find Monsieur Rochambeau, hands on hips, watching her.

'Carry on, carry on,' he said, leaning in for a closer look. Then, without further comment, he walked away. Jasmine frowned, concentration broken. Was he confirming his suspicions that she would never attain the requisite standard? Another unpleasant middle-aged man trying to ruin her life. She bit her lip. No point in getting downcast about it. She'd just have to try harder. Her pencil moved across the paper, as she tried to force her mind to focus. She was endeavouring to capture the contrast between light and shade rather than drawing the outline shape, slowly building up the image as her eyes darted between the paper and the plaster cast head. Leaning back to look at what she'd drawn so far, she thought she'd done quite a decent job in spite of the professor's absence of enthusiasm.

She hoped Lachlan would arrive soon. His presence would offer a welcome distraction from the constant replaying in her mind of Bernard Courbet's mouth moving down to claim hers. Jasmine felt sick at the memory. Of course she wouldn't tell Lachlan what had happened. She couldn't tell anyone. It was comforting that Marielle had been sympathetic, but Jasmine wanted no one else to know. It made no difference that she'd done nothing wrong – she was awash with shame. The last thing she wanted was Lachlan to think badly of her – or worse – feel pity towards her.

It was almost eleven when Lachlan strode into the covered courtyard. He barely glanced at her. Jasmine sensed immediately he was in a bad mood.

'I have things to do in my studio. Carry on with what you're doing and I'll see you later.' Without another word he walked off.

It was nearly two when, with no sign of her tutor returning, and with her stomach rumbling, Jasmine left the school to find something to eat. She walked up to the corner of the Rue Bonaparte and as she passed Les Deux Magots, she peered through the window, hoping in vain to spot Stan inside. She crossed to the other side of the road and decided she might as well try Café de Flore. To her delight, Stan was sitting at the rear of the room, a cup of coffee in front of him, smoking and staring into space, an empty notepad on the table.

'No writing today?' she said. 'May I join you for a few moments?'

'Jazz! Great to see you. Sure! Sit down. I need some distraction from the pressure of an empty sheet of paper. I don't seem able to get a word down today – not a one. The Muse has deserted me.'

'I won't stay long. I need something to eat but then I must get back and finish my work.'

A waiter appeared and Jasmine ordered an omelette.

'How's it going?' Stan ground the butt of his cigarette into the ashtray.

'It's beastly,' she said. 'I'm trying to do a pencil drawing of some old man's head. It's horribly complicated as he has lots of hair.'

'Must have been even harder for the poor sculptor then.'

'Gosh, I suppose that's true.' She smiled at him, already feeling better. 'Thank you for introducing me to your friends last night. I'm moving into the same place as Corinne this evening.'

'Tonight! Wow! You move quickly. Couldn't wait to get away from the fine ladies and fancy poodles in Passy?'

'I wasn't comfortable in that apartment. Madame Courbet made it very clear I wasn't welcome.'

'The Lutèce is a bit rough and ready, like most places in the Quartier, but there's a friendly crowd there and it's cheap, as long as you don't mind slumming it.' He gave her a broad smile. 'The plumbing in Paris hasn't moved on much since the Romans left. But at least they change the sheets occasionally at the Lutèce.'

'I don't mind at all. I may be privileged myself, but in Africa and Malaya I've seen how the native people live and if they can, I can. Everyone seems to manage all right here in Paris. Why should I be different?'

'That's the spirit, girl.'

'Where do you live, Stan?'

'I have a *chambre de bonne* in a building a couple of streets from here. The room is lousy. Ice cold in winter and like a furnace in summer. But the other inmates are friendly enough. A lot of my fellow Americans, as well as many other nationalities. I'm next door to a sax player from New Orleans. No extra charge for all that jazz music. He plays in a club near the Sorbonne.' He leaned forward. 'You ever eat soul food, Jasmine?'

'I'm afraid I don't know what it is.'

'It's black people's food. Born out of slave rations. Fried chicken, pork, catfish, lots of greens, cornbread. That sort of thing. Cheap, filling and tasty. Lots of spices too.'

'Spicy suits me. Growing up in Asia I always loved the local cooking.'

'Then I'll take you along to Chez Inez and you can eat you some soul food and hear you some jazz. You like jazz, Jazz?' He looked eager.

She laughed. 'I think so. I need to live up to my name.'

'You ever heard musicians playing live?'

Jasmine shook her head.

'Then you got a whole new experience coming up. We'll have ourselves a party. You gonna love Inez's place.'

Jasmine ate her omelette. How did the French make omelettes taste like the food of the gods?

'When are you going over to the Lutèce?' Stan asked.

'This evening. I'm going to get a taxi as there's a lot to carry.'

'What time?'

'I'll be finishing at the school about six. But—'

'Which floor are you on in the Lutèce?'

'The fifth.' She gave a little groan.

'Then you definitely need a hand. I'll come and find you at the Beaux-Arts about six then.'

Feeling better than she had since the previous night,

Jasmine returned to the school to continue work on her drawing.

When she entered the covered courtyard, Lachlan was standing behind her easel, examining what she had done. 'You're trying too hard,' he said at last. 'Did you spend all day just working on this one drawing?'

Jasmine stared at him, uncomprehending. She'd been rather pleased with it.

'I'm not your professor until term begins. This part of the process is not meant to be tutored.' He turned to face her. 'The whole point of these two weeks is for you to do what all the other students have already done and produce a series of twenty classical drawings. Once the term starts I will be teaching you and your colleagues how to improve. That's when the training in technique will begin.' He sounded impatient.

'But...'

'For the rest of the day I want you to do a series of quick studies. As many as you can manage. Concentrate at this stage at getting the proportions right. The more you do, the better you'll get.' He frowned. 'I'd like you to work at the Louvre tomorrow rather than in here.'

'I see,' she said, but she didn't.

'Teaching starts next term. Not before.' His tone was brusque, formal, distant. 'I'll be in my atelier if you need anything, but I'm afraid, Jasmine, you're on your own from now on.' With that, he turned on his heel and left the courtyard, his footsteps echoing along the corridor back to his studio.

Jasmine stood stunned, her eyes welling up. Why was he being so cold? So businesslike? So unfriendly? What had she done to offend him? When they'd parted the previous day, he'd been affable. Even suggested a drink. Could that be why – because she said she was meeting someone else?

She tortured herself with questions. Did this mean she was going to lose her place next term? What possible chance would she have without Lachlan's help, when she was unaware of even basic concepts like the thing he'd explained to her yesterday about foreshortening? Surely, all the other new students would have had some foundation training. Was it because Monsieur Rochambeau simply disliked her?

Jasmine wiped her hand across her eyes. Perhaps it was out of her reach, but she was going to give it her all and go down fighting. If she wasn't good enough, it wouldn't be for want of trying.

It was already three o'clock. Only a few hours left so she needed to make the most of them. She pushed her hair away from her face, tucking it behind her ears, and reached for a pencil. Taping a clean sheet of paper to her easel, she moved the easel in front of a plaster cast of a fragment of intricately folded robes from which two feet emerged; the upper body was absent. Jasmine set to work on a new drawing.

On her third drawing, Jasmine had lost track of the time, until the caretaker arrived to tell her there was a black man waiting outside. His expression was dubious. 'Shall I tell him to leave?'

'Oh, my goodness,' she said, 'Of course not. I didn't realise it was so late. Has he been waiting long?'

'Fifteen minutes. Since six. I told him he couldn't come inside.'

'He's going to help me move my luggage to my new lodgings.' She nodded her head in the direction of the pile of cases.

'*Alors, bien,*' the man said, clearly assuming that Stan was a porter.

She decided there was no point in disabusing him.

'I'll let him in then.' The porter went off to find Stan.

Jasmine scrambled to put away her materials and apologised profusely when her friend appeared.

'I'm so sorry if the porter was rude to you,' she said, 'I should have told him to expect you.'

Stan shrugged. 'No problem. I'm used to it.' Then he gave her a wry smile. 'I can put up with casual rudeness from a concierge. It's nothing to what he'd be dishing up to me if he was an American and we were Stateside.' He picked up the two heaviest suitcases as if their weight was insubstantial. 'Can you manage the rest?'

'I've got off lightly.' Jasmine had only her portfolio, the satchel containing her art materials and a small holdall. She followed him outside onto the Rue Bonaparte.

'Is that why you decided to live in Europe? I mean, people being prejudiced towards you in America?'

'You could say that.' He glanced at her sideways. 'My family came from the South. Moved north to Chicago. My father needed to work to feed the family. We were dirt poor and with no way of earning in Mississippi during the Depression.

'What did he do in Chicago?'

'Worked as a meat packer.' Stan hesitated then said, 'Decided to move us all to the Midwest after the Klan lynched my uncle.'

'Lynched?'

'Strung him up from a tree and hanged him. But only after they'd mutilated his naked body in front of a cheering crowd.'

'Oh, Stan!' Jasmine's skin crept. 'That's horrible. Savage. Why did they do it?'

'Hatred. Simple as that. My uncle had done nothing. No crime. Sometimes they don't even bother to find an excuse. When they do, it's a lie anyway. I was only a kid and didn't see the lynching but my father never got over it. It wasn't just the job that made him move to Chicago. It was about his family's survival.'

'Did the men who lynched him get punished?'

Stan gave a hollow laugh. 'You kidding? Under those long

white robes and pointy hats there are judges and cops and teachers and doctors.'

'But why?'

'Pure unadulterated hatred of the black man. As if it wasn't enough to have captured and enslaved my ancestors and bought and sold them in the market like cattle, once they were free, those people keep on wanting to destroy us. They see black skin and want to wipe us off the face of the earth.' He turned to look at her. 'That's some level of hate to make a townful of men want to torture and murder a man just for existing.'

Jasmine could feel his suppressed anger as he strode along beside her. She was uncertain whether to ask him more questions, feeling he might find her naive and ignorant as well as out of her depth. Biting her lip, she said nothing, and they walked on in silence.

At the Lutèce Madame Trenet was snoozing, mouth open, behind her desk and there was no sign of anyone else.

'You know your room number?' Stan put down the cases.

'Thirty-six.'

He leaned over the wooden counter and plucked the key from the board behind the elderly woman, who didn't even stir. He tossed it to Jasmine. 'Lead the way, lady.'

Five minutes later they dragged the cases inside the cramped bedroom and the two of them sat side-by-side on the edge of the bed catching their breath.

'Thank you, Stan, that was frightfully kind of you.'

'Happy to be of service, ma'am.' He gave her a mock salute.

Jasmine was relieved the sombre nature of their earlier conversation had passed, but couldn't stop thinking about what Stan had told her. Most of her life she had been surrounded by people of different races. While they'd frequently been regarded as inferiors by many white colonials, she'd never imagined that people might be capable of hating people with a different skin colour to the extent of wanting them dead. Then she remembered how Amir's mother had been shot in cold blood by the loathsome Lieutenant Ellis. The only motivation he could possibly have had was hatred too. Hatred and contempt that led him to assume the worst possible motives of everyone with a browner skin than his. She had to ask Stan more about his experiences in America, but now was not the time.

'You hungry, Jazz?'

'I am, actually.'

'Then let's go grab us some soul food, like I promised.'

'On one condition.'

'Oh, yeah?'

'I'm paying. After what you've done for me this evening, it's the least I can do.'

'You'll soon be as poor as the rest of us if you go round making gestures like that. But as it's usually a case of choosing between eating or smoking I won't be saying no.'

'Good. That's settled then.'

Chez Inez was in the Rue Champollion off the Boulevard Saint-Michel, just a few minutes from the Lutèce. As they headed there, Stan told her it was run by a woman called Inez Cavanaugh, a jazz singer and a fellow Chicagoan. 'It's early so the place won't be hopping yet. We can eat and talk, then enjoy the music later.'

Jasmine loved her first experience of soul food, relishing the spicy fried chicken, the cornbread and greens. Eschewing the suggested beer, she drank water.

'You're quiet this evening, Jasmine. Something on your mind?' Stan's eyes showed concern.

'I was thinking how things here in Paris are very different from what I expected.'

'What did you expect?'

She gave him a sheepish smile. 'I don't know really.' Hesitating, she added, 'Being on my own is harder than I imagined it would be. I miss my family. Having my mother around to talk to.'

'You know you can always talk to me, girl. Not the same as your mammy but better than no one. I'm like a great big sponge. I'll soak up what you say but never tell anyone else.' He placed his palm over his heart then took a Gauloise from the packet and lit it, blowing the smoke up towards the ceiling. In the corner of the room a man began playing the piano. Quiet, lilting soulful music. The place was beginning to fill up.

Jasmine decided to tell him about what had happened the previous night with Monsieur Courbet. She needed a confidant and she liked and trusted Stan.

'The husband where I've been staying... he...' She looked down, now wishing she hadn't started.

But Stan guessed what was coming. 'The man from Passy made a pass?' Then, evidently realising that making light of what happened was not making Jasmine feel better, he added, 'I hope he didn't hurt you, sugar?'

She smiled sadly. 'No he didn't hurt me. I managed to kick a glass of vintage Bordeaux over a priceless antique carpet and while he was recovering from the shock I barricaded myself in my bedroom.'

Stan started to laugh, then stopped himself. 'It must have been frightening. I'm glad it didn't turn into something worse. Must have been a shock.'

'I'll get over it,' she said ruefully. 'Are all Frenchmen like that?'

'I'm no authority on the subject, but I guess some of them are. For a young foreign woman to be alone in Paris at such a tender age is unusual. I suppose he felt he had the right to try it on.'

Jasmine snapped. 'If I hadn't kicked the wine over he'd have gone through with it, I'm certain. He pushed me onto my back on the sofa and was on top of me. I couldn't breathe and wasn't strong enough to fight him off.' She felt the tears threatening and gulped them away.

'I'm sorry.' He inhaled slowly, savouring the smoke. 'Don't let him put you off Paris. One bad apple.' He shrugged. 'As to how to avoid the unwelcome attentions of French men, you're better off asking Corinne than me. But I promise you this, Jasmine, if that man ever comes near you again, you let me know and I'll sucker punch him. I may look small and skinny but I know how to fight.' He fiddled with the packet of Gauloises on the table in front of him. 'That was one thing my daddy taught me. Said a man needs to be able to defend himself. Didn't want what happened to his brother happening to his son. People might not have walked through the streets of Chicago with white robes and burning crosses, but the everyday racism there was insidious. Maybe the French don't particularly like negroes but they treat us with indifference. That's fine by me. All I ask is to be left alone.'

'Did you ever consider going back to America after the war ended?'

'When you get used to living in a place where there's no segregation, it's hard to contemplate going back to one where the colour bar is all around you. The French may treat us with disdain, but they tend to show disdain to everyone who is not one of them. That air of superiority extends to white folk like you who just happen to have the misfortune not to be born French.'

Jasmine laughed. 'Really? As bad as that?'

'Well, maybe not all Frenchmen but certainly Parisians. Yet, at the same time, they have a love of "otherness" – a fascina-tion for things they perceive as exotic and different. Like jazz.' He jerked his head in the direction of a couple sitting at the bar. She was white, wearing a figure-hugging dress and smoking. He was black, in wide trousers with an open-necked white shirt that highlighted the darkness of his skin. He had an arm draped loosely over her shoulder and bent his head to kiss the woman. A long lingering kiss. 'They'd never be able to do that in public in the United States.' Stan shook his head, his eyes a mix of bitterness and sadness.

The band struck up. A woman stepped onto the small platform and began to sing.

'That's Inez.'

The song was sad, wistful. Gershwin's *Somebody Loves Me*. Jasmine's eyes filled with tears at the poignancy of the lyrics, grateful that the lighting was too dim to reveal her emotions. It made her think of her family – and of Howard Baxter.

To Jasmine's relief the pianist moved into an upbeat tempo and a bassist and a sax player ambled onto the stage to join them. The music swung into a medley of melodies. Jasmine immediately warmed to the mixture of lyrical soarings and foot-tapping rhythms.

Carried away by the music, she forgot her loneliness and feelings of misery. She was here. In Paris. In a night-spot. Listening to jazz music. There was nowhere else she would rather be.

August 1949

Mary Hyde-Underwood pulled her daughter onto her lap, after Frances attempted to run onto the cricket pitch and join the players. It was the time of day when usually the little girl would be taking an afternoon nap, but the excitement of being in George Town meant the toddler was resisting Mary's attempts to pacify her.

Amir bounded up and announced he was going to get one of the ice creams that were being served to the children.

'Me go with Amir!' Frances wailed. 'Please, Mummy!'

'Let Amir go with his friends, darling. He'll be back soon. I'll take you myself for an ice cream in a moment.'

But Frances was having none of it. She wriggled out of her mother's grasp and ran to join the gaggle of older children heading for the clubhouse.

'She's getting wilful,' Mary said to Reggie, who was fully padded up and sitting beside her in a deckchair, waiting for his turn to go into bat.

'She's excited. And you know she hates being separated from Amir.'

'The poor boy deserves a bit of peace.' Mary swatted an insect away before it could settle on her arm. But Amir didn't seem perturbed at Frances tagging along. He happily hitched her up into a piggyback and carried her in the direction of the clubhouse.

Mary looked up at the play, not that she was interested in cricket, unless her husband was on the field. That was looking less likely today as Howard Baxter had scored over forty runs and the opposing side looked unlikely to get him and his current partner out.

'Old Howard's a darn good player,' said Reggie. 'Don't know why he doesn't play more often. He puts the old crocks like me to shame. They only roped me in as there was no one else.'

Mary gave him an indulgent smile. 'Nonsense, darling, stop fishing for compliments. You caught that fellow out when you were fielding. And bowled out another chap. Don't do yourself down.'

'It'll be over before long anyway, the rate Howard's batting. His half-century is coming up any minute.' Reggie leaned forward as the bowler made his run.

'Well I'm jolly glad he's staying with us tonight. We don't see nearly enough of him,' said Mary as there was a thwack of leather against willow and Howard sent the ball over the boundary.

'Six! He's done it! Half-century!' Reggie, like most of the spectators, jumped to his feet cheering.

'Mary! How frightfully good to see you!' The speaker was a matronly woman with over-plucked eyebrows. 'I spotted you from the other side of the field and simply had to come and say hello.'

Mary blinked up at the woman, shielding her eyes from the sun. 'Good afternoon, Mrs Crawley.'

'You two are veritable hermits, hiding away at the top of the island. We'd love to see more of you in town. Of course Charles occasionally runs into Reggie at the club, but you never seem to come into George Town yourself, dear girl.'

As Mary was about to reply, Amir and Frances reappeared, each with an ice lolly. 'Do give Amir some peace, Frances,' Mary said. Turning to the boy, she added, 'Here, I'll take her for a while. You go and watch the match with your pals.' She lifted Frances onto her lap and Amir raced off to join the other boys where they were lying on their stomachs at the side of the pitch.

'Awfully good of you to take that native boy into your home,' said Mrs Crawley. 'And him a poor orphan. Although I hear his mother was a terrorist.' The woman lowered her voice and spoke conspiratorially. 'Aren't you worried he'll be a bad influence on little Frances?'

Mary stared at her. 'What are you saying? His mother was *not* a terrorist but was murdered in cold blood by a British officer who should have been court-martialled, jailed and thrown out of the army.'

'Really! Not the done thing, Mary, to speak that way about one of our own, and particularly about a brave officer doing his duty to protect us all.' Her nostrils flared. 'I must say, Mary, I think you and Reggie are taking a grave risk allowing that little girl to spend so much time with a child of another race. You never know what kind of habits she might pick up.' Mrs Crawley puffed out her chest. 'He looks a charming boy, but...' She lowered her voice. 'Not one of *us*. He'd be far better off with his own kind.'

Mary took a deep breath to control her temper. 'And you'd be better off minding your own business, Mrs Crawley. Good day.' She reached down into her handbag to find a handkerchief and busied herself wiping orange ice lolly residue from Frances's chin.

Any response Mrs Crawley might have made was drowned out by a loud cheer from the opposing side and polite clapping as the man who was in bat with Howard was run out.

Reggie rose, smiled at Mary and nodded at the indignant Mrs Crawley. 'Excuse me, ladies, but my moment of glory awaits.' He strode purposefully onto the pitch.

When Mary turned round, Mrs Crawley had already gone. 'Thank God for that,' Mary said to herself.

That evening the Hyde-Underwoods and Howard Baxter gathered on the veranda at Bella Vista. The two men were enjoying pre-dinner *stengahs* and Mary was sipping a glass of iced water.

She had just told them about Mrs Crawley's behaviour during the cricket match.

'Take no notice of her,' said Reggie. 'Talking claptrap. I always tune out when that old biddy gets started. Can't abide the woman. Not keen on her husband either.'

'It's the sense of superiority I can't stand. As though the accident of British birth gives her the right to lord it over everyone else. It's intolerable that she sees Malays and Chinese as inferior. In fact, it's utterly horrible.'

'Don't let her upset you, Mary,' said Howard. 'Not worth getting yourself wound up over a dinosaur like her.'

Reggie reached across and squeezed his wife's hand.

'But she said Amir's mother was a terrorist. She called him a native.'

'Clearly has no idea he's half-white and is Doug's son. Maybe you should have told her.' Reggie took his pipe up and lit it.

'It's none of the woman's business. And that would be

pandering to her game. Why should the fact that he's half-white make him a better person?' Mary put her cup back on its saucer with a clatter. 'She ruined the day for me.'

'Come on, old girl. Don't spoil Howard's brilliant achievement by letting that old witch detract from what was a ruddy marvellous afternoon.'

Mary smiled. 'Sorry. Of course. We need to raise a glass to you, Howard. What was it in the end – eighty-nine not out? And you too, darling.' She smiled proudly at Reggie. 'Fifteen runs not out, one man bowled out and one caught.' She counted the triumphs on her fingers. 'Plenty of life in the old dog yet!'

'I have some news to share.' Howard put down his tumbler. 'I'm leaving Batu Lembah. I only found out this morning. Remember, I mentioned that Sir John Hay was on his annual visit to Malaya and I was asked to drive him round the district to all the estates?'

They nodded, both leaning forward.

'My area manager asked to see me at the Guthrie's office this morning. He's travelling down to KL this afternoon for more meetings next week with Sir John, who leaves for London on Wednesday. He told me I'd made a good impression on the big man and they want me to take a post as acting manager at a huge estate down in Johore. The manager there is on sick leave in England. Heart attack. There's a strong possibility he won't return to Malaya and unless I mess up, I could get the job permanently. It'd be a massive promotion.'

Mary clapped her hands. 'Bravo! You clever chap!'

Reggie leaned forward and banged Howard on the back. 'This calls for another celebratory snifter, don't you think? Sir John's no pushover. You must have really impressed him.'

Howard brushed off the compliment and said, 'I'll be sad to leave BL. And most of all I'll miss being near you two, and Amir and Frances. It'll be a wrench not being able to jump in the car and nip across to Penang.'

The Hyde-Underwoods exchanged glances. Mary smiled. 'A fresh start for you, Howard. New faces. New challenges.' She looked down and studied her entwined fingers in her lap. 'Time to get on with your life. Meet a nice girl. A new beginning. A chance to forget about Jasmine.'

Howard's brows lowered. 'Maybe I don't want to forget her. Maybe I can't.'

'No harm in trying, old chap,' said Reggie. 'You never know, once you're away from the places that remind you of her, you may see things differently. Mary's right. Nothing wrong with a new start. Look at the two of us. Neither of us expected we'd end up with each other and be so happy. You never know what's around the corner.'

Mary reached over and patted Howard's hand. 'At least keep an open mind. Give it a try.' She looked him in the eye. 'I'm presuming you still haven't heard from her?'

He shook his head and his lips formed into a tight line.

'Then it's definitely time to move on. Don't throw your whole life away wishing for something that will never happen. I know it's hard to face it, but Jasmine's in a different world now. You may have both been fond of each other, but the longer she's gone, the more likely you are to grow further apart. You're a good man, Howard, and have so much to offer the right woman. Forget her.'

'You're right. Absolutely right.' Howard swigged the remains of his whisky. 'Time to accept that Jasmine simply doesn't care for me and never will. And yes, as you say, it's a chance for a new start.'

EIGHT

PARIS

August 1949

It was cold in the Louvre. The days were chillier now autumn was on the way. Here in the vast draughty interior Jasmine was glad she'd remembered to put a sweater in her satchel.

Her first night at the Lutèce had passed without incident. When she'd returned after the evening with Stan at Chez Inez, she'd gone straight to bed, tolerating the rather lumpy mattress and grateful that there was no risk of Bernard Courbet pushing open her bedroom door.

She'd left the hostel that morning without seeing Corinne, who must have been still sleeping. The autumn term hadn't yet started at the Sorbonne and Jasmine had no idea what Corinne's movements were. Stan had told her that most habitués of the Left Bank fled every day to the cafés to seek warmth and company, rather than staying in cold hotel bedrooms, so maybe that went for students too. As well as being unheated, the rooms were grim, and didn't tempt their occupants to linger.

Jasmine was sitting in front of a statuette of a naked Zeus.

She'd done a few rapid warm-up sketches and was now allowing herself an hour to do a more detailed drawing. At least there were no complicated folds of fabric to worry about, although Zeus's head was encircled with copious curls and his chin sported a luxuriant beard. Not to mention the plentiful hair that his manhood rested in – but she was leaving that until last.

Remembering Lachlan's impatient outburst yesterday, Jasmine concentrated on getting the shapes and proportions right. She would tackle the light and shade and texture later. With a sting of hurt pride, she replayed his words. It was hard not to feel he'd abandoned her when he'd said he was no longer prepared to help or tutor her until term began. What had she done to bring about such a change in attitude? Then she reminded herself that it was the summer break for staff as well as students. Yet he'd been more than willing to spend time with her before.

As she squinted and stared, frowning in concentration, Jasmine wished she was outside in the fresh air. It would be warmer in the early autumn sunshine than here in this echoing, deserted gallery. She longed to be sketching real living people: the *clochards* clustered on the *quais*, the children playing games or sitting with their feet dangling in the Seine as they floated paper boats. Or those long barges passing by on the river, many with washing on clothes lines strung the entire length of the boat. She'd always loved painting washing lines – and remembered the splash of random colours in the intense Malayan sunlight: saris, *baju_kurungs* – or in Africa the bright cloth of Kenyan *kitenge*. Here in Paris, lines tended to be hung with white undergarments, blue utility overalls or dull faded dresses. But even that, and the chance to splash paint onto paper or canvas would be preferable to the strict discipline of what she still believed to be copying the works of others.

'How's it going, hen? Time for a coffee?'

Jasmine jumped in fright.

'I'm on my way to the École so thought I'd drop by and see how you're getting on,' Lachlan said. 'Tell you what. I'll treat you to a hot chocolate.'

Still bristling from his abruptness the day before, Jasmine hesitated. But Lachlan had already turned and was moving away down the gallery, so she put down her pencil and followed him.

They went to Angelina's in the Rue de Rivoli. Jasmine was awed by the grandeur of the belle époque interior with its painted murals, chandeliers and glass-panelled ceiling. The hot chocolate was thick, rich and creamy, cloying in Jasmine's mouth. But perfect for warming up bones chilled in the cold interior of the Louvre.

To her surprise, Lachlan made no reference to his behaviour the previous day. It was as if it had never happened. 'How are you getting on?' he asked.

Before she could respond, he added, 'Come into the school on Friday afternoon and I'll go through your drawings with you. I'll give you some pointers and we can discuss which ones to submit to Beetle Brows and the rest of the selection committee.'

'What happens if he rejects them? Will I have to leave immediately?' The shame of returning to Africa would be unbearable. 'Or is there another school here in Paris that might take me? I know it won't be the Beaux-Arts, but maybe if I do a foundation year somewhere else they'd reconsider me next year.'

Lachlan stared at her. 'What the devil are you talking about? You're in. Your portfolio determined that. Doing the classical drawings is just a formality. Can't have anyone bending the rules.'

Jasmine didn't know whether to laugh or cry. 'I don't understand. Monsieur Rochambeau said I had to complete the drawings or I wouldn't get in.'

'Correct.'

'But you're now saying it doesn't matter. I'm in anyway.'

'No. He said you have to *complete* them. Whether they're good enough doesn't enter into it. That's what you're here to learn. Besides, they will be good enough.'

Jasmine was confused. Was he playing games with her?

'Look, we admit students whom we believe have talent. But if none of you had anything to learn from us what would be the point? Doing the classical drawings tells us how competent you are technically. Shows us what needs working on. We already know you have raw talent.'

'I see.' But she didn't. Instead, she felt a mixture of anger and frustration. All the worry she'd gone through. All the agonising that she'd fall short of the required standard, when he was now telling her she'd already met it. Why hadn't they told her this from the start?

Lachlan was staring at her and she felt herself reddening. Under his intense gaze, she felt that little lift in her insides and wondered again what it would be like to be kissed by him. But he'd been curt and abrupt yesterday. She wasn't about to forget that.

As though reading her thoughts, he said, 'Old Beetle Brows tore a strip off me yesterday. He's not happy that I've been working with you before term begins. Wants to see your drawings completed without any more guidance from me.' He rolled a cigarette then lit it. 'Conveniently forgets that most of the other students will have done foundation courses and had plenty of teaching. But who am I to argue with him? It'd only make it tougher for you if I did.'

'Do you think he might try to prevent me being accepted?'

Lachlan smiled. 'Och, I told you. You're already in. Keep the heid. He's just a miserable old man who likes to throw his weight around. You're a damn good artist, Jasmine. I can see that even if the auld fool canna.' He puffed on his roll-up, then abruptly stubbed it out in the ashtray. 'You'd better get back to the Louvre. You do need to get those twenty drawings done, even if they aren't perfect.' He pushed back his chair. 'I'll see you on Friday afternoon. Come to my atelier.' Then he was gone, leaving her wishing he was still there.

Jasmine was in a bar off the Boulevard Saint-Michel. It was almost midnight and the place was packed. She was squashed into a booth with Corinne, another girl named Sophie from the Sorbonne, and three young men, all students. Jasmine was tired, having spent the evening straining to understand the nuances of the conversation, the frequent use of argot and the intensity of the debate. They were discussing politics: the problems in the North African colonies, or communism, or de Beauvoir's treatise on feminism, but she'd given up trying to follow the subtleties. The topics seemed to be interchangeable, as they all provoked raised voices and impassioned debate. Jasmine yawned and longed to go to bed. It wasn't that she was uninterested in these subjects. It was rather that trying to discuss them was too exhausting when she felt ignorant of the facts and disadvantaged by the subtleties of the French language. She suppressed a yawn. Tomorrow was her review with Lachlan and she wanted to be on her best form for that.

There was no sign of the others wanting to eat, so she decided to leave them to their discussions and head back to the Lutèce, where she had a packet of biscuits in her room.

'Hey, Jasmine!'

She looked up and saw Stan Tyson. His arm was linked through that of a companion. A few inches taller and of a sturdier build than Stan, the other man was as blond and pale-skinned as Stan was dark. The contrast immediately made Jasmine want to paint them together. Stan's friend looked Scandinavian. Handsome, but in a rather bleached-out way. Insipid next to Stan.

'This is my friend, Lukas. He's a musician. Plays the clarinet.' Stan looked up at Lukas proudly. 'You hungry, Jasmine? We're heading over to Les Halles for a bite to eat. Wanna come?'

Corinne and the others were still arguing and hadn't even looked up. Jasmine was grateful for an excuse to escape.

Despite the lateness of the hour – or rather the earliness of the morning – the wholesale food market at Les Halles was a buzz of activity. Wooden handcarts, vans and lorries blocked the streets around the market halls. Black-capped *porteurs* in overalls rushed about, unloading and stacking crates of produce. Women sorted fruit and vegetables and piled giant cauliflowers into gravity-defying pyramids on the pavements. Under their feet, cabbage leaves, crushed pea-pods and squashed cherries stained the road surface. The air smelled of vegetables, the pungent scent of garlic, the sharp saltiness of fish and the sickly stench of blood. Strongmen – *les forts* – carried the carcasses of cattle and horses on their backs, wearing oversized hats to protect their heads and shoulders. Jasmine was transfixed by the men as they moved past, carrying their burdens from lorries into the meat pavilion, where they suspended the carcases from hooks. It was hard to believe they were each carrying the dead weight of an enormous beast single-handed.

'Those guys have to pass a test of strength before they get the job,' said Stan. They need to carry a weight of two hundred kilos for sixty metres.'

'How heavy is that?' Jasmine still didn't understand French weights and measures.

'Over four hundred pounds.'

She did a mental calculation. 'That's more than thirty stone! How is that possible?'

'They are very powerful,' said Lukas, smiling in appreciation, one eyebrow lifted.

The market pavilions were nineteenth-century iron and glass structures and Jasmine thought their elegant soaring metal pillars beautiful. But the market spilled out beyond their confines onto all the surrounding streets, in a dense and chaotic spread.

'There's been a market here since the twelfth century,' Stan told her. 'Used to be for all sorts of goods but now it's only food.'

Jasmine stepped aside to dodge *un fort* in a bloodstained apron, carrying what appeared to be a dead horse on his back.

'The produce comes from all over France. Emile Zola described Les Halles as "the belly of Paris". And talking of bellies. I could eat a horse myself.' Stan rubbed his stomach.

'Please no! I don't want to eat horse-meat.' Jasmine pulled a face.

'Don't worry. I don't either. You'll find the best and cheapest food in all Paris here,' said Stan. 'You haven't lived until you've tasted the onion soup and the snails in butter.' He took Jasmine by the arm and steered her towards a building opposite the market halls. 'Butter may be rationed but the farmers and merchants here have access straight to the dairies so there's plenty to be had. If you know where to look Paris is one giant black market anyway.'

They entered through the battered metal and glass door of a *bistrot* into a narrow room that opened into a larger space at the rear. The man in charge knew both Stan and Lukas and greeted them like old friends. They introduced him as Marius.

'This place has been going since Marius's father opened it in the 1890s. The beating heart of Paris.'

Before long, a bowl of piping hot onion soup, covered with toasted bread and an enormous amount of cheese, appeared in front of Jasmine, as well as a dish of snails in their shells. The soup was delicious and the heavy amount of garlic and butter in which the escargots were served was enough to compensate for her initial squeamishness about eating the gelatinous creatures.

Behind its steamy windows, the café was crowded. To Jasmine's surprise she saw a group of fashionably dressed socialites there, as well as several students and assorted night owls, all mingling with market traders. The latter were seizing a break before the frenzy when buyers arrived at around four in the morning: sturdily-built women as well as men, the women in headscarves and overalls as well as woollen coats, and the men in dirty aprons and black berets or caps. The sound of horns, braking lorries, revving engines, the crash of crates, and the cries of the traders penetrated the *bistrot* from the street outside. Jasmine knew she would need to come back to Les Halles with her sketch-book. Looking around her now, she wondered about the lives of these people. Many had been working here in the market since the previous century. Most had lived through two wars and the German occupation.

When they finished their food, Stan and Jasmine lingered over a *pichet* of wine, while Lukas moved across to the aluminium-topped bar to engage one of *les forts* in conversation over a brandy.

Stan looked meaningfully at Jasmine. 'Lukas has a weakness for strongmen.'

Jasmine stammered, 'Is he your...'

'We're friends and occasional lovers. I have no claim on him though.'

She felt herself blushing and struggled to find another topic of conversation.

But Stan must have realised she was uncomfortable with any allusion to his homosexuality, as he quickly steered the conversation onto different ground by asking her how she was settling into life in Paris.

Jasmine hesitated a moment, unsure of herself.

'Look, it's pretty clear to me that you come from the kind of family where you live in a comfortable home. Servants?'

She nodded.

'Hot running water?'

Another nod.

'So living in a dump like the Lutèce can't exactly be a bed of roses. It's different for me. I lived in a Chicago tenement. Paris isn't that different – and comes without the race hatred.'

'It's my choice. All students have to live like this. Why should I be different?'

'I didn't say you should. Just that you might not find it that easy.'

She smiled at him, but said nothing. One thing she had promised herself when she embarked on her European adventure, was that she'd never complain. Coming here was the fulfilment of a dream and nothing was going to detract from that.

Stan leaned back in his seat and studied her. 'I thought you looked like you needed rescuing tonight. Corinne and her friends can be intense.'

Jasmine smiled. 'Thank you. Corinne is delightful on her own but as soon as she meets her Sorbonne friends it's all passionate debate. I find it hard to keep up.'

'Those guys are fond of the sound of their own voices.' Stan broke a spent match into small pieces and deposited them in the ashtray.

Realising the lateness of the hour, Jasmine got up and said she must leave. 'I have an important meeting tomorrow afternoon with my tutor and have to prepare for it. So I need at least a few hours' sleep.'

'I'll walk you back.' Stan glanced in the direction of the bar. The Swede and the strongman had disappeared. 'Looks like Lukas made a new friend.' He followed Jasmine out of the *bistrot*.

·   ·   ·

The meeting with Lachlan didn't happen. Instead, Jasmine's tutor asked her to hand over the portfolio of classical drawings and told her to wait in his atelier while the admissions committee reviewed it.

'But I thought you were going to go through it with me and choose the best,' she protested.

'Change of plan. Beetle Brows insists on seeing the lot and right now.' Lachlan took the collection of drawings from her. 'Keep yer head on, hen, you'll be fine. I'm in your corner. It's a wee formality so everyone can see where you sit on the spectrum compared with the other students. We're just establishing the baseline for each student so we can measure how they develop and progress.' Then he rushed away.

If that was meant to console her, it had the opposite effect. Jasmine paced up and down the studio, heart racing, as the clock on the wall ticked. Eventually, she wandered over to look at what Lachlan had been working on. A large canvas rested on his easel, covered by a white cloth. She lifted the edge of the cloth tentatively and saw it was a portrait of a nude woman, sitting, legs akimbo, her labia exposed, leaving nothing to the imagination. Executed in a violent melange of heavily-applied colours, the painting exuded anger and ugliness rather than sensuality. Jasmine was shocked. It had an air of violence.

She lifted the fabric higher to reveal the model's face, and to her surprise and dismay, she recognised Corinne Deschamps. Dropping the cover as though it had delivered an electric shock, Jasmine backed away and went to sit by the window overlooking a small courtyard garden. It was raining again.

She asked herself why she was shocked. After all, Corinne had told her she modelled at the Beaux-Arts. Yet she had never seen her here – certainly not while Lachlan had been working on the painting. Had he painted this elsewhere? Or had he been working from memory? From preliminary sketches done on another occasion?

She went back to the easel and lifted the cloth again. The painting was raw, direct, and she sensed an intimate relationship between artist and subject. Corinne's head was back, her hair, usually pulled back into a ponytail, was a tumble of unkempt locks. One hand was behind her neck, her small breasts thrust forward, her lips apart and her eyes sending a message of provocation, of abandon, of desire. Then Jasmine noticed an unmade bed behind Corinne, a tangle of sheets trailing onto the floor. She had not modelled it here in the atelier then. Whether Corinne had been making love or was about to, the artist had clearly intended to convey that impression.

A dart of jealousy pierced her. Corinne was having a relationship with Lachlan. Was she his girlfriend? His mistress? His muse? A sour taste filled Jasmine's mouth. Why hadn't Corinne mentioned it? Or had Lachlan turned a simple studio life study into a bigger, uglier, more dramatic story? If so, it was clearly the artistic realisation of something he imagined or desired. The painting was charged with meaning.

Jasmine knew nothing of such matters. Her entire romantic experience comprised one brief but passionate kiss in a car with a man who was now dead, and protestations of love from Howard Baxter. She felt ignorant, naive, childish. Out of her depth.

Wanting to escape, she ran from the room, seeking the toilets at the end of the corridor. Once safely inside a cubicle, she sat down on the seat and told herself not to be foolish. Why shouldn't Lachlan and Corinne be having a relationship? And why should she have expected them to tell her? She had never seen them together. Why would Lachlan even be aware that Corinne was her friend? But she had told Corinne that Lachlan was her teacher, hadn't she? She tried to remember whether she'd mentioned that she had a crush on him. Of course she hadn't. She'd told no one. Thank goodness!

Blood rushed to her face as she realised what an idiot she was to have entertained the notion that Lachlan might be interested in her. When he'd said goodbye to her at the Tour Saint-Jacques that first night, he was probably on his way to meet Corinne.

She was a silly teenage girl, lacking any worldly wisdom. Corinne, in contrast, was a feminist, a woman of the world, self-confident, French. The kind of woman who thought nothing of taking her clothes off to pose for hours in front of a roomful of students. The kind of woman who would take them off and make passionate love to Lachlan Robertson.

Stop torturing yourself!

Jasmine splashed water on her face and ran a comb through her hair before leaving the ladies' room. When she got back to the atelier, Lachlan was there, bending over a table where he had laid out her drawings. He looked up and smiled. 'All done,' he said. 'You can relax now.'

Jasmine moved over to join him, aware she was shaking with nerves – a new fear at being around him now she had this secret knowledge. Not that she had any intention of mentioning it. She'd die first.

'The challenge of a clean white sheet of paper daunts most students, when they start out,' said Lachlan. 'Not you. You're not afraid to begin. To position your figure on the paper with confidence. To use the space. To make the shape work in the space.' He looked at her quizzically. 'I don't know whether it's instinctive or whether you think it through beforehand. Maybe you can tell me?'

'I don't understand what you mean.' Jasmine lacked the vocabulary to speak 'art'. It was a foreign language, full of arcane concepts. The way Lachlan spoke, his fluency, the terms he used, overwhelmed her, making her inarticulate. He looked at a drawing and spoke of lines and curves and Golden Ratios, of form and tone and structure. She struggled to make any connection between his words and her work. And right now, all she could think of was that three feet behind them was an intimate portrait of her friend, either before or after making love. Jasmine wanted to be anywhere in the world at this moment except here, facing her tutor while struggling to express herself coherently.

Lachlan picked up another drawing, tapped it with the back of his fingers and said, 'What I'm trying to say is you begin well. You don't rush in when you start a drawing and close off your options. And yet, you don't appear to hesitate. It's as though you have an uncanny ability to see exactly which aspects you want to emphasise and which to suppress, without experimenting, or thinking it through. Am I right?' He looked at her, searching for an answer in her face. 'Tell me, Jasmine, what exactly goes through your head when you begin a drawing?'

She was tempted to say the sooner started, the sooner finished, but she knew he wouldn't want to hear that. Instead of these cold clinical drawings, these disciplined copies of ancient artworks, she thought of how she'd sketched freely and loosely before coming to Paris. It was as if the city and the school had put constraints on her, shackled her to deliver others' expectations rather than fulfilling her own creative passions.

'I suppose I have a sense of how I want it to look when it's finished, and I set out to get there.' She thought of the portrait she had painted of Bintang – or even the quick sketch of Howard Baxter she'd done when they met on the passage from Ceylon to Penang more than a year ago. She tried again. 'You know... light falling on the side of a face, throwing the other side into shadow...' Her voice trailed off. 'I don't know. The shapes, I suppose, the patterns.'

Lachlan pulled one of her drawings towards him and pointed to the series of studies of the head of a long-dead Roman. 'These, for example.' He picked up another larger version of the same head and placed it beside the first sheet.

'Walk me though the process you used to get from these exploratory sketches to this final one.'

She stared at him; her mind blank.

'What I mean is these five initial sketches are all from the same angle.' He sounded impatient. 'I'd understand if you'd been experimenting with different ones.'

'No. I knew I wanted that one.' She gestured towards the smaller sketches. 'Here I was only trying to make sure I understood exactly how the shape would fit in the space.' She hesitated. 'This will sound silly, but I also wanted to be certain which bits were the most important.' She looked down, wishing she'd never started. 'Which bits should be in the spotlight. Otherwise it's just copying. I had to make it mine. Have I done it wrong?'

'No. You work from intuition. You know exactly how to interpret a subject. It will be interesting to see how you use this to capture the essence of a living subject, not a motionless plaster cast. It's only a wee while till you get to work with a life model.'

Jasmine could not suppress a groan. 'Until then more copying.'

Monsieur Rochambeau's voice came from behind her. The principal looked at her coldly as he came into the studio. 'Not merely copying. Seeing. Learning. It was good enough for Leonardo da Vinci and Michelangelo, Miss Barrington, yet you consider it beneath you. You clearly have a very high opinion of yourself.' The principal narrowed his eyes. 'Even Cézanne and Degas saw the value in studying and, yes, in copying the work of great classical masters, but you, an eighteen-year-old girl, find it beneath your dignity.'

He moved towards her. 'You will earn the right to self-expression only when you've proved beyond doubt that you have the skill and technique needed to deploy that expression.' He jerked his head up as though to give himself extra

height. 'Your contempt for rules does you no credit, Miss
Barrington. In the words of your own English master painter,
Sir Joshua Reynolds, "Rules are not the fetters of genius, they
are the fetters of men with no genius". That sentiment
equally applies to girls.' He nodded at Lachlan, then left the
room.

'He hates me.'

'Don't be dramatic. That's just how he is. You've passed the
untutored classical drawing stage with flying colours, but he
doesn't want you resting on your laurels before you've earned
them.' Lachlan brushed his hair away from his eyes. 'You've a
lot to learn, hen, but by God I'm going to relish teaching you.'

He walked across the room, reached into his jacket pocket,
took out his tobacco and rolled a cigarette. 'And the good news
is there will be lots more drawing of plaster casts.' Lachlan took
a long draw on his roll-up and gave her a knowing look. 'Stop
fighting it, hen. Recognise that you need to learn technique –
and yes, understand the theories too and concentrate on
perfecting them. You have your whole life ahead to express your
creativity. With technique at your disposal, you'll have even
more freedom to use your imagination. You won't have to waste
so much time struggling to work out for yourself the things that
study and practice can make instinctive. When all this is second
nature, it will no longer feel like a constraint – it will set you
free.'

Jasmine gazed at him, enraptured. She was in! She'd passed.
Nothing else mattered.

September 1949

Term had begun. The previously empty courtyards and echoing
corridors of the Beaux-Arts now teemed with students and staff.
It was overwhelming. After having the place almost to herself

these past weeks, Jasmine felt an intruder in these hallowed halls.

Lachlan's atelier students were a mixture: Robert, an Englishman; Rod, an American on the GI Bill; Yelena, a Russian woman; Giancarlo, an impossibly handsome Italian; the rest were all French – one woman and three men – and finally Jasmine. She couldn't help a slight sense of resentment that she would no longer have her tutor to herself. Instead of working in peace without fear of her work being seen by anyone other than the staff, she would now be drawing and painting in a roomful of people. Competitors. That made her edgy and uneasy.

Their days were to be divided between cast drawing in the morning and life drawing in the afternoons. For the life sessions, sometimes several ateliers were grouped together to make best use of the model. The prospect of this made Jasmine even more self-conscious: she didn't like the idea of working surrounded by so many others in a crowded space. Yet, the chance to draw from a living, breathing model after those weeks of inanimate plaster casts was a joy.

Like Corinne, one or two of the life models were students, supplementing their meagre finances, but the majority came from Paris's underbelly: prostitutes, *clochards*, the unemployed. Sitting in front of these frequently tragic-looking figures, Jasmine wondered about their lives outside the atelier. Their sad, emaciated faces, haunted eyes and shabby clothes were more interesting than the clear bright complexions of the student models. There was something liberating about sketching them – doing rapid charcoal sketches of their naked bodies after the hours of meticulous reproduction of the plaster casts. Rather than the rigorous draughtsmanship the classical drawings demanded, she could move her charcoal across the paper with freedom and spontaneity.

These life classes were tranquil. Peaceful. Everyone worked

in silence, in a collective companionship that Jasmine found lacking the rest of the time. The haunted faces of the dispossessed subjects contrasted in her mind with the smiling Malayan and Kenyan villagers she had once drawn, and created a hollow sense of longing. A longing for sunlight, colour, laughter, simplicity. Many of those villagers had been poor too, but they had had an inner joy and exuberance that was lacking in the subjects in front of her now. Yet still she preferred to draw them than the bored students and the noble Graeco-Roman gods and emperors.

After classes, she often wandered along to the bar in the Rue Jacob where Stan worked several evenings a week. She would install herself at a table in the corner, sketch-pad in hand and draw the habitués, some of whom were flamboyantly-dressed homosexuals, and none of whom paid her any attention, so she was free to sketch unobserved. Sometimes, in quiet periods, Stan would join her.

'How was your day?' he asked one evening, sliding into the banquette opposite and topping up her glass from a bottle.

'Good,' she said. 'I'm loving the life classes. Won't you get into trouble giving me free drinks?'

He gave a little smirk and said, 'The owner has a crush on me. I can get away with murder.'

She smiled. 'I'm so glad I met you, Stan. You're my only real friend in Paris.'

He studied her. 'That makes me happy for me but sad for you. Are you very lonely here? Missing home?'

'I miss my family.' As she said it, she remembered she had an unopened letter from her mother in her satchel. She burrowed into her bag and pulled it out, waving it at him. 'Thanks for reminding me. I've got a letter from home and I haven't read it yet.'

'Then I'll leave you in peace to enjoy it.' He smiled and went back behind the counter.

She tore open the envelope, her heart lifting as she saw there was also a brief note from Hugh. She read Evie's letter first, her eyes welling with tears and her heart longing to be with her mother, to fling her arms around her and tell her how hard it all was here.

Evie's letter was cheerful, full of small incidents than made Jasmine feel nostalgic – how Kichinga had been stung by bees while hanging out the washing but fortunately suffered no long-term effects, how Hugh had won two races at his school sports day, and little snippets of information about everyday life in Nairobi. Arthur had added a few lines at the bottom of the letter, wishing her well and asking how the course was going. He had evidently not heard from the Hendersons about their return to England and was surprised to hear about Jasmine's transfer to the Courbets' apartment. She hadn't wanted to upset her parents by telling them about Bernard Courbet's attempted rape or the standard of accommodation at the Lutèce. She'd told them the new address but none of the details. There was no point in having them worry about her when they were thousands of miles away.

Hugh had illustrated his letter with tiny drawings in coloured pencil showing his triumphs on the sports field. He had also included several corny jokes. Jasmine smiled, imagining him regaling everyone at the breakfast table with them. Annoying little pest as he often was, she wished he was here for her to hug – even though he'd pull a face.

It was painful to imagine life carrying on as normal in Nairobi while she was here, so far away from them. Not so long ago, she'd been desperate to leave Africa, to escape from the bonds of family and live for a while in Penang. And now, here in the City of Light, fulfilling her ambition and dreams, she ached to be under the African sunlight, living an uncomplicated life, surrounded by the people she loved best. But there was no point pining for something she couldn't have. She was doing what she'd always dreamed about: living in Paris and studying at one of the best art schools in the world. How dare she feel miserable?

But it was not just homesickness driving Jasmine's malaise. It was Lachlan, too. Now that he was teaching a full class, she missed being the sole focus of his attention. Most of the other students were older than her and she felt she had little in common with them and wasn't part of the gang. That was her own choice – she'd turned down one or two invitations to go out with the group after class ended. She was also avoiding Lachlan, slipping away before he could approach her. It was the same with Corinne.

There was no reason for her to feel so hostile towards her French friend. Corinne's lifestyle was not one Jasmine would choose for herself, but that she had the sort of relationship with a man that Jasmine wouldn't contemplate outside marriage was not a reason to give her the cold shoulder. Jasmine had listened to Corinne on many occasions talking about the repressive state of matrimony and the need to exercise freedom as a woman. While she didn't share Corinne's views, she didn't condemn her for them.

And yet, now that she had found out about Corinne's relationship with Lachlan, it was all too real and too upsetting. No matter how much she tried, Jasmine couldn't stop her gaze from following her tutor as he moved around the atelier, discussing students' work, or explaining concepts to class. She tried to forget him, but every time he entered the room, her heart almost arrested at the sight of his thick dark hair, falling heavy on his brow and curling over his collar, his narrow hips and long legs, and the deep brown eyes that, when they fixed on her, made her feel she was the only woman in the world. The beard had gone since term started, and she wasn't sure whether or not she missed it. Still, she day-dreamed about how it would feel to be kissed by him.

One evening, when Jasmine returned to her lodgings straight from the art school, wanting to write letters home, she opened her bedroom door to find Corinne sitting on her bed, waiting for her.

Surprised, and not a little annoyed, Jasmine stopped in the doorway. 'What are you doing in here?'

'Waiting for you. You've been avoiding me.'

Jasmine sensed her face flushing. 'I've been very occupied with classes.'

'In the evenings? I don't think so.'

'Sometimes I spend time with Stan. It's good to relax and speak English with him after concentrating on my French all day.'

'You said to me your teacher is Robbo. He's Scottish.'

Jasmine's face burned. 'He's half-French, actually. But then you'd know that better than I do.' She couldn't control the note of sarcasm.

Corinne frowned and jerked her head back. 'Why would I know that?'

'Come on, Corinne. Stop pretending. I know you and Lachlan Robertson are having a love affair.'

Corinne spluttered. 'What are you talking about?'

'I saw the portrait he painted of you. It was quite obvious you'd been making love. There was even a bed in the background. The sheet was trailing over the floor. And the way you were sitting. It was...well... it was obscene. It wasn't a studio life pose. It looked as though it was painted in what must have been his apartment. You looked like a...'

Corinne gave a hollow laugh. '*Une putain*? Is that the word you're searching for? You are thinking I look like a prostitute? You're crazy. Me and Robbo? That would be a joke if it wasn't so very rude.'

'Stop lying, Corinne. I'm not stupid.'

'No. But you are jealous.' Corinne leaned back against the

cracked plaster wall behind the bed. 'I am not having any romantic or sexual relationship with Lachlan Robertson. For money or not. Not now. Not ever.'

'So why ...?'

'Why has he painted me looking like a *putain*? I think you'd better ask him that.'

Corinne jumped off the bed and moved towards the door. 'You do not need to worry about me stealing him from you. I have no interest in Lachlan Robertson – nor in men at all. Hadn't you realised? I prefer women. But happily, not you.' Corinne opened the door and went out, leaving Jasmine mortified.

After a sleepless night, tossing and turning with embarrassment at her *faux pas* with Corinne, Jasmine went into the school early. The autumnal morning was crisp. She hurried along the empty streets, past the street cleaners as they washed away the dirt and detritus of the previous night and day.

In the atelier, she wanted to snatch time to work on something of her own before the obligatory cast drawing session began. If she was lucky, she had about an hour here to work undisturbed on the preliminary charcoal studies for a series of paintings she intended to create. As there was little scope for personal projects during the normal working day, she'd decided to come in every day at this time – and possibly stay late in the evenings. Each year there was a series of open competitions for works to be hung in the Salon des Expositions at the École and Jasmine wanted to have something to submit for consideration. Perhaps as a first-year student, she didn't stand a chance – but others had achieved it and she wanted to give it her best shot. She had mapped out these works in her head and couldn't wait to get started on them.

It was quiet and chilly in the building. The janitor didn't

light the furnace until the last possible minute, but Jasmine had remembered to bring a warm jumper and a small woollen blanket she'd picked up in a street market. Once she began drawing or painting, she was in her own special world, sealed off from such trivial considerations as cold and discomfort.

Lost in concentration, she was unaware of Lachlan's presence until he spoke. 'You're here early, Jasmine. What are you working on that has to be done in secret?'

She spun round to face him. 'It's not in secret. But obviously I can't do it in class.' She wanted to say that he knew all about working in secret himself, covering up his work with a white cloth, but she held back.

'Let me look.' Lachlan held a hand out for her sketch-pad and reluctantly she handed it over.

He flipped through the pages, frowning and nodding. 'Interesting composition. Tell me more.'

She sucked in her lips. She didn't want to tell him. 'I'm not sure yet.' Jasmine would not admit she already had a clear idea of how she would paint the works. In her mind's eye, they were finished paintings, and she didn't want his interference or suggestions.

Lachlan tapped a finger on one sketch. 'This is good.' It was a drawing of the *clochards* huddled on the quays of the Seine, clustered together, bodies pressed close to preserve warmth. There was another of barges, bedecked with washing, and a third of children sitting on the stone quay, legs dangling over the water. 'Keep it up, Jasmine. Smashing work, hen.'

It was the first time he'd called her 'hen' since term had begun. She swallowed, unexpectedly uncomfortable about the resumed intimacy.

Jasmine looked around. The large painting of Corinne under the white sheet was no longer in the studio. Lachlan must have removed it when classes started.

'I saw your painting of Corinne,' she said, the words tumbling out before she could stop them.

Lachlan's brow creased. Then he smiled, puzzled. 'Corinne?'

'Corinne Deschamps. She's a philosophy student at the Sorbonne. I live next door to her at the Lutèce. You had a painting of her on the easel. I imagine she must be your girlfriend.'

'I don't have a girlfriend.' His expression was inscrutable.

'I assumed ... but Corinne says I was wrong.'

'Why were you looking at the painting? Why do you think it had a cloth over it?' His voice lacked the warmth of a few minutes earlier.

'You're my teacher. I wanted to see your work. I thought I might learn from it.'

'And did you?'

'I didn't like it,' she said, deciding she had nothing to lose from honesty. 'I found it crude.'

He gave a little snort. 'Crude? The subject matter or the execution?'

'Both.' She looked down. 'I found it ugly. Unsettling.'

'Good,' he said. 'That's exactly what I wanted to convey.'

'Did you show her the painting?'

'The model? No. Why should I?'

'You made her look like a prostitute. I don't think she'd be thrilled about that.'

'She's paid to sit. Models have no right to see or comment on the works that result.'

Jasmine wished she hadn't brought the subject up. But he was right, of course. Corinne was fulfilling a contracted service. The school was paying her, not the other way round. 'It seemed to have been painted elsewhere. There was a bed. It looked like...'

'That was the idea. While you are all drawing or painting

the models as an exercise, we teachers sometimes use them to incorporate in other works. That was one of a series. Portraits of fallen women.'

'But Corinne isn't a fallen woman.'

'Maybe not. But I thought she made an excellent subject.'

'Did she sit like that? I mean, with her legs splayed open?'

'I can't remember. It was last term, before the summer. I worked on it over the long vacation. Look, Jasmine, why all the fuss?'

She bit her lip. 'Because after I saw it, I accused her of having an affair with you. I thought you and she...'

'Did ye now? You've quite an imagination.'

'It didn't take much imagination.' She risked a smile.

'And what did your friend say?'

'She was mad at me.'

At that moment, the studio door opened and Antoine, one of the male French students, walked in, ending the conversation.

NINE

STATE OF JOHORE

November 1949

Howard was relishing his new role. The Redmond Rubber Estate was enormous – more than twice as big as Batu Lembah. He had jumped from being the assistant manager on a much smaller plantation, to being the man-in-charge with four assistant managers and a team of juniors and controllers. A meteoric rise within Guthrie's, and likely to cause resentment in some quarters.

The district was almost entirely given over to rubber, apart from the occasional tin or bauxite mine. Redmond was roughly equidistant from Kuala Lumpur and Singapore, so – in theory – he could access both cities in his free time. But Howard was ambitious, hard-working and strangely resistant to the lures of dance halls, cinemas and parties. Instead, he spent what little free time he allowed himself at the local club, about a ten-mile drive from the estate. There he could get a game of tennis, swim in the pool, have a few beers and enjoy a game of cards with other planters. Otherwise, he avoided social activities and flung himself wholeheartedly into his work. He had a lot to prove and wanted to show that taking a chance on him had been the right decision by Guthrie's and Sir John Hay.

On top of the normal duties of a plantation manager, there was a constant need to exercise vigilance against enemy activity by the communist insurgents. Not only to protect Guthrie's interests, but to ensure the safety of the hundreds of rubber tappers and their families. The estate was close to two large communist fighting cells, and the insurgents lost no opportunity to strike terror wherever they could.

Today, Howard had been covering a distant section of the estate, and now stood close to the perimeter fencing, watching as an RAF plane flew overhead. The aircraft banked and turned, then flew low over the adjacent jungle, dropping a stream of propaganda leaflets in its wake. He'd read in the *Straits Times* that a million of them were being dropped across the country to encourage the insurgents to surrender. There were assurances that terms would be favourable – meaning avoidance of the death penalty for all but the most grievous of crimes. He thought of the trade unionist, arrested and hanged six months ago for being in possession of a pistol and ammunition. It appeared the British authorities were reducing their thirst for revenge, preferring the deterrent of imprisonment. Too late for that poor chap, though.

Howard turned away from the fence and headed back down between the lines of rubber trees to a section where a gang of workers was clearing away undergrowth. If the vegetation wasn't cut back regularly, the jungle would reclaim the land and choke the rubber trees, preventing tapping.

He glanced at his watch. The men were packing up for the day. Time for a quick shower, before jumping in his jeep and heading to the nearest small town, Bukit Kepong, where some of the planters and local police gathered once a week to share news over a beer.

.   .   .

When he arrived at the bar, there were already half a dozen planters and miners there, along with the local police chief, a Malay, Sergeant Bin Mohammed Shah. Howard bought a beer for himself and one for another planter who had arrived at the same time, a chap called Bert Carter, whom Howard had met on his last trip to the club in Segamat.

They joined the group, sitting round two tables that were shoved together.

An American mining engineer, Wayne Clark, was next to Howard. He looked up and nodded at Howard and Bert as they sat down. 'I tell you, you Brits need to get a grip on this situation. I don't mean you personally, but the darn British government. We're almost at the end of the year and if you reckon up the score-card, it looks like the commies are wiping the floor with you.'

'Steady on, old chap,' said Carter, an old-timer in Malaya, who had survived imprisonment by the Japanese in Changi. 'They're armed to the hilt with our damned guns. Should never have trusted the blighters. They may have been on our side against the Japs but they're twisty little sods, those Chinese. You can't trust them as far as you can throw them.'

Howard glanced over at the Chinese man who owned the bar and was busy polishing glasses behind the counter, pretending not to have heard.

'That's uncalled for, Bert,' Howard said. 'Most Chinese are thoroughly decent men, and we'd be in trouble without them on the rubber estates. My tappers are hard-working and loyal. Don't tar them all with the same brush as Chin Peng and his ilk.' He was referring to the notorious leader of the insurgents, a man who had fought beside the British and had been flown to London after the war to be invested with honours, but who now killed his former allies at every opportunity.

Carter harrumphed and moved his chair sideways to create a gap between his and Howard's. 'Only been here five minutes, and he's already sounding off like he's an expert. He needs to remember he's only an acting manager. Pennington will be back once he's got over his heart problem.'

Another planter spoke up. 'Come off it, Bert. Pennington won't be coming back. He's bloody lucky to be alive. Back in Blighty for good if you ask me. And this chap's right. My Chinese coolies are hard-working men who hate the commies as much as we do. Not all of them are in thrall to Chairman Mao or to Chin Peng.' He leaned across the table and offered a hand to Howard. 'I'm Donald Miller. You can call me Don. Pleased to meet you, son, and welcome to the district. I know O'Keefe, the *tuan* up at Batu Lembah. He speaks highly of you.'

'Shall we get down to business, gentlemen?' The speaker was the local police sergeant. He outlined all the recent insurgent activity in the area. 'An officer from the army will be joining us later. Apparently he wants to give you all a briefing on security plans.'

'Never mind the darn plans,' said Carter. 'Anyone else here wondering why the government in Westminster and the Colonial Office are doing damn all? There's nothing in the British press about what's happening here.'

'And precious little in the local press,' said Don. 'Seems fishy.'

'It's a conspiracy of silence,' said another planter. 'They're acting as though they're not interested.'

'They're not.' The American scraped his chair back and went up to the bar. 'It's because we're fighting a civil war and you lot call it an emergency. What the hell do you expect?'

'Come on, Clark, you know as well as we do if we used the word "war", London would implode. The rubber companies don't want their insurance premiums to go through the roof.' Ron tilted back in his chair.

'There's definitely something up,' said Carter. 'You're right, Don, it's fishy.'

Speculation was cut short by the arrival of the British army officer. The man swaggered into the room, looking about him as if surveying his newly-acquired kingdom, staking out his territory. He oozed arrogance from his brilliantined hair to the small, clipped moustache that garnished his upper lip like a furry caterpillar.

Howard hoped the man wouldn't recognise him. They'd met on the voyage between Colombo and Penang, when Lieutenant Ellis had attempted to court Jasmine. Although 'courting' was the wrong word for what he'd done, compelling her to dance with him and persistently trying to persuade her to spend time with him when it was clear she had no interest in him, a man old enough to be her father. Months later, he'd attacked her in her studio at Bella Vista, trying to force her to kiss him. And Howard was all too aware that Ellis had been responsible for the cold-blooded murder of the mother of Jasmine's half-brother, Amir. Reggie had said the man was doing a desk job near Ipoh, but here he was, in charge of an active unit here in Johore. Howard tried to hide his loathing and avoided the officer's gaze.

Ellis stood at the end of the table, his mouth shaped into a smile, eyebrows raised, as he waited for someone to vacate a seat or bring one to him. The overall impression was one of a gladiator who had just fought another contender to the death and was now waiting to accept his laurels.

Howard would have liked to lunge at him. Hurt him, punch him, knock that sneering expression from his face. He wanted Ellis to suffer. He wanted to punish him for killing that innocent woman and depriving Amir of his mother. For being a self-serving, insensitive brute. And most of all, for assaulting and insulting Jasmine.

Carter was the first to break, rustling up a seat and shuffling his own chair sideways to accommodate Ellis at the head of the table. Howard would have liked to flatten Carter too.

The lieutenant ran his eyes around the room, as though taking the measure of each individual and finding them wanting. The men waited expectantly.

Ellis's eyes settled on Howard, trying to place him. Howard recognised the moment the penny dropped, when contempt caused that twitching lip to curl, revealing the crooked stained teeth behind. But Ellis clearly decided not to claim any past acquaintance and moved on without comment.

'I'm Lieutenant Ellis, the new commanding officer in this district. I'm here to root out the nest of communist vermin that's been operating in the area and making your lives miserable. I'll soon have the situation under control. These people need to see a show of strength and I'm going to give them one.'

The men round the table exchanged glances. Howard took another swig of beer.

Ellis went on, ignoring the presence in front of him of Sergeant Mohammed Shah. 'The local police aren't up to the job. Not their fault. They're all Malays. This calls for the superior brain of the white man.' He tapped the side of his head. 'When it comes to finely honed skills, I, gentlemen, had mine tuned in the heat of battle. My troops operate as a well-oiled machine. They're champing at the bit to get out there and sort out the little yellow bastards. To drive them out of their filthy jungle rats' nest and restore order.'

The initial scepticism on the faces of the men had been transformed into a mix of amusement and disgust. It was the American, Clark, who spoke up first. 'You ever been in the jungle, Ellis? Ever had leeches crawling through your undershorts and feeding off your balls?'

Before Ellis could answer, Don Miller chipped in. 'You're an experienced jungle tracker, are you? Know how to spot booby traps before you walk into them and get your head sliced off?'

'Speak Malay or Chinese?' Carter asked. 'Understand the

lie of the land, do you? Like Sergeant Bin Mohammed Shah here? He was born and bred in the state of Johore and knows every man, woman and child for miles around.'

Ellis's contempt was visible. His eyes raked over the police officer. 'That's just the problem. Telling good from bad. When you've known people since childhood, it's easy to assume they're good men. But the only good communist is a dead communist.'

The sergeant remained silent, his expression impassive.

'When it comes down to it, I don't trust any of the natives,' said Ellis. 'They'd sell their own mothers for an extra bag of rice or a few dollars. No, gentlemen, what's needed here is discipline and fighting spirit. I fought at El Alamein and then served in the military police in Palestine. I know how the terrorist mind works.' He gestured dismissively towards the police sergeant. 'All due respect, but this fellow is a country policeman. Used to dealing with the odd petty thief or settling arguments about cows, but not up to the job of stamping out the commies.'

Clark scraped his chair back, got up, and went to stand in the open doorway to the street. He turned to address Ellis. 'Around here we judge a man by his actions, not by how big his mouth is. Everyone in this room has a lot of respect for Sergeant Mohammed Shah, or Jamil, as those of us who are fortunate to know him well, call him. I also respect all the men of the Federation Police who work for him. Malaya's finest men. You, sir, are an unproven outsider.' He took a step forward. 'And let me give you one tip for the job that lies ahead of you. This sure as hell ain't the deserts of El Alamein or Palestine where it's open country not dense jungle. So, until you have something concrete to offer us, I for one have better things to do than sit here listening to you, Mr Big Shot Brit. I'll see you guys next month.' With that, he left the bar.

The other men returned their attention to their beers. Carter went over to the counter and came back with three bottles, handing one to Howard and another to the police sergeant.

'Anything else you've got to say to us, Lieutenant Ellis?' asked Don Miller. 'Only we'd like to discuss business. *Rubber* business.'

Ellis stood, his smug expression indicating he had been impervious to the snub. 'I'll be seeing you all again soon. I plan to visit each plantation to review your security measures. Meanwhile, you'll find me at the district HQ in Segamat.' He picked up his cap, put it on, and left the bar.

'A well-oiled military machine?' scoffed Miller after the officer had gone. 'The man's an idiot.'

'A dangerous idiot,' said Howard.

TEN

PARIS

November 1949

Jasmine was in the Luxembourg Gardens with Stan. For the past few weeks she'd been down in the dumps, and had been avoiding Lachlan and her fellow students, slipping away whenever someone suggested going to a bar after their studies ended.

It was a crisp Sunday morning in November, and traces of frost lingered on the lawn where the watery sun hadn't yet reached. She was only here with Stan now because he'd come to the Lutèce, hammered on her door and convinced her she'd feel better if she joined him for a walk.

'You can't stay in bed all day feeling sorry for yourself, Jasmine. Come out and see the world.'

So she'd flung on some clothes and walked with him through the streets to the park. Under the now russet-red chestnut trees, men wrapped in scarves and coats squared off against each other across tables, playing chess. In the central Grand Bassin, children sailed toy boats on the ornamental expanse of water, and strains of music drifted across the park as a concert got under way.

They were sitting on metal chairs, positioned to catch the gentle sunlight, Stan reading a novel, and Jasmine in fingerless gloves, sketching a pair of elderly chess players battling in silent concentration. Her mind was racing as she thought about Lachlan and the way he'd cooled towards her. Ever since she'd told him she hated his work and accused him of having an affair with Corinne. She silently cursed Antoine for walking in on them before she'd cleared the air properly with her tutor. And how much of the conversation had Antoine overheard? Was her argument with Lachlan now common knowledge among the other students? Suddenly, she felt very alone and wished she'd never come to France.

Stan closed his book and leaned back to gaze up at the sky. 'This is my favourite place in all Paris,' he said. 'Sometimes I sit here all day long, watching the world go by.'

It was as if he were reading her mind, giving her a reason to see things through a different lens. She looked around her at the spread of the park, at the chess players, at the children playing, the couples taking a romantic stroll along the rows of pleached trees.

'I love it, too,' Jasmine said. She moved her head in the direction of the chess players. 'Do you think they came here to play throughout the war?'

Stan shrugged. 'Probably. I imagine most Parisians did their best to live as normally as possible, despite the German army crawling over the place. A form of defiance.' He fumbled in his jacket pocket for a cigarette. 'There was serious rationing. The Germans shipped most of the produce off to Germany, treating France as a great big larder, and leaving the French to eat boiled cabbage.'

'Where did you serve, Stan?' She put down her pencil. 'You've never told me about your time in the war.'

'And you've never told me what you did either.' He lit the

cigarette. Like many former GIs, he had one of those Zippo lighters that were supposed to stay lit even in a high wind.

'That's because as soon as the Japanese began bombing the island where I lived, we were evacuated. My mother, brother and I were put on a train along with the rest of the people from Penang – well, the Europeans, unfortunately not the locals – and sent to Singapore. We were lucky. They took us straight from the train to the port and put us on a ship to Australia. So I spent the rest of the war swimming in the Indian Ocean and playing on the beach. Mummy's best friend, Mary, who was with us when we were evacuated, wasn't so lucky. They kept all the women without children in Singapore, and by the time the city fell, there was a huge scramble to get away. The Japs captured her ship and sent the passengers to prison camps in Sumatra. Most of them died there, including Mary's mother. Mary never talks about being a prisoner of the Japanese. Nor does Arthur – or Mary's husband Reggie.'

'Who's Arthur?'

'My adoptive father. He and Mummy married after the war. His wife died in the Camp Mary was in. He was a friend of Daddy's. Arthur fought behind the lines in Malaya and got captured, too. I don't know exactly what happened to him. I'm not sure even Mummy knows.' She drew a finger across her lips.

Stan took a long draw on his cigarette. 'I can imagine why he wouldn't want to talk about it.'

'Can you?' She looked at him intently. 'I'd have thought it would help to get something like that off your chest. I'm sure it was pretty grim.'

Stan exhaled a long stream of smoke, his expression troubled. 'I was with the guys who liberated the concentration camp at Dachau. Until I die, I'll never forget what I saw that day. I find it hard to talk about. God only knows how the survivors cope.'

Jasmine bit her lip, aware that Stan had turned away. She

didn't want to press him, so she waited to see if he'd volunteer more.

'It was the smell at first.' He let out a deep sigh. 'I still remember it. It took days before I stopped smelling it – it seemed to go with me. Like nothing I've ever known. If I live to be a hundred, I won't forget that smell and what I saw that day.'

'What kind of smell?' Her voice was barely a whisper.

'It was coming from a train. Outside the camp gates. The Germans had packed three thousand prisoners from the camp at Buchenwald into a few dozen carriages and sent them to Dachau to avoid the American advance. Instead of taking days, the journey took weeks. By the time the train got to Dachau most of them were dead and the camp guards left their bodies to rot inside the carriages.' He took in a slow, prolonged lungful of air. 'But that was nothing to what we saw once we went inside the camp.'

Stan drew on his cigarette and put back his head as he exhaled, his eyes following the plume of smoke as it spiralled into the air above him. 'They were the walking dead. Skin and bone, barely able to move. Skeletons. Not an ounce of muscle. You could count every rib. Hip bones sticking out. Some had stomachs swollen like balloons.' He shook his head, and turned to look at her, the pain of the memory clear in his eyes. 'Every goddamn bone in their bodies on display. They could hardly stand, let alone walk. They were dying in front of us. And they weren't just starving, they were riddled with disease. Typhus. Lice.' His voice trailed away.

Jasmine reached out and took his hand. 'If you don't want to talk about it...'

'I want to talk about it. But if you don't want to listen...'

'I'm here,' she said simply.

'It's the guilt. That's what I didn't expect.'

'Guilt? The Germans?'

'No!' He almost spat the words out. 'Mine. Ours.'

'What do you mean?'

'Not for killing the German guards. I wasn't one of those who did that, but believe me, Jasmine, I'd have killed those bastards with my bare hands if I'd had a chance. Some of the company mowed a bunch of guards down. Shot them dead as they were surrendering. Yes, it was wrong, but I understand why they did it. If you'd seen what we saw, anyone would get why we were mad with rage.' He ground the stub of his cigarette into the gravel with his heel. 'No. My guilt is for what we did to the survivors. We just didn't know. No one warned us.'

Jasmine squeezed his hand gently, then let it go.

'They were clinging on to life by a thread. So we gave them all our food. Candy bars, beef jerky. Anything we had we pressed on them, saying "Here, eat, eat". We only wanted to help them. They were dying of hunger, so we gave them food.'

Jasmine sucked her lips inward, wishing she knew what to say to ease his pain.

'We weren't medics. We hadn't a goddam clue. Those poor bastards fell on those Hershey Bars like they were manna from heaven. All that fat and sugar when their organs were in failure? Made them sick. Some of them died. We were killing them with kindness.' He scuffed up the gravel with the edge of his shoe, burying his cigarette butt. 'I've no idea how many of them survived.' Stan bent forward, elbows on his thighs. 'We moved on a few days later and the medics and the Red Cross came in to care for them. Most of them spent months in camps before they were fit enough to be released.'

'What did you do after that?'

'Mopping up. Mainly in southern Germany. Keeping order. Overseeing bomb-site clearance, security patrols. That kind of thing.'

'When did you get out of the army?'

'Three years ago. Late '46. If the Japanese hadn't surrendered, we were slated to transfer to the Pacific in '45. When most of the company were demobbed back to the States, the army reassigned some of us and kept us in Germany.'

'After you were demobbed, you stayed in Europe?'

'Nothing for me back in the USA. Seeing what the Nazis did to those Jews, I wasn't going to go back into a society where there's race-hate. In America they don't herd black men into concentration camps but there's many who'd really like to.'

'Did many soldiers remain over here?'

Stan shrugged. 'Most couldn't wait to get home.' He expelled the air from his lungs with a deep sigh. 'Including my friend. My special friend.' He closed his eyes. 'He was an officer, a captain. We fought together in the Italian campaign, then in Operation Dragoon, invading the south of France.'

They stopped speaking for a few minutes as a family group approached, one small child running up in front of Stan and Jasmine and squatting down to pick up a bird feather. The little girl waved it like a trophy, oblivious to her mother's lament that it was dirty.

Once the family had passed on, Stan picked up his story. 'I saw some terrible things in the war. Nothing to compare with Dachau, but some of the fighting in Italy was brutal. Yet, I can honestly say it was the happiest I've ever been and probably ever will be. Sometimes, Jasmine, it's as if that war gave me a preview of the hereafter. Dachau was a vision of hell. Not like that painting *Pandemonium* in the Louvre. There's something pure about those flames. Dachau was the opposite of that. Everything ugly. Every foulest stench, every gut-wrenching taste. Nothing came close.' He turned to look at her. 'Sorry. I shouldn't be laying all this on you.'

'It's OK. I want to listen. Go on.'

'Well, in all the horror and death and destruction, the months I spent with Jeff were the sweetest, most joyful I've ever known.' His voice choked as he struggled to control his emotions. 'I sometimes think what we had with each other cancelled out so much of the pain. I thought it would last forever. I thought we'd be together forever.' He bent forward, elbows on his knees, eyes downcast. 'But *he* knew it wouldn't last. He must have known all along.'

'But you said he went back, so he didn't die?'

'No, he didn't die. Only to me. But *I* died. Or something inside me did.'

'What happened?'

'First chance he could, Jeff returned to the States. Back to his old life. Back to a place at Harvard Law School, back to his Waspy family, his home in Westchester County and the girl he'd met in high school. I never saw it coming. He let me believe we had a future together.'

'You'd made plans?'

'Nothing specific. No one makes plans when they're fighting a war. But there was an assumption that we were going to stay together.' Stan's mouth set hard. 'We loved each other.'

'Did other people know about your relationship? I mean in the army?'

'Hell, no! Uncle Sam has no time for perverted homosexuals. It's not the American way. Not apple pie and Uncle Sam. The US military isn't exactly in the *avant garde*. So we were careful. Very careful. But I'm sure you don't want to hear all this, Jasmine.'

'I do. It must have come as a terrible shock when Jeff said he was going home.'

'The worst betrayal. It was like someone hacked off my arm and left me bleeding. The pain of losing him; that and the realisation that while he'd been my entire world, I wasn't enough for him.'

Jasmine reached for his hand again.

'But how could I have expected to be? A short, ugly, black kid from the slums of Chicago? What did I have to offer, compared with a prosperous future as a lawyer and the cosy façade of the all-American family?' Stan closed his eyes, hiding his pain.

'He said he couldn't let his folks down. Asked how he could look his mom in the eye and tell her he was in love with another man. "What would become of us, Stan?" he asked me. "It was a beautiful dream while it lasted, but in the end, it was just an escape from the war."' Stan turned and looked at her. 'Imagine what that felt like.'

His eyes were full of tears. 'But it wasn't like that for me. I loved him, and I truly believed Jeff loved me. Hell, I *know* he loved me. But I wasn't enough for him. You see, Jasmine, no matter how many times I've tried to tell myself to get on with life and forget about Jeff, I can't. I just can't. In those fifteen months we were together – fifteen months, one week, and four days – we were everything to each other. But he walked away to have his society wedding to an empty-headed, pretty girl, join his father's law practice, and raise a family. All to keep his folks happy.'

'Does he know you're in Paris? Have you ever heard from him?'

Stan shook his head slowly. 'No, and I never will. I'm safely behind a door. He's closed it, turned the lock and thrown away the key.'

Jasmine didn't know what else to say. It was tempting to offer platitudes, but she knew there'd be no comfort in them. Stan would see them for what they were: hollow attempts to stick a plaster on a severed artery. She released his hand and they lapsed into silence.

Jasmine hadn't seen Corinne since their falling out weeks earlier. At first she'd been annoyed, until she realised the French girl had perhaps been justified in taking offence. As time went on and she hadn't so much as glimpsed her erstwhile friend – not even passing her on the stairs of the Lutèce – Jasmine decided to apologise and try to make peace. Better to swallow her pride and admit she might have made a mistake.

Nervous, she knocked on Corinne's bedroom door. It was a Sunday morning, so she assumed it would be a good time to catch her at home. Getting no response, she knocked again. Louder. There was a sound of movement from within. The door swung open.

Standing on the threshold was a scowling man with his bedsheet wrapped around him, a tousled mop of unkempt hair and bloodshot eyes. '*C'est quoi ce bordel?*' he snapped, adding another expletive that Jasmine didn't understand.

She stared at him, shocked. It was Antoine from Lachlan's atelier. Was he sleeping with Corinne, too? So much for her claim that she preferred women.

'I was looking for Corinne,' she said, trying not to look beyond Antoine to the bed behind him. 'Is she there? Maybe I should come back later when you've...'

'Who's Corinne?'

'The girl who lives here.'

'*I* live here. There's no girl. Who are you? Don't I know you?' He stood back, appraising her. 'You're the English girl in Robertson's atelier.'

'Yes. Jasmine Barrington. I live in the room next door.' Jasmine looked at the man in perplexity, then dropped her eyes, trying to avoid staring at his very hirsute chest.

'Right. Well, I live here. Now you know.' He moved to close the door with one hand, scratching the area of the bedsheet covering his balls.

'How long? I mean, when did you move in?' she asked, determined to get some answers.

'About two weeks ago. Now can I go back to sleep?'

He gave her a menacing look. Muttering an apology, she

retreated, and the door slammed. She was about to open her own door when Antoine reappeared. 'Wait! Your friend left this. It was under the bed. I've no use for it.' He tossed a book at her. She caught it, breaking a fingernail. The door slammed again.

Back in her room, Jasmine sat on the bed shaking. She glanced at the book in her hands. *Le Deuxième Sexe* by Simone de Beauvoir. Well, hadn't she planned to buy a copy, anyway? She might as well read this one until she found out where Corinne had gone.

But not right now. She hadn't the stomach for reading. She lay back on top of the bedcovers and stared up at the cracked ceiling and the rickety pipework.

Everywhere she turned and everything she did seemed to lead her up a blind alley. She'd accused her only female friend of having an affair with her teacher. She'd thought the worst of Corinne – with no real justification. Practically called her a tart. Then not content with that, she'd jumped in and said more or less the same to Lachlan – and since then had experienced a noticeable cooling of relations between them. And now, it seemed, unwittingly, she'd angered one of her fellow students.

How had she been unaware the man had been staying in the room next to hers for the past two weeks? She'd blindly assumed it to be Corinne. What had possibly made her think it would be acceptable to disturb anyone early on a Sunday morning? Even Corinne?

It was a virtual certainty that she'd alienated one of her fellow students for no reason. If only she were back in Nairobi, relaxing on a lounger on the veranda beside Mummy and Arthur while they all listened to Hugh telling them the latest of his feeble knock-knock jokes. Or sitting on another veranda in Penang as Reggie sipped his customary *stengah*, Mary talked about what had happened at the little village school and the fireflies glowed in the dark and cool of the evening. Even being with Howard Baxter. What she'd give right now to see that smiling handsome face. She'd even put up with him being big-headed about his boring old rubber production numbers. Maybe Jasmine had nothing in common with Howard, but at least he was kind and he cared about her.

Thoughts of Howard took over. She'd been too hasty in tearing up his letter without replying. The image of Antoine standing half-naked in the doorway morphed into one of Howard. Jasmine thought of the afternoon they'd spent together at the beach. She'd really liked him then. He hadn't been corny. Hadn't made a pass at her. He'd just talked to her in a way that wasn't at all arrogant, opening up to her about his unhappy childhood and the difficult relationship he had with his father. Then they'd swum in the warm water of the Strait of Malacca. Howard's skin had been tanned by the sun, not the pasty white of Antoine's. Howard's chest was firm, with a fine line of darker hair running between his pectorals down to where it disappeared into his shorts, whereas Antoine's was thatched with dark hair like a gorilla. And Howard would never be so crass as to scratch his balls through his bedsheet and yawn, mouth wide like a hyena.

Put Howard out of your head! He's gone. History. Part of a life you've walked away from. Like it or not, she must adapt to her new life here. Just because she'd got off on the wrong foot with Lachlan and Corinne, and now this Antoine chap, didn't mean that she was incapable of finding some people to become friends with. And she had Stan. Lovely, sad, lonely Stan with his tragic memories and his abandonment by the man he loved. Jasmine might not have understood what drove a man to prefer other men – or in Corinne's case other women – but she could tell that Stan truly loved his lost Jeff and surely the world would be a far better place if there were more love, whatever form it took.

In Malaya, where the Emergency was showing no signs of

ending, Jasmine was all too aware that people were consumed with hatred and mistrust of each other to the point of cold-blooded killing – as far as she could see, on both sides. That thought reminded her that, as a white planter, Howard's life was constantly in danger. Those awful, steel armour plates he had to fix onto his jeep, the gun he carried in his belt, the armed guards on the gates, the barbed wire. She'd been rotten telling him not to write when he was facing danger every day.

But hadn't she already been through all this and made her decision? Carrying on a long distance friendship with Howard by letter would be cruel. It would be mean stringing him along, getting his hopes up that one day she might go out with him. And she couldn't go out with him unless she was ready to accept that meant a long-term commitment. They knew each other too well for that. It might even mean marriage eventually. Jasmine didn't want to be a planter's wife. She was married to her art. No room for a husband. Her life was here, like it or not, so she jolly well had to get on with it.

She rolled onto her stomach. The grimy window looking onto the airshaft let in so little light it was impossible to tell whether it was cloudy or sunny outside; a problem exacerbated by the birdlime from Parisian pigeons streaking the glass.

Jasmine was shivering. Either she'd have to climb back into bed or venture outside to find a warm café to sit in. Or she could take a brisk walk along the river or over to the Île St Louis, which she hadn't yet explored. If she took her sketch-book, there'd be no time to feel lonely. After all, she was only in Paris for one reason: to become a better painter. She didn't need friends and certainly didn't need a boyfriend. Best to put it out of her head and stop feeling so jolly sorry for herself, like some wretched lovelorn girl in the novels the girls at her school used to pass round.

She would rise above it all. Dedicate her life to her art. Who needed people? Of course, she'd keep some room for Stan, as he was a kindred spirit. But that was all.

Jasmine gathered her materials up, shoved them into her satchel, and went to put on her coat. There was a knock on the door. Opening it, she saw Antoine, now wearing a pair of trousers and a roll-neck navy blue sweater under a heavy greatcoat.

'I was abrupt with you just now. I'm not great in the morning. At least until I've drunk coffee, and especially after a late night. Some of us went dancing at Le Caveau de la Huchette and I now have the worst hangover. Let me buy you a coffee. Since we're neighbours and in the same atelier, we might as well get to know each other. Antoine Laroche, *à ton service, Jasmine.*' He gave her a brief salute. '*Ça marche?*'

Taken aback, Jasmine merely nodded. 'Okay. I'm sorry I woke you up. I was about to go out for a walk anyway, so why not?' As soon as she'd said it, she regretted it. What if this chap got the wrong idea and thought she was interested in him? Or what if he was like Monsieur Courbet and she'd have to pile the furniture against the door?

Antoine must have noticed her hesitation, as he added, 'Come on. I don't bite. And just to avoid any misunderstandings, I have a girlfriend in Cabourg, where I come from.'

Relieved, she shrugged on her coat, wrapped a scarf around her neck, put her satchel over her shoulder and followed him down the five flights of stairs to the street.

They walked down the Boulevard Saint-Michel towards the Seine. Antoine, hands deep in his pockets, said nothing and Jasmine went along with the silence. Eventually he turned off the boulevard, steering her towards a small café in a side street. Inside, he ordered one coffee and two *cafés au lait* with croissants, without consulting her. She wondered whether someone else was joining them, but it appeared not. He swigged back the shot of coffee quickly, smiled and said, 'That's better. I feel half-human now.' Turning his attention to the milky second coffee, rather than drinking it, he dipped pieces of croissant into the cup and ate them hungrily, stuffing them inside his open mouth. Jasmine stared at him. He hadn't shaved. His hair looked as though it had never said hello to a comb, but he wasn't bad looking. Not her type, but there was a definite Gallic *je ne sais quoi* about him.

The coffee had loosened his tongue. 'Where did you learn to speak French?'

'At school. Then I went to classes at the Alliance Française in Nairobi. That's where my family live. In Kenya.'

'Pas mal,' he said. Evidently as close as he could manage to a compliment about her command of his language.

'I watched a lot of French films too.'

His eyes lit up. 'Which ones?'

'I loved *Les Enfants du Paradis* and went to see it twice.'

He nodded, gravely. 'What else?'

She tried to remember the titles. *'Dedée d'Anvers.'*

He curled a lip slightly.

'Yes, it was grim, wasn't it? Rather seedy. Although Simone Signoret was very good.'

'Best thing about it. But the film's not as good as *Le Quai des Brumes* which it shamelessly copied.'

'I haven't seen that.'

'Carné directed it.'

'Who?'

'Marcel Carné who made *Les Enfants du Paradis.'*

'Then I'll definitely have to see it.'

'Bien.' He threw some coins into the saucer to settle the bill. *'Alors,* we will walk through the flower market and then along the *quais* to see what treasure we can find among the *bouquin- istes.* Last week I found a first edition of *Les Fleurs du Mal.* A bargain. Later, we will walk back to Saint-Germain and spend the afternoon at the cinema. They are showing *Au-delà des*

grilles. Clément won Best Director at Cannes and Jean Gabin is in it.'

None of this meant anything to Jasmine, who stared at him, unsure how to respond. He seemed to relish bossing her about, making decisions for her and being her personal film critic. But was that so bad? At least she was getting an introduction to Paris from a Frenchman, even if he came from Normandy.

The flower market on the Île de la Cité proved to be a joy. It was a riot of colour under the grey skies and against the backdrop of the front of Notre Dame, its façade charcoal-hued from centuries of smoke and grime. It was the flower sellers themselves who interested Jasmine. She leaned against a wall, took out her sketch-book and began some rapid studies.

Antoine stared at her in astonishment. 'Why are you doing that? It's Sunday. Don't you take time off? We're not at the École now.'

She returned his gaze, equally surprised. 'Because I love to draw and paint.' It had never occurred to her people might construe it as eccentric. 'It's why I'm here. Every day offers chances to draw. Why on earth wouldn't I seize them?'

He grunted. 'You're one of "Them"! Someone who joined the school full of misty-eyed passion, intent on becoming the next Picasso.' He shook his head, his eyes a mixture of pity and contempt. 'Let me save you the trouble, Mademoiselle Jasmine. There are several reasons to rule that possibility out. First, Picasso is a genius. Second, he is a man. You, on the other hand are a girl. And an English one at that.' He twitched his mouth in contempt. 'You don't have a chance. Nothing personal, as I'll admit I don't have a chance either. In fact, none of us has. Forget your starry-eyed dreams and get the most out of living in Paris. Do enough to get through the three years without getting thrown out, then go home, settle down and get a job teaching at the local art school.'

Jasmine was about to protest, to say that she wanted to enter a painting in the *Salon des Moins de Trente Ans* – an open art competition for under-thirties. but Antoine spoke again before she had a chance. 'Unless...' He looked her up and down, taking in her clothes and looking down at her shoes. 'Yes. In your case, enough money to carry on playing at being an artist. At least until you get bored – or get married and start having babies.'

He reached for her sketch-book, took it from her hands and put it into her satchel, doing up the straps. *'Allons-y!* Let's have a treasure hunt among the *bouquinistes.'*

It was pointless protesting. So, she went along with him and, as he began squirrelling among the stacks of books in the little green wooden boxes on the quayside walls, she extracted her drawing-pad and began to sketch again. This time he rolled his eyes and returned his attention to the quest for a rare edition.

They worked their way along, first on the right bank, before crossing over and continuing on the left.

'How long have they sold books here?' she asked.

Antoine shrugged. 'Centuries.' He asked one of the book-sellers. 'Apparently since the sixteenth century.' The man said something else, but she couldn't catch the words. Antoine laughed. 'He says the Seine is the only river in the world that runs between two bookcases.'

'Extremely long bookcases!'

'All governed by statute. Each *boîte* has to conform to strict measurements.'

Antoine's slow trawl for buried treasure produced nothing. 'Just as well. At least I don't have to skip a meal to make up for splashing out on a book. Some days I get lucky, most not. *Dépêche-toi!* We need to get to the cinema.'

ELEVEN

PARIS

December 1949

Jasmine's friendship with Antoine was thriving. In the atelier she'd detached herself from her fellow students, preferring to block them out and focus single-mindedly on her drawing. Yet the atmosphere in the studio had been more relaxed since Antoine had befriended her. His acceptance of her appeared to make the other students more affable. Not that Jasmine actively sought the friendship of any of them. Detachment fostered calm. Calm fostered concentration and hence observation. And that made her drawings better.

Antoine continued to boss her about and Jasmine let him steer her on trips to the cinemas along the Boulevard Saint-Germain. She shared his passion for films – if not his intellectual dissection of them. For her, the magic was the darkened room and becoming lost in the story playing out on the screen. Words were not needed. Better to let the experience soak in and ferment.

Trips to the cinema with Antoine were also doing wonders

for her command of the French language so she no longer strained to follow conversations.

Why Antoine had chosen to study fine art puzzled her. His interests clearly lay elsewhere. In the studio his work was competent and meticulous, like a skilled draughtsman's, but he took little interest in it. He would have been more suited to studying philosophy or literature. Apart from analysing films, his great joy was in devouring the dense tomes he dug up from the *bouquinistes*. Occasionally he persuaded Jasmine to join him in dim-lit *boîtes* on the Left Bank, where groups of students engaged in fierce debate of arcane topics. She invariably ended up pulling out her sketch-book or, when Antoine had confiscated it, as he sometimes did, drawing on the back of the menu or on a paper serviette.

She asked him what had inspired him to study art.

'My father's an architect. He studied at the Beaux-Arts too. Won the *Prix de Rome*.' Antoine narrowed his eyes. 'He's a hard act to follow. Since I was a baby, he's been determined that I study architecture here. My act of rebellion was to apply for fine arts instead. By the time he found out, it was too late.'

'Why didn't you want to be an architect?'

'Would you?'

'No.'

'*Voilà!* It's the same for me. I enjoy art. There are worse ways to pass the time. I get to be around interesting people here in Paris and I won't have to go into the family firm and live in my father's shadow.'

They were with a large group of fellow students heading for an end-of-term drink in a bar somewhere in the Quartier Latin. There was just one more day of term left and most of the students would be leaving Paris the following evening.

Tonight, the debate centred on whether the true meaning of a piece of art was best articulated by the artist who created the work, or by the critic who sought to interpret it. Antoine was making the case for the critic. He argued that artists lacked the necessary detachment to contextualise their own work and draw out the underlying meaning. This stance provoked angry ripostes from other students, who accused him of intellectual arrogance and a bourgeois sense of superiority.

'How dare you imply I'm too stupid to know the true meaning of my own work?' Giancarlo, the Italian from the atelier, thumped the top of the table; the wine glasses shook. 'You think I work blindly, using only intuition? It's an insult. You imply all artists are stupid and need much cleverer people to explain what our work is about. *Che palle!*'

'Maybe you intended something specific, but just like your lousy French, it gets lost in translation.' Antoine took a sip of beer and gave the Italian a smug look. 'What you end up with is quite different from what you set out to convey. That's where the critic comes in with a cold objective appraisal.'

Marie-Claire, a student at the Sorbonne and a fellow inmate of the Lutèce, interjected, 'Not only the critic. Anyone. Even a child. People can look at a work of art and see all kinds of things, often completely different from the artist's original intention. People bring something of themselves to a painting, so in a way, the artist no longer "owns" his work. It becomes whatever people choose to make of it.'

'*Absolument!*' Antoine chinked glasses with her.

'*Conneries!* You're saying we artists are like Rousseau's noble savage. That's so insulting,' said Jean-Luc, another of Lachlan's students. '*Va au diable,* Antoine!'

The debate raged on and Jasmine gave up trying to follow it. What did it matter? Why should she care? It was one of the things about being here in Paris that she disliked: the way everyone seemed to draw intense satisfaction from pointless intellectual argument. She wished she were alone in the studio now. Free to lose herself in painting.

A chair scraped on the tiled floor and Lachlan Robertson

slipped into a seat next to her. Jasmine felt that familiar tug in her stomach – it happened every time she saw her tutor. Lachlan's arrival broke the circular flow of the discussion but, after a few minutes, the debate resumed and Jasmine realised Lachlan was watching her as he drank his beer, apparently uninterested in the heated argument around him.

'You're quiet,' he said. 'Not interested in the topic of the day?'

She hesitated, wary of stepping into a trap and making a fool of herself and uncertain where she stood with him. 'It seems rather pointless. All the circular arguments. I can't get worked up about it. Yet it raises such passion.' Her eyes roamed over the others round the table, who were arguing with the blind fervour of saints courting martyrdom. When her gaze returned to Lachlan, he gave her a lazy grin. Her stomach flipped.

'Want to get out of here?' he asked, his voice low.

Was he serious? But he was already pushing back his chair, so Jasmine grabbed her coat and followed him outside.

It was raining, so they hurried without speaking through the Quartier, heading west. They emerged from Rue Jacob into Rue Bonaparte and through the gates into the École des Beaux-Arts. She followed him into his atelier, where he shut the door behind them.

'I hoped I'd find you there. You looked as though you wanted to be rescued,' he said at last. 'Did you?'

'Thank you. I did.'

'You realise, of course, you'll now be the object of speculation among your fellow students.' Lachlan shrugged off his wet *canadienne* jacket and helped her off with her coat. He flung the coat behind him onto a chair and moved towards her. 'We might as well provide some justification for them talking about us.'

He ran the palm of his hand down her cheek and a shiver

shot through her body. Before she knew what was happening, his mouth was on hers and he was kissing her. Soft, gentle, tender kisses. The sensation of his lips against hers sent shock waves through her. She wanted it to go on and on. She was giddy with joy but he drew back and fixed his dark brown eyes on hers, his hands resting on her shoulders. 'Ye've nae idea how long I've wanted to do that.'

She murmured, 'Me too.' Then they were kissing again, more searchingly, with increasing passion and – on Jasmine's part – all the pent-up emotion and desire she had held within her for so long. Her hands went up and her fingers tangled in his hair. He pulled her closer and kissed her more intensely. She was caught in a whirlwind. Lost. Drowning. Yet desperate for it to go on.

A hard bulge in the front of his trousers pressed against her. Insistent. Sending ripples of desire through her body.

She was afraid, but she didn't want to stop. Couldn't stop. It was glorious. Her whole body was on fire. A tingling sensation coursed between her legs as he kissed her until she couldn't breathe. Never before had she experienced anything like it. A kind of madness fuelled her. A deep-rooted need for him.

Then, out of nowhere, a little voice sounded an alarm in her head.

If they didn't stop now, she had no doubt where this was going to end. And Jasmine wasn't ready for that – even if her body was crying out for it.

Lachlan's hand slipped under her sweater and cupped her breast while the other hand caressed the curve of her bottom. He drew her tightly against him, his hungry mouth more urgent.

A gasp escaped her, and Jasmine pulled away. 'We mustn't. We have to stop. Before...'

'Before what?'

'You know.' She was suddenly shy. 'I've never done this

before. I've only kissed one other person. And then only once. I can't...'

Lachlan stared at her, brow creased. Then he pushed his still damp, overlong hair back from his brow and gave her a smile as he released a long breath. 'You're enough to drive a man mad, Jasmine.'

'I'm sorry.'

'It's okay. I understand. We'll take it slower.' He moved away from her and went over to sit on a chair. 'I've waited a long time for this, I'll just have to wait a wee while longer for you to catch up wi' me.' He bent his head, took a deep breath and exhaled slowly.

He looked so handsome, sitting there, in a white shirt with the top buttons open – he never wore a tie. His thick, dark hair was glossy under the studio light. Jasmine swallowed, overcome by the knowledge that he wanted her. Actually wanted her. How often had she fallen asleep at night dreaming of Lachlan? And the reality was so much better. It was all she could do not to run to him and let him fold her in his arms again.

'Tonight, when I heard that idiot Laroche inviting everyone for a drink and saw you leaving with them, I couldn't take it any longer. I had to come and find you,' he said.

'I didn't know,' she said. 'I'd no idea you felt that way.'

'Of course you did, hen.' He gave her a wry smile and her stomach did another somersault. 'You couldn't possibly not know.'

'I thought you were angry with me.'

'Angry? Why on earth would ye think I was angry?' His brow creased.

'When you stopped helping me before term started and banished me to the Louvre. And then when I accused you of being with Corinne.'

He took out his tobacco and deftly rolled a cigarette.

'I'd have told you that you were barking up the wrong tree

about that life model, if that fool Laroche hadn't burst in on us before I had a chance. Then I forgot. The idea of me having an affair with one of the models was so daft. Too ludicrous for me to remember.' He pulled a face, then lit up, drawing the smoke deep into his lungs. 'I was more amused than angry. As for the Louvre, I told you what that was about. Rochambeau tore a strip off me for helping you. I have to make my living and it means keeping on the right side of old Beetle Brows. And ye ken well enough that he's not exactly your biggest fan, Jasmine.' Lachlan's lips made a hard line and he shook his head, ruefully.

She hadn't actually known that. While Rochambeau had been cold and aloof as well as strict in his enforcement of the school's entry requirements, Jasmine had convinced herself his animosity wasn't personal. *All* the students found him arrogant and dismissive. She'd imagined his belittlement of her, and her work, was no greater than that he showed towards her fellows. Lachlan's words now were a savage blow to her self-confidence.

Lachlan went on, apparently oblivious to her shock. 'Ye have nae idea how hard I fought to keep you on the course. If it had been up to Rochambeau, you'd not have been allowed to submit your drawings late, and then, if it had been his decision alone, you'd never have been admitted once you'd submitted them.'

'But... but you said before... that doing the classical drawings was a formality and I'd already been selected on the basis of my portfolio.' The joyous feeling of being with Lachlan was rapidly being replaced by a desolation that she was the only student in the school on sufferance and her work was viewed as substandard.

'True. That's exactly what I argued with him. The decision on the portfolio was a majority one and as far as doing the drawings later – last year another applicant who'd had no access to classical works was allowed to do what you've just done, so I had precedent on my side.' He took another long draw of his cigarette. 'But ye need to know that your position here is down to me being in your corner. We both need to keep on the right side of the boss.'

'I see.' She was miserable. Deflated.

He jumped to his feet and moved towards her. 'And in that context we need to be careful. We don't want Rochambeau to see us together. Romantic entanglements between staff and students are frowned upon. At best, he'd move you into another atelier. At worst I'd lose my job and you'd get thrown out. And we wouldn't want that would we, hen?'

She certainly didn't want that.

Lachlan cupped her chin in his hand, bent down and brushed her lips lightly with his. Again a shaft of fire ran through her body. He put his hands on her shoulders, holding her at arms' length. 'I have to go now, beautiful girl. I'm going to Scotland for the Christmas break to see my father. I'll be back in the first week of January. How about we meet on the evening of the fifth of January? It's a Thursday, the week before term begins. At the Tour Saint-Jacques. Eight o'clock. We can have a bite to eat then take the evening as it comes. What do you say?' He gave her one of his broad smiles, his eyes shining.

She couldn't help herself. It had to be yes.

They left the school separately and Jasmine trudged slowly in the direction of the Lutèce. Her cold, gloomy bedroom was not an enticing prospect, so on impulse she stopped at the Place de l'Odéon, bought a cinema ticket and went to see a film.

In the dark of the picture house, captivated by the magic of cinema, she hoped to stop dwelling on what had just happened. The film was about the murders of five champion cyclists on the *Tour de France,* each of them killed while wearing the yellow jersey. After each murder, the killer placed a red tulip beside the body of his victim.

But Jasmine couldn't sustain any interest in the whodunnit. Rather than following the police inspector and the woman sports writer as they endeavoured to unmask the culprit, her mind returned to the atelier and Lachlan. To the sensation of his lips on hers, the memory of his gently probing tongue, his hands touching her under her woollen jumper, her fingers tangled in his hair.

She thrilled at the knowledge that he wanted her and that she herself was capable of feeling that same way, with a raw passion and a hunger that was completely new to her. Wanting it to go on and on, to fall inside the kiss, to give herself up to it, to give her body up to Lachlan. And now she had a yawning void in front of her while the object of her desires was out of the country. The prospect of weeks without even so much as a glimpse of Lachlan was unbearable. Then she told herself that the enforced separation would make their reunion all the sweeter. She pictured herself running into his arms when they met at the Tour Saint-Jacques. He would sweep her up and swing her around before devouring her with kisses.

Jasmine had always imagined she would wait until she was married. She remembered Evie telling her that she could only lose her virginity once and that it was important to choose the right person to give it to. That man was surely Lachlan.

But the more she thought about that, the less comfortable she felt. Her reading of Simone de Beauvoir had led her to the conviction that her virginity was not a precious gift to bestow upon a man and that the old-fashioned idea of marriage was a form of slavery. A line from the book had been haunting her and she thought of it now: *'It is not women's inferiority that has determined their historical insignificance, but their historical insignificance that has doomed them to inferiority'*.

If Jasmine herself were to break free of the label of insignificant woman, she couldn't afford to subjugate herself to a man. And the worst form of subjugation was surely marriage. Wasn't it?

Giving up trying to follow the film, Jasmine closed her eyes and pondered her dilemma. Hadn't Antoine so flippantly, in his comparison between her and Picasso, listed the fact that she was female among the barriers preventing her from achieving artistic greatness? Any visit to the Louvre underlined the validity of that assertion. She couldn't remember a single example of a work by a woman artist hanging there.

The odds were stacked against her. If she were to have the slightest chance to make even the smallest ripple as a painter, she had to dedicate her whole life to it. That ruled out marriage and children.

But ruling out being subjugated within a marriage didn't mean she should deny herself the pleasure that had been all too evident this evening. De Beauvoir refused to marry but had not abjured relationships. She and Sartre were lovers. Openly. So, why shouldn't she, Jasmine, take a similar, modern approach? Take pleasure with a man outside the tyranny of marriage?

Abandoning the film, Jasmine walked out of the picture house into the cold night air of the Place de l'Odéon. It was raining again, and the headlights of the few passing cars illuminated the puddles on the surface of the road.

Was she getting ahead of herself? Lachlan had kissed her, not offered to marry her. He was an artist and probably 'modern' in his attitude. He hadn't tried to force himself on her. And if he meant what he said and was prepared to take things slowly, it might be possible to have the kind of relationship with him she dreamed of. Two kindred spirits united in a passion for art and each other.

If Jasmine were to lose her virginity to Lachlan, it would be because she'd made a conscious choice to do so. It wouldn't be a gift to a man as Evie had described it, but her own gift to herself. She was living among bohemians, artists and intellectuals, so it was logical that she should shrug off the trappings of the bourgeois traditional patriarchy and instead embrace a life where she called her own tune rather than dancing to that of a man.

No. She wouldn't forgo the delights she was certain lay in store for her with Lachlan. She was an independent woman. And yes, she would also be a great artist. Why not?

Filled with a newfound energy, Jasmine half-ran through the streets towards the Lutèce. She would carry on reading de Beauvoir's book but, more importantly, she had work to do.

The curriculum of the École des Beaux-Arts gave no place to painting in the first year. But there was nothing to prevent Jasmine working in her own time on the ideas that had been buzzing around her head for weeks.

Her room was cramped and dark and quite unsuitable for painting large works. She'd speak to Lachlan about working at the weekends and in the evenings in his atelier. No more sitting around in crowded bars listening to pointless arguments. Jasmine's spare days would be filled with painting, and her nights... she smiled inwardly as she imagined what her nights might hold.

TWELVE

Following her tryst with Lachlan, Jasmine spent the Christmas holidays struggling to keep him out of her head. Wrapped in a heavy coat, a woollen hat and a thick scarf, she prowled the banks of the Seine, sitting on the cold stone slabs while she sketched frantic, rapid drawings of the *clochards*, the *bouquin-istes* and the passing barges, trying in vain to banish the memory of Lachlan's mouth on hers.

Her focus was on composition, experimenting with how she would place the forms on the canvas when she came to start painting. She had in mind a large work, looking across the Seine from one bank to the other, the *clochards* huddled together against the walls of the quay to keep warm. The painting would be of night-time, with the people grey, ghostly shapes, and the surface of the river faintly illuminated by streetlights and a starry sky. She wanted it to be bold, dramatic, arresting. The ideas in her head were like a heap of sand that her fingers sifted through, seeking out and sorting through the grains in search of a gem worth extracting and exploring.

Perhaps there would also be a companion work, this time by

day. Children playing, women washing clothes, men bent over a game of cards, an accordionist, a couple dancing. Blocky shapes, soft-edged, rounded, curving lines.

Jasmine remembered the painting Lachlan had done of Corinne – all hard edges and acute angles. Yesterday, she'd happened to pass an art gallery on the Rue du Faubourg Saint-Honoré and had noticed a large painting propped on an easel in the window: a portrait of a naked man. The subject was sitting with legs wide apart, his manhood on full display, dangling like a long thin sausage, from a thicket of pubic hair. The pose and the painting's ugliness reminded her of Lachlan's portrait of Corinne. Crude, sharp angles, hard-edged, defiantly devoid of curves. The artist had signed his name in the same angular zigzag style as the painting. Bernard Buffet.

Buffet was a legend at the Beaux-Arts. A prodigy. He'd started at the school when just fifteen and last year at only twenty, not long after graduating, he had won the prestigious *Prix de la Critique*. Jasmine gazed at the painting through the plate glass window. It depressed her. If this was great art she might as well give up now. While Buffet might have meant those angular shapes to convey poverty, suffering, deprivation, Jasmine saw only a cold cruelty and a kind of self-regard in the mannered nature of the work and the flamboyance of the signature. It made her wonder whether Buffet had been one of Lachlan's pupils and had borrowed something of Lachlan's style. But that was unlikely. Buffet was already one of the most acclaimed artists in Paris, as the exhibition here at the exclusive Galerie Drouet-David testified. Anyone exhibiting in such a place must be a spectacular success. Lachlan, on the other hand, was merely a tutor.

Jasmine was clear about one thing. The kind of paintings she wanted to produce were the antithesis of these. Hers would be bold, rich and full of strong shapes. If that didn't wash with the critics or with Monsieur Rochambeau, then it was too bad.

Why then did she want to paint the *clochards*? Why choose a subject that was a reminder of suffering and poverty? But Jasmine had perceived joy too on the quays of the Seine, in contrast to the miserable faces of the life models. These homeless people laughed, lived, played and made the best of their pitiful circumstances. Maybe the deprivations they experienced now were minor compared with what they had endured during the war years; the absence of a roof over their heads a minor inconvenience when it meant freedom. They reminded her of the villagers in the *bomas* in Kenya. The mud huts, the shaved heads and the subsistence living told one story, but the joyfulness of the children at play and the women laughing as they prepared food, told another.

Other ideas for paintings formed in her head. Instead of the grey architectural backdrop of Paris, she would call upon the wide, open plains of the Masai Mara and the lush green vegetation of Penang for inspiration. The vibrant colours. But most of all, the soft, bold, feminine shapes. She craved the chance to paint these instead of following the rigid discipline of the atelier.

Jasmine had been dreading Christmas. She expected to feel completely isolated and alone, so far away from her Nairobi family and her Penang second family. She fretted that the parcels she had sent might not arrive in time. It was hard to bear the thought of tramping around Paris alone on Christmas Day, knowing the rest of the population would be warm behind closed doors, enjoying celebratory Christmas meals.

A parcel had arrived from Nairobi a few days before Christmas, and she put it aside to open on Christmas morning. She dreaded the prospect, knowing it would make her even more homesick. On Christmas Eve she planned to go to bed early and remain there all of Christmas Day, hiding from what she thought of as a hostile world. If only she could have accepted Arthur's offer to pay for her to come home – but the enormous

distance had made it unviable. By the time she arrived she'd
have needed to turn around and come back.

Jasmine lay on her stomach on the bed, reading *Le Deux-*
ième Sexe, hoping it would make her drowsy enough to sleep.
But it was impossible to concentrate. There were so many
words she didn't understand, and she was beginning to get a
headache.

The trouble with being alone in her tiny room was that
there was nothing to stop her dwelling on Lachlan. Putting the
book aside, she ricocheted between annoyance with him for
building her up only to abandon her for weeks, and mounting
excitement at the prospect of their planned meeting in the new
year. Life was rotten. It was cruel – offering up pleasure only to
snatch it away before she could reach it.

But she couldn't possibly stay in bed all day tomorrow.
Better to be out and about and on the move. At least she'd have
the streets to herself. It would be a chance to draw buildings
and practise what she'd learnt about perspective. She was
pulling off her jumper to climb into bed, when there was a
hammering at her door. Had Lachlan decided not to go to Scotland? Her heart did a somersault in her chest and she wrenched
open the door.

It was Stan. He was wearing a red Santa hat and a beaming
smile. 'Come on, Jazz, there's a gang of us going to Midnight
Mass at Notre Dame.' Behind him on the narrow landing was a
motley crew of half a dozen individuals, some of whom she had
seen in the bar where Stan worked and others who were
complete strangers. Among them was Corinne, standing with
her back to Jasmine, staring down the stairs, a clear signal that
she was there on sufferance only and had no wish to renew her
friendship with Jasmine.

'Come on. Get a move on or we'll be late.' Stan gave her a
nudge.

Setting aside her concern about Corinne's presence, Jasmine put her coat on and followed them out.

The cathedral was bathed in light, like a celestial building. Inside, the dark interior was transformed by a multitude of burning candles, shimmering and shining, the smell of burning wax mingling with the scent of flowers and incense.

The organ boomed sonorously, and the massed ranks of choristers sang *Silent Night*. To Jasmine's surprise they sang in English. She watched spellbound as a sea of altar boys in white cassocks surrounded the archbishop and priests as they processed to the altar; the music changed to *Adeste Fideles*. One of the altar boys held aloft an open book – presumably a Bible – resting the weight of it against his head as the archbishop sang from it in Latin and the choristers' voices swelled. The phrase 'heavenly choir' no longer seemed a cliché. She was mesmerised watching from a distance as the choirmaster – also in ecclesiastical vestments – conducted the singers with expansive gestures as though he were throwing himself body and soul into the music. His efforts paid off: Jasmine was transported by the beauty of it.

Looking around her at the vaulted ceiling, columns and soaring roof, blackened by centuries of burning candles, she got a visceral sense of the history of this place. How many people over hundreds of years had stood where she stood now and witnessed the Christmas service? The vestments worn by the priests and bishops were heavily and sumptuously embroidered – just as they would have been back in the Middle Ages. She imagined the sung Latin Mass was also unchanged. As the congregation queued to partake of Holy Communion, each kneeling at the altar rails to receive the host on their tongue, the choir broke into a French hymn Jasmine remembered from her time at the convent school – *Il est né le divin Enfant*. She realised her eyes had filled with tears. Beside her she could see Stan was similarly moved.

Afterwards, as they emerged into the Parvis Notre Dame, Jasmine commented that she hadn't realised he was religious.

'I grew up in the church. Pentecostal not Roman Catholic. My grandfather was a preacher. My whole family were church-goers. I had no choice.'

'You still believe in it now?'

Stan linked arms with her. 'I guess I never stopped believing in God but I long since stopped believing in churchgoing. A Pentecostal service is a bracing experience – speaking in tongues and falling down on the floor. But I always enjoyed the singing. There's nothing as powerful as a gospel choir in full throat. But it doesn't compare to the magic of Notre Dame at Christmas. You liked it?'

'I loved it.'

'You coming to the Bar Antibes tomorrow? We're going to have a Christmas dinner for waifs and strays.'

'Will it be open on Christmas Day?'

'No. At least not to the public. We're having our own private party.'

'And you're inviting me?'

'Didn't I just do that?'

'I can't think of anything I'd like more.' She threw her arms around Stan and hugged him. 'You've no idea how grateful I am. I expected to spend Christmas alone in my room. I thought—'

'You thought you were the only person alone in Paris at Christmas. Hell no! Bring anyone else along. We've enough food to feed an army.'

Everyone in the group appeared to live on the Left Bank so they walked along in a crowd. Somehow Jasmine ended up beside Corinne. Her former friend turned to her and said, '*Joyeux Noël,* Jasmine.'

Jasmine returned the compliment, relieved that the ice had

been broken. 'Look Corinne, I'm sorry about what I said to you. I jumped to conclusions. It wasn't fair on you, and it wasn't fair on Lachlan either.'

Corinne sniffed. 'Certainly not fair on me. And him? He deserves no sympathy.'

Jasmine narrowed her eyes, suddenly uncomfortable. 'What do you mean?'

'Oh nothing. *Ce n'est rien.* I just don't like the man. That's all. No particular reason.' Corinne shrugged then smiled. 'So, what have you been doing lately?'

'Working hard most of the time. I sometimes go to the pictures. Antoine, the chap who moved into your room at the Lutèce, is in my atelier. He loves the cinema so we often go together.' Then, keen that Corinne shouldn't get the wrong idea, she quickly added, 'We're just friends. He's getting married when he finishes school.'

Corinne didn't seem interested.

'How about you, Corinne?'

'I moved in with some people from my course. It's basic but there is much space. An old warehouse. The building owners have no use for it so we have it for a very low rent. I am working on the weekly student newspaper – *Hebdo Latin*. Our office is in the same place so it is very convenient.'

'That's terrific,' Jasmine said, uncertain what else to say. 'Is it in the Quartier?'

'Montparnasse.' Corinne frowned. 'I don't suppose you need some studio space, do you?'

'I'm hoping I can use the Beaux-Arts at the weekends. I'm going to ask Lachlan after the Christmas holidays. It's so much more convenient if I can store everything in one place.'

Corinne shrugged.

They had reached the Lutèce, so Jasmine said goodbye to the group. *'A demain. Joyeux Noël,'* she called.

Corinne quickly scribbled her address on a scrap of paper and pressed it into Jasmine's hand. 'I won't be there tomorrow, but if you change your mind about needing some space, come there any time and I show you.' She gave her a wave and hurried after the others.

The following morning Jasmine opened her Christmas parcel. From Hugh, there was a pair of wooden carved animals, a giraffe and a lion, accompanied by a drawing she supposed was a self-portrait, his arms aloft in victory and a medal round his neck. The self-portrait bore no likeness to her brother but it made her smile. On the back, Hugh had written *I won the 500 yards and only just missed winning the hundred-yard dash. But I don't mind being second as Roger Cunningham came first and he's my best friend and anyway I beat him in the 500 so that's fair.* Jasmine wished horrible little Hugh was here right now so she could give him a great big hug – from which he would desperately try to wriggle free. She propped the picture against a pile of books on the chest of drawers, where she could see it when she woke each morning.

There was a long letter from Mummy, a short one from Arthur. She read them before turning her attention to the two gift-wrapped parcels. Arthur's first – a delicate silk scarf in a vibrant mixture of colours, which she draped loosely around her neck. She'd wear it to the waifs and strays party that day. Evie's gift was in a velvet box. Jasmine flipped it open to find a rope of pearls. She held them up against her throat. She'd always coveted her mother's pearl necklace and now she had one of her own. It was perfect. Jasmine couldn't imagine a gift she'd like more. She decided to save wearing it until her evening with Lachlan, when she'd need something to make her feel special and to give her confidence. And it would go perfectly with the pearl ring Evie had given her last year, on the ship from Ceylon to Penang. She put the pearls back in the box and placed it inside a pocket in her suitcase on top of the wardrobe, where she also kept the ring.

She got dressed, ready to set off for Bar Antibes. Christmas had turned out to be so much better than she had expected.

THIRTEEN

STATE OF JOHORE

January 1950

Howard slumped into a chair and eased off his wet boots. The rain had soaked all the way through, so he tugged off his socks as well.

He glanced at his watch. Almost time for the news on Radio Malaya. Recently it hadn't seemed worth tuning in as there was so little coverage of the progress of the Emergency. Suspiciously little. Across the table, Alan and Roger, two of Redmond's assistant managers, were already in place, waiting with bored expressions as Billy, the junior assistant, fiddled with the dials.

But tonight, it was a different story. The news was shattering. The British Prime Minister, Clement Attlee, had announced in Parliament that the British government was recognising the Chinese Communists, under Chairman Mao Tse-tung, as the official government of China in place of the Nationalists.

'He's got to be kidding.' Roger's mouth was wide in disbelief.

'Hitting us below the belt.' Alan pounded his fist on the table. 'Here we are, trying to supply the Empire with rubber while fighting off a communist insurrection and the morons in Whitehall bloody well anoint those Chinese bastards who are no doubt fuelling the troubles here.'

'Shut up and let's listen.' Howard leaned forward, elbows on the table, straining to hear.

Sir Henry Gurney, the High Commissioner to Malaya, began speaking. Jaws slack, the men listened. 'Nothing that may happen in China will weaken the determination of the people of this country to eliminate militant communism here.'

The men around the table groaned.

'What a load of utter bollocks!' Roger's contempt was evident on his face as well as in his choice of words. He got to his feet, not stopping to right the chair he had knocked over as he went out of the room, cursing.

'They've sold us down the river. Bandits running amok here, while back in Blighty they're rolling out the red carpet for Chairman Mao.' Alan shook his head.

Howard, still relatively new in the role of acting manager, was reluctant to show his own emotions – which were pretty much the same as the other men's. 'We all know politicians are fools. There's no point in losing sleep over it. It is what it is. We need to get on with it.'

'Yes. Singapore all over again. We shouldn't have expected anything more. They let us down then and they're letting us down now. All we're good for is swelling their coffers, but when it comes to defending us, we can go hang as far as they're concerned.' Alan was an old hand who had spent the war years incarcerated in Changi prison. A bachelor in his fifties, he was all too aware he would never rise any higher in the Guthrie empire. With nothing to return to in Britain, Alan was content to carry on as an assistant manager in the adopted country he loved. Howard liked the man, relied on him, and was grateful Alan had shown no resentment at being overlooked for the top job.

'As for Gurney, he's weak and indecisive.' Alan got up and switched off the wireless; the news had now moved onto other topics. 'We need someone to take a hard line with the bandits and make sure we're safe to get on with our business.' Seeing Howard wasn't going to be drawn further, he said, 'I'm going to the club for a few beers. Want to come along, *Tuan?*'

Howard didn't really. But he recognised the need for solidarity. 'Good plan! Give me ten minutes for a quick shower and I'm with you.'

The club was more crowded than usual. The news of the recognition of Communist China had brought planters and tin-men out in force. Their wives too. Howard wished he'd stayed at Redmond for a couple of beers and a quiet night in. He was engrossed in George Orwell's *Burmese Days* and would have preferred to spend the evening following the tribulations of Flory, the main character in the book. Instead, he sat at the end of the bar and passed the time by silently comparing his fellow colonials with characters from the novel.

He'd been stupid to agree to come here tonight with Sam. Now he'd have to sit it out until his colleague was ready to return, as they'd travelled together in one armoured jeep. It looked as though the news today had made everyone determined to make a night of it. He took another gulp of beer and resigned himself to a long wait.

The door to the bar opened and a group of British army officers came in, along with three young women. He recognised one of the men as Lieutenant Ellis. A bloody awful evening looked like it could get even worse.

Ellis swaggered up to the bar, his voice stentorian as he ordered drinks for the party he'd arrived with. The women, in their twenties, were wearing khaki trousers and white shirts and Howard detected Australian accents. He watched from a distance as Ellis held court. The women appeared more amused than impressed by the lieutenant's braggadocio. To hear him speak, anyone would imagine he was battling the communist insurgents single-handedly.

Howard glanced up and happened to catch the eye of one of the women. She smiled. Before he could look away, she detached herself from the group and moved down the bar to join him.

'On your ownsome, stranger?' Her Australian accent was soft and musical. 'You a rubber planter?'

Howard smiled and stretched out a hand. 'Howard Baxter, Acting Manager, Redmond Estate.'

She took his hand, her grip firm. 'Betty Fletcher. My friends and I are volunteers. Getting some work experience helping out over here. We're trainee nurses and teachers.'

'Which are you?'

'Nurse. At least that's the plan. As long as being here doesn't put me off.' She jerked her head in Ellis's direction. 'That fella's been trying to scare the pants off us. Telling us the commies are all over the place, ready to blow us to high heaven.'

'Well, it can be a dangerous place.'

She gave him a cheeky smile. 'I hope you'll look out for me, then.'

Was she flirting with him? Howard had been living like a monk since he'd arrived in Johore. Or to be more accurate, since meeting Jasmine Barrington on the passage to Penang over a year ago. A harmless flirtation with a pretty Australian nurse might be just what he needed.

He bought Betty a drink. She took it with one hand and

placed the other on his arm. 'It's hot as hell in here. How about we go and sit out on the veranda and you tell me all about yourself. You'd be doing me a big favour by helping me get away from that big-shot Brit with his talk of tommy-guns and jungle warfare.'

Howard groaned. 'Ellis has never been near the jungle, let alone conducted jungle warfare. He's a paper pusher.' As soon as he'd said it, he felt bad. Betty would think he was interested in her and putting the competition down. 'Sorry. I'm probably talking out of turn, but I came across him up north a few times. He travelled out to Malaya on the same ship I did. Let's just say, we don't see eye to eye.'

Betty smiled. 'I like you already, Howard Baxter.'

He led the way through the crowded room and out through the French doors. A few men were sitting out there, chewing over the day's news about China. Howard steered Betty to the far end of the veranda, out of earshot. They sat on a pair of rattan armchairs and listened to the sounds of the night: bullfrogs and cicadas and the drip of rain through the trees and down the metal drainage chains suspended from the veranda roof.

'Where in Australia are you from?' he asked, eventually.

'I'm a city girl. A Sydneysider. You been there?'

Howard shook his head.

'You should go some time. It's a bonzer place. All the advantages of a big city but with the beach right on your doorstep. You like swimming?'

'I love it. There's a pool here at the club but it's not the same. I miss the beach.'

'Best beaches in the world in Australia.'

'So I've heard.'

'As long as the sharks or jellyfish don't get you.'

She gave a little chuckle and smiled at him. Her face was

pretty in a healthy, outdoorsy way, tanned and freckled from the sun.

'And where are you from, Baxter?'

'Ceylon. My family are in tea. My father's a planter.'

She seemed amused. 'But you chose rubber instead. Contrary, are you? Or do you like the smell of latex?'

'I prefer the smell of tea actually. But there was nothing for me in Ceylon. My father doesn't believe in delegation.'

Betty nodded, then swatted at a mosquito. 'I get the picture. And is there a Mrs Baxter around?'

'My mother is very much around. In Ceylon.' Howard smiled, aware he was being evasive. Or perhaps tuning into Betty's flirtatiousness.

She seemed about to say something, but must have thought better of it. Howard turned to look at her. He could picture her playing tennis and swimming competitively. Her suntanned arms were firm with clearly defined muscles. He could imagine her hitting long, strong returns from the baseline to win tennis matches or powering ahead in a freestyle race. An Australian version of the redoubtable Miss Joan Hunter Dunn in the poem by Betjeman.

'You don't say a lot do you, Howard Baxter?'

He gave a dry laugh. 'I'm not usually renowned for my silence. But the political situation is on my mind I'll admit. And to be honest, I've only recently been put in charge at Redmond and the responsibility is weighing on me a little.'

'Not up to the job?' She gave him a wink.

'Just conscious I'm on trial.'

'You look pretty capable to me, mate.'

Her Australian, in-your-face style of speaking took some getting used to after the more reserved British, but he decided he liked her. It would be impossible not to. That broad smile and those bright eyes were captivating.

Inside the club, someone had put a record on the gramophone and a few people were dancing.

Betty jumped to her feet. 'Want to cut a rug, as you poms say?'

Howard couldn't remember the last time he'd danced. Maybe it was time he gave it a go. He took her proffered hand and followed her back into the clubhouse.

FOURTEEN

PARIS

January 1950

On the first morning of the new term, Jasmine rushed into the École at an early hour. She hoped to find Lachlan alone and ask him about using the studio out of hours. When she walked in, he was sorting through large pencil drawings taken from a portfolio chest at the rear of the studio. He looked up at her and smiled; her insides contracted.

'You're early this morning, hen.'

'I was hoping I'd catch you alone.' She took off her coat and hung it up.

'Not a good idea to meet alone in here. I told you that. I'll see you tonight. And I canna wait, darlin'. It'll be hard enough getting through today with you sitting there looking beautiful and me imagining what I want to do with you...'

'I didn't mean that.' She gave him a shy smile, embarrassed that he was so openly referring to what had passed between them and what might lie in store. 'I just wanted to ask if I can work on a large painting here in the atelier in the early mornings and after class finishes at night.' She saw he was frowning, and added, her voice trailing away. 'And at the weekends... but...'

He tightened his lips and shook his head. 'If I allow you, they'll all want to do the same. The place will be full of work that's off the curriculum and there'll be nae room to move in here.'

'But I thought we all were expected to do our own work in between classes.'

'Aye. You are. But you need to do it elsewhere. If there's nae room where you're living, you need to find a bigger place. Or get together with other students and rent a shared studio space. God knows, Jasmine, there must be plenty of places that are uninhabitable but would be usable as a studio.' He folded his arms and looked at her. His face was the tutor's face now, no trace of the lover's.

She bit her lip. 'I see. I'll have to ask around.'

'You do that. But, as far as the painting goes, I'd also caution you not to try running until you've learnt to walk.' He turned away and went back to sorting through the drawings.

It was a kick in the teeth.

Getting through the morning drawing class was torture. Lachlan took them into the Cour Vitrée to draw the enormous casts of the Parthenon columns there. They'd been studying perspective and, while reluctantly, she had to admit the cast drawings of torsos, heads, limbs and even cuirasses had helped her awareness and understanding of how the human body could be portrayed convincingly, the detailed drawings of plaster pillars left her cold. Lachlan meandered between his students, throwing in a comment here or a suggestion there, but he said nothing at all to Jasmine.

When it was lunchtime, she fled from the school and into the Rue Bonaparte, then walked, hands in her coat pockets, onto the Boulevard Saint-Germain, seething with anger and humiliation. Why had Lachlan denied her the chance to work in the atelier? It seemed petty and unjustified. He was playing games with her, like a cat with a mouse.

She felt a hand on her arm and turned to find Stan beside her.

'Hey! Jazz. Where are you going in such a hurry?' he asked. 'Wanna join me for a coffee? It'll give me the perfect excuse to delay the moment I try to put pen to paper.'

She felt a rush of relief at his friendly face. 'That sounds super. As long as you don't blame me for your under-production.'

At Café de Flore, Stan went straight through the crowded interior and bounded up the stairs to the wood-panelled upper floor. 'They now reserve a table up here for me where I can work undisturbed.' His beaming smile testified that he was proud of this symbol of acceptance. 'It's quieter and Boubal, the manager, likes having writers around.' He indicated a table. 'It used to be Apollinaire's. He spent his entire days here, writing and talking to his friends. It's a huge honour to inherit his space.'

Today Stan was imbued with energy and enthusiasm. The smile rarely left his face. Seeing him like this lifted Jasmine's own spirits. 'By the way, I want to thank you again for rescuing my Christmas. I dread to think how glum it would have been, spending it on my own.'

Stan waved a hand dismissively. 'It was fun, wasn't it?'

They requested coffee and, always hungry, Jasmine added a couple of *omelettes aux fines herbes* to the order. 'My treat,' she insisted.

'You looked down in the mouth when I ran into you just now. What's up, Jazz?'

'I asked my tutor if I could use the studio at the weekends and he said no.' She pulled a face. 'I need plenty of space as I want to work on a large canvas.' She sighed and gave him a rueful smile. 'My trouble is I have too many ideas and, apparently, I'm trying to run before I can walk.'

'Is that a bad thing?' He jerked his head back, surprised.

'I didn't think so. It doesn't stop me focusing on the classwork and surely there's no such thing as painting too often.'

He raised an eyebrow. 'One thing I've learnt is it's harder to encourage a writer or artist than to dissuade one. I can't think of a single reason why anyone would want to discourage you from working on your passion. Never mind walking, Jasmine, just run. Fast as you can.'

Jasmine smiled, then looked down. She couldn't argue with that, but it made her doubt Lachlan. And she didn't want to doubt him at all.

'What kind of space do you need to work on this creation?' Stan leaned forward, elbows on the table.

'Somewhere with plenty of natural light. A roof. Four walls. That's about it. Running water is ideal but not essential. Somewhere I can store my work and materials. Somewhere safe.'

Stan leaned back against the banquette. 'Maybe I can help. The place is very basic. An attic space, up several flights of stairs. It's in Pigalle. You know – below Montmartre. There's natural light but it's from skylights. It's damp, dirty, and God knows what else goes on in the building. You'll need a padlock for the door and an ability to go up and down the stairs without paying attention to the other people you might pass. Maybe some earplugs too. But there's plenty of room, and as long as you don't mind putting buckets under the skylights when it's raining, it's pretty good. A Belgian friend of mine who's just moved back to Antwerp had it and as far as I know it's available. He was a sculptor.'

'I'll use the rainwater to clean my watercolour brushes.'

'Then why don't I show you the place tonight? I warn you though. Pigalle's not the most salubrious of areas.'

'Tomorrow?' she asked. 'I have plans tonight.'

Stan gave her a wink. 'I won't ask. Tomorrow it is.'

Lachlan kept his distance throughout the afternoon and Jasmine began to wonder whether their evening was off. Disconsolate, she packed her things into her satchel and was putting her coat on when he came up behind her and whispered, 'See you tonight.' He went out of the atelier leaving Jasmine shivering with the sensation of his warm breath on her neck.

She rushed back to the Lutèce, relief and excitement coursing through her, wanting to change into something pretty. Most of the time she dressed as unobtrusively – and scruffily – as possible, so as not to stand out among her fellow students, most of whom were impecunious. Her inheritance from her late father and the allowance she received from Mummy and Arthur made her relatively well off and she didn't like to rub others' noses in her good fortune.

But tonight was different. It would be Lachlan alone. Tonight, she'd make a special effort. Her wardrobe of winter clothes was scanty, so she put on a floral frock her mother had bought her in Ceylon. It was rather summery, so she'd need to add a cardigan – but immediately she felt more feminine than she did in the slacks and baggy sweaters that were her usual attire at the École. All she had in her tiny room at the Lutèce was a hand mirror, so she was unable to check the total effect. She put on some lipstick, brushed her hair, added Evies's pearls, and hoped for the best.

As soon as Jasmine crossed the Pont au Change, her nerves increased. What did the evening have in store? Who was she about to meet – the warm, friendly and encouraging Lachlan, or the one who gave her the cold shoulder? But as she approached the Tour Saint-Jacques all she could think of was how much she wanted to experience being kissed by him again.

At first she thought he wasn't there. Her wrist-watch told her it had already gone eight. Disappointment hollowed out her stomach. Was she about to be stood up? If Lachlan was making fun of her she wouldn't be able to face him again in the atelier. Her skin prickled at the thought of the humiliation.

But he was standing just around the corner of the tower, half hidden by a news-stand. He was wearing his usual canadienne jacket with its double set of leather buttons, sheepskin lining and collar. This style of jacket seemed to be *de rigueur* among men who chose to signal their *avant garde* credentials: Jean-Paul Sartre always wore one. It looked more stylish on Lachlan than on the philosopher, whom she was now used to seeing holding court in the Flore or wandering along Rue Bonaparte, where he lived. Lachlan's brown hair almost reached to the wool of the collar. He hadn't shaved and his face was darkened by stubble. As she walked towards him, he broke into a smile that made her bones liquefy. Everything was going to be all right.

They went towards the Marais. Jasmine had hoped Lachlan would take her hand but he strode along purposefully beside her, his hands stuffed into the pockets of his jacket, so she had to walk faster than usual to keep pace with him.

Jasmine hadn't been to this area of Paris before. The former aristocratic district had fallen on hard times since its pre-Revolution heyday, with most of the beautiful *hôtels particuliers* now neglected and in disrepair. As she looked up at elegant frontages, she tried to imagine how the area must once have appeared in past centuries. The area had also been a Jewish quarter since the end of the Revolution, with a thriving garment industry and a large art nouveau synagogue, which had survived an attempt to blow it up by right wing Nazi collaborators in 1941.

Lachlan took her along a narrow street to what she would never have guessed was a restaurant from its exterior. Jasmine followed him inside, barely able to see, it was so poorly lit. A glum-faced young man was seated behind the counter, reading a newspaper in Arabic. There were just four tables for customers. The man greeted Lachlan with a barely perceptible nod then disappeared behind a beaded curtain into what must have been the kitchen. Jasmine wondered why Lachlan had chosen the place. They were the only people there.

'I hope you like Moroccan food,' he said as they sat down.

'I've never tried it. But I like most things.' She realised she was actually hungry despite her nervousness about spending the evening alone with him.

'Spices?'

'Most definitely.'

He looked at her over steepled fingers. 'That's a relief. Not a lot of women do, in my experience.'

Was this some kind of test? She hoped that meant she'd passed. 'I grew up in the Far East. Our cook was Malay Chinese. Penang has a wonderful mixture of different cuisines. The only food I can't bear is the kind of thing we had to eat at school when we were in London after the war. It was bland and tasteless. Meat and two veg. Watery soup. Stodgy puddings. Grim.' She was aware she was blathering, nerves firing at being alone across a table from Lachlan.

'To be fair, the rationing in Britain was pretty extreme. I can tell ye, there were times when I was living in Glasgow when I thought I'd die of starvation, the portions were so small.'

He chuckled but Jasmine couldn't help remembering what Stan had told her about liberating Dachau. Lachlan clearly had no conception of what real starvation was.

The young man brought over a jug of water and a *pichet* of wine, his face still expressionless. Neither of them had ordered anything and no menu was offered.

'Shouldn't we ask him for the menu?' she whispered.

'No need. We get to eat whatever they've cooked.'

'Gosh!' She said. 'How exciting.' But she wasn't sure she meant that.

The food when it arrived was piled on a large metal tray from which they helped themselves into bowls. Piles of fluffy couscous, little spicy sausages, tender chicken and a sauce that contained chickpeas and tomatoes.

After a couple of mouthfuls, Jasmine looked up. 'Mmm,' she said. 'Absolutely delicious. Such subtle spicy flavours. I love it.'

She was rewarded by a wide smile from Lachlan. Jasmine tried not to stare at him but her eyes couldn't stay away from him. His thick wavy hair looked freshly washed, although the stubble on his face indicated he hadn't shaved since that morning. It was impossible not to wonder if it would be scratchy when he kissed her. *If* he kissed her.

To avoid fixing her gaze on his face, she dropped her eyes to study his hands as he served himself another helping of the food. But it was almost as bad. He had long fingers and she remembered the feel of them caressing her, cupping her breast and her buttocks. She struggled not to reach out and touch those fingers, to interweave her own with his.

She finished eating, unable to manage all of the enormous portion Lachlan had piled on her plate. Trying to calm her racing heart, she took a gulp of wine. It coursed through her veins warming her inside. She lifted her eyes to take in his beautiful face again and the heat spread through her.

Jasmine realised for the first time that he bore an uncanny resemblance to the actor Gérard Philipe. The same thick lustrous hair, hypnotic eyes, a perfect straight nose and a small cleft to his chin. She and Antoine had seen Philipe in a film the previous week. *Une si jolie petite plage* had belied its chirpy title – no pretty little beach but a rainswept empty one, out of season. It had been dark, brooding, depressing and she'd loved every minute of it – especially the performance of the enigmatic stranger in a raincoat, played by Philipe. Now Jasmine wondered if her fascination had been subconsciously because of the star's resemblance to her tutor.

She asked Lachlan if he'd seen the film.

'No. I never have time to go to the cinema.' It was said in such an abrupt way that it left her in no doubt that he wasn't interested in the subject. Instead, she asked him about his family.

'Not a lot to tell. During the First World War, my father fought at the Somme and was badly injured. For some reason he was treated in a hospital in Amiens rather than a British field hospital. He met my mother there. She was visiting her brother Raoul, who had also been wounded. Raoul was in the next bed to my father's and was in a coma, so my mother passed the time practising her English on my father.'

'How romantic.'

Lachlan shrugged. 'Raoul died, so Dad comforted the bereaved sister. They married when the war ended and she went to live with him in Glasgow. I was born the following year.'

He was thirty, Jasmine realised. Twelve years older than her. Not that it made the slightest difference to how she felt about him. What did age matter when two people were destined for each other? If anything it added to his attraction. Perhaps she was running away with a romantic idea – but she didn't think so.

'What did your father do after the war?'

'Same as he did before. A schoolteacher.' Lachlan gave a small sniff and she wondered whether it was a sign of contempt, but he added, 'Like me. Teaching's in the genes. Although Dad taught Biology to grammar school boys.' He refilled their glasses. 'The artistic genes are from Delphine.'

'Delphine?'

'My mother. She never allowed me to call her "*Maman*". Delphine has always been a free spirit. Probably why her marriage to my strait-laced Church of Scotland father was doomed.'

'I'm sorry. They're not together?'

'The marriage barely survived the first year. I reckon the only reason it did was she fell pregnant with me. She stuck around until I was four, then headed home to Paris.'

'I'm so sorry. That's terribly sad.'

'She didna adapt to life in Scotland. The church. The cold weather. The short days in winter. To playing the schoolmaster's wife... och, Jasmine, the woman wanted a life for herself.' He lit a cigarette. 'She loved to draw and paint. She hated the kirk and the whole way of living that she was expected to follow. Used to tell me it was like having a poker up her arse.'

Jasmine recoiled in surprise as Lachlan quickly added. 'Forgive me, I've sometimes a way of talking that runs away with itself.' He gave her a disarming smile.

'What happened? When she went to Paris? Did you go too?'

'Och, no. The old man would never have allowed that. His only son! I stayed in Glasgow. But I got to spend the holidays here in Paris. And summers on the Côte d'Azur.'

Jasmine listened, spellbound, leaning closer.

'After I finished school, Dad wanted me to go to his university – St Andrews. But I wouldna have it. I got a place at the Glasgow School of Art on the foundation course, then I came to the Beaux-Arts.' Lachlan picked up his wineglass and twirled the contents round absently. 'He was furious. Blamed Delphine. Raged and ranted. He said I'd betrayed him. Stabbed him in the back with a dagger furnished by Delphine.'

'So, you were in France during the war?'

'Yes.' He looked away. 'That was the killer blow as far as

Dad was concerned. He wanted me to find a way to get back to Britain and join the army. Serve as he had done.'

'Did you try?'

'Try what?'

'To come back to fight Hitler, of course.' Jasmine frowned, puzzled that he'd even asked the question.

'No, I stayed in France.'

Jasmine was taken aback. It was too horrible to imagine that he would have been on the side of the Vichy government and Hitler. She looked across at his handsome face and then it dawned on her. Being bilingual, he would have been a perfect asset for the Resistance.

She gazed at him with new admiration. 'You were a special agent for the Resistance Special Operations, weren't you?'

'I prefer not to talk about what I did during the war. It's all just history now.' He lit a cigarette and looked at her with a faint smile playing about his lips. It made her shiver with anticipated pleasure. Her already strong feelings about him now increased. On top of everything else she added courage and self-sacrifice to the growing tally of his qualities.

Lachlan reached across the table and took up her hand, weaving his fingers through hers. This time the shiver ran through her whole body. He stubbed out his cigarette with his other hand and called for the bill. After he'd paid, he said, 'Let's get out of here.' His voice was husky and his eyes were locked on hers.

Reminding herself of her decision to let whatever should happen between them take its course, she smiled up at him and let him steer her out of the restaurant. They were still the only customers.

They walked, her hand wrapped in his, along the quays of the Seine. She wanted to ask where they were going but decided to wait and see. Perhaps he was taking her to a small romantic *boîte* to talk and drink wine, while they told each other everything about themselves. Or maybe they'd go to his apartment. She expected the former but secretly hoped for the latter. It would be wonderful to see where Lachlan lived, to see him surrounded by his own things. To sit beside him on a sofa while they kissed, until inevitably he would take her by the hand and lead her to his bedroom. The prospect was terrifying, but nerves were understandable. If their emotions got the better of them and she gave herself to him then so be it. It was happening more quickly than she'd imagined – she would have preferred to take things more slowly. But when the chemistry between two people was as strong as this, it was an inevitability. And she had to admit she'd be relieved to get it out of the way.

It was chilly but he held her hand inside the pocket of his jacket, and she luxuriated in the touch of his fingers around hers. The dark bulk of Notre Dame, crouched like a mythical beast on its island, was silhouetted against a full moon, the central spire soaring skyward between the two solid towers at the front and the glorious flying buttresses at the rear.

Lachlan led her down some stone steps and onto the quayside. The lampposts all along the riverbank sent yellow pools of light shimmering across the black empty water. There was no one about. Just the distant throaty roar of a motorcycle or the occasional passing car. He steered her gently towards a shadowy section of the quay wall, unreached by the radiance shed by the ornamental street lamps. With his hands against the wall on either side of her face, he leaned down and looked into her eyes. Jasmine felt as though she were falling off the edge of the world and she could feel her heart racing. He brushed his lips softly and teasingly across hers. She could barely breathe.

'God, you're beautiful,' he said, then kissed her again. It was a long lingering kiss that rapidly intensified. His hand moved to the buttons of her coat and he eased them open, slipping his hand inside where it moved under her woollen cardigan, his open palm covering her left breast so she could feel each finger through the cotton of her dress. She could hear his breath, ragged, uneven. He pressed up against her. The cold stone of the wall behind her back contrasted with the warmth of his body through her thin summer dress. She gasped, her nerve ends firing, her legs barely able to support her.

Lachlan moved his hand slowly downwards across her stomach, sending her nerves into a Dervish dance, before dropping down to scoop up the hem of her dress. She felt the touch of his cold fingers as he moved up her nylon stockings towards the bare skin at the top. He ran a finger under the line of one suspender up to where it disappeared under her knicker elastic. The soft pad of his finger traced the line along the crease of her groin, following the edge of her pants. Her whole body shivered. It was an exquisite sensation to be touched in this way, where no one had touched her before. While his hand continued to caress the skin between her stocking tops and her underwear, he kept kissing her and she kissed him back with growing urgency. Breathing was barely possible. Then his hand moved between her legs and a finger stroked her through her knickers, sending ripples through her entire body. Jasmine gave a little cry of surprise and pleasure. Then his hands moved under the elastic and, touching her there, right between her legs, he worked a finger inside her. A surge of heat like an electric shock – only pleasurable – went through her and she cried out again.

At the sound of approaching footsteps, Jasmine went rigid, clamping her legs shut and pulling away his hand.

'No. Not here. Not like this.' The beauty of the moment suddenly became furtive and sordid. They were on a public street where any passing stranger might see them. She felt ashamed, dirty. Like a lady of the night. A common prostitute. Not here in public, in the street. She cried out, 'Please stop, Lachlan. I can't. There's someone coming.'

'Who cares? They've no idea who we are.' He moved his

hand under her dress again but she jerked it away. Lachlan stepped back, his expression plaintive. 'Come on, Jasmine. There's nowhere else we can go. I didn't think you a prude.'

His words stung.

'But it makes me feel cheap. Behaving like this in the street.'

He smiled. 'Don't be daft. This is Paris. The city of love. I thought you were a woman of the world. It appears I got that wrong. I thought you cared for me. I must have got that wrong too.' He looked into her eyes, disappointed. His own eyes were full of longing. 'Did I get it wrong, Jasmine? Don't you care for me?'

This made her feel as though she had been mean. He was like a small child who had been let down and denied the treat promised to him.

'Of course I do. I'm mad about you. I've never felt this way about anyone before.'

'Then prove it to me, my darling.'

She didn't know how to respond. In one moment, she had gone from a feeling of bliss to one of misery. Lachlan was looking at her, puzzled, as though her behaviour was unfathomable. He must think her a child. Naive, unsophisticated. Then she told herself he'd be right – she was exactly that.

Mortification descended on her like a pall. So much for being a modern woman. She wondered what Simone de Beauvoir would have done – but decided she would never have got into a situation like this in the first place. Madame de Beauvoir would be calling the tune, not leaving it to the man. But Jasmine couldn't see herself throwing her weight about. And certainly not with a man like Lachlan.

'We could go back to my room at the Lutèce,' she said, hesitating.

Lachlan shook his head, took out a cigarette and turned away to light it between his cupped hands. He turned back to face her and gave her a sad smile. 'I can't go back to the

Lutèce with you, hen. Half my atelier live there. We canna risk that.'

'What does that matter? I don't care what they think. We have nothing to hide. I'm an adult. This is Paris. Let them say what they like about me.' She stood, hands on hips.

He stared at her, frowning.

'What's wrong?' She was unsure of herself, on shifting ground. Suddenly emboldened, she asked, 'Why don't we go to *your* apartment?'

'Never mind. Forget it. I'll see you tomorrow.' He started to move away.

Jasmine grabbed at the sleeve of his jacket. 'Please, Lachlan. Why are you being like this? So impatient? Look, it's just that I don't feel comfortable here where anyone passing can see us. Please. I'd love to see where you live. We can take our time. I'd be more relaxed since we'd be alone there.'

'That's just it, darlin', we wouldn't be.' He looked at her with a doleful expression like a wounded puppy. 'Didn't I tell ye? My mother is staying with me. She's having some renovation work done at her place and I agreed to put her up for a wee while.'

'I don't mind – I'd like to meet her.'

He stared at her, frowning again and she wondered why he seemed so ill at ease. Eventually he said, 'Some other time maybe.'

Desperate for the evening not to end this way and wanting to recreate the warmth of a few moments ago, Jasmine had an idea. 'I'm getting a studio. A writer friend of mine found it for me. It was a sculptor's but he's gone back to Belgium. I'm going to see it tomorrow. It sounds perfect. If I take it – which I'm sure I will – next time we could go there to be alone. It will be wonderful.' She reached for his hands. 'Because, Lachlan, I do so want to be alone with you.' She gave him a shy smile.

He smiled back and stroked a finger down her cheek. 'Why

do I have the feeling that if we do that you'll have yet another reason to let me down.'

'Let you down?' She stared at him, appalled. 'I don't understand.'

'Driving me crazy, desperate to make love to you, then putting on the brakes. You can't do that, Jasmine.' He shook his head and ran one hand through his hair. 'It's plain wrong. To get a man all fired up and then leave him stranded. Cruel.' He took a long draw on his cigarette, then threw the butt of cigarette down and ground it out.

His face was lit up momentarily by the headlight from a passing car on the road above them. She was struck again by how impossibly handsome he was and she felt the pull of desire for him. Yet again she'd messed everything up between them. Why was life so complicated? All she wanted was to be in his arms again and right now she felt as though a barrier had descended between them.

Lachlan, as though reading her thoughts, moved closer. He ran the palms of his hands down the sides of her face. 'I'm sorry, sweet. It's my fault. I shouldna have put you in this position. You're so innocent, so beautiful. A nice, well brought-up girl. I should have been more responsible – but I canna help myself. The very sight of you sends me over the edge.' He smoothed back her hair from her forehead and looked into her eyes. 'You've never been with a man have you? That's why you're so jumpy, so nervy.'

She gulped, blood rushing to her face, and shook her head, wishing the ground would open up beneath her. 'No, but—'

'There's no buts about it.' He shook his head, eyes sad. 'It'll kill me but I think perhaps it's better we don't see each other again outside of classes. I'm too old to play teenage dating games.'

Her heart almost stopped. 'No!' she said, panic rising. 'Please. It's just—'

'You're not ready for a mature relationship, Jasmine. Don't worry, I quite understand why.' He stroked her cheek again with the back of his fingers. 'But it's a terrible shame as I'm awful taken with you. Ever since the day you first walked into my studio.'

Jasmine gasped.

'I tell you, lass, the sight of ye took my breath away. I canna get you out of my head, you must know that. I'm so wild for you I've pushed you too far too soon.'

He gave a long low sigh and Jasmine moved towards him and laid her head against his chest. He stroked her hair again and she could feel the beat of his heart through his thick canvas jacket. 'The man in me wants to take you to a room, lock the door behind us, undress you and spend the rest of my life making love to you.'

Jasmine moved her head back and looked up at him. 'Really? You do?'

'Oh, yes.' He said it like a protracted sigh 'You've nae idea what it's like trying to teach the class with you sitting there, when all I want to do is tell the lot of them to get out so I can do all kinds of unspeakable things to you.'

Jasmine swallowed, wondering what that might involve.

'But, then the teacher and responsible adult in me takes over and tells me I ought to forget you. You're young, you're beautiful and you're unspoilt and I know I should leave you that way.' He let out another long heartfelt sigh. 'But I canna bear to think of another man being the one to introduce you to the pleasure of making love. No, Jasmine, I'm too selfish for that. I want you all for myself.' He eased her away from his chest and looked down into her eyes. 'I knew from the first moment I clapped eyes on you that I wanted you. I've fallen for you real bad, darlin'. You've nae idea! I thought there was something special between us, from that very first day. I thought you felt that way too, but clearly I was wrong.'

Jasmine shivered with joy. Lachlan made her dizzy. She never knew from one moment to the next where she stood with him. She told herself that's what made it special, exciting, unpredictable – like being led blindfold down a steep mountain trail. All she knew was that the idea of not being with him would send her into abject despair.

'You're not wrong, Lachlan. Not at all. I think about you all the time.' She wanted to confess that she was in love with him but she was hesitant in the face of his volatility.

He put an arm around her and turned to lead her along the quayside. She leaned against him, luxuriating in the feel of that protective arm, her head resting against his shoulder. They reached Châtelet and he stopped, turning to kiss her. It was a soft fleeting kiss, a teasing brushing of his lips over hers.

'We'll say goodnight here, darlin'.' Looking in the direction of the Pont au Change, he added, 'You know which way you're going?' He jerked his thumb in the opposite direction. 'I'm that way.' Fixing her with those deep brown eyes, he whispered. 'Let me know when you've got that studio sorted. By the way, where is it?'

'Near Montmartre. Boulevard de Clichy.'

Lachlan raised an eyebrow, then smiled and said, 'Perfect. Absolutely perfect.' He kissed her again, then, before she could protest, he was walking away towards Boulevard Sebastopol.

Jasmine stood rooted to the spot, staring after him, utterly bewildered and unable to suppress the disappointment that he hadn't offered to see her home. She couldn't imagine Arthur leaving Evie to walk alone through the streets of Paris late at night. But then she couldn't imagine Arthur trying to seduce her mother in the street either.

Shivering with the cold, she went across the river and the Île de la Cité to the Left Bank. As she walked, she told herself to snap out of it. After all, Arthur and Evie were of a different era. Jasmine and Lachlan were part of a new modern generation.

Not for her the stiff formalities of old-fashioned courtship, marriage and children. She had a bright new future awaiting her, one where she would become a successful artist and live a free bohemian lifestyle unfettered by constraints. Despite the ups and downs of this evening, she was determined that bright new future would have Lachlan at its centre.

Walking briskly up the Boulevard Saint-Michel towards the Lutèce, she told herself she must read another chapter of *Le Deuxième Sexe* before she went to sleep.

FIFTEEN

STATE OF JOHORE

February 1950

In late February a shocking event brought the horrors of the Emergency closer to Howard and the people of the district.

Sergeant Jamil Bin Mohammed Shah, the local police chief for the Bukit Kepong area, was a key figure in the planning and management of the response to the communist insurgents. As well as attending the daily Emergency briefings of the regional defence council, known widely as Morning Prayers, the sergeant often met the planters informally in a small local bar, to keep them up to date on security measures. As a Muslim, he didn't join them in their ritual beer consumption but frequently stayed for a game of cards.

Ever since Sergeant Shah had been treated with contempt by Lieutenant Ellis on the evening Howard had first met the police officer, Howard had warmed to the Malayan and enjoyed his company. Shah was a good source of information on local sentiment regarding the communists. Keeping pace with how the tappers and their families were reacting to the security measures and how much the communists were active in each area was essential to Howard's effective running of the Redmond Estate.

Shah lived and worked along with his team of about fifteen Federated Malay Policemen and their wives and children, in the remote Bukit Kepong police station, a wooden building on the banks of the muddy Muar River. At dawn on 23rd February around two hundred guerrilla fighters came out of their jungle camps and surrounded the building, demanding that the occupants surrender. When the police refused, a pitched gun-battle followed. The insurgents were armed with automatic weapons, while the heavily outnumbered police had only rifles and shotguns but were determined not to give in. Reinforcements from two other police teams were ambushed on their way to assist, thus removing the possibility of support for Shah and his beleaguered men.

Two of the wives took the guns from the bodies of their slain husbands and continued the fight. Two other women were captured, a mother and daughter. When still the police refused to capitulate, these hostages were put to death.

The battle ended when the attackers set fire to the police station, burning it to the ground before fleeing back into the jungle.

Twenty-three lives were lost: policemen, civilian guards, auxiliary police, two wives and two children. Only four policemen and nine family members survived the attack. Among the dead was Sergeant Shah, the chief of police.

Far from demoralising the local population, the attack strengthened their resolve that the insurgents must not be allowed to prevail. For the locals, the slaughter of policemen and their families who had courageously refused to surrender, was viewed as something they wanted to live up to. The insurgents, in contrast, were perceived as ruthless cowards.

For Howard, the news was a bitter blow. It was one thing to

read reports of enemy activity, but quite another when it involved someone you knew and respected.

At the club, the night after the incident, the planters gathered at the bar. Funerals had taken place, as was customary, on that same day. Howard and many other British residents had been present to pay their respects to the fallen policemen and their families.

At the end of the room, Betty and several of her nursing and teaching volunteer colleagues were sitting together at a table. As soon as she saw Howard arrive, Betty detached herself from the group and came over to join him.

'Was it grim?' she asked. 'I mean the funeral.'

Howard nodded. 'I knew several of them, especially the chief. He was a good bloke.'

'One of my pals taught one of the dead kids.' Her mouth was a taut line.

Before he could reply, he heard a raised voice behind him.

'I say, old chap, that's completely uncalled for.' The speaker was Bert Carter, a retired planter who had chosen to remain in-country. 'Those men were incredibly brave.'

Howard turned round: Carter was addressing Lieutenant Ellis.

Ellis threw the old-timer a look of contempt. 'Come on! They were a bunch of amateur idiots. The Keystone Cops. Trying to be heroes. If they'd had any sense, they'd have left the job to those of us who know how to deal with the enemy. Properly trained soldiers.'

'Those chaps were outnumbered ten to one. And you weren't there, were you? How could they possibly have hoped to hold out? Just a few rifles against sub-machine-guns?' Carter stood, hands on hips, glaring at the British officer.

The conversation around the bar had ceased and all eyes were now on Ellis. He gave a hollow laugh. 'Are you a bunch of pinkos in here then? That's what it looks like. Maybe you can't stand to know the truth.'

Howard sensed Betty's restraining hand on his arm but brushed it off. 'And what might the truth be? Come on. Let's hear it.'

Ellis gave a snigger. 'We all know if we want to get a job done properly, we can't trust natives to do it. Anyone who disagrees with me is deluding himself. They're all the same. From Khartoum to Cairo and Baghdad to Bombay.' He tapped the top of his head. 'Lacking brainpower. Fit only to obey the white man's orders.' He looked around him at the sea of faces. 'You know the answer as well as I do. The government should stop pussyfooting around and send in the RAF to bomb the blazes out of the jungle. That'd sort the bastards out. But instead, they insist on keeping up the charade of involving the Malay police, keeping the sultans happy and talking about winning damn hearts and minds.' Evidently noticing that his words were gaining no traction with his audience, he added, 'You're not military men so you don't understand these things. The Yanks had it right when they dropped the big ones on the Japs. Otherwise most of you would still be locked up in Changi. Or more likely dead.'

At once, Bill Carter took a lunge at the lieutenant, landing a punch in his solar plexus.

Ellis doubled up, his face contorted.

Howard and another man restrained Carter, who was about to go in for a second blow.

Betty moved between the men and stood in front of Ellis. 'OK, sir, lots of big deep breaths. Nice and slowly. You're only winded. You'll live.'

Ellis did as she suggested, then snarled at her. 'Get out of my way.' Swagger stick under his arm and lip curled, he moved to the door, where he turned to deliver his parting shot. 'No wonder the Japs walked straight in and took over the country.

You're a bunch of lily-livered has-beens.' He pushed through the door.

It felt like the pressure had been released from the room.

'What a bastard that bloke is.' Betty's Australian accent punctuated the stunned silence. She turned to look at Carter. 'Nice punch, mate. I'd have liked to give him a bashing myself.'

She rolled her eyes at a surprised Howard. 'I mean it,' she said, her voice modulated to address him only. 'The bastard got what was coming to him. Sometimes I wish I wasn't a nurse, having to do the right thing.' She looked at him, frowning. 'I'm surprised you didn't deck him yourself.'

'Believe me, Betty, there's more than what he said just now to encourage me. But taking a pop at him tonight would achieve nothing apart from getting me banned from the club. Ellis is pond life. He'll get his comeuppance one day and it will be more than a few punches in the bar of the club.'

Betty cocked her head to one side. 'I hope you're right, mate.'

For a moment Howard wondered whether Betty thought he'd chickened out, but then she smiled cheekily. 'How about you and I go and get some air out on the veranda while everyone else is putting the country to rights in here?'

Howard needed no encouragement. He picked up their glasses and followed Betty outside.

April 1950

Howard and Betty were playing tennis. The game was mixed doubles at the club, and they were trouncing the opposition. He glanced across at her as the opposing woman, the wife of the local doctor, slammed the ball straight into the net, and Betty blew a kiss to him. He and Betty were well-matched as players, each having an almost instinctive understanding of what the other would do next.

It was match point in the final set and Howard served a powerful shot which by a miracle was returned and landed just inside the baseline where Betty, bending and swooping down, reached it with her racket and sent it pounding back over the net. It was so fast and so deftly done that the pair on the other side of the net were taken by surprise; the ball bounced high and off the court before they'd even realised Betty had managed to return it.

Afterwards in the clubhouse, Howard showered and changed, then went to sit at the bar, waiting for Betty to emerge from the ladies' changing room. He bought a couple of beers and settled down to enjoy his. The game had been played in blistering heat and high humidity, so the beer was welcome. As he drank, he reflected how much he enjoyed Betty's company. Everything was easy with her. No tension. No drama. She was effervescent, like champagne, always smiling. Fun to be around. Meeting Betty had been just what he needed after moping over the unreachable Jasmine Barrington for so long. He'd not been moping so much over Jasmine since Betty had bounced into his life. That had to be a good thing.

Betty came into the room. She took the glass of beer he handed her and chinked it against his. 'We make a good team, Howie. Those poor suckers didn't know what had hit them.'

He smiled. He only wished that Betty wouldn't persist in calling him Howie. She'd claimed it was impossible for her not to, as all Australians had a deep-rooted pathological tendency to create diminutives of words and names. He decided to try one more time. 'Look, Betty, I know it goes against the grain for you, but I really can't abide being called Howie.'

'Well I can't possibly call you Howard, mate. It's a bloody awful name.' She swigged another mouthful of beer, then bent forward and kissed him lightly, teasingly. 'Sorry, but it is.'

It had never actually occurred to Howard that his name might be a handicap in life. But even if it was, he was damn sure he'd never answer to Howie. It sounded like a character in a comedy show on the wireless.

Betty tilted her head on one side and studied him thoughtfully. 'I know. I'll just call you Baxter. How about that?'

He smiled and shook his head in defeat. 'I suppose I can live with that.' He chinked his glass against hers again.

'You'll have to.' She leaned in and spoke in a whisper. 'You want to find a quiet place for some canoodling?' Her hand slipped into his.

'Lead on!' he said.

There was no one else out on the veranda. It was midweek, when the club was usually quiet. It was unusual for Howard himself to take time off from work. The couple they had played had made their excuses and left straight after the match. The only other people in the club were a few planters at the bar, no doubt expressing their outrage about the progress of the Emergency – or lack of it.

Howard and Betty leaned against the balustrade. It was now dusk, and they listened to the evening chorus of crickets and bullfrogs. Fireflies twinkled like fairy lights among the line of trees that bordered a sluggish brown river.

'Funny old place, Malaya,' said Betty. 'Mile after mile of endless jungle. It's so different from back home.'

'No jungle in Australia, then?'

'There's rainforest up in Queensland but I've never been up there.' She sighed. 'I miss the sea. And the beauty of Sydney with all those inlets and coves and crystal-clear blue water. I miss the beaches. And I hate the godawful rain we get here every bloody day.'

Another thing Howard had needed to get used to was Betty's tendency to swear. He'd been taken aback at first, thinking it odd for a woman to talk like a navvy, but she'd just laughed when he took her to task for it.

'Hell, Baxter, why should the men have all the fun? We Aussies like to tell things how they are. We're not like you stuck-up pommies. Strewth, when I listen to the planters' wives sometimes, I want to get on the next plane back to Oz. They're so prim and proper. Anyone would think they're waiting in line to be presented to His Maj and the missus.'

Howard laughed then pulled her into a kiss which she met with enthusiasm. Reluctantly, he stopped before he got too carried away. 'You want to grab something to eat?'

'You buying?'

'Of course I am. What do you take me for?' He kissed her quickly again. 'Come on, let's find a table before they close the kitchen.'

After the meal of beef rendang, which Betty ate with healthy relish, she put down her cutlery and looked at him, her expression serious. 'How long have we been seeing each other, Baxter?'

He thought for a moment. 'A couple of months I think.'

'Exactly fourteen weeks.'

He smiled at her. 'You've been keeping count? Is it like a prison sentence? You hoping for time off for good behaviour?'

Serious now, she looked at him intently. 'Something's come up. I have to decide whether to stay here in this godforsaken town in the middle of this war that's not a war, or go back to Australia where a position's come up that I can apply for. It's in a small hospital about twenty miles up the coast from Sydney. I could go the beach every day. And it's a good move for my nursing career. Bu ...'

Howard stared at her, shocked. He realised he didn't want to think about life here without Betty. Those fourteen weeks had flown by in a flurry of tennis games, weekends spent swimming at the club pool, walks by the river, drinks at the club or in small local bars. Betty had even managed to lure him to the occasional party and had often come out to Redmond at weekends with her girlfriends to join Howard and his team of assistants for lunch and open-fire cook-outs. How quickly he'd taken it for granted that she would be around. The idea of her going left him feeling hollow.

'You're going back to Australia? Leaving here?'

'I'm thinking about it.' She began to play with her fingers, unusually nervous. 'Look, Baxter, I didn't plan this – I didn't expect a chance like this to come along so soon.'

'I see,' he said, miserable.

'But...'

He looked up, afraid to acknowledge the hope that the little word 'but' carried.

Betty turned to look at him. 'Hell, I'm no good at this kind of stuff, but this is the point where you're supposed to jump in and say you don't want me to go.'

He leaned back and blinked, nervous. He hadn't seen this coming. It was all too soon. But the thought of life here without Betty to brighten it up was not a pleasant one. He drew a long slow breath and said, 'I don't want you to go.'

Her eyes were on his, her expression expectant. Clearly he was supposed to say more than that blunt statement of fact.

He was squirming. 'But I'm being selfish. I know how much nursing matters to you. And how much you miss your family. And those beaches. And how much you hate the rain here.' Howard realised he was scrabbling about, hoping she would contradict him but she didn't.

There was a long silence.

'I'm going to powder my nose.' Betty got up from the table and went out of the room. Howard was left feeling that he'd been set a test and failed it.

SIXTEEN

PARIS

January 1950

Jasmine bumped into Antoine on the landing, so they walked to the school together. She had suffered a turbulent night, unable to sleep as her brain raced, re-running everything she could remember about the previous night. As they walked, Antoine kept up a monologue, but she was only half-listening. They were crossing the Boulevard Saint-Germain before she realised he was talking about his girlfriend and how he was going home to Cabourg the following weekend.

Trying to sound casual, Jasmine said, 'You must miss her a lot.' Seizing the opportunity she added, 'May I ask you a personal question? You and your girlfriend – have you? Do you? You know...'

He looked at her sideways, amused. 'Get to the point, girl. Are you asking me whether we sleep together? Of course we don't. I respect her too much for that. Cabourg is a small town and I care about Françoise's reputation. She'd never agree to have sex before marriage, and I would never demand it. I intend to marry her when I finish my studies.'

'So, you're still…You've never…'

'Of course I have.' He looked at her as if she were half-witted. *'Sacré dieu*, Jasmine, I am twenty-four, not twelve. Of course, I have been with a woman.' He shrugged. 'Just not with Françoise. She is a good girl from a good family.'

'How then? When? Why?' She reached a hand to his arm to slow his pace down.

'Merde, you ask a lot of questions. The first time was with a girl I met when the government sent me to work in Belgium on the S.T.O.'

'What's that?'

'A scheme implemented by the Vichy government on behalf of the Nazis. The *Service du Travail Obligatoire.* Basically, slave labour. The deal was meant to be that for every three workers sent to Germany the Germans would release a French prisoner of war. I was lucky to avoid the coalmines and was put to work in a factory that made paint.'

'And the girl?'

'She was a Belgian working on the packing line in the same factory.'

Jasmine stared at him wide-eyed. 'And you fell in love?'

He gave her a pitying look. 'Love had nothing to do with it. In war things happen that wouldn't happen in peace. We were all doing forced labour. When you have nothing much to live for, you take your pleasures where you can. Don't judge me, Jasmine.'

'You did that with a woman who meant nothing to you but not with Françoise? That seems odd if you love her. Or don't you?'

'Of course, I love her! It's because I love her that I respect her. When I'm home in Cabourg, we do things without going the whole way. The important thing is that technically she will be a virgin on our wedding day. For Christ's sake, Jasmine, don't ask me to give you a biology lesson and draw you diagrams.'

She blushed, then emboldened, said, 'And here in Paris? Are you faithful to her?' She was thinking of the noises she had sometimes heard through the thin walls of the Lutèce.

Antoine folded his arms and looked at her with an expression of disdain. 'I've slept with a couple of students. No one you'd know. There are plenty with loose morals. There's no danger Françoise will find out. It doesn't mean anything.' He wiggled his eyebrows. 'You want to volunteer your services?' Seeing the look of horror on her face, he laughed and added, 'And I masturbate a lot.'

Aware that her skin was burning, Jasmine hurried through the gates of the École where she was swallowed up by the crowd of students.

That day, there was no evidence of Lachlan the lover. He was back in tutor mode, keeping her at a distance. But at least Jasmine had the consolation of what he'd told her last night – that he deliberately avoided her in class because he found her presence distracting and arousing. Knowing this didn't stop her feeling insecure – especially when he lingered in conversation with the Russian girl, Yelena, who, Jasmine had to admit, was beautiful, in spite of her cold eyes and aloof manner.

As soon as classes finished for the day, Jasmine went to meet Stan, excited about seeing the studio he'd offered to show her. As well as a place where she could paint the large canvases she had in mind, it would be a secret refuge for her and Lachlan. That thought both thrilled and terrified her and sent anticipatory sparks fluttering through her body. But she had a queasy feeling at the pit of her stomach when she remembered what Antoine had said about respecting his girl-friend too much to expect her to sleep with him. She knew it was double standards. Exactly the kind of thing de Beauvoir referred to. One law for men and another for women. Jasmine preferred to identify with the existentialist rather than the girl from the quiet provincial town. In fact, she felt sorry for

Françoise, who was blissfully ignorant of her fiancé's infidelities.

The approach to the prospective studio was along a street full of cafés, bars and neon-lit nightclubs. It seemed the building housed what was known as an *hôtel de passe* – a hotel which rented out rooms by the hour – effectively little more than a legalised brothel. As Jasmine followed Stan up the narrow staircase, they were watched by scantily-clad women peering out from doorways, some of whom called out to Stan and gave him lascivious looks. They viewed Jasmine with undisguised suspicion.

Stan explained that after the war the old *maisons* had been closed down by law, along with pimping and the organisation of prostitution. In consequence, the former *maison* owners had opened these hotels to allow prostitutes to operate within the law without walking the streets.

'How do they find their customers, then?'

'They hang out in bars. In this area everyone knows what they're up to. Pigalle is the centre of Paris's nightlife. Some of these girls have regulars who book in for the same time every week – like making a regular hotel reservation. The ones we passed on the stairs were no doubt on the lookout when they heard us coming, presuming we might have been their customers arriving.'

'Gosh,' she said, pulling a face. She didn't want to run the risk of anyone mistaking her for one of 'the girls'.

'Everyone has to make a living somehow, Jasmine. Some people are desperate and have no choice.'

'I suppose so.' But she couldn't help shuddering at the idea of selling one's body in order to survive. 'Just as long as no one thinks that's why I'm here too.'

Stan chuckled. 'There's no risk of that. And should anyone dare to presume, I'm pretty sure they'd soon be put right, won't they?'

'You bet they would.'

The prospective studio was an attic with crumbling plaster walls on which patches of mould spread like spilt ink. The walls had no windows, but the ceiling was almost entirely composed of skylights, looking out onto a night sky lit by a watery moon. The building was at the bottom of the hill of Montmartre and Jasmine could make out the dark shadowy shapes of other buildings climbing the steep hill and the reflection of the coloured lights from a night club on the other side of the street.

She wondered what Evie and Arthur would make of her renting a studio in a place like this. But they'd never need to know.

'It's perfect!'

'Really?' Stan looked dubious. 'You don't mind trekking all the way over here every weekend? It's not very convenient from where you're living. To be honest, it's a bit of a dump. If I'd realised it was this bad I'd never have suggested it.'

'I'll just have to get used to taking the Métro.'

'I guess if it's only in the hours of daylight,' he said, hesitant. 'I don't want you wandering alone along the Boulevard de Clichy after dark. You wouldn't even think of doing that, would you, Jazz?'

'Don't worry. I need natural light to work. It's not as if I'll be living here.'

'It'll be hot as hell in summertime too.'

'I'm from Malaya. I'm used to heat.'

Stan shrugged. 'Then I'll ask the landlord to arrange for the keys and find out about the deposit. How about we go for a celebratory drink?'

'Not just a drink. I'm treating you to something to eat as well, Stan. You've more than earned it.'

'No need to do that. It's my turn. You paid when we went to Chez Inez.'

'And you paid when we went to Les Halles. So we're square

and I want to do it as a small thank you. So please let me. But let's go back to our side of the river.'

'Deal!'

They emerged from the Métro at Place de la Concorde and walked through the Tuileries Gardens. The night sky was cloudless and inky black, illuminated only by a pale moon. The ground under their feet was hard and frost dusted the lawns with a thin coating which shimmered in the moonlight. They walked briskly over the Pont Royal to a little place near the Beaux-Arts that Stan recommended.

Inside, they sat near the rear of the restaurant and Jasmine rubbed her cold hands, before perusing the menu.

Stan leaned forward and said, 'I recommend the *blanquette de veau* – and if you've room for it afterwards they do an excellent *tarte tatin*.'

'I've never tried either,' she said, 'but I trust you.'

'You won't be disappointed. Now tell me what's new with you, sugar?'

'Oh, nothing particular.'

'How's the painting? Still drawing those old broken statues?'

Jasmine pulled a face. 'Yes, but we do get to draw living breathing people in the afternoons. I really like that. And I have to be honest – the classical drawing has taught me a lot, even though I'm never going to love it.' She reached into her satchel and pulled out her sketch-book. 'Want to have a peek?'

'You bet!' He turned the pages slowly and gave a long low whistle. 'You're the real deal, Jazz. These are impressive.' He turned another page. 'Hey! This is me! When you do that, girl?'

'While you were serving in the bar. It's just a quick sketch.'

'Well, you've got me to a T.'

'You should sit for me some time and I'll paint your portrait. You could send it home to your family.'

Stan's face broke into a huge grin. 'Really? My mother

would be so proud to have a real painting of me on the wall. Hell, Jazz, she'll likely invite all the neighbours and her friends from church to admire it and she'll use it as an excuse to throw a party.' He roared with laughter at the thought.

'And she'll have something to remember you by. She must miss having you around.'

Stan's grin turned into a rueful smile. 'Yup, you're right. I don't give enough thought to the fact that she misses me real bad. It would be a fine thing to do.'

'Good, then that's settled. As soon as I've set up the studio, you'll be my first sitter.'

'I'd be prouder than you can believe.'

The *blanquette de veau* arrived and lived up to its name, being entirely white.

'They don't cheat here and throw a few carrots in, like lots of places do. Gaston takes pride in following the old ways.'

Jasmine tried a forkful and declared it delicious.

They drank white wine with the meal and in between courses Stan refilled her glass from the bottle. 'Any romance in your life then, Jazz? Surely there must be? A beautiful girl like you, here in the city that believes it invented love.'

She was aware she was blushing.

Stan noticed her pink face and laughed. 'I thought so. Who's the lucky man? That guy in the heavy overcoat I saw you with the other day heading towards Odéon? I was in Brasserie Lipp with a friend and saw you passing.' He gave her a wink.

'No! That would have been my classmate, Antoine. He has the room next door to mine at the Lutèce. We often go to the pictures together as we both love films – there's nothing between us. He has a girlfriend back home whom he intends to marry.'

'So, who is it?' He was grinning like the Cheshire cat.

She hesitated then reminded herself Stan was her closest friend in Paris, and he'd trusted her enough to tell her about his own doomed love affair. After all, didn't she need some advice right now?

'Actually, there is someone. My tutor.' She bit her lip, nervous about Stan's reaction.

He raised one eyebrow. 'Your tutor? Teacher's pet, eh?'

'It's not like that. In fact, he completely ignores me in class. He spends less time with me than with any of the other students.'

Stan said nothing, but fixed her with his large, hooded eyes, his forehead creased by the slight trace of a frown.

'What?' she said. 'Don't look at me like that!'

'Like what?'

'As though I've done something wrong.'

'Have you?'

'No!'

'Well then.' He raised the eyebrow again. 'No need to be so defensive.'

Jasmine leaned back, watching as Stan lit a cigarette. After he had drawn on it and slowly expelled a plume of smoke, she said, 'It's one reason why I need to rent the studio.'

'Yeah, you said he won't let you work at the school over the weekends.'

'Well, there's that too, but the main reason is to have somewhere private to meet.' She looked down. 'He doesn't want to risk coming to the Lutèce as it's crawling with students.' The waiter brought the *tarte tatin*. 'And there's nowhere else.'

Stan gave her a quizzical look.

'His mother's staying with him while her apartment is renovated.'

Stan took another long draw on his cigarette. 'So, this is a serious relationship, is it? Not just a casual thing?'

'Of course, it's not casual.'

'Seems to have happened mighty fast, Jazz. I mean to get to

the point where you are taking on a studio in order to have clandestine meetings with your lover.'

'It's not like that.'

He said nothing but kept his eyes locked on her.

'I'm in love with him.'

'Glad to hear it. But I still think it's mighty fast.'

'Not when two people love each other.'

'He's told you he loves you then?'

Her cheeks burned. 'Well, not in so many words.'

'I see. So, it was him you were seeing last night?'

'Yes. He took me to a Moroccan restaurant in the Marais. But afterwards...'

'You had nowhere to go?'

'Exactly!' She hesitated, then decided to trust Stan. 'We were kissing and... you know ... on the quayside. But someone came past. I didn't feel comfortable doing that in the street. And he wouldn't come back to the Lutèce with me and couldn't invite me to his place because of his mother, so we said goodnight at the Pont au Change and I told him I'd sort the studio out so we'll have a place to be together.'

Stan jerked backwards in his chair, aghast. 'This guy left you to walk home alone? At night? And he expects you to do the same from Pigalle of all places? Hell, Jasmine, that 'aint right.'

'What do you mean?'

'I mean no decent man would let a young woman he's supposed to be in love with walk through the streets alone at night. And a decent man would certainly not expect you to rent a room so he could be with you there. At your expense. Come on, girl!' He ground out his cigarette in the ashtray and immediately lit another. 'Hell, Jazz, you a virgin?'

Her face was on fire. 'It's none of your business.' She sat upright in her chair and put down her spoon.

'That's a yes then.'

'What if it is? I won't be for much longer.'

'And you think that's something to be proud of?' He looked at her intently.

'I don't believe in the bourgeois trappings of false morality. I am an independent woman, and I control my own destiny.' Jasmine said the words with all the dignity she could muster.

Stan laughed.

'Why are you laughing at me?' She glared at him across the table.

'Because you're spouting nonsense. That's not you speaking. Not you from the heart. You're too good for all that. Say what you really feel, not what you think you ought to feel or what you've read in a damn book.'

'I don't know what you mean.' Tears threatened but she sniffed them away.

Stan leaned forward and took her hand in his. 'You are a beautiful soul, Jazz. You don't have to pretend to be someone you aren't. And you certainly don't have to behave as though your virginity is a burden you have to cast off as soon as possible.'

Her skin was hot, and she felt a mixture of anger and bewilderment. She snatched her hand back. 'I don't know why you're saying that. Why you're being so cruel.'

'I'm not being cruel. I'm your friend. I don't want to stand by and witness some chancer taking advantage of you.'

'Lachlan's not a chancer. Whatever that's supposed to mean. He was a war hero. He fought in the Resistance...'

'He told you that, did he?'

'Not in so many words.' She twirled a lock of hair through her fingers and avoided Stan's gaze.

'Look, sugar, every darn Frenchman claims he was a Resistance fighter. Makes you wonder how the Vichy government managed to hold on to power and how the Nazis weren't run out of France before they'd crossed the border. As for all the

Jews that were rounded up and shipped to the death camps... all the agents who were betrayed and shot. Come on!'

'Lachlan's not a Frenchman. He's half-Scottish. And he didn't make any claims. I worked it out. It's obvious. He was here in France during the war and bilingual. His father wanted him to go back to Britain and join up, but he refused. There can only be one reason why.'

'I can think of one too, but it doesn't involve joining the Resistance.'

Jasmine folded her arms. 'I don't know why you're being so horrible. You haven't even met him.'

Stan took her hand again. 'I don't need to meet him. All I know is he's supposed to be your teacher. He's in a position of trust but he's taking advantage of you.'

'He's not!' She was indignant. 'You're treating me like a child.' She jerked her hand free again.

'You said his mother's staying with him. You met her?'

'Not yet.'

Stan gave a long sigh. 'The guy leaves you to walk home alone, asks you to rent a studio so he can meet you in secret, refuses to court you properly and in the open, fails to show you respect. Look, I've never dated a woman, but I sure as hell know that if I did, I'd treat her special. I wouldn't expect her to go to bed with me as my reward for buying dinner. I wouldn't leave her to walk home alone. And I wouldn't want to meet her in secret as though we had something to hide. Believe me, Jasmine, I've had to live my entire love life in secret and it isn't something I'd recommend. What d'your folks say about this fella?'

'I haven't told them. It's none of their business.'

'Of course it is. They love you and care about you.' He drained the bottle into their glasses. 'You deserve to be treated with respect. This guy isn't doing that. You may not like me for saying it, but believe me, I'm saying it because you're my friend and I care about you. You're a nice girl. You deserve better.'

'Maybe I don't want to be a "nice girl". Maybe I want to be treated as an adult.'

'Well, I won't be a part of it. I'm not getting that key for you. If you want a studio that's one thing, but a sleazy love nest is another. And a place to use for painting during the daylight hours is not the same as you wandering the streets of Pigalle alone at night. Sorry, but I won't do it.' He thought for a moment. 'Where does this guy live?'

She flushed again. 'I'm not sure. Somewhere off Boulevard Sebastopol.'

'Other side of the river. Just like that studio is. How very convenient for him and a trek across Paris for you.'

'That's not fair. He didn't suggest that particular place. You did.'

'I wish I hadn't. If I'd known what you intended using it for I'd have kept my mouth shut.'

Jasmine turned away, feeling tears rising. Mortified, she remembered what Antoine had said that morning about Françoise. He was a hypocrite, sleeping with other women, but she couldn't deny that he had stressed how much he respected his girlfriend.

She picked up her glass and drained it. Glancing at the bar, she saw a couple there, sitting on high stools, drinking cognac. They were clearly lovers. They gazed at each other, oblivious to the rest of the world. As Jasmine watched, they leaned in to kiss. The man put some money on the counter, then wrapped his arms around the woman and helped her down from her perch. They left the restaurant, arms entwined, her head on his shoulder. Jasmine felt a pang of envy. She imagined it was Lachlan instead of Stan on the other side of the table. Her stomach fluttered at the thought of Lachlan leading her out of the place like that couple, taking her to his nearby apartment to make love to her.

But Lachlan didn't live nearby. She had no idea exactly

where he lived – other than it was somewhere northerly. And he wasn't about to take her there. She wondered if his mother's presence was an excuse. Surely, if he was serious about Jasmine he'd want her to meet Delphine? She looked up to see Stan watching her; suddenly she wanted to get away from him and be alone. Why was the world so complicated? And why did she have a sneaking feeling her friend was right?

More than a week passed before Jasmine exchanged a few words with Lachlan – and those words related to her drawing, not to their relationship. Every time she'd tried to grab a few moments alone with him, he'd rushed off, claiming he was late for a staff meeting, heading to an appointment at a gallery, or she'd found him deep in conversation with one of the other students. Jasmine was certain he was going out of his way to avoid her. As a result, her morale was fragile and her confusion growing greater each day.

Finally, they spoke. Lachlan came up behind her as she was reading the notices on the board in the corridor. It was late and there was no one else about. He stood so close she could feel his breath against her cheek.

'Did you get it?' he asked.

'Get what?' Puzzled, she thought he must be referring to something in his lesson that afternoon.

'The studio in Boulevard de Clichy.'

'It wasn't suitable.'

'Pity. It sounded ideal.'

Trying to suppress her irritation, she said, 'It was too far away. And the area wasn't very nice.'

'The area was good enough for some of the greatest artists. But not good enough for you, eh?' His eyebrows were raised. 'Toulouse-Lautrec, Van Gogh, Picasso.'

He'd failed to point out that they were all men. Affronted she said, 'It was in the red light district.'

Lachlan smiled knowingly. 'Ye didna think Mummy and Daddy would approve – is that it?'

'Of course not.' She bit her lip.

As though reading her thoughts, he said, 'I'm sorry.' He looked around him, checking there was no one else in the corridor, then stretched out his hand and stroked the side of her face. 'I didnae mean to be short with you, darlin', but it's a bitter blow. I can't begin to tell you how much I want to be alone with you, beautiful girl.' He ran his hand through her hair, then turned her around to face him, holding her gaze.

'Ye've no idea what it's been like these past days. I'm at breaking point. The sight of you in front of me each day. The way you crease your forehead and bite your lip when you're concentrating – it pushes me to the brink. I want to tell the whole class to pack up their things and get out of the atelier. No man should have to go through this torture day after day. You barely give me a glance, Jasmine. It's driving me crazy. It's cruel.'

He closed his eyes and expelled the air from his lungs.

She stared at him, shocked. What did he mean? She wasn't ignoring him. It was the other way round.

He raised his hand and pushed a lock of his hair back from his brow. Jasmine wanted to reach up and touch it, run her fingers through it as he had just done to her. She looked away, afraid to keep her eyes on his, afraid that her legs would give way under her.

'We're meant to be together. Ye canna deny it. Please, darling girl, don't torture me.' He reached for her hand and drew her into the studio. Inside, Jasmine couldn't stop herself. She lifted her hands and tangled them in his hair as he bent down and kissed her. It was a tender kiss, soft but searching, lingering yet growing in intensity as she responded.

Lachlan pulled away first. 'It's nae good, hen. We canna relax here. Too risky. Rochambeau is looking for an excuse to boot you off the course. I canna risk that happening.'

Jasmine gasped. 'What? Why?'

'I dinnae ken for sure. But it seems he has it in for ye, Jasmine. Jealousy, I imagine. He canna bear women. And he thinks English ones are even worse. It's nothing personal. Just a case of being the wrong gender and the wrong nationality. But I promise you, darling, I'm in your corner, fighting to keep you on the course.'

Jasmine took a few steps back and her knees hit the edge of a chair. She righted herself and sank into it gratefully. 'I'd no idea,' she said. 'No clue that he resented me so much.'

'He's old school.' Lachlan shook his head. 'The old fool believes women shouldna be here at all. He thinks you're taking a place a man should have. It's daft, but he's from the Great War generation. Thinks women should only be in the kitchen and the bedroom.'

Jasmine stared at Lachlan, her brow furrowed. 'So why did he agree to let me in?'

'He caved in under pressure.' Lachlan smiled. 'I can be very persuasive when I put my mind to it. He didn't have a case other than blind prejudice. I told ye darling, I'm in your corner!'

'But I'm not the only woman. What about Yelena and Mathilde – and Lisette?'

Lachlan crossed his arms. 'Mathilde and Lisette are French. And perhaps...'

'What?'

'Perhaps he is attracted by Yelena. After all she is Russian and I suspect Rochambeau has communist sympathies.'

Jasmine's mouth fell open. 'Monsieur Rochambeau a communist? He's the last person I'd have thought that of.'

Lachlan shrugged. 'Many of the French are communists. A side-effect of being occupied by the Germans. It's not enough that they abhor fascists; for many Frenchmen there's a compulsion to go in the opposite direction.' He knocked a Disque Bleu out of its paper packet and lit it. 'It was different in Britain. You never got invaded.'

Jasmine was taken aback. 'I wouldn't know. I wasn't in Britain. Not until after the war. We certainly got invaded in Penang.'

Lachlan took her hand in his. 'Of course, you did, hen. I'm sorry, I forgot that.' He stroked the back of her hand, then lowered his head and kissed her palm, sending waves of electricity through her.

'I'm that wounded. Cut to the quick that you didn't rent that studio. It sounded perfect.' He gave a long sigh, clutching her hand as he did so. 'God, woman, I'd tear the clothes off ye now if I could – but I know better. Is there nae chance we can ever be safely alone together?' He shook his head, his hand gripping hers like a vice.

'I've had another idea,' she said, realising there was a solution to their problem. 'Over Christmas a friend offered me some studio space in Montparnasse. Why didn't I think of that before? It might still be available.'

Lachlan's brow furrowed and his eyes narrowed. 'Montparnasse?' He sucked his lips inwards. 'It's crawling with artists and students there. I'm not sure it's a good idea. And it's a canny distance to travel.'

'Not from here,' she said, before realising he must mean from wherever he lived.

She was about to ask him where that was when he glanced at his watch. 'Got to dash, darling. Delphine's a bit under the weather and I promised I'd pick up some medicine from the pharmacy. We'll have to talk about this another time.'

'Your mother's still staying with you?'

'Aye. It looks like it'll be some time. The renovation work is extensive and with her being poorly.'

'I'd love to meet her.'

'Och, you don't want to meet her while she's ill. She's cranky enough at the best of times and when she's sick she's a hard woman. I wouldna inflict that on you, darlin'.'

'When she's feeling better then?'

'Aye, one day,' he said vaguely.

Lachlan smiled. He had a way of smiling that turned her insides liquid. Picking up his jacket, he left the studio, leaving Jasmine deflated.

As she trudged despondently from the École towards the Lutèce, Jasmine lurched between elation at the memory of kissing Lachlan, and utter dejection at what she could only describe as his dodging and weaving. One minute he was gazing at her with a loving expression and the next he was treating her not only as a stranger but as someone to be avoided.

She couldn't help being uncomfortable about his keenness on her renting the studio in Pigalle, even when he must have known it was awkward for her to get there and he obviously knew it was in an insalubrious area. All his concerns seemed to be for his own reputation, with scant regard to hers.

Jasmine tried to imagine Arthur behaving that way towards Evie. Impossible. Yes, they were of another generation, but she'd always found her adoptive parents open and forward thinking. Jasmine had seen Evie as a role model and there was no denying that her mother would be unlikely to approve. If only Lachlan would meet her halfway. He appeared to want to mould everything to fit his own convenience without making any allowances for hers.

As for this business with Monsieur Rochambeau – Jasmine rarely saw the principal but when she'd passed him in the courtyard a couple of days earlier he had nodded and offered what, for the stern-faced man, was a near-smile. If he was intent on throwing her out of the school surely he wouldn't be smiling? But perhaps it was a smile of satisfaction – a smile of anticipation that he would soon be telling her she must leave. There could be no other possible explanation. Lachlan wouldn't lie about this.

She passed a small café-bar and heard a rapping on the glass. Turning, she saw Antoine behind the steamed-up window, where he'd wiped part of the glass clear. He was alone, nursing a beer, so she went inside to join him.

'How was Cabourg?' she asked. 'I haven't seen you since you got back.'

'*Superbe!* I'm now officially engaged to be married.' He beamed. 'Françoise and I are marrying in the summer.'

'Congratulations! That's super news,' she said. 'But I thought you intended to wait until you'd finished your studies?'

'Change of plan.' Antoine took a slug of his beer. 'I realised how much I miss her. There's a place available in the autumn term teaching art at the local *lycée*. They interviewed me and I got the job. They don't mind that I won't be finishing here. Just a year at the Beaux-Arts is prestigious enough for them.'

'Your father?'

'Not pleased about me not finishing. He wanted me to try for the *Prix de Rome*.' Antoine gave a sardonic chuckle. 'No chance of me winning that. But since I'm a disappointment in not following him into architecture anyway, it makes little difference. And he adores Françoise. As does *Maman*. So, my friend, I will soon be an old married man. I'm counting the months now.' He reached into his breast pocket and pulled out a photograph. 'Here's my girl.'

Jasmine took it. Françoise looked young, fresh-faced, with her hair in a neat bob - very gamine and pretty. She handed the small photograph back to him. 'She looks lovely. You make a perfect couple.'

'*Merci,*' he said. Looking bashful, he added, 'We've been

sweethearts since we were small children. Our mothers are friends. As we've grown up together, we know all there is to know about each other.'

Not quite all, Jasmine thought, remembering what Antoine had told her about his sexual adventures. But she said nothing.

'I'm ready to settle down and have a family. Françoise will make an ideal wife.'

The words rushed out before she could hold them back. 'But do you love her? Truly love her? So, you can't bear not being around her... so you think of her all the time? And will you make her an ideal husband? Surely it works both ways?'

He took another slug of beer. 'I'm fond of her and I respect her, and she will make the perfect mother to our children. That's what matters. And she's pretty, affectionate, fun to be with – and a great cook.' He jerked his shoulders in a shrug. 'If the passion dies eventually, I'll just have to find it elsewhere. I'm a practical man. Marriage is about more than sex. As for what she thinks of me... I can promise you I'm the biggest catch in Cabourg.' He made a noise that was half snort, half laugh.

Jasmine stared at him, horrified. 'I'm sorry,' she said, lamely. 'It doesn't sound terribly romantic.

'Don't be sorry. I'm a lucky man. I can't wait to be married. This last long weekend drove me crazy, having to behave like a gentleman, as Françoise is always quick to remind me.' He gave another dry laugh. 'But what about you, Jasmine? You're a pretty girl. Even beautiful. Isn't there someone in your life? Maybe back in Africa?'

She shook her head. 'No there's no one there.'

'That other place you were. Malaya?' He signalled to the waiter to bring them more drinks. 'Or maybe here in Paris? Come on, Jasmine, you can tell me.'

She'd had more than enough lecturing about Lachlan from Stan, so she certainly wasn't about to confide in Antoine too.

But Antoine was enjoying teasing her. 'Come on, tell me.

'There was a chap in Malaya I was fond of, but not in that way. He wanted to write to me when I came here but there was no point in pursuing it so I never gave him my address.'

'No point? Why?'

'Because he's on the other side of the world. It's pretty clear he wants a wife, and it would have been unfair to string him along.'

'Didn't you like him?'

'Yes, I liked him... a lot. But it was pointless. I have no intention of becoming a rubber planter's wife, living in the middle of nowhere. I intend to dedicate my life to my art, not to being someone's wife and having lots of babies. Besides, we have nothing in common. He's not artistic at all.'

It seemed a kind of betrayal to be belittling Howard like this. Right now, she'd like nothing more than to be with him. With Lachlan everything was so complicated, so difficult. And he seemed to expect her to make all the effort, to make life easy for him. Howard would never be like that towards her. He would never leave her to walk home alone. Never make demands that she should give way to his desires. But then she had never so much as kissed Howard. That led to her wondering what that would be like – and why he had never tried. But she knew the answer to the second question. Howard was not the kind of man who would kiss a woman if doing so was going to be unwelcome. And he had always made one thing clear – his intentions towards her were both serious and honourable.

Antoine snapped his fingers in front of her. *'Attention!* From the look on your face perhaps you like this *mec* more than you're admitting. But since he's out of the way in Malaya, my advice is to have some fun while you're here in Paris. How about Giancarlo?' He frowned. 'No, I think he is seeing Mathilde. But there are others – Robert, Didier, Guillaume.'

'Stop! I'm not interested in any of them. Nor I imagine are any of them interested in me.'

Antoine rolled his eyes. 'They're not blind. But I am certain there's someone. That dreamy expression in your eyes most of the time. Come on, tell me.'

'You're imagining things. It's probably just because I'm anxious about the course.'

'Anxious about the course? *Bordel de merde!* What do you have to be anxious about? You may not be the next Picasso but you're easily one of the best in the atelier. Maybe not at the classical drawing but you're not the worst – and your life drawings are *formidable*.'

His words took her by surprise. *'Tu es fou!* Crazy. Are you trying to make me feel better before I get thrown out?'

Antoine pulled a face. 'Now who's crazy? Why would you get thrown out?'

'Monsieur Rochambeau hates me.'

Antoine put down his beer. 'He hates everyone! Don't take it personally. There's no reason for him to pick on you in particular.'

'It's because I'm a girl, and I'm English and come from the colonies. Apparently, he's a communist.'

Antoine laughed. 'For a start half of Paris is communist, but Rochambeau is probably the most unlikely candidate. He's a friend of De Gaulle's. Where did you hear this nonsense? Is all this just to force me to tell you how good you are? '

She stared at him open-mouthed. *'C'est vrai?'*

'You know it's true. In fact, I was wondering if the Scotsman was giving you extra lessons after class. I couldn't help noticing you leaving with him at the end-of-term drinks.'

The blood rushed to her cheeks. To cover her confusion, she took a sip of her beer.

Antoine leaned forward. *'Merde,* That's it, *n'est-ce pas?* You and Robertson. You're lovers!'

'Of course, we're not. He's our teacher.'

Antoine shrugged. 'What's that to do with it?' He reached across the table and nudged her arm. 'I should have guessed. That's why you barely speak to each other in the atelier. You are definitely lovers.'

'Please, Antoine, stop it. We're not lovers.' Her defences crumbled and she squeezed her nails into her palms. 'That's just it. I don't know what we are or where I stand with him. Please don't tell anyone at the Beaux-Arts – I'll be in trouble if Monsieur Rochambeau finds out.'

'Why this obsession with Rochambeau? *Il s'en fiche.* As long as you're discreet. *C'est normal.*'

'Nothing's happened so there's nothing to find out anyway. We had dinner once. That's all.' Then, seeing Antoine's doubting expression, she decided she might as well get a male point of view. 'He wants to take it further. I told him I was renting a studio. But then I didn't go ahead with it and I think he's disappointed in me. He wanted us to be able to meet in private.' Jasmine was aware she was blushing again.

'I had no idea you were so modern, Jasmine. I presumed you were the classic English girl – all prim and proper. How very clever to have an affair with the tutor.'

'Please, Antoine, I told you. We're not having an affair. Not yet. Maybe not ever. And it's certainly not to be clever.' She gave in to a long sigh. 'I don't know what to do. What to think. I keep remembering what you said about not sleeping with Françoise until you're married, and it made me think I should wait until I'm married too.'

'Françoise is different. She's a provincial girl, unsophisticated. A girl like her would never dream of travelling across the world to a strange city in order to study. It would be unimaginable. You're an artist. We live by different rules. A different morality. You've said you don't want to be a married woman and settle down to have children. I doubt as a woman you'll ever be a successful artist – but if you don't care about being poor and are prepared to dedicate yourself to it you could be a great one. So if that's your choice, who cares about morality?'

Antoine glanced at his watch. 'If we hurry we can make it in time to see the new Yves Allégret film. Simone Signoret is in it.'

Jasmine followed him out of the bar. Maybe immersion in a good film might take her mind off what she was increasingly seeing as a painful decision.

February 1950

Jasmine made her mind up. She'd talk to Corinne about renting the studio in Montparnasse – assuming it was still available. Regardless of Lachlan, she needed space to work. Antoine's comments about her ability had fuelled the fire in her to paint. And his words had hit home about her making a choice between a husband and family and her art. She would choose art. Jasmine tried not to hear the little voice inside that suggested maybe with Lachlan she might find both.

As soon as she walked into the former warehouse, she knew this was the right place for her. The ground floor housed the *Hebdo Latin* office – although office was a generous term for what was a chaotic arrangement of tables, chairs, and a large duplicating machine. The space had been divided horizontally by a mezzanine floor.

Corinne waved her arm around. 'This is where we produce the magazine. Four of us are sleeping up there.' She pointed to the mezzanine, which was accessed by a metal ladder. 'Simple but very cheap. I'll show you the room that's available.'

Jasmine followed the French girl across the *Hebdo* office to a door in a partition wall. They went in and Jasmine gasped. The space was huge – with no mezzanine so it benefited from the full height of the warehouse. Floor to ceiling windows ran the length of one wall.

Corinne gave a rare smile. '*C'est spécial, n'est-ce pas?*'

Jasmine had to agree it was indeed special.

'It is not cleaned since the warehouse closed so you'll have some work to do.' She indicated a pile of empty cardboard boxes heaped in one corner and the cobweb-covered windows.

'I suppose I can find a window-cleaner – it's a bit too high for me. Only I'll need lots of light.'

Corinne shrugged. 'I'll ask around. So, you want it then?'

'Oh, yes!'

The rent was a pittance and they shook hands on the deal.

'Bernard!' called Corinne. 'Your turn to make the coffee. And one extra for my friend, Jasmine, who is going to be our new neighbour.'

While the coffee was being brewed, Jasmine sat down on a battered sofa beside Corinne.

'Terrible about Stan, isn't it?' said the French girl. 'I did not know he was so unhappy.'

Jasmine jerked her head back. 'What do you mean? What about Stan?' She realised it was a couple of weeks since she'd seen him.

'I thought you knew. I know you're friends. He's in the hospital.'

'What?' Jasmine's hand flew to her chest, and she stiffened. 'I've heard nothing. What's happened to him? Which hospital?' She jumped up. 'Tell me! I need to go there.'

Corinne reached out, took her hand and drew her back down onto the sofa. 'Calm down. Drink the coffee first. Bernard, *dépêche-toi!*'

'I don't want any coffee. Please just tell me, Corinne.'

Corinne sighed. 'He tried to kill himself. Took a knife to his wrist, but fortunately he didn't make a very good job of it. He's at the American Hospital in Neuilly.'

Jasmine didn't wait any longer. She rushed outside and ran towards a nearby taxi rank, where, to her relief, two or three cabs were waiting. The trip took half an hour and cost almost all the cash in her purse.

A stern nurse tried to turn her away, but Jasmine's distress was evident.

'Please. I'm his fiancée,' Jasmine said, desperate to gain access.

The nurse made no effort to hide her disbelief. 'If that's the case, you need to do a better job of taking care of him.' But she softened a little in the face of Jasmine's genuine distress. 'You can have ten minutes. No more. He's very weak. Don't upset him or I'll have you thrown out.'

Stan's bed was at the far end of the ward. His eyes were closed and at first Jasmine thought he was asleep. Sensing her presence, he opened them, but turned his head away. He looked small, vulnerable, weary.

Jasmine pulled up a metal chair and sat beside his bed, reaching for his right hand. The left one was swathed in bandages. 'Oh, Stan!' she said, her voice barely a whisper. 'I only just heard.' She wanted to ask him why he'd done it, but it felt intrusive – and somehow she thought she already knew.

With Stan there was always an undercurrent of sadness, even when he was at his most jovial. If only the heartless Jeff were able to see what lasting harm his betrayal and abandonment had done. While something else might have triggered Stan's desire to slash his wrist Jasmine was certain that the underlying cause was a broken heart. Jeff's behaviour had been cruel; clearly the loss and pain were still present even after five years.

Stan opened his eyes again. 'I didn't make a very good job of it, did I?'

'I'm glad you didn't. Very glad indeed.'

He gave her a watery smile.

'When will you be out?'

'They say in a couple of days. Once I get my strength back.' He jerked his head at the intravenous drip.

'I'll visit every day.'

'You don't need to do that but you're a sweet girl, Jazz. A true friend.'

'Oh, Stan I wish you'd talked to me. I can't bear to think of you not being around. You're my dearest friend here in Paris. And my first friend.' She began to cry.

Stan squeezed her hand in response. 'I'm afraid you'll have to get used to me not being around, sugar. Don't worry, I'm not going to try and kill myself again. But I need to get away. Paris isn't good for me.'

'Where? Why? When?' Jasmine's shoulders slumped.

'Some friends have offered me a place to stay in the South of France. It's warmer there and I'm craving some sunshine.' He closed his eyes again, momentarily. 'And to tell you the truth, Jazz, I'm weary of Paris and even wearier of Parisians.'

'I know how you feel. I long for some sunshine myself.'

'Any time you care to escape for a vacation, you can come and find me in Provence. It's a painter's paradise.'

Jasmine forced herself to smile but inside she felt empty. Stan was special. She got on well with Antoine – but even though she saw him more often than Stan, it was a more superficial friendship. Her kinship with the American was perhaps because they were both outsiders. He had turned his back on his country of birth and she felt unclaimed by any – except perhaps Malaya – and both would always be outsiders to the French.

In early March, the night before Stan was due to leave Paris, they met for dinner. Jasmine asked if they could go to Chez Inez again. It was a place she couldn't imagine going to with anyone else.

When they had eaten he leaned across the table and took her hand in his. She could see the still livid scars on his wrist. He stroked the back of her hand with his other. 'Don't change, Jasmine. Don't let Paris change you. You are a beautiful person. Yes, you're beautiful to look at, but it's more than that. It's something that comes from inside you, radiates out of you.'

Jasmine pulled a face.

'Don't be like that. I mean it. You have such strong inner confidence. And *joie de vivre*. But a quietness too. A still centre. Stay true to yourself, girl.' He smiled, eyes shining. 'And come and visit me when you need to see the sea and the sunshine.'

He released her hand and took a sip of his beer. 'You still seeing that teacher?'

'I see him in class every day.'

'That's not what I mean, and you know it. You sleeping with him?'

She looked away. 'No. He doesn't seem to be interested anymore.'

Stan said nothing.

'I'd never have expected you to be a moral guardian, Stan.'

'What's that supposed to mean?'

'It means you're hardly in a position to criticise me. You sleep with different men. Why should I be different? Besides I'm an artist and this is Paris. Most of the students in my atelier are having sex. Even the chap who has the room next to mine – he cheats on his fiancée.'

'I'm not talking about the other students, I'm talking about you. And I'm not saying you shouldn't be sleeping with men. Just that particular one.'

'Well don't, or we risk ruining your last evening.'

'You're right. I'm sorry. I should never have brought it up.'

Jasmine cupped her hands under her chin and gazed across

the table at Stan. 'I haven't done that painting for your mother yet.' She frowned. 'I wanted you to sit for it, but I'll have to work from the sketches I have of you.' Studying his face she added, 'I need to lock an image in my head of you as you are right now so I can do you justice. It's got to be a good enough likeness to make your mother happy.' She reached into her satchel and pulled out her sketch-pad and a pencil. 'Here, write your mother's address down so I can send it to her.'

'You sure, Jazz? You'd do that for me?'

'I've never been surer, my dear friend.'

Easter 1950

Now that Stan had left Paris, Jasmine felt desolate, abandoned. Not that she blamed him for leaving – that was perfectly understandable. But in Stan she'd found someone who expected nothing from her and gave so much in return. Life in Paris would have been unimaginable without him. She'd learnt so much from him – about the night life of Saint-Germain-des-Près, jazz music, soul food, life as a GI – and what it meant to be shunned for the colour of his skin in one's own country. She'd also learnt that a man who loved other men rather than women was not someone to be feared or despised. Stan had proved to be more sensitive, cultured and kind than anyone else she had met here.

Jasmine was now spending every weekend working in her studio. The lighting was too poor for her to paint at night, during what seemed to her an endless winter. Not for the first time, she sent up a silent prayer of thanks to her late father for her inheritance. The income from it, while not large, enabled her to buy the canvases and materials she needed. Her first priority was the painting of Stan. Painting his portrait made her feel close to her departed friend – and she was determined it would make his mother happy. Flinging herself into a fury of work, she found consolation in her art for the emptiness caused by Lachlan's continued evasiveness.

Corinne was rarely around – other than on press day for *Hebdo Latin*. While she had a room of sorts upstairs, Jasmine had the impression she rarely slept there, but didn't enquire further. Corinne was friendly enough, but there was that certain Parisian distance, an unspoken assumption that they could never be close friends. Jasmine remembered a conversation she'd had with Stan when he'd told her that she mustn't expect to become close to the French: no matter how hard one might try, how charming and friendly they might be in response, they always found a way to keep one at arm's length. While Corinne would happily invite Jasmine along with groups of her friends, include her in the fierce debates they so often indulged in, the French girl revealed nothing of herself nor expressed more than superficial curiosity about Jasmine's life or emotions.

In the Montparnasse studio, Jasmine painted with passion, energy and complete absorption. Alone, she was never lonely as long as she was working, and the solitude made her calm. She knew the work she did in that big empty room to be better than anything she was producing at the school. In Lachlan's atelier, most of the time she felt anger towards him and her fellow students and a kind of hatred towards herself for feeling that way. Lachlan's presence was a distraction. She struggled to concentrate, to lose herself in her work as she did here in Montparnasse. Listening to him as he explained concepts to the class, watching as he moved around the room, giving comments to his students; she was angry with herself all the time because of the power he exerted over her.

Time moved slowly for Jasmine. She was longing for the last semester of the academic year to end so she could return to her family for the summer months. It seemed a lifetime until term was due to end in late June.

Lachlan was careful now not to exclude her from his critiques, but his feedback was impersonal, noncommittal, lacking in the enthusiasm he had shown towards her when she was first in Paris. He continued to avoid being alone with her. She marvelled at the variety of techniques he employed to do so.

In early May, at the end of one of the life drawing classes, he made an announcement. 'I've some exciting news about the *Médaille d'Or*, ladies and gentlemen. You have your first opportunity to enter your work into a competition and I urge you all to do so. A still-life or a portrait. The submission date is in four weeks. Any medium.'

One of the students, the Italian, Giancarlo, raised his hand. 'Does it have to be work done here in class?'

'No. It can be, but you're encouraged to submit work you've done in your own time.' He thought for a moment. 'And you can use the studio here after hours. I know most of you don't have anywhere else to work.'

Jasmine smarted. Hadn't Lachlan told her weeks ago no one was allowed to use the school out of hours? She glared at him but to her surprise he smiled in response. Pushing her annoyance aside she realised she was excited. Not about Lachlan, but about the chance to enter her work into a competition. Just a week ago she had finished the portrait of Stan. When it was done she'd stood back and assessed it. Her usually over-active critical voice was forced to acknowledge that it was her best work ever. Now she had a chance to prove herself. To show what she was capable of away from the sterile and hostile atmosphere of the atelier.

After his announcement, Lachlan called across the room to Jasmine as she was packing away her materials. 'I'd like a wee word with you, Miss Barrington, if you wouldn't mind waiting behind.'

She sat, clutching her satchel to her, until the last student left. It was interminable. She could feel herself shaking.

At last he came towards her, his face lit up by that hypnotic smile. 'I think it's time I came and had a look at that studio of yours. How about eight this evening?'

As soon as they were inside the studio, Lachlan kicked the door shut and pulled her into his arms. His mouth was on hers, his hands moving over her body and her heart raced in response.

'My God, darlin', you're so gorgeous. I've missed you,' he said.

But this time Jasmine was determined not to fall under his sway. She jerked herself free. 'Stop. You've come to look at my work, haven't you?'

'Of course, I have. Later.' His mouth was on her neck.

Jasmine pushed him away. 'Not later. Now! I want you to look at my work. I want to win this competition.' Her own words surprised her, but then she repeated them in her head. She *did* want to win. More than anything, including being kissed by Lachlan. She wanted to win for Stan as well as for herself.

Lachlan gave a heavy sigh but turned to look at her work. There was a line of canvases – portraits of the Seine *clochards* intended as preparatory studies for her planned larger work, a self-portrait, one of Corinne, another of Antoine, a painting of an old lady sitting on a burlap sack selling caged birds at the Marché des Oiseaux, and the largest canvas, the portrait of Stan. It was full-face and behind him was the shadowy impression of the Eiffel Tower – an *homage* to their first encounter on the terrace of the Trocadéro.

'It's a friend of mine. Stan has just left Paris to live in

Provence. I've painted it as a gift for his mother in Chicago, but I'd like to enter it in the competition before I send it to her.'

Lachlan said nothing, but moved along the line of paintings, giving them each a cursory glance. Eventually he stopped in front of the portrait of Antoine. 'Maybe this one. It's not a bad likeness.' He shrugged and pointed at one of the *clochards*. 'Or this. Now come here.' He reached for her.

Jasmine stepped aside, frowning. 'The one of Stan is the best. You must see that.'

'Yes. If you think so.' He pulled her into his arms. 'You know I love all your work, darlin'. Choose whichever you want. We all know Giancarlo's going to win the prize.'

Jasmine stiffened and drew away from him. 'Why? Are you telling me it's already been decided?' She felt sick.

'He's the best in the atelier. Well, apart from you, hen. If it were up to me, you'd win hands down. But there's a panel of judges and our friend Rochambeau is the chair.' He planted a kiss on her hair, then moved his lips to her brow, dusting her face with light kisses until he found her mouth.

Jasmine pulled away from his embrace. 'Stop. Please, Lachlan. This is serious. You're my tutor. I need your guidance and advice. The competition really matters to me.' She bit her lip. 'But you're telling me I might as well not bother to enter.'

'Och, I didna say that.'

'But you meant it.'

'It's not just down to Rochambeau – although his opinion carries the most sway. I'll be putting a word in for you. I've told you before, darlin', I'm in your corner and I'll be lobbying the rest of the panel.'

'I'm not asking you to be in my corner. I just want to be treated fairly. But you haven't even bothered to look at my paintings properly.'

'That's because I'd rather look at you, sweet girl.' Seeing she was unimpressed, he sighed. 'Very well.' He turned and walked again along the line of canvases. 'Truth is they're all very good. Maybe not as good as you're capable of but any one of them is a credit to you.' He glanced back at them. 'And they're all better than the work you've done in my atelier.'

She wanted to say it was little wonder why, but thought it best not to antagonise him.

He adopted a pleading tone. 'Look, Jasmine, you canna expect me to give you special treatment. It wouldn't be professional.'

'I've not asked you for special treatment, just for your opinion on my work. I'm not asking for you to vote for me to win. Just to give me your expert opinion as my tutor as to which of these pieces is my best effort.' Jasmine folded her arms protectively across her chest. 'You don't actually care, do you? Even in class you never give me any guidance. Not like when we first met, when I was doing the classical portfolio. You taught me so much. Now you barely glance at my work.'

Lachlan closed his eyes and expelled a protracted sigh. 'Do ye nae get it? I've taught you all I can. You're a better artist than I am and you're not yet at the end of your first year. I'm afraid to critique your work because it's so special and I'd hate to crush that. You learn so fast. Everything I've taught you, girl. You're like blotting paper, you soak it all up and understand it instinctively. I never have to tell you more than once. Unlike most of them.'

Jasmine swallowed. She hadn't expected that.

'God, woman, ye've nae idea, have you? I'd like to punch that fool Rochambeau on the nose for his narrow-minded, short-sighted attitudes to women and to you in particular. What else can I say?'

Jasmine was stunned. She slumped onto the battered old sofa that stood in the corner of the studio. 'You mean that? Really?'

'Of course, I mean it. I'd never lie to you, hen.' He collapsed into the seat beside her, his head jerked back to stare at the ceiling.

Jasmine looked at him, her heart hammering. 'So which painting?'

Lachlan sighed. 'The one of the negro. The bird seller too. Enter them both.' He turned to look into her eyes, his hands moving to cup her face. 'Now, at last, can I make love to you?'

SEVENTEEN

STATE OF JOHORE

May 1950

For months, Sir Henry Gurney, the High Commissioner of Malaya, had been trying to persuade the sultans to grant title deeds to agricultural land to the hundreds of thousands of mainly Chinese squatters, so they could be enticed to move away from their camps. These were mostly close to the jungle that ran like a spine the entire length of Malaya, and hence close to the influence and coercion of the communist insurgents. Now at last, in the person of former general Sir Harold Briggs, Gurney's newly-appointed civilian Director of Operations, resettlement could be put into practice. Briggs's strategic plan was to cut off the supply routes to the communists by moving the squatters into so-called "new villages" safely protected from the incursions of the insurgents.

While most of the squatters were subsistence farmers, many also worked on rubber estates as tappers and the idea of moving them some distance away was unpopular with the planters. Neither Briggs nor Gurney would be moved from their conviction that resettlement was essential to prevent the "bandits", as they were known by the British, from succeeding in their armed insurrection.

If the resettlement operations were unpopular with the planters they were the source of fear, anger, and shock in the squatters themselves.

Howard was dreading the day ahead. He had received a visit from the local civilian district officer, and the local police chief, to inform him that the squatter camp adjacent to the Redmond Estate was to be cleared before dawn the following morning. Under the Briggs Plan, these operations were kept secret until the last possible moment to prevent the insurgents infiltrating the camps and hence the new settlements, and to use surprise to limit resistance from the squatters themselves. While the operation was to be carried out by the civilian authorities, there would be British army troops there to help out, drive the trucks, and shift goods and furniture for the unwitting squatters.

The police sergeant had assured Howard that the new village offered significantly improved facilities compared to the squatter camp, including a school, a clinic and social hall. All very well, Howard thought, but these families regarded their primitive camp as home.

At four in the morning, the troops and police arrived and while the villagers slept, they threw a cordon around the area where the camp adjoined the estate. Howard watched, fearing the worst, as gradually the inhabitants woke up and began to go about their usual early morning activities before dawn, oblivious of what lay in store. Women went to light camp-fires to cook the rice for the breakfast and men moved towards the river to perform their daily ablutions. Howard could hear babies crying as they woke and wanted to be fed. Children began to play. Beside him in the half-light was a Chinese Malayan, the local Chinese Affairs Officer. The man was there to translate but as the *tuan besar*, Howard was the figurehead for the estate and was expected to announce the bad news. He had a smattering of Chinese and reasonable Malayan, but wanting to avoid making errors and, with the CAO beside him to translate, he decided to speak in English.

'As some of you may be aware, the government has been creating new villages with brand new facilities. Schools, clinics, meeting halls. Supplied with electricity and safe from the bandits who have been extorting money, rice and other supplies from you and terrorising families throughout the country. You will each receive a large plot of land on which to grow food, keep livestock and source the materials to build your own house. This plot of land will be yours to pass on to your children and their children. You will also receive a sum of cash to tide you over until your first harvest.' What he didn't mention, but knew only too well was that the village was surrounded by a seven-foot-high wire fence and perimeter lights. It was designed to keep the bandits out – but inevitably would also have the effect of keeping them in.

As the CAO translated Howard's words, the wailing began. Cries of grief, anger, defiance, despair were swelled by the howls of babies and small children and a chorus of barking from dogs, as if in sympathy with their masters' plight. Howard had to raise his voice to be heard.

'We all hoped this wouldn't have to happen, but it's for your own protection.'

One of the tappers shouted angrily in English 'No, *Tuan*. We no go. No one help bandits here.'

Howard took a gulp of water from his flask before responding. 'Maybe you haven't been helping them. But it's only a matter of time before they try to force you.' He paused while the CAO translated. 'You've heard what's been happening. The shootings, the burnings, the children murdered when people refused to help them. Mr Wong is now going to tell you more about what you can expect in your new village.'

Howard felt like Judas. He knew these men well. He understood that for them and their families, home was more than bricks and mortar. This camp might be basic and primitive, but they had lived there for years. It was familiar. Now they were being herded like cattle into the unknown. In the regular Emergency briefings or the local war council, and at 'Morning Prayers' which, as *tuan* of one the largest estates, he attended, he'd made a suggestion that was rejected. He'd proposed one or two of the tappers be taken to view the new village, ahead of the change, so they could speak to the other families as trusted leaders. Better to hear the virtues of their new home from them than from a white man and a local official. But secrecy was critical, the District Officer had maintained. This was a non-negotiable part of the Briggs Plan. If Chin Peng and his cohort got word of an imminent resettlement, they would have time to infiltrate, thus defeating the object of the entire enterprise. The humanitarian benefits of resettlement, while touted to the villagers, were clearly insufficient motivation in their own right.

Howard stepped forward again to tell the people what was about to happen next.

'All those of you who work as tappers at Redmond will be paid as if you'd done a normal day's work, but your work today is to settle your families into your new homes. You'll see there are a lot of soldiers here today. They're not here to harm you but to help you. Use them to carry your furniture, to help the elderly among you to get onto the trucks. We need to start now. We will do this in family groups. Who's first?'

No one moved.

One of the men shouted, 'Never. I will not leave.' He began to run but was immediately apprehended by one of the Malay policemen.

The CAO stepped forward and spoke rapidly. The response was immediate. Hands shot up into the air.

Howard looked at the Chinese man. 'What did you just say?'

'I tell them best plots go to who arrives first.'

From then on the operation proceeded smoothly. Howard was intensely relieved at the behaviour of the British troops, who evidently found shifting furniture and lifting old ladies onto the backs of the scores of trucks more palatable than marching through dense jungle, up to their waists in water and bitten by leeches. Most of them were young men on their National Service; they went about the task with patience and good humour.

Into the midst of the orderly process a jeep roared up and to Howard's dismay, Lieutenant Ellis jumped out. His distaste was further heightened when Howard noticed a third pip had now appeared on Ellis's sleeve, indicating the man had been promoted to captain. So much for Reggie's belief he was destined to remain in a desk job in disgrace after his cold-blooded murder of Amir's mother. Howard, having no wish to engage in conversation with the man, went to talk to the occupants of the first loaded lorry which was about to depart.

But Ellis was clearly intent on making his presence felt. 'Who's supposed to be in charge here?'

The civilian district officer stepped forward. 'That would be me, Captain.'

'What the hell is going on here? My men are soldiers not a bloody furniture removal firm.' As he spoke, a pair of squaddies rushed in front of the huts in hot pursuit of a runaway cockerel. 'We're here to fight a war not to round up chickens.' Ellis raised his voice and barked at the men. 'Stop wasting time. The sooner you fools get these natives loaded on the trucks and out of here, the sooner we can get back to what we're supposed to be doing.'

Howard could take no more. 'And what might that, be, Ellis?' he said. 'Shooting innocent mothers dead in front of their children?' He moved closer to Ellis, then took a small step back – he'd forgotten about the man's appalling halitosis. 'I'd remind you that this operation is under the management of the local civilian authorities and the military is only here to assist. Some-thing, I might add, your men have been doing with charm and good nature. Now I suggest, Captain, you let the lads get on with the job.'

Without waiting for a response from the dumbfounded Ellis, Howard went to reassure an elderly lady who was anxious she might not be allowed to bring her caged birds on the trans-port. He led her to join the line of people waiting to board a truck and once she and her cage were safely installed, he moved on to deal with the next problem. Hearing a screeching of tyres, he was gratified to see Ellis depart.

EIGHTEEN

PARIS

Early May 1950

Jasmine's assumption that everything would be different when she and Lachlan made love proved to be a delusion.

She had expected a romantic and intimate experience, but their lovemaking was a bitter disappointment. Not for Lachlan – he was the cat who'd got the cream. But for Jasmine it was a curiously unemotional experience. She'd been detached, as if watching herself from a distance. It was painful – but she'd expected it would be. What she hadn't anticipated was that she would be almost incidental to the process as far as her lover was concerned. He went about deflowering her with an efficiency and enthusiasm that appeared to centre entirely on his own pleasure rather than hers.

She'd made a special effort for his visit, wearing a new dress, teamed with the Christmas pearls. But Lachlan couldn't wait to divest her of her clothing and in his enthusiasm managed to catch his hand in her necklace. Impatiently he jerked it free, breaking the string and sending pearls bouncing across the studio floor.

Jasmine jumped up to gather them, but he pushed her down onto the couch, saying, 'Leave them. I'll pick them up later and get it mended for you.'

When he'd finished, he took his pouch of tobacco and began to roll a cigarette. 'All right?' He glanced sideways at her.

As far as she was concerned, it was far from all right. Jasmine had never experienced such a sense of loneliness with another person. If she was detached from herself, it was nothing compared to how detached she felt from him. How many months had passed with her longing for this moment and how utterly different was the reality from her dreams? Was that all he had to say for himself? She didn't want to cry in front of him but the urge to do so was overwhelming. Squeezing her eyes tightly shut, she tried to think of something to distract her from the misery coursing through her. She took some gulping breaths, hoping it would calm her.

At least her virginity had been dispatched. It had begun to feel like a burden. But inside, she didn't feel any different from how she'd been before. No, that wasn't true. She felt worse. Hollow. Bereft. Used. She gave a little sob and buried her face in the sofa cushion.

'Och, what's wrong darlin'?' He drew on his cigarette. 'Settle yersel' doon. It always hurts women the first time. Next time it'll be more fun.'

Fun? What did fun have to do with it? She didn't want fun. She wanted to be swept off her feet and overcome by passion and love. She wanted him to gaze into her eyes and tell her he loved her.

To her dismay, Lachlan ground out the butt of his roll-up but instead of taking her in his arms again he reached for his trousers and pulled them on.

'What are you doing?'

'I need to get moving. I told you this studio wasn't in the most convenient of places. I've a long walk home now.'

'Not yet... it's not even nine o'clock.' She stared at him, in disbelief that he intended to leave her like this. She wanted another chance – this time she wouldn't be so nervous. Maybe it had been her fault. If she could try harder ... ask him to tell her what to do. What he wanted. She stretched a hand out to him, but he moved out of her reach.

Lachlan pulled his shirt over his head then drew her upright and gave her a slow lingering kiss that set her on fire again. He ran his fingers over her cheeks and smiled at her in that way that always melted her insides. Surely, he'd have to stay now. How could he possibly leave her like this? But Lachlan brushed his fingers through his hair, pushing it back from his brow, his attention already elsewhere. He grabbed his jacket. 'I'll see you in the atelier on Monday.'

'On Monday? But it's Saturday tomorrow. I thought we...'

'Enjoy your weekend, darlin' girl.'

Then he was gone, leaving Jasmine struggling to believe that he'd been there at all. But the soreness between her legs and the scattering of precious pearls across the floor testified that he had. She flung herself back on the battered sofa and gave in to the tears.

Over the following weeks, Jasmine lurched between joy and misery. Lachlan didn't visit her in the studio again despite promises to do so soon. Instead she had to content herself with a few stolen kisses when no one else was in the atelier and one furtive and highly uncomfortable encounter in a store cupboard, which made her feel cheap, but appeared to excite him greatly.

When she got him alone in the atelier and begged him to visit her studio, he shook his head and said, 'If you want to win the gold medal you need to spend all your free time working in preparation for it. We can't risk anyone seeing me with you and telling Old Beetle Brows that I've been giving you extra tuition. That would scupper your chances, sweetheart.'

'But I've already decided what I'm entering. The painting of Stan and the one of the bird seller. The work's done.'

He cupped her breast in his hand and kissed her softly on the mouth. 'You must never be satisfied, darlin'. You're capable of even more. I want you to show your full potential and even though you probably canna win the competition, I need you to give it your very best shot.'

'I can't paint every waking hour,' she said, hearing the tone of desperation in her voice. She didn't want to sound whining.

Lachlan shrugged. 'I thought you were serious about being a painter. But maybe you're just a hobbyist after all.'

'And I thought you were serious about me, but you never seem to want to see me.'

Lachlan wrapped his arms around her. 'I want to see you all the time. I can't stop thinking about you, hen, imagining what I'm going to do with you next time we make love.'

Jasmine shivered. She couldn't stop imagining either. The problem was there was too much imagination and not enough reality.

Every day she missed Stan more. Missed her family. Missed someone to confide in. She had hoped that would be Lachlan, but he remained elusive, declaring how much he wanted her, but telling her nothing about how he felt. And their one experience on the unsprung settee in the studio had been far from fulfilling. Jasmine longed for the luxury of a bed, where she wouldn't feel sordid and sleazy.

She raised the question of their meeting at his apartment, but Lachlan told her it was out of the question as the concierge would almost certainly spot them and he risked losing the place.

'Besides, Delphine is still there. The works she's having done are dragging on. Apparently there's a shortage of skilled craftsmen. And to tell you the truth, I'm worried sick about the old girl. She's still not in good health. It's why I need to be around so much. Please understand, darlin'. I can hardly throw a sick mother out.' He stroked her hair and kissed her again.

Jasmine, wretched, threw herself into a frenzy of work. She channelled her disappointment, her anger and her loneliness into her art. Setting aside her unfinished work portraying the *clochards* on the banks of the Seine, she turned away from everything that was around her here in Paris. She wanted to reject the city in the way she was increasingly feeling the city was rejecting her. The self-doubt had begun to cripple her ability to paint, so instead she drew on her imagination and began to work from memory.

Over the remaining weeks leading up to the competition she worked on a series of paintings recalling her time in Penang. One large canvas was a self-portrait in which she was standing at her easel in the little studio Reggie had created for her in the grounds of Bella Vista. The subject she was painting was Bintang. Painting him from memory made her sad, wistful. Her feelings for him had been so raw and real at the time but now seemed rather sweet, innocent and dreamlike. She'd been a different person then. Naive. Innocent. Trusting. The anguish and bitter-sweetness of how she'd felt about him seemed unreal now – a nostalgic echo from her adolescence. Life had seemed so complicated and difficult then – but in comparison with how she felt about her life now it had been simple.

There were several Penang paintings. Most were light and bright and bursting with colour. Village women sitting chatting as they prepared vegetables, mended clothes, fed babies. Two were much darker than the self-portrait with Bintang. Closer to the darkness that seemed to be enveloping her every day here in the city of light.

She stood in her Montparnasse studio, hands on hips,

studying the painting of Stan. The decision was clear – she
wouldn't share Stan with an audience who neither knew nor
understood him. The painting had been promised to his mother
and Jasmine didn't want to delay sending it any longer. The fact
that she believed it to be her best work was immaterial – indeed
a further reason to parcel it up and send it to Mrs Tyson at once.

Decision made, Jasmine stacked the *clochards* and the
flower seller against the wall. Her entries for the *Médaille d'Or*
would be entirely drawn from her Penang works. If the judges
of the Grand Salon didn't like them, it was too bad. She selected
four paintings, all in oils. The entry form required her to name
them for the catalogue. *Self-Portrait with Young Man, Women
at Work in the Kampong, Shot by his Comrades* and, with a
heavy heart, *Boy Mourns his Murdered Mother* – her portrayal
of her half-brother, Amir, grieving over the dead body of his
mother. Jasmine still wanted to win the gold medal but not at
the cost of her own integrity as an artist. If the committee
rejected her work, so be it. Those paintings had been hewn
from her heart and that was all there was to it.

The weekend before the painting competition, Antoine
suggested they take a picnic to the Bagatelle Gardens in the
Bois de Boulogne. It was a glorious spring day and Jasmine had
never been to the gardens before so she readily agreed. Getting
out into the sunshine and spending some time with a friend
might cheer her up.

Picnic was a dignified term for the simple lunch they
brought with them to the gardens: a baguette, a box of Pont
l'Evêque cheese, a pair of apples and a bottle of cheap *vin
ordinaire*.

They took the Métro to the Pont de Neuilly and walked
from there to the park. The Château de Bagatelle was a former

eighteenth-century hunting lodge built in sixty-three days by Marie Antoinette's brother-in-law, the Comte d'Artois, as a result of a bet she made with him that he couldn't build it within three months.

'Was he executed too, during the Revolution?' Jasmine asked Antoine.

'No. He escaped the day the Bastille was stormed. Fled to England. He bided his time until eventually everyone else was dead and Napoleon exiled, so he became King Charles X.'

'French history is so gruesome,' she said. 'All that guillotining.'

'You English did your fair share of chopping heads off monarchs. You just employed messier methods. If I had to be executed I'd rather face Madame Guillotine than be hacked at with an axe or hanged like you English.'

Jasmine shuddered. 'I can't begin to imagine how terrifying it would have been kneeling at the scaffold, waiting for the blade to fall while the crowd cheered and heckled.'

'They didn't have long to wait. They had so many aristocrats to despatch that it was like a production line.'

'Every time I walk past the Conciergerie I think of Marie Antoinette in her prison cell praying she wouldn't be executed too. Can we talk about something else, please?'

They walked around the gardens. Like much of post-war Paris they were rather neglected. The authorities were prioritising building and rebuilding homes. Sports playing fields took priority over pleasure gardens. Nonetheless, Jasmine loved the place with its tall trees, lakes, bridges, and rocks. The Comte's château with its domed roof was in need of repair, but she thought it romantic – if rather sad.

They found a spot in the sunshine near a waterlily-covered lake and sat down to eat their meal.

'This was a terrific idea, Antoine. I love picnics.' She

washed down her bread and cheese with a slug of wine. 'This cheese is delicious.'

'From Normandy,' he said, his expression smug. 'Like all good things.'

Jasmine ignored him. 'Everywhere's so much more beautiful when the sun shines.' She leaned back against the trunk of a tree, extending her legs out in front of her. 'Are you entering anything for the *Médaille d'Or?*'

'No point. I haven't a chance.'

'You don't know that.'

'It's a foregone conclusion. Giancarlo will win if anyone in our class does. But more likely someone from another atelier will.'

'That's so defeatist, Antoine. Surely you have a piece to put in? It's not fair to whoever wins if no one bothers to enter.'

'Maybe I'll chuck something in then. If it keeps you happy.' Antoine rolled onto his stomach and began chewing a blade of grass. 'What about you?'

She hesitated a moment then said, 'Actually I'm entering four pieces. They're all works I did in my own time.'

He gave a derisive laugh. 'You're mad. Is that what you've been doing every weekend? Is that why you hardly come to the cinema anymore? Why waste your time, Jasmine?' Then his expression changed as something occurred to him. 'Is Robertson giving you extra lessons?'

'Certainly not. In fact he hasn't seen any of the paintings I plan to put in.'

'You're kidding. You're sleeping with the man. You must have shown him.'

Mortified, she snapped, 'What are you talking about?'

'Don't give me that look,' he said. 'Everyone knows about the two of you.' He held his hands up, palms raised. 'Marcel is even running a book on when his wife finds out.'

Jasmine felt the ground rock under her. 'His wife? Lachlan doesn't have a wife.'

'*Merde*! Not only does he have a wife but two children and another on the way. That's probably why he's been desperate to get inside your underwear.'

She slapped him hard across the face.

'What's that for? Didn't you know? You must be the only one who doesn't. Everyone knows his reputation. He picks a girl in his atelier every year, seduces her then moves on.'

'You're making it up.' She grabbed at his arm, desperate for him to laugh and say he was pulling her leg.

'Ask anyone at the school if you don't believe me. He's married to a Frenchwoman called Hélène. She was once one of his students.'

Jasmine gasped, unable to take in what he was saying. She scrambled to her feet and ran away as fast as her legs would carry her, heedless of the tears coursing down her face. It was impossible that Lachlan was married. Unthinkable. Unbearable.

She ran until her legs gave way, then she walked, unaware of where she was going until after circling round a lake, she emerged from the Bois de Boulogne. When she saw the number 16 on a street sign she realised where she was. Panic seized her. The last place she wanted to be wandering around late on a Saturday afternoon was Passy. Bumping into either or both of the Courbets would be a terrible end to what had turned into a disastrous day. She stopped a woman and asked the way to the nearest Métro station. Ten minutes later she was clattering down the steps into La Muette.

Happily, the train wasn't crowded. Jasmine collapsed onto the wooden seat and stared blindly out of the grimy window at the dark void beyond.

Reluctant to return to the Lutèce and risk Antoine seeking

her out, she went to the studio and curled up on the battered sofa. But this was worse. She was alone but surrounded by memories of the time Lachlan had been here with her. Lying here alone in a cold warehouse was stupid. She'd be better going back to her room and refusing to answer the door if Antoine knocked.

She went into the empty *Hebdo* office to exit the building but as she reached the door it opened and Corinne walked in.

'What's wrong? You look terrible. Are you ill?' Corinne narrowed her eyes. 'You've been crying. What's happened?'

'Nothing,' she said. 'I'm going back to the Lutèce.'

But Corinne barred her way. 'Not like that. Come with me. I did something nice for someone and they gave me a bottle of cognac. A drink will make you feel better.' She took Jasmine by the arm and steered her towards the stairs up to the mezzanine.

It was like a dormitory. Three mattresses on the floor were separated from each other by washing lines draped with old threadbare sheets.

'Not much but it's home and it costs nothing thanks to the rent paid by *Hebdo* and you.' Corinne sat down on one of the mattresses and gestured to Jasmine to join her. She took the promised bottle of cognac and two chipped tumblers from a wooden fruit crate which served as storage and poured some into each glass. 'I'm sad too. My boyfriend broke with me.'

Jasmine was puzzled. Corinne had used the term *petit ami* which she knew meant boyfriend. Perhaps she'd misunderstood. She repeated the words, frowning. 'You told me you preferred women.'

Corinne smiled. 'I say that when you accused me of having an affair with your teacher.'

As soon as she mentioned Lachlan, Jasmine started to cry again.

Corinne put an arm around her. 'But never mind me. What's upsetting *you*?'

'I'm the one who was having the affair with him,' she said between sobs. 'But Antoine told me today, Lachlan's married. But it isn't true. It can't be true.' She looked at the French girl, desperately hoping for reassurance that Antoine was lying – but knowing she wasn't about to get it.

'I'm sorry you've been hurt, Jasmine. But that man is *un connard*. That painting you saw was how he tried to shame me into having sex with him. Before you are in Paris. I was modelling in his atelier and he kept asking me to stay behind. He is a handsome man but I know his type and know he is married, so I refuse. Not long after I met you I am going to see Mademoiselle Daudin to ask her to put me on the list of models for this year and I see him on the way out. He said he had something to show me and asked me to come to his atelier. He show me the painting. It was so ugly. It made me feel contaminated, dirty. He said he wanted to exhibit it and everyone would believe we were lovers so we might as well be. He tried to force himself on me, so I give him my knee in his groin and run away. That's why I never go back there. I stopped doing life modelling after that. He is not a good person.'

Jasmine stared at her in shock.

'When you accused me of having an affair with him and said you'd seen the painting, I took it out on you. I'm sorry for that.'

'Did you sit for him with your legs wide open and your head tilted back?' Jasmine still didn't want to believe it.

'Of course not. I wouldn't. All I did in his atelier – and in the other ateliers when I model there – were the usual poses. Naked, but never like that. It was pornographic. I tell you the man is horrible.' She paused and her lips tightened. 'You're not having an affair with him, Jasmine, surely not?'

'So, Antoine wasn't lying? He is married?'

'With children, as far as I know.'

Jasmine dissolved into more tears.

'Look, it's not the end of the world. We all make mistakes. Unless... you're not pregnant, are you?' Corinne looked at her with a mixture of sympathy and shock.

'No. I'm not. He made sure of that.' Jasmine began to shake.

Corinne wrapped her arms around her. 'You're not the first and you won't be the last woman to be tricked by a handsome man, but I'm very sorry.' She shook her head. 'It's my fault. I should have warned you about him. But I never expected you'd fall for him. You always seemed such an intelligent and sensible person.'

'And now you discover I'm a stupid little girl who has messed up her whole life.'

'No, you aren't, and no, you haven't. You're a beautiful, clever and talented woman who is far too strong not to come through this and learn from it. Don't let the bastard have the satisfaction of doing this to you. You're so much better than him. And a better artist. Even I can see that.' Corinne splashed more cognac into the glasses. 'Come on. Drink up. You haven't taken a sip yet. It will make you feel better. We will both get very drunk tonight. Men aren't worth crying over, *mon amie.*'

Jasmine took a sip and felt the burning warmth of the cognac course through her veins. Corinne was right. Men weren't worth crying over. She'd cried her heart out over Bintang and now over Lachlan. Neither deserved her tears.

On Monday morning Jasmine arrived at the École early and went straight to the outer office where Mademoiselle Daudin kept guard over the principal's domain beyond.

The secretary looked up at her and smiled. 'Mademoiselle Barrington, how may I help you?'

'I need to see Monsieur Rochambeau.'

The secretary raised an eyebrow. 'Is there a problem? Is it to do with the *Médaille d'Or*? I've had two students in here already asking for an extension, but tomorrow is submission day and Monsieur Rochambeau has been very clear that entries must be made by tomorrow or not at all.' She gave Jasmine a regretful smile. 'Perhaps next year you will be ready in time.'

'I'm not entering.'

The woman jerked in her chair, surprised. 'Not entering?'

'I'm leaving the school. That's why I want to see Monsieur Rochambeau.'

The secretary gazed at her in astonishment. 'Leaving? But Mademoiselle Barrington, he will not be happy to hear that. From you of all people.'

Jasmine looked down. She didn't want to have to explain herself to Mademoiselle Daudin as well as the principal. All she wanted was for this to be over so she could make the arrangements to return to Nairobi and admit to Evie and Arthur that it had all been a mistake.

'I know I should be grateful to be here and that Monsieur Rochambeau believes I shouldn't be, so it's better I admit defeat now, rather than wait to be humiliated.'

Mademoiselle Daudin got up from behind her desk. 'Wait here.' She knocked on the principal's door and went inside, shutting it behind her.

Jasmine stood in front of the desk. The ashtray was already full despite the early hour – Mademoiselle was a prodigious smoker. She looked around her at the neatly-stacked shelves, the framed photograph of a couple that appeared to be from the turn of the century, presumably the secretary's parents in their youth.

The door opened. 'He'll see you now.'

Inside the professor's study for only the second time, Jasmine was nervous. Rochambeau was standing in front of the window, which gave onto a small paved courtyard with a tree at its centre. She didn't dare sit down.

'My secretary informs me you wish to leave the École and

that you will not be entering for the *Médaille d'Or*.' His tone indicated suppressed anger.

'I'm grateful for the chance to attend the school and for your agreeing to admit me even though you consider my work doesn't merit it. I've tried to do my best and I'm sorry it's not good enough.'

He turned to look at her, his heavy eyebrows meeting in a deep frown. 'What are you talking about?'

'I know you agreed to admit me against your better judgement. I truly believed I could prove you wrong but I realise I can't, so it's better I leave now.'

Rochambeau moved to the other side of his large oak desk and sat down. He waved a hand for her to do the same. All Jasmine wanted to do was get this over with and make her escape. She perched on the edge of the chair like a nervous sparrow.

'And what makes you think you have to prove me wrong, Miss Barrington? You think I am a poor judge of talent?'

The blood rushed to her face and her palms were sweating. She laid them flat on her thighs and swallowed, wishing she weren't so crippled by nerves in his presence. 'No, sir. I'm sure you are very good judge. That's why I'm leaving. It's pointless for me to keep trying to prove you wrong.'

His frown deepened. 'And you know exactly what I'm thinking, do you? Are you blessed with psychic powers?'

This was not going the way she had predicted. All she wanted was to get the ordeal over.

'Of course not. But Mr Robertson said——'

'Ah, Mr Robertson. I thought he might have something to do with this.'

'I know he has tried to convince you of the quality of my work, but——'

'But he has told you I am blind to it?'

She twisted her hands together. Looking up, she saw he was still frowning and anger swept through her. Telling herself it no longer mattered what this man thought of her, she said, 'Yes. I know you never wanted to admit me to the École. I know you dislike me because I am female and British and come from the colonies. I can't help who I am or where I was born, and I've worked as hard as I possibly can. Harder than anyone else in my atelier. I've given everything to this. Every weekend I've spent painting. Every moment I can. I had four pieces ready to enter the *Médaille d'Or*. But I've gone as far as I can and I realise I'll never be able to overcome your prejudice.' Emotion welled up inside like hot lava. 'I'm desperately unhappy here. So, what's the point of carrying on? Better to stop now after this first year. I miss my family. I'm so lonely and feel utterly miserable.' She broke into tears, fumbling in her satchel for her handkerchief. 'May I go now, please?'

'No, Miss Barrington, you may not.'

He was cruel to prolong her torment. She wiped her eyes.

'I wish to see the four works you'd intended to enter for the prize. You can show me now.' He leaned forward, about to get up from behind the desk.'

'They're not here. I did them in my own studio.'

'And where might that be?'

She told him it was in Montparnasse.

Rochambeau rang a bell on his desk and Mademoiselle Daudin reappeared.

'Make some time in my agenda for today. You can postpone the syllabus review meeting until later in the week. I will be going to view Miss Barrington's work.'

Jasmine gasped. 'You want to see my work?'

'I'd like to know whether it is of a similar standard to the work you have done in Robertson's atelier.'

She stared at him. 'You've seen my work?'

'Of course. I see everyone's. That is my job.' He bent over the diary Mademoiselle Daudin was holding out to him. 'Three o'clock.' He tapped the page, then turned to address Jasmine. 'Leave the address with Mademoiselle Daudin and I will see you there later.'

Scarcely able to breathe, Jasmine did as instructed then rushed out of the school. Why, if he thought her work so poor, was he bothering to cancel a meeting in order to visit her studio? Was he a sadist who enjoyed humiliating students? She needed to get back to ensure all the work was displayed in its best light.

The *Hebdo* office was a hive of activity – today being press day. Corinne was sitting behind a battered typewriter, hammering away with two fingers. She looked up when Jasmine entered. 'How did it go?'

'I don't know.'

'*Tiens*! You must know. Did you speak to the principal?'

'Yes.'

'*Alors*?'

'He's coming here this afternoon. He wants to see the pieces I'd been intending to enter.'

Corinne leaned back in her chair. 'Did he say why? How did he react when you told him you were leaving?'

'It was all very confusing. He said he'd seen my work in the atelier. When I said there was no point in me keeping trying to impress him he accused me of trying to read his mind.'

Corinne grinned. 'He must like it then.'

'But why did Lachlan tell me the man has it in for me?'

'Why do you think – all part of his plan to make you in thrall to him.'

'But—'

'Don't say but. You'd better get ready for the great man's arrival. What time will he be here?'

'Three.'

'I'll let him in. I'll make sure we keep the noise down while he's here.'

Jasmine gave Corinne a hug. 'Thank you so much.'

Rochambeau stood in front of the canvas depicting the death of Amir's mother, his hands clasped behind his back. The scene depicted was in sunlight, the grass a vivid green under a cloud-less blue sky, the tall trees surrounding the lawn a darker dapple of green. In stark contrast, Nayla's body lay on on the ground, the purple of her *cheongsam* blackened with the blood from her chest. Beside her corpse, Lieutenant Ellis in khaki shorts stood with a box camera to his eye as he captured an image of his own handiwork. But the focus of the painting was a diminutive figure in white, Jasmine's half-brother, Amir, gazing down in disbelief at his mother's dead body.

'You witnessed this?' said Rochambeau, looking shocked. Jasmine nodded.

He moved on, muttering under his breath, examining the portraits of Bintang and stopping in front of the painting of the villagers at the *kampong*. The expanse of ground here was bare, painted in browns and ochres, surrounded by a dense wall of trees. Jasmine had painted the women in close-up, a group of simple shapes, wearing colourful garments, heads veiled. Their cross-legged posture created a pattern of outlines and colours as the women squatted on the bare ground with baskets of fruit and vegetables around them, while in the background children were at play.

Jasmine was increasingly nervous as the principal studied each painting in turn but said nothing.

Eventually he turned to look at her. 'Miss Barrington, has your tutor seen this work?'

'Some of it. Not all.'

Rochambeau shook his head.

Jasmine held her breath, waiting for him to tell her she was right to give up her hopes of an artistic career.

'Your work reminds me so much of Amrita's.' He shook his head again. 'An exceptional understanding of form and colour. Simplicity of composition. Symmetry. You have an ability to capture an individual in a portrait so that one feels one is looking inside and seeing their soul.' He gestured at the painting of Stan, which she had moved to the corner out of the way, ready to parcel up. 'This one. I look at it and see pain in the young man's eyes. Sadness... Quite exceptional. Are you entering this too?'

'Not that one. It's promised to his mother.' Jasmine's words were barely above a whisper, scarcely able to digest what Rochambeau was saying. 'Who did you say my work reminds you of?'

'A friend of mine. She died. Far too young. Only twenty-eight.' To Jasmine's surprise, his eyes brimmed with tears. 'Amrita studied at the Beaux-Arts and was the most outstanding student of her year. She won the *Médaille d'Or* three years in a row and was accepted into the Grand Salon. Her death was a tragic loss.'

'Amrita? She was Indian?'

'Half Indian, half Hungarian. Amrita Sher-Gil.'

Jasmine had never heard of her but didn't like to admit it.

'She was a stunning beauty. Broke a lot of hearts.' He shrugged. 'Including mine to tell the truth.'

'When did she die?'

'During the war. 1941. Nothing to do with the war though. She was living in India at the time. It was very sudden. I still find it hard to believe.' He coughed and moved back to look again at the paintings. 'Like you Amrita had a strong sense of form and colour. I think that's why she went to India. She wasn't born there but she had an affinity for the place and her work there was freer and bolder and simpler. My most treasured possession is a small portrait of the woman who eventually became my wife.'

He moved across the room to where Jasmine's Paris paintings leaned against the wall. He examined each in turn. 'Very good but lacking the vibrancy of the others. I think you respond more to the colours of the tropics, *oui*?'

Dumbstruck, she nodded.

'Nonetheless they are exceptional works. This one in particular.' He indicated the old woman from the Marché des Oiseaux. 'A beautiful sensitive portrait.'

Rochambeau looked at his watch. 'I must go. But before I do, Miss Barrington, I want you to promise me you will enter these works in the competition.'

'You think they're good enough?'

'No more false modesty. You must know yourself that they are.'

'But Mr Robertson—'

'Is a good teacher but a man constrained by his own shortcomings. He will never be more than a competent artist himself.' He sniffed. 'His work is derivative. He can be jealous of students whose natural talents are self-evident.' He sighed. 'I had misgivings about assigning you to his atelier. If I had understood your talent for French would prove almost the equal of your talent for painting I would have put you elsewhere. We tend to give Robertson the English speakers. I see how he has shattered your confidence. Was he scathing about your work?'

'No.' Jasmine hesitated, then her anger at Lachlan rose inside her. 'No. He told me it was good but that you didn't agree. He said he had to constantly fight on my behalf.'

Rochambeau narrowed his eyes. 'Really? *Au contraire*. Now I must go. I expect to see those paintings again tomorrow. I hope you will reconsider your decision to leave. If you do, I am minded to move you to another atelier next year. One of our former students, Bernard Cathelin, would be a very good teacher for you. His style is different, but he shares your feeling for colour. He has been teaching here since he graduated.' He put on his hat and with a nod, left the studio.

After he'd gone, Jasmine slipped onto the settee in a dazed state. Had that all really happened?

NINETEEN
STATE OF JOHORE

May 1950

Since Betty had told Howard about the job offer in Sydney, there'd been an unspoken tension between them. Life here without her was a grim prospect, but something made him reluctant to raise the subject. He had the clear impression Betty was hoping he would suggest marriage but Howard didn't feel certain enough to take that step. After all, they'd known each other less than six months. It felt wrong to discourage her from pursuing what was clearly a tempting job offer, but equally wrong to be catapulted into marriage with undue haste. Why did she want to rush things? Yet Howard knew it was unreasonable to encourage her to turn the job down if there was a possibility he wouldn't eventually propose.

He lay on his bed, staring up at the ceiling fan, retreading the same ground in a loop of ever-repeating thoughts. Betty was a wonderful girl. She was fun to be with. She'd brightened his life and he found her attractive. Easy to talk to, she was down-to-earth, and they had so much in common. Why then was he hesitating?

But it was nothing to do with Betty. It was everything to do with him. His hesitation wasn't due to any doubts that she would be a good wife, that he could make her happy and they could build a life together. Rather it was the sense of pressure, of being pushed prematurely into marriage when he wanted to move at his own pace.

If he didn't grab his chance now, he risked losing Betty forever. He'd be unable to stand in the way of her returning to Sydney and he'd probably spend the rest of his life regretting her slipping through his fingers. Time was moving on. If he didn't act soon, it would be too late.

He thought of Alan and old Carter, lonely bachelors hanging out at the club with no one to go home to. Or Flory in *Burmese Days* who destroyed his chance of marriage and ended up killing himself.

Howard turned over and punched his fist into the pillow. He hated being cornered. Eyes closed, he tried to picture himself walking down the aisle with Betty, sitting across the table from her as she served him a meal, having children with her. But no matter how hard he tried to see Betty, however clearly he fixed her image in his mind's eye, it always morphed into an image of Jasmine.

He had always intended to wait for Jasmine. Even though she'd told him it was pointless. Even though she'd not written him a single letter since she went to Paris. Deep inside, he continued to harbour a faint hope that once she finished her studies they'd meet again and she'd feel differently. It was probably folly. But he had to accept that he couldn't possibly marry Betty when he was in love with someone else. It wouldn't be fair on her. Yet he couldn't let things drift – he owed her an explanation.

His mind made up, he drifted off into a troubled sleep.

· · ·

Steam was coming off the jeep's armour plating as Howard drove through the torrential rain. The inside was like an over-heating boiler and he brushed the sweat away from his brow. As he drove, he mentally rehearsed what he would say to Betty in the club that night. He had no desire to hurt her feelings, but he wasn't going to be dragooned by guilt into such a life-changing decision. If she decided to go back to Sydney, he'd be disap-pointed, and would miss her dreadfully, but so be it. Howard believed marriage was forever and he had to be sure first.

He was on his way to a local security meeting in Segamat. While he understood the need for these regular meetings and considered them essential, today he'd have preferred not to have this diversion. Since the displacement of the people from the squatter camp, rendering them out of reach of the insurgents, Alan had told Howard that he suspected there was an infiltrator among the Chinese tappers. Accessing ordinary people and coercing them into giving food and money was vital to the survival of the communists, whose camps were deep in the jungle. Howard himself believed Alan was mistaken but he needed to investigate. Having insurgents or members of the *Min Yuen* among the workforce would defeat the purpose of the new villages.

The rain rendered visibility poor, and Howard had to drive at a slower speed than he would have liked. It was never wise to dawdle on these roads where an ambush could be waiting around every corner.

As he rounded a bend, he saw in front of him at an angle partly blocking the road, a small white truck with a Red Cross painted on the sides. He slammed on the brakes, steering into the inevitable skid. Just ahead of the truck, in the middle of the road, lay the body of a British soldier.

Ambush. Were there still bandits waiting and watching? Then he recognised the registration of the medical van. It was

Betty's. Abandoning caution, he grabbed his pistol and dashed through the driving rain towards the vehicle.

The driver was slumped forward over the steering wheel, a patch of bright red marking the exit wound in the back of her head, the hair around a blood-soaked mess. Howard's heart almost stopped.

Betty. Dead.

Rain blurring his vision, he felt for a pulse but there was nothing. It looked as though she'd been killed instantly. He let out a groan of anguish.

He looked past the body, then ran round to the other side of the truck. An angry voice came from the footwell. 'Do it! Get it over with. Kill me if you're going to, you bloody commie cowards.' Howard cried Betty's name in a flood of relief and emotion. He jerked the door open. She was tucked down into the footwell, convulsed in blind terror. He squatted down and reached for her, taking her hand in his. 'It's all right, Betty. It's me, Howard. Come with me. We have to get out of here before they come back.'

'No!' Her breathing was ragged and her upper body shaking. 'Charlene. You have to help Charlene.'

'She's beyond our help. Bullet through the head. Betty, for God's sake, we have to get out of here. My jeep's just behind.'

Betty was weeping but put up no resistance as he lifted her and carried her to his jeep. He gunned the engine and moved forward, skirting past the Red Cross truck and the body in the road. 'We have to get to Segamat and raise the alarm. The army or the police will pick up the bodies.'

Beside him Betty sobbed quietly.

Eventually, when she'd calmed a little, he asked what had happened. 'Where did the dead soldier come from? Was he travelling with you?'

'No. The army guys showed up later. There were only two bandits. We came round the corner and they jumped out in front of us so we had to stop.' She wiped the back of her hand across her eyes. 'They wanted medicines. Nurses have to help people no matter what side they're on. We were going to hand over bandages, disinfectant, that sort of thing. And then the army truck came along. A Tommy was driving, and the passenger was that horrible creepy officer. You know the one. Always trying to get into the girls' knickers.' Her voice oozed contempt.

'Ellis,' he said. 'What happened next?'

'Ellis takes a pot at one of the CTs and gets one of them in the knee. The injured guy's screaming and shouting. The other guy takes aim at Ellis but Ellis shoves the Tommy out of the jeep so the bandit mows the poor bastard down. But now Ellis is in the driving seat. He spins the jeep round and buggers off.'

'He left you there?'

'Yes. Then a helicopter went over and the bandits must have thought it was after them as they starting shouting at each other. I couldn't see as I'd ducked down when they shot the soldier, but Charlene was about to try and drive us out of it. The wounded bandit shot her. Then you showed up. I thought you were them coming back to kill me.'

'Thank God for the helicopter.'

Betty started crying again. 'It should have been me. Charlene only drove today as I had a letter from home and wanted to read it. She hates driving. It should have been me. It's my fault.' Her sobbing intensified.

By now they'd turned onto a wide open road with no potential ambush spots, so Howard pulled over to the side and took Betty into his arms. 'It's all right now. It's over. You're safe.' He stroked the top of her head and held her against his chest. 'It's not your fault, Betty. Blame the men who shot Charlene. And Ellis for abandoning you both.' He dropped a kiss on the top of her head, overcome with relief that it wasn't her draped over the steering wheel of the medical truck with her brains blown out.

In that moment he told himself he loved her. He lifted her chin up and kissed her slowly. 'Will you marry me, Betty?'

After dropping Betty at the hostel in Segamat where the Australian nurses and teachers lived, Howard drove straight to the security meeting. It was held in the police station and chaired by the local police chief. The attendees were other policemen, an army sergeant, a man who he surmised was from Special Branch and an assortment of planters. Ellis was on his feet, holding forth.

Howard stood in the doorway, unobserved, listening in disbelief as the newly-appointed captain recounted a very different story from the one Betty had just told. He painted himself as the hero of the hour, claiming to have single-hand-edly chased the bandits into the jungle.

'Has he mentioned the dead soldier he left in the middle of the road and the nurses he abandoned to their fate?' Howard said, trying to control his anger.

Ellis looked round, his face distorting into a scowl when he saw it was Howard.

'Go on, Ellis, tell everyone exactly what happened. How you ran away like the coward you are.'

'How dare you? You weren't even there. And it's *Captain* Ellis.' Ellis looked around him as though expecting someone to back him up.

'I *was* there – on my way here from Redmond.'

The other men were staring at Ellis, who said, 'Then you'll know there was nothing more I could do. Corporal Browning was dead.' He looked in appeal at the men round the table. 'Apparently this idiot thinks I should have got out of my jeep and let the Chinks murder me too.' He stood up and opened his arms wide indicating he was a target.

Howard moved further into the room. 'Corporal Browning

was dead because this man pushed him out of the jeep to distract the bandits while he made his getaway. And what about the nurses? Tell everyone how you left them to the mercy of the terrorists while you saved your own skin.'

'What nurses?' Again, Ellis looked around at the audience of men, all of whom were frowning.

'The ones in the bloody great white van with the red crosses painted on the sides.' Howard fixed the man with a gimlet stare. 'One of them, the driver, had her brains blown out as you were driving away. The other survived, but no thanks to you. If a passing RAF helicopter hadn't put the wind up the bandits, she'd be dead too. And she happens to be my fiancée.'

A murmur went round the table.

Howard's anger could no longer be contained. Ever since he'd first set eyes on Ellis, he'd loathed the man. 'Where women are concerned you've got form, Ellis. Remember the Malayan woman you shot dead in front of her eight-year-old son at the Hyde-Underwoods' place on Penang? Your motto seems to be shoot first, ask questions later. Remember Miss Barrington, a guest of the Hyde-Underwoods, who you tried to assault?' Howard moved towards the captain, planting his hands on the table. 'You should have been court-martialled then, but the army evidently looks after their own as they sent you here and promoted you. But I'm about to make some phone calls, if Police Sergeant Must bin Ahmad will kindly let me use his telephone. Your card's been marked for a long time, Ellis, but this time I'll make it my business to ensure you don't get away with it.'

Ellis got to his feet so quickly he knocked his chair over. Kicking it out of his way, he moved to the door. He stopped and pushed his face into Howard's so Howard took the undiluted force of his foul breath. 'I'll get you, Baxter. Maybe not today or tomorrow, but I'll get you. Watch your step because I'll be waiting for you.'

Howard stepped back to create some much-needed

distance. 'Are you threatening me, Captain? I hope you all heard that, gentlemen.'

With his face contorted in contempt, Ellis pushed past him and left the station. The sound of his jeep driving away at speed penetrated the room.

'Right,' said Howard. 'That phone, Police Sergeant?' He turned to the army sergeant, 'Would you mind joining us, Sergeant? I need your help regarding who to ask for at divisional HQ.'

When Howard got back to Redmond later that day, he had no chance to tell his deputy, Alan, about the events on the road to Segamat or how he'd reported Captain Ellis to his commanding officer and taken Betty to make a formal statement to the police, as requested by Lieutenant Colonel Rochester. He didn't even get round to mentioning that he'd proposed to Betty and she'd agreed to marry him. As soon as he walked into the estate office, all eyes were on him.

'What's wrong? What's happened?'

Alan's mouth formed itself into a grim line. 'There's no easy way to say this, *Tuan*, but it's bad news. Your father had a heart attack and I'm sorry to tell you he passed away. Guthrie's have been on the blower and you have compassionate leave. The office in Singapore is arranging a flight to Colombo for you. You need to get yourself there as soon as you can.'

Howard stared at Alan. It made no sense. His father was invincible, indestructible.

'Sit down. Drink this.' Alan handed him a brandy. 'You must be shocked.' One of the junior staff jumped up and offered his seat to the *tuan*. 'I'm so sorry, sir. Was he very old?

'Sixty, I think. Or maybe fifty-nine. I'm not sure.' He swallowed, numb. 'When did it happen?'

'Early this morning,' said Alan. 'That's all we know.'

'My mother...'

'Is there anyone else at home? Any other family?'

'Just the servants. My sisters live in England.'

'Then it's good that you can get there quickly to be with her.'

'Right,' said Howard, still in shock. He slugged the brandy back. 'I'd better pack a bag.'

TWENTY

PARIS

May 31st, 1950

On the day of the preview exhibition for the prize-giving, Jasmine was leaving the Lutèce, when the concierge told her she had a letter.

It was from Mary. Shorter than her usual detailed epistles, as though written in a hurry. She read as she walked, smiling at the mentions of Frances and Amir, and the enclosed photograph of Amir giving his little sister a piggyback. Mary had signed the letter and then added a postscript:

Reggie's just received some news this afternoon via the Guthrie's bush telegraph. Howard Baxter has lost his father. Heart attack. Poor chap heard just after he got engaged to be married to an Australian nurse. I know you haven't been in touch since you went to Paris but I did get the sense before you left Penang that you'd become pals, so I thought you might want to send condolences and congratulations. So rotten for the poor man to have such terrible news just when things had started looking up for him. Goodness knows when the wedding will happen – I

imagine they'll feel obliged to postpone until his mother is able to
face it. So sad. He's flown to Ceylon to sort out the funeral and
support Mrs Baxter and I don't have the address. I'll forward it
when I hear from him, but meanwhile if you want to drop him a
line I'd suggest writing, care of Guthrie's in London or
Singapore.

Jasmine stopped dead. Howard was getting married. Howard, the man who had declared his love for her within hours of their meeting when her ship docked in Colombo. Howard, the man who'd embarrassed her by giving her a recording of *When You Were Sweet Sixteen*. Howard who had saved her life when a terrorist had been about to shoot her. Howard, without whom she'd be dead and buried.

She ought to be happy for him, so why did she feel like she'd been punched in the stomach? Then she felt awful because of his father dying. With a sudden rush of emotion, she remembered the afternoon they'd spent at the beach when he'd told her his father resented him for being alive when his older brother had been killed in the war. As he'd opened up and told her his feelings about being in his adored older brother's shadow and how he had always been a disappointment to his dad, she'd felt close to him for the first time. A lifetime ago. She'd been a child then. Now she was a woman who'd been seduced and deceived. Now she was older and wiser. But she felt what was akin to grief in the knowledge that Howard now belonged to someone else.

It wasn't as if she were interested in Howard herself. Of course she wasn't. Hadn't she spent most of the time whenever she was with him thinking about how much he irritated her by being such a know-all, for being too handsome for his own good, and for being groaningly corny – especially about his feelings for her?

But today, on a cloudy morning in early June, alone in Paris, she could imagine nothing nicer than Howard being beside her as she trudged towards the École and the judgement of the *Médaille d'Or*. To have Howard beside her, encouraging her, looking at her paintings and declaring them all to be stunning – not because they were – but because she'd painted them. To have someone here beside her who saw her for who she was – without assessing her artistic and bohemian credentials. Someone with whom she didn't have to pretend. Someone who might have loved her – and yes, perhaps, someone, if she'd given herself the chance, she might have loved back.

She dug her fingernails into her palms. What a fool she was. Why was it only now when Howard was beyond her reach that she was entertaining the possibility she might love him? What was wrong with her? Other people fell in love and married in a completely straightforward uncomplicated way. Antoine for example – maybe he'd had adventures with other women but he'd been sure all along that he wanted to spend his life with Françoise. Evie and Arthur. Mary and Reggie.

Then Jasmine remembered Stan and his tragic love affair with Jeff. That had been anything but straightforward. Or the nasty and cynical *mariage de convenance* of Bernard and Claudine Courbet. Corinne's recent breakup. And most of all, Lachlan Robertson cheating on his wife and family. Maybe failed relationships were the norm. It was another reason to throw herself entirely into her art.

Even if today, at the judgement of the gold medal, her work was overlooked, she would go on. Perhaps not here in Paris where she felt stifled, sad, out of place. But in Nairobi or Penang. Many great painters never even went to art school at all – Jasmine remembered that first conversation with Lachlan when he'd told her about Henri Rousseau. He'd never had so much as a day's schooling. And hadn't she been happy painting in her studio-shed at Bella Vista – happier than she'd ever been here in Paris?

No matter what happened today, she decided she would dedicate the rest of her life to painting.

As for Howard, what had changed? She hadn't been in touch with him for months. She'd already consigned him to history. That he was getting married to someone else didn't matter, to her. Did it? But she wished Mary hadn't dropped that little bombshell into her letter.

Jasmine's nerves were raw as she entered the school's exhibition gallery. She hadn't seen Lachlan, having avoided going into the École since Antoine's revelations. The last thing she wanted was to run into him now, when the entire school and most of the Paris art establishment was gathered for the vernissage.

Entering the large space, she gasped at the sight of her work hanging on the wall opposite. Her canvases were larger than most of the entries from the other first-year students. To her delight and amazement people were clustered in front of them.

Antoine emerged from the throng and approached her, 'Hello, stranger, are you still avoiding me?' He touched her arm in a conciliatory gesture. 'I want to apologise. I honestly thought you must have known. When you reacted like that I realised you didn't. I'm truly sorry, Jasmine. I hope you'll forgive me.'

'How could you think I'd have an affair with a married man?' Her mouth formed a tight line. 'It feels like you don't know me at all.'

Antoine looked down, his expression rueful.

'Were they really taking bets about his wife finding out?'

He nodded. 'I'm sorry.'

Her lip trembled so she took a large intake of breath. 'I feel such an idiot for believing him.' She glanced across the room and realised her fellow students were all looking at her, sniggering and nudging each other, clearly talking about her. Anger bubbled up inside her. Heart thumping and adrenaline coursing through her veins, she was about to cross the room to challenge them, when she felt a tap on her arm. She spun round to find Monsieur Rochambeau standing there with another man whose face she recognised from the corridors of the school.

'Allow me to introduce you. Miss Jasmine Barrington, Monsieur Bernard Cathelin. Bernard, you must come and see Miss Barrington's work.' Taking each of them by the elbow the principal steered them across the gallery towards the painting of the Malayan village women.

Out of the corner of her eye, Jasmine saw Antoine staring at them with his mouth open in astonishment.

The next hour passed in a blur as various people pressed forward to meet her and discuss her paintings. Other teachers, gallery owners, critics and patrons. Jasmine had no time to take in the significance of it because as soon as one person moved away another was waiting to speak to her.

She was answering questions about her work from a critic for a fine art magazine when a voice behind her said, 'If you're writing this up, Pierre, I hope you're going to mention that Miss Barrington is my protegée. She's come on remarkably well since joining my atelier, haven't you, Jasmine?' Lachlan put a proprietorial arm around her shoulder. She wanted to say it was no thanks to him but, with no opportunity for her to explain, the art critic would deem her arrogant. Instead, she shrugged Lachlan's hand off her shoulder and said nothing.

Surprise turned to annoyance on Lachlan's face. He continued to stand there, butting in to reply on her behalf as the critic attempted to ask her questions.

Eventually the man took a card from his breast-pocket and handed it to Jasmine. 'Perhaps you'd like to come to the office and we can talk properly. I'd very much like to feature you in my column on emerging talent. Meanwhile, I wish you good fortune in the competition.' He gave her a little bow and moved away.

Lachlan grabbed her arm and pushed her towards the door. 'We need to talk.'

Unable to resist without causing a scene in the crowded gallery, Jasmine allowed him to steer her out of the room. A door led from the corridor to a small courtyard. Lachlan opened it and they went outside.

'What the hell was that about? Why were you so rude? After all I've done for you. Pierre Lafitte is an eminent critic. What must he have thought? And if it hadn't been for me, Rochambeau would have never agreed to you getting four works hung.' He was still gripping her arm.

'Take your hands off me. You can stop right there. I know everything. I'm no longer the docile little girl, grateful for every word that comes out of your lying mouth. Did you honestly think I'd never find out?'

Lachlan brushed a hand through his hair, assumed a puzzled frown and changed the timbre of his voice to a softer more conciliatory tone. 'I dinnae ken what you're on aboot.'

'Do I have to list it all? Let's start with Monsieur Rochambeau and how you told me he didn't want me in the École and was going to have me thrown out.'

Lachlan raised his palms up. 'All true, hen. The man's not reasonable, but you can see I won him round. Otherwise you'd never have been in the show today.'

'Apart from the flower seller, you'd never even seen those paintings before. The reason they're on the wall is because Monsieur Rochambeau came to my studio and asked me to enter them.'

Lachlan's jaw dropped.

'You led me to believe that you were the only person who saw my talent. You did that while at the same time undermining my confidence in my work. But that wasn't enough, was it? You also undermined my confidence in myself as a woman. You lied to me. You concealed the fact you have a wife. A *pregnant* wife. You are despicable.'

'Aw, Jasmine, you're blethering. Yer off yer head.' He made a snorting sound. 'Look, you knew it was only sex, hen. I made ye nae promises.'

'Only sex? You're beneath contempt. You knew I'd never have had anything to do with you if I'd known you were married. That you have children. How could you? I was a virgin and you took away more than that. You destroyed my respect for myself and you ruined my faith in human nature.' Tears of anger threatened but she was determined not to break down in front of him. 'Did you know the whole atelier knew about us? They were laughing at me. That's why I told Rochambeau I was leaving. I expected him to be pleased. Turns out he wasn't.'

'Ye didna tell him about us sleeping together?' He looked uncomfortable, even anxious.

'Sleeping? There wasn't any sleeping. You treated me like a prostitute. So no, I didn't tell him that, I still have a vestige of self-respect. But I told him you'd explained that he wanted me out of the École. Turns out that was a tissue of lies. I'm going home to Nairobi for the rest of the term because I can't stand to be a minute longer in the same place as you. If after the summer break I decide to come back I will be joining Bernard Cathelin's atelier. Goodbye Lachlan. You broke my heart but somehow I think I'm going to recover very quickly.'

Lachlan tried to grab her arm, but she stepped away. She went back into the school leaving him standing there, slack-jawed, looking after her.

It was the first time Jasmine had been inside the Salle de Prix for a prize giving. The student body and staff were crowded into the semicircular space. The main attraction was the announcement of the winner of the *Prix de Rome*, which would be at the end of the proceedings.

She sat at the back, apart from the other students from her atelier, hoping she would be able to slip away unobserved when the session was over. It was impossible not to marvel at being in this room, gazing down at the brilliantly colourful *hemicycle* that followed the curved wall of the room. She shivered in the knowledge of all the great artists who had sat here on these wooden seats, waiting like her to hear the judgements on their talent.

The first honour went to Bernard Cathelin. The applause was deafening when he was called forth to accept the Florence Blumenthal prize. The American benefactress had established a foundation to reward and nurture French creativity and foster cultural exchanges between France and the United States. The young Beaux-Arts teacher looked astonished as he went up to be formally presented. The annual award – a cash prize of six thousand francs for two years – was awarded across literature, painting, sculpture, decorative arts, engraving and music, so Cathelin's win as a painter was an exceptional honour for both him and the École. Cathelin looked stunned but gratified. Jasmine got to her feet with the crowd to applaud. On the far side of the *hemicycle*, she noticed Lachlan. His expression was as stern as the stone statues in the Grand Cour. He's jealous of his colleague, she thought. Good.

She turned her head away, not wanting this special occasion to be marred by thoughts of her former tutor. The longing for home and family was now unbearable. For normality and stability – and for clean sheets, hot water and people with no hidden agendas. There were only four weeks of term left and Monsieur Rochambeau had agreed to her cutting it short. 'You've done more than enough to justify your inclusion next year. Enjoy the summer, Miss Barrington and take time to think. I hope when you've had some time with your family, you will be ready to return to us in September.'

Lost in thought as she was, she almost missed her name being called out from the podium in front of the *hemicycle*. The gold medal. Her painting of the Malayan villagers had been judged the best in her year. Stunned, she went forward to accept the honour. She glanced to where Lachlan had been sitting, but he was no longer there.

Two days after winning the *Médaille d'Or*, Jasmine left by train for Marseille, where she was to join a ship for Mombasa. But first she wanted to see Stan. He was living in a small coastal town about thirty-five kilometres from Marseille as the guest of two women friends he'd known when they'd lived in Paris. A train from Marseille stopped there and Jasmine had written to Stan to ask him to arrange for her to stay in an *auberge*.

She'd left her artworks and some of her belongings in Paris, storing them in the studio in Montparnasse. She'd paid Corinne rent in advance for the entire summer in order to store it and to ensure she retained the studio in case she decided to return for the second year at the École. While she was far from certain she would return, at least it kept her options open and should she change her mind she could arrange for her things to be shipped out to her.

When she arrived at the station in La Ciotat, Stan was waiting for her on the platform, a beaming smile on his face. He wrapped her up in a tight hug then insisted on carrying her suitcases.

'Oh, Stan, lovely Stan, I've missed you so much. Let me get a good look at you.'

He released her from the hug and she took a step back and studied him.

'You look a whole lot healthier and happier than the last time I saw you. Evidently being down here suits you,' she said.

'I'm not disagreeing with that, Jazz. Everything's much less complicated here. Beryl and Flora, the women I'm lodging with, treat me as a surrogate son and spoil me. I'm writing every day and the words are flowing like never before. I've almost finished the first draft of my book.'

Jasmine clasped her hands in delight. 'That's wonderful news. And you don't get bored here?'

'Not at all. I've developed a taste for long walks in the hills and around the Calanques.'

'What're the Calanques?'

Between here and Marseille – rocky coves and inlets in the limestone cliffs. Apparently, they're like fjords but as I've never seen a fjord it's not that helpful.'

'I've never seen a fjord either.' She laughed then said again, 'It's super to be with you again, Stan.'

'Has it been bad?' His voice was concerned.

'Terrible.' She gave him a rueful look. 'I messed things up completely.'

'Don't tell me. The teacher.'

She nodded.

'We need to find a nice harbour view and a glass of something cool then you can tell Uncle Stan all about it.

Half an hour later, having deposited her bags at the harbour-front *auberge*, they were sipping ice cold *citrons pressés*. Stan told her he barely drank alcohol these days. 'I don't miss it. I feel fitter and healthier – mind as well as body.' He smiled. 'I blamed Paris for my state of mind. But I've come to realise it was my state of mind that made me hate Paris. Here there are no complications, few temptations.' He laughed. 'I'm like a monk. I write and walk every day. Just fresh air, the sea smashing against the rocks, open skies, people who are warm-hearted but let you live without judging – everyone minds their own business. It's calm, quiet, and I can focus on writing without all the distractions. And do you know, Jazz, I find such solace in getting the words on the page. It had come to be a chore in Paris. Here it gives me joy.' He took a sip of his drink and lit a cigarette. 'Enough about me. Let's hear all about what's happened with that man. I've a feeling it doesn't have a happy ending.'

So, she told him. As she shared her humiliations with him, some of the burden lifted from her. He reached across the table and squeezed her small white hand in his large black one. 'I'm sorry you had to go through that.'

'It wasn't all bad though,' she said brightly and told him about Monsieur Rochambeau and how she'd won the *Médaille d'Or*.

'Hell, Jazz! You saved that till last, girl? You're a wonder. Didn't I tell you, you'd got talent? And that reminds me, did you ever send that painting to my mom?'

'Of course.'

'Just wait till I write and tell her she has a work of art by a gold medal winner at the best art school in the world!' He punched one fist into the palm of his hand. 'Beryl and Flora want you to come to eat with us tonight. When they hear that, they're going to want to crack open a bottle of champagne. You're going to love those old gals.'

That evening they enjoyed a delicious bouillabaisse prepared by Beryl, a plump American of middle years with a passion for French cooking. Flora was a tall thin Scotswoman who chain-smoked and played the piano. Both welcomed Jasmine with warmth and urged her to visit them again when she returned to France. After the two women retired to bed, Stan walked Jasmine back to her hotel.

'You're suddenly quiet,' he said. 'What's up?'

'I'm just sad about saying goodbye. And I was thinking of something else that's happened and feeling sad about that too.'

'Come on, girl, you can't drop that into the conversation without telling me more. How about we have a nightcap by the harbour?'

She nodded, reluctant for the evening to end.

They went to a quiet bar on the waterfront where they sat at a small metal table by the water's edge. The evening was warm but with a gentle breeze coming from the Mediterranean.

'So, what gives?' asked Stan once they had ordered.

'There was someone. Before I came to Paris. I met him on the boat to Penang. I convinced myself I didn't like him, but...'

'But you liked him more than you felt comfortable about?'

'Exactly! How did you know that? I didn't even work that out myself until it was too late.'

Stan nodded. 'Go on.'

She stared past the bobbing boats, creaking on their moorings in the harbour, to the horizon where the moon washed a pale golden glow over the ink-black sea. She took a sip of the cognac she'd ordered. 'He's getting married. To an Australian girl.' Her lip trembled. 'Oh Stan, I thought he'd always be there. He told me he'd wait for me, but I was cruel to him. Told him to get on with his life as I intended to get on with mine. I pretended I was being unselfish, setting him free to settle down with someone else. And now he's doing just that, and I don't want him to.' She twisted her glass round in her hand. 'You're probably wondering why I was so stupid. I certainly am. I pretended he was part of the boring old past and I was about to embark on an exciting adventure in Paris with no time for the likes of him.'

'Is he a painter too?'

Jasmine laughed. Her cognac went down the wrong way and she started coughing. 'No. A rubber planter. Imagine! That was the problem. My late father was too. I ran Howard down because he was different from me. I believed I wanted to be with interesting arty people, like Lachlan. Look how wrong that was. I've seen how shallow and empty some of those people are. Howard's not like that at all. He's different.'

'Different can be good.'

'All Lachlan did was pretend to build me up while all the time he knocked me down. Howard doesn't understand art, but he's always encouraged me. May I have a cigarette?'

'You don't smoke.'

'I don't care.'

'It'll make you cough.'

'Let me have a puff of yours then.' She reached out and took it from his fingers. One puff later she handed it back. 'Yuck. That's disgusting. How can you possibly enjoy that?'

Stan shrugged.

'Howard stopped smoking because of me you know.' She gave a hollow laugh. 'I told him it was a disgusting habit and he quit on the spot. I'd never have dared ask the same of Lachlan. I've never even so much as kissed Howard. We almost did when I left to return to Nairobi to apply to the Beaux-Arts. On the quayside. I think if we had, I wouldn't have got on the ship. And I know it sounds odd, but I think he knew that too.'

'He wanted you to leave?'

'No. He knew it was my dream and he wanted me to live it.'

'Sounds a good man.'

'The best.' She heaved a long sad sigh. 'All it would have taken was for me to write him a crummy letter every now and then – or even sent him a blooming postcard. But oh no, Miss Too-Clever-By-Half here tells herself he's not good enough. Just because he doesn't sit around in Left Bank bars all day talking about art. And now it's too late.'

'Is he already married?'

'No. He got engaged and then the same day his father died so he had to go off to Ceylon to care for his mother and sort out the family affairs.'

'Then it's not too late.'

'What do you mean?'

'If you really love him, you have to tell him. Sounds to me like he stopped waiting for you when you didn't give him an ounce of encouragement.'

She dropped her head.

'But if he really loves you, and I'd hazard a guess he does, he needs to know you feel the same way. Maybe he'll still marry this Australian girl but at least you'll have given him the chance not to. What've you got to lose, Jazz? If you do nothing he'll marry her. But if there's the smallest possibility you've got to grab it. He sounds a great guy, and they don't come along very often.'

'I don't know where he is.'

'Then find out, girl.'

'By the time I get to Nairobi it might be too late.'

'So, go to Ceylon and find him now.'

She looked at him wide-eyed. 'The ship I'm on goes there. I'm due to get off at Aden and change ships for Mombasa. I suppose I could stay on.' She thought for a moment. 'Mummy and I first met him in a hotel in Colombo. He was with his parents and the waiter told us they often stayed there. Maybe the hotel will give me the address. Then I can write to him.'

'Telephone him. Tell him you're in town and must see him. As our CO in the military used to say every time we went into battle – *Carpe diem!*'

'Seize the day,' she said, remembering her hated schoolgirl Latin. 'You're right. I have to.'

After she had embarked on the SS *Himalaya* and changed her destination for Colombo, Jasmine began to doubt her decision. The voyage would take three weeks and she believed there was little possibility that Howard would still be in Ceylon by the time she arrived. Funerals took place almost immediately in the

Far East and even though it was likely he would spend some time comforting his mother, Guthrie's wouldn't spare him indefinitely from his job as the manager of one of their larger rubber plantations. But something inside made her take the risk. If he wasn't in Ceylon then fate was telling her to give up but until then she would do as Stan had prompted and grasp fate by the hands.

As soon as the ship landed in Colombo, Jasmine was almost paralysed with nerves. But now she was here she had to be brave. The next passenger ship for Mombasa wasn't due to depart for three days and she needed to send a telegram to warn Evie and Arthur she was delayed. She wouldn't tell them the reason why.

In a fit of sentimentality, she decided to splash out and stay at the Galle Face Hotel. It was there that she'd given Howard the brush-off when they'd first met. If Howard refused to meet her now, it would be poetic justice.

On the quayside, she breathed in the scent of the East. It was invigorating being in the tropics again. The roar of traffic, the blare of horns, the rumble of double-decker buses, and the cries of the street traders. She climbed into a taxi, enveloped by the heat of the day. Petrol fumes mingled with salty air from the ocean and the sweetness of spices and flowers. And the colours. Turquoise sea. Azure sky. White colonial buildings. A rainbow of cotton saris. Jasmine's heart lifted after the drabness of Paris. It was such a contrast to the murky grey Seine, the grime-encrusted run-down buildings, the huddled masses of the homeless. In the tropics she felt she had come home.

The car swept into the driveway of the Galle Face Hotel and pulled up beside the elegant arched portico. To her relief, there was a single room available. It was bitter-sweet to be here alone when last time she'd shared a room and a few happy days with Mummy. After unpacking a few things, she went back downstairs and, suppressing her nerves, approached the desk clerk. 'I'm trying to contact Mr Howard Baxter. I understand his parents were regular guests here.'

The clerk offered a polite but noncommittal smile.

She pressed on. 'Mr Baxter's father has recently died and I'd like to offer my condolences. Please would you give me the family's address or even just the telephone number.'

The clerk's expression was of dignified gravity. 'I am sorry to hear of Mr Baxter's loss but I'm sure you can appreciate the hotel policy is to preserve the privacy of all our guests, madam.'

Desperate, Jasmine said, 'I've travelled from France. I was supposed to be going to Mombasa via Aden, but I stayed on board because it's really important I speak to Mr Baxter.' She leaned forward, hands in a gesture of supplication. '*Really* important.'

'I'm very sorry, Miss Barrington.'

She was about to walk away, disconsolate, when the clerk said. 'I am reluctant to intrude upon Mrs Baxter at a time of bereavement but I will telephone the Baxter residence and request that one of the staff discreetly mentions to young Mr Baxter that you are staying here and would like to speak with him. We can't be sure the message will reach him in the circumstances, or that he will return the call. I'm afraid that's all I can do.'

'Will you let me know if you hear anything? If he calls?' Her heart raced – did this mean Howard was still here? Did the clerk know that? Her hands were clammy, leaving a damp trail on the counter.

'Of course, Miss Barrington. May I help you with anything else?'

Jasmine remembered her broken necklace, took it out of her satchel and asked where she might get it repaired.

'I can help with you with that. Leave it here. It will be ready by tomorrow afternoon.'

Something was going her way. At least she wouldn't have to hide it from Mummy.

'Will you be dining in the restaurant this evening, Miss Barrington?'

'I'd prefer something light in my room. Just a salad. About seven o'clock.'

'Our pleasure.'

She went to her room and lay down on the bed. Almost immediately the telephone rang, and she almost stopped breathing.

'Miss Barrington, I telephoned the Baxter residence, but I am afraid Mr Baxter is not at home.'

'Did they say where he was or when he was coming back?'

'Alas, Miss Barrington, the person who answered the call did not offer that information.'

Jasmine put the receiver back in the cradle and turned over onto her stomach. Howard must have already returned to Malaya. Why had she let Stan talk her into this fool's errand? If she'd stuck to her plans, she'd be home with Mummy and Arthur by now. Instead, she was utterly miserable, alone in a beautiful hotel with no one to share it.

The salad arrived but she had no appetite. She rolled off the bed, went to the window and opened the shutters. To her surprise her room had a small balcony and a sea view. She stepped out where the breeze from the water lifted her hair and her skin felt the tang of salt. It was dark, a pale moon, but the sky was pierced by a million stars. The sound of the waves crashing on the rocks below the hotel lawns was a lure, calling to her.

A few minutes later, Jasmine was walking along the beach. She kicked off her shoes and carried them, luxuriating in the feel of the still-warm sand between her toes. Further up the beach, dark silhouettes of palm trees bent towards the water and the white caps of waves were luminescent against the black of the night sea. She wanted to burn the image of this empty starlit beach onto her brain to summon up in the future. Already she was envisaging how to recapture the moment in a painting – her abject loneliness in the midst of beauty.

She sat on the sand, hugging her knees. The enterprise had been foolhardy from the start. Even if she had managed to track him down, Howard would probably have brought his fiancée with him to Ceylon for the funeral. Attempting to barge in on him in the midst of preparations to bury his father was a crass thing to do.

Everything she attempted in life she made worse. Everything except her art. Until Stan had encouraged her to come here she'd made up her mind to concentrate on that alone. She'd been crazy to change her mind. After all, she had no claims on Howard. She'd never been his girlfriend – no matter how much he might once have wanted her to be.

Choking back tears, she chided herself not to be pathetic. She was on this earth to paint and that would have to be sufficient. Much better to use her few days in Ceylon to draw, to swim, to relax – not to wallow in self-pity and tell herself she should never have come.

The pounding waves were too loud for her to hear approaching footsteps; she almost jumped out of her skin when a hand touched her shoulder.

Howard eased himself down onto the sand beside her. 'What are you doing here, Jasmine?'

Her heart almost burst through her ribcage. She stared at him in shock. 'I'm on my way back to Nairobi,' she said, her courage failing her. 'Mary wrote to tell me about your father. I'm so sorry.'

'Thank you. As you know, we weren't close. But I wasn't expecting it.' His voice sounded odd, as though he was choosing his words carefully. He wasn't even looking at her but staring out at the ink-black, night-cloaked sea. 'The funeral was a couple of days ago. I'm glad it's over. My mother found it very hard. She's still in shock.' He sifted sand through his fingers.

'What will she do?'

'She's decided to live in England. Probably best. My sisters and their families are there. They couldn't get here for the funeral.'

'I'm sorry,' she repeated, realising she must sound fatuous. But why was he being like this? Cold, clipped, impersonal.

'I came into Colombo to meet the family solicitor. Dad's death was sudden. No sign of illness. There's a lot to sort out. I booked in here as it's a four- or five-hour drive back to the Central Highlands. The desk clerk told me you were here and that you wanted to get in touch with me. I got him to ring your room and when you weren't there, I guessed I'd find you out here.'

'You know me so well,' she said, her voice barely a whisper. Then deciding to get it over as quickly as possible, she adopted a false, cheery tone. 'Mary also told me you're getting married. Congratulations.'

'Thank you,' he said. He was still staring out into the nothingness of the ocean.

'What's she like?' Jasmine asked after a long silence, trying to keep her voice steady.

'You'd like her. She's very likeable. Easygoing, fun, kind, funny. A great girl.'

Jasmine wanted to howl. She dug her fingernails into her palms to distract herself from the pain inside.

'Trouble is, I don't love her,' he said, turning to look at Jasmine for the first time since he'd sat down. 'I mean, she's a wonderful girl and she'll be a good wife. But I don't love her. I'll never love her, no matter how hard I try.' He gulped, keeping his eyes on Jasmine. 'I can never love her because she's not you. I lived such a long time on hope. A kind of blind belief that one day you'd feel the same about me as I do about you, but I'm lonely, Jasmine. I know it's probably wrong to marry her but the alternative seemed worse. Betty will never be you, but I've gradually come to accept that I can never have you, because you will never love me.'

She was about to speak but he continued.

'I run a business. I'm fearless in the face of bandits. Yet I fall to pieces in front of you.'

'Shut up, Howard.'

'I'm sorry – I'm doing it again aren't I? But I can't help myself.'

'Shut up and let me speak.'

He stared at her, his eyes full of anxiety.

Jasmine looked into them. 'I love you too.'

He gazed at her, disbelieving. 'You're not just feeling sorry for me? Making fun?'

'I'd never do that. I've had enough of people lying to me. I'm weary of trying to be someone I'm not. *You* know me. I don't need to pretend. You know all the bad things about me, and you still love me. Well, I do too. Love *you* I mean.'

Howard gasped. He moved to pull her into his arms.

She put her hands up to keep him at arms' length. 'Wait. You need to let me finish.'

'I'll end it with Betty.'

'It's not about Betty. When I tell you the terrible things I've done, you won't want me anymore. I can't have secrets from you. All the time in Paris, I was trying to be somebody I'm not. Trying to be sophisticated. I've been such an idiot. I'm just a silly immature girl who pushed you away. The person I love most in the world.'

Howard started to speak.

'No. Hear me out,' she said. 'When I tell you what a mess I've made of my life you'll be glad you had a lucky escape.'

'Never.' He gazed at her intently. 'Nothing could stop me loving you.'

Jasmine closed her eyes and took a long slow breath. 'I slept with my tutor. I allowed him to seduce me. No – I actually encouraged him. He was a married man although I didn't know that at the time or I'd never have gone near him. He lied to me. Everyone else knew. It just shows what a stupid, shallow person I am. It was sordid and I'm ashamed. So, there you have it. I'm no longer the innocent virgin. I'm a fallen woman.' She started to cry.

Howard gathered her into his arms. 'Yes, Jasmine, you're a fallen woman. You've finally fallen for me. That's all that matters. I don't care about your rotten tutor. Well – that's not true as I'd like to beat him to a pulp for hurting you and taking advantage of you. And most of all for making you feel bad about yourself. Never do that, Jasmine. Whatever he did to you, you're still *you*. The girl I fell in love with across the dining-room of the Galle Face Hotel without even speaking to you. The girl I made an utter fool of myself over to the point that I managed to drive you away.'

He took her hand and looked into her eyes. This time she didn't turn away. 'I love you with every fibre of my being, my darling girl. And I realise I'm now running the grave risk that you'll accuse me of being corny, but I can't help myself.'

'You mean it? You still love me despite that? In spite of me behaving like a cheap tart?'

'Of course I mean it. I may be flippant and corny and put my foot in it all the time, but one thing about me that is never going to change until my dying breath, is how much I love you, Jasmine. All I want is to spend the rest of my life with you. And no, let's get something crystal clear – you're not a cheap tart.'

She relaxed a little then said, 'What about Betty?'

'I'll have to break the engagement. I'm going to feel an absolute cad as she doesn't deserve to be jilted. She'll be hurt and upset but she'll get over it. She's a great girl and she'll find someone worthy of her. But that's not me.' He stroked a hand over Jasmine's hair. 'To be honest, I was about to break up with her because I couldn't stop thinking of you, even though you'd made it clear it was hopeless. I knew it was wrong to marry her while I was in love with you. But then she got caught in an ambush and her friend was shot dead in front of her.'

Jasmine gasped.

'I was the first person to drive up after it happened. I thought it was Betty who was dead at first. It was very emotional. Traumatic. In the heat of the moment, I proposed.'

'Does she love you?'

'She's very fond of me. We had a lot of fun together. But... there was never the connection between us that there is between you and me. Even when you're angry with me.' He smiled sheepishly. 'Especially when you're angry with me.'

He took Jasmine's hand. In that moment she knew she never wanted to hold anyone else's. She wanted to cry out with joy.

'I think she may actually be relieved. She wants to be back in Sydney. She'd been hinting about me getting a job in Australia. Now my father's dead and I have the family tea business to run I'm anchored to Ceylon forever. I'll be leaving Guthrie's. Not something she's likely to be thrilled about.' His face fell. 'I haven't even asked how you feel about Ceylon?'

'I know I'd be very happy here,' she said, then added, 'but if it's with you, I'd be happy anywhere. If you'll have me.'

Howard lifted her face and kissed her slowly but with growing passion. It was a kiss that wiped out every kiss that had preceded it. The realisation that she didn't want to kiss anyone that way but him, sent a warm glow through her. For the first time in her life, she had found home. It wasn't a country, a nationality or a building. It was Howard.

'Thank you for loving me when I had no right to expect it. When I was so beastly,' she said.

'Loving you isn't difficult. It's like breathing.' He kissed her again then drew back, frowning. 'Your course – I haven't even asked how it's going. Apart from the vile tutor.'

'I won a gold medal. Best in my year. I had four paintings on show and a posh gallery is interested in showing my work.' She gave him a rueful smile. 'But I was very unhappy in Paris.'

'I wish you'd told me.'

'So do I. But something my American friend, Stan, said rang true to me. He left Paris to live in the South of France. He blamed Paris for all his problems, but eventually realised they were actually inside him. I think the same's true for me.'

Howard held her against his chest, stroking her hair.

'I told Principal Rochambeau I wanted to leave. He's let me go home before term ends and told me to think about it over the summer. He's wants to put me under another teacher.'

'I hope he doesn't mean that literally.'

Jasmine swatted at him. 'Don't worry. I'll never look at another man again. And anyway, I won't be going back.'

'You're giving up before you get your degree?'

'Of course.'

'It's killing me to say this, but I think that's a bad idea. You owe it to yourself to finish your studies, Jasmine. You'll never have another chance.'

'What about us? Don't you want to marry me?'

'More than anything. But I'll have to be patient and wait for you. And this time it'll be different as I'll know you're coming back to me. I'll be sure you love me. And who knows? This time, I might even have the odd letter to look forward to.'

Jasmine stared at him. 'You'd do that for me? Let me go?'

'I love you, Jasmine. That means making sure you do whatever you need to be happy. One thing I understood about you from the beginning is that painting is a huge part of your life. Without it you wouldn't be you. We'll have the rest of our lives together. I can't begrudge you finishing the course. I'll miss you more than you can imagine but better that than have you always regretting not finishing.'

She wiped a tear away. 'I'll go back on two conditions.'

'Tell me.' He looked nervous.

'That you won't complain when I write to you every single day. And that you marry me before I leave.'

Howard twisted onto his knees in front of her and took her hands in his. 'I'll marry you the moment we can get a licence.' He kissed her again. 'Tomorrow I'll bring you up to the plantation. You need to see what you're letting yourself in for and you'll meet my mother. She's going to be delighted. She still asks me about the beautiful girl we saw in the Galle Face Hotel. The girl I couldn't keep my eyes off. But tonight—' Jasmine could see his eyes were shining. 'Now we're officially engaged to be married, I'm going to spend the night showing you exactly how much I love you.'

He took her by the hand, pulled her to her feet and they walked hand in hand along the sand towards the golden lights of the Galle Face Hotel.

A LETTER FROM THE AUTHOR

Huge thanks for reading *Jasmine in Paris*. I hope you enjoyed your time with Jasmine there – and with Howard back in the Malayan peninsula. If you want to join other readers in hearing about my new Storm Publishing releases and bonus content, you can sign up for my mailing list here!

www.stormpublishing.co/clare-flynn

If you enjoyed this book and could spare a few moments to leave a review that would be hugely appreciated. Even a short review can make all the difference in encouraging a reader to discover my books for the first time. Thank you so much!

If you'd like to sign up to my mailing list for updates and extra content, you can sign up here!

www.subscribepage.com/r4w1u5

When I left Jasmine walking up the gangplank to sail away from Penang and her friend Howard at the end of A Painter in Penang, I was already sure I was going to follow her to Paris. I didn't realise then what fun it would be. I lived for a couple of years in Paris – in the heart of the Latin Quarter so many of the places Jasmine visits were already familiar to me. It was great to revisit them – even though it had to be virtual as I wrote the book during lockdown. I had such a great time – watching YouTube videos and going on live virtual tours through the city

– wandering around the Luxembourg Gardens and the Louvre. I also enjoyed learning about the Ecole des Beaux Arts and the *atelier* system. Writing it was a great opportunity to discover new music, artists and places. I loved writing about Stan – who many readers will guess was based on James Baldwin – although I changed lots of things about him. Baldwin, like Stan, used to write upstairs at Café Flore, lived in a hotel near the Beaux Arts and liked to hang out at Chez Inez. Jasmine also gave me an excuse to watch some fabulous contemporary French movies. One of the reasons I love writing historical fiction is that every book becomes a complete cultural immersion!

Thanks again for being part of this amazing journey with me and I hope you'll stay in touch – I have so many more stories and ideas to entertain you with!

Clare

clareflynn.co.uk

facebook.com/authorclareflynn

x.com/clarefly

Printed in Great Britain
by Amazon